Congratulations Tashfin!
I hop[e]
ne[xt]

JESTER BOBBITY

— Jester

MAKER

⚱

• *IT'S TIME FOR AN AMBUSH* •

This is a work of fiction. All the characters and events portrayed in this book are fictional, and any resemblance to real people or incidents is purely coincidental.

Maker – It's Time for an Ambush. Copyright ©2017 by Gary Fisher. All Rights Reserved. First Printing: 2017. The editorial arrangement, analysis, and professional commentary are subject to this copyright notice. No portion of this book may be copied, retransmitted, reposted, duplicated, or otherwise used without the express written approval of the author, except by reviewers who may quote brief excerpts in connection with a review.

United States laws and regulations are public domain and not subject to copyright. Any unauthorized copying, reproduction, translation, or distribution of any part of this material without permission by the author is prohibited and against the law.

May be purchased for educational, business, or sales promotional use.

Cover Art designed by Damonza.com

ISBN-13: 978-0692999523

CHAPTER: 1

The moment you relax, sigh, put your feet up, that's when there will be a knock at the door.

"*Burn*," I growled, and a small bottle appeared in my hand. I didn't look at it; I didn't have to. "Come in," I called out, gripping the glass bottle a little tighter. If whatever coming through the door of my office proved to be a threat, the contents of the vial would turn it—and possibly the entire block—into a torch. Funny that summoning a fire potion always caused a slight chill in the air.

It didn't look like a threat. It looked like a man in glasses and a dark suit and tie; a mop of neglected light brown curly hair above hunched shoulders and a slow cautious stride. He wasn't the type you'd normally see strolling around this neighborhood. I still didn't move. It looked human, but there was never any way to be certain. Lots of things *looked* human.

"Mr. uhh Maker?"

"Come in. Have a seat."

In the few steps between the door and the chair, he looked at me and then quickly looked away again—twice. One of those looks had a timid half-smile attached. The kind of smile people used when they wanted to be polite and didn't know what else to do. After all, he was staring down a two-hundred-twenty-pound, muscular, grumpy, black guy.

He only took a few steps, as the room wasn't large. In fact, this "laboratory" was my smallest. I had five of them in abandoned buildings all over town. This room had just enough space for a couple simple wooden chairs, my desk, and a table against the far wall that looked like something out of a chemistry lab—or an old Frankenstein movie. All the furniture was used, beat up, or dug out of a dumpster.

I was sitting with my hands behind my head, feet up on my second-hand IKEA Brusali desk, waiting for him to try something that would end in a murder. I stashed the vial a few inches up my coat sleeve.

He sat down and immediately launched into a rushed torrent of words: who he was, who had referred him, and why he was here. His eyes darted around, and his breathing was fast and shallow. All very un-monster like behavior.

I took a deep breath and stopped paying attention. Relaxation was far more important. Tension was a way of life, but it was also a good way to get dead. Besides, everything Mr. Robert Blan was saying, I'd heard before. Seriously, Bobby Blan? Kindergarten must've been hell.

I focused on the sun caressing my face. It was streaming through the window behind him. Sunlight was always a comfort. The things that went bump in the night didn't bump quite so hard in daylight. Most of them, anyway.

"…and so… like, he said you could help me."

I was getting popular with the just past college crowd. Blan was about my age, maybe a little older. His suit was cheap—like everything else he was wearing. His glasses had tape on the side, and his short brown hair was unkempt. He was a nerd right out of someone's favorite sitcom.

I knew what he meant by "help." He wanted me to give him

an advantage that no one else had so he could cheat at life. In some circles that would be immoral, but I have a rule that dictates my sense of morality. I stole it from Scarlett O'Hara—the bit about never being hungry again. Most people have never been starving before. In the vignettes of my childhood that I could remember, it wasn't unheard of to miss a week of meals.

I'm not above love potions, money potions, make this guy grovel or that bully go away hexes. Weight loss potions, beauty marks—even breast and penis enhancement. Whatever keeps the lights on. I've even been known to pull a rabbit out of a hat at kid's parties when I get desperate enough.

"Let me make sure I have this," I said. "You have an interview with some firm in Research Triangle Park. You get the job, and you're set for the next forty years. You don't get the job, and life as you know it comes to an end. Complicating this relatively simple matter is that you're a socially awkward, anxious kinda guy who's guilty of solipsistic introjection, dissociative imagination, and generally learned all the wrong lessons from the internet. You came to me because you want enough charisma to get through the interview without breaking out in hives. That about right?"

Blan flinched. Like, actually flinched. Apparently, he didn't like hearing what someone thought when they didn't pull their verbal punches, but few people did. I found it was a good test of someone's character. If they couldn't take hearing something that was painfully obvious to everyone else, it was kinda hard for me to take them seriously.

Life was a crucible; for me at least. As a result, I didn't have much sympathy for people who chose not to see how good they had it.

He didn't even answer; just dropped his eyes and nodded. I sighed. "Everyone thinks magic can solve their problems. Well it can. It will just create bigger and more difficult problems in the process. Then, you think 'Hey, more magic!' It's like a drug that way, soon you'll be wondering how you can even brush your teeth without it."

"Well I just—"

Cutting him off, I continued, "For instance, have you even bothered to think about how you're going to maintain this persona once you get the job?"

"I—"

"Is there a second interview? A third? Will you be back for the inevitable yearly performance review? What happens when your new boss ambushes you in the toilet? He'll take the urinal right next to yours and strike up a conversation about the Pickadilly merger. Then you'll wanna walk around with a potion in your pocket all the time. No doubt, you'll wanna ask that cute new receptionist out at some point. First date? First love? Up for a promotion? Meeting the in-laws for the first time? Wedding? Baby? I can put courage, charm, fame, and money in a bottle. That doesn't mean you should drink it."

I palmed the fire potion. I was fairly certain by now that I wouldn't need it. Blan sat there processing, while I pretended to root around in my nearly empty desk. The drawer had a few glass and plastic bottles, but everything magical was in my pack at the base of my chair.

My pack was a simple thing: black leather, unassuming, spectacularly old and spelled to be light as a feather. It made me look like I was off to college. The reality was, it held my vast collection of magic implements—and if Dr. Who doesn't mind, yeah it's bigger on the inside.

I didn't realize how big it had gotten over the years. I once went inside, and it was like a small bank vault in there. If not for air, water, and the inherent hazards of living in an extra-dimensional space, I'd have moved in. It was nicer than my apartment.

"*Charmer…*" I said, as if I were looking through the drawer, making sure a few glass bottles clinked together. A chill went up my spine, and a new vial appeared between my fingers as if by… drumroll please… Magic!

I sat back up and tossed him a small glass vial with a cork stopper. It was centuries old. I had a source that could get me a few hundred of those bottles from Mongolia once a year. They were ancient; great for potions. I leaned back in my chair again with my hands behind my head and my feet up on my desk.

"That will turn you into a silver-tongued devil for about an hour. Don't change the way you talk or behave—don't bother. The potion will make sure everything you say or do is taken in the best possible light."

He reached for his wallet, and I held up a hand. "Like any good dealer, the first one is free. Like a bad dealer, I'm going to give you a disclaimer: Don't drink it." He nodded and got up to leave. He was staring at the potion; thinking so hard he didn't even say thanks. I guess that was my good deed for the day.

This lab was a place for people to come and see me. I kept semi-regular hours here, but I wouldn't if I didn't need the money. Potions were big business and nearly all profit. A few months to get the formulas just right, make them in bulk, then sell them off. The charmer potion Blan wanted was only twenty dollars, but that didn't matter when I sold two or three a week. It was by far my best seller. That and love potions. The disclaimer was much longer for those.

Almost always, the poor guy or girl came back because the person they loved turned out to be the "jealous type." One man had just escaped after his new wife locked him in their house.

I explain that superficial love is a fear of loss; that they should know how someone will handle that particular neurochemical cocktail first. I tell them that genuine love is based on vulnerability, generosity, and shared experience. Even if they could induce those feelings in someone, it's all gonna end badly unless they feel the same way. No one listens.

That's why I charge everyone five thousand dollars for love potions. With an additional five-thousand-dollar deposit up front for the "undo" potion they will inevitably need afterward. I found out years ago that it just made life easier. Only one person had ever not needed it. I hadn't had the heart to tell her that it was because he loved her already; although I did refund the ten grand.

I closed the door on Mr. Blan. If he *was* just out of college, then we were about the same age. Still, he was a child in other, less obvious ways.

I went back to my desk, threw my feet up, and continued my relaxation endeavors. A sigh changed into a yawning-stretching combination and I hoped for another lazy day in the sunlight. I spent most of my days relaxing and studying, or at least I tried to. It wasn't easy sometimes. People always had problems.

I could never sit long before someone walked in with a problem magic had caused, or one they thought it could fix. In their mind, the fact that I was one of the only wizards around meant it was my job to do something. They were half right. I'm happy to dole out cures to people's pathetically small problems—but only when the price is right.

For all the problems magic couldn't solve, I had my pistol tucked in a holster under my arm at all times, and under my pillow when I slept. A custom Desert Eagle .50 caliber and a clip full of hollow points. It was the Dirty Harry pistol for millennials, except I had seven in the clip, one in the chamber—and no one ever felt lucky.

Against all rules of gun safety and good sense, I kept it chambered. I had also long ago gotten rid of the safety, trigger guard, and anything else that would keep bullets from flying immediately. Most people preach "ready, aim, fire." My credo was "ready, fire, aim, fire, fire." I get their heads down first, then I worry about finding a way to shoot them in it.

I picked up my phone again. I'd been reading up on ancient

mythologies and their influences across cultures, when a woman's voice came from behind me.

"Daddy I got a boo boo."

My hand instinctively went to my gun and fired while it was still in its holster under my arm. The advantage being, it was already pointed behind me. I felt the powder burns forming on my ribs. Looking on the bright side, I was still alive to feel it.

My coat was bulletproof, but only if the bullets came from the outside. I heard a pane of glass shattering, the thunk of the round hitting non-reinforced concrete and a ricochet—though it couldn't have happened in that order.

I was out of my chair and had the Desert Eagle unholstered before I had finished wincing. I turned and raised my weapon only to have it twisted out of my hand. If it still had a trigger guard, it would've broken my finger. The pistol fell to my desk before I could even think to squeeze off another round. The magazine had been removed, and the slide pulled back. A gun without bullets would do me no good.

I was about slam down my fire potion and torch the whole building when I saw that it was Zora. She was a caramel skinned woman with long black hair in a braid that went down her back. Zora worked out daily, watching cartoons while she did it. As a result, she had the look of a blood-splattered cappuccino flavored fitness model.

Her real name wasn't Zora, of course. When she met me, and found out what names could do, she quickly started going by Zora Wade Theresa Kenpatchi—which were all names of anime swordsman she liked or something. She was carrying her Japanese katana slung on one hip and looked up at me with a huge grin. The grin pulled at a wide jagged scar that began just above her jawline and ran down her left side. The scar was a few shades darker than she was, and therefore impossible to miss. That had been a particularly bad day. She was wearing a once-white tank top and once-tan cargo pants; both now ruined and covered in blood.

She had asked for a hair growth potion a couple years back. All her hair was falling out because obtaining magical knowledge is an unforgiving process. It had grown the hair on her head, and in a lot of other places too. For a while she looked like the 1940's wolfman.

I panicked for a moment, seeing all the blood. I thought I may have shot her, then I realized even this close that was nearly impossible.

Zora's power was speed. She was like Quicksilver on steroids. Like me, she only did a couple things, but she did them *really* well. She had probably come into my lab, closed the door, and moved behind me all in the span of a blink.

"How many times have I asked you not to sneak up on me?"

She sounded genuinely thoughtful. "Few hundred or so. I swear I'll stop just as soon as it's not funny anymore… or if you ever manage to kill me. That would put the brakes on my bullshit quite quick actually." She was smiling, like usual—which was a bad sign, also like usual. I closed my eyes and let out a sigh. I could hear her breathing hard and smelled the gore all over her. Half of her long black hair was loose from its ponytail, also spattered with blood. "Anyway, I think I need a bandage."

"What happened?"

"I got bored." She laughed, then collapsed in the other chair, wincing as she held her arm tightly.

"Are you kidding me?" I snapped, "You were supposed to watch them."

"I did watch them. I watched all the way up until they died screaming. I even watched for a minute or two after. Felt kinda pointless."

I threw up my hands. "And you couldn't text me? What was so hard about sticking to the plan?"

"Maker," she said calmly, emphasizing each word, "I'm bleeding to death. I would like a bandage please."

"*Gauze*," I said. A paper wrapper that you could find in any hospital room appeared in my hand, and I handed it over. Zora ripped her pants open at the thigh, and I noticed she had made a tourniquet from an old belt. She spat on her leg and scrubbed the wound with her bloody pants, prompting me to grab a bottle of water off my desk. I set to work cleaning it properly, while she explained what had happened.

"Blueboy was in the warehouse, like you said." Blueboy was a fairy with long wild blue hair—hence the name. He looked like a Comic-Con reject. Fairies came in all shapes and sizes; this one happened to be human looking. They also came in every spectrum of motivation from benign incorruptible seraphim, to those spawned from the depths of hell.

We didn't know if Blueboy was in town for business or pleasure, but I assumed it was nothing that polite society would approve of. I had foregone finding out exactly what it was when I saw he had a squad of goblins in tow. The benign fairies seldom had a reason to visit Earth, and never made noise when they did. These goblins went out every night vandalizing, trespassing and jaywalking. They were obviously looking for something, so we'd planned to kill Blueboy and ambush the goblins on their return at dawn. Simple.

"I was watching most of the day and didn't see much movement. You said they were in and out of the place. I figured if I saw an opening, I could go in and kill him. Goblins would be easy to hunt down if he wasn't there giving them orders."

"And what was wrong with waiting until tonight, when they would all be gone?!" The cut was down to the bone and looked jagged as if someone had gone in with something large and dull, then ripped it out sideways. Whatever it was had torn an artery. The gauze would take care of it. She was going to be limping for a day or two, but at least it was clean. I stood up and crossed my arms, frustrated she was hurt… and worried more than anything.

She ripped open the gauze package with her teeth. The cleaner you could keep the bandage, the better this particular magic worked. Zora was careful to ease it out of the package without touching it.

As soon as the bandage touched her skin, the magic activated. Any wizard would feel the faint discharge of power in the air. This was a magical tool, so it wasn't the shock of bone-deep ice you get casting a spell—but you could notice a chill this close.

The threads from the gauze dug into her skin, and she slowly released the tourniquet with a sigh. "Better make that two bandages," she said, inspecting her bloody left arm. There was a trickle of bright red mixed in with the duller darker shades.

"*Gauze*," I said again. "You need to be more careful. These aren't easy to make. What if I had been out?"

"You have six left and the ace bandage. You would've said if you used one," she said dismissively, focusing instead on cleaning her arm. She was right of course. That was annoying.

"That's not the point." I snapped

"You wanna hear the damn story or not?" She growled. Zora was either a fellow wizard or the misbehaving little sister I never wanted. It was often hard to tell which. At times, she was the most sane and rational person I'd ever met. Other times she was a bloodthirsty lunatic who reveled in chaos and spent *my* time and talents keeping *herself* out of trouble. She was also my apprentice.

We glared at each other in silence for a few moments before she finally looked away and spoke, "Fine."

"I think what I wanna hear is 'It won't happen again Maker.'"

She carefully slid the second bandage onto her arm and looked up at me. "That doesn't sound realistic at all, but if you still wanna hear it…" She grinned, the way she did when she wanted to unnerve people and entertain herself. There was no warmth in that smile; it was more like the look you would get from an excited grizzly bear who just realized you were edible. I sighed and let it go. She was still alive. That was enough for the moment. "Anyway, I went in when I saw him leave with six goblins in tow. I knew that we could hit them tonight, but nothing wrong with taking down a few before that."

"Actually, there's a lot wrong with that idea but go on,"

"Well six of them left, so I figured if your count was right there would only be three inside." I didn't say so, but for her, those were actually pretty good odds. "I snuck in through the roof and found them all in the same room talking about something in Fae. I got two before they could move. I was interrogating the last one—not an easy thing to do when they only speak crappy Fae and crappier Mandarin. I was making some headway at least, until Blueboy walked in. He shot me before I got my bubble up. Him and nine goblins in close quarters was… a strain."

"Nine? I thought you killed two?" I said.

"Yeah, funny thing about that. I was trying to peel, and every time I did, one of the headless or gutless goblins would get up again. I assumed that Blueboy was doing that somehow so I feinted a few times and managed to put a scratch on his leg. He got distracted for a second. Then the, somehow, not dead goblins hesitated. Then they all died. Then I left. Then it was now."

"Anyone see you leave?" I reloaded my gun, chambered a round and shoved it back in the holster.

"Nah, I left at speed 'cause I was rushing here. Got swag though." She smiled, nodding to an army-style duffle bag behind me. I hadn't noticed it before.

"So, you were bleeding? Arterial bleeding? And you took time to ransack the place?"

She sounded as incredulous as I felt. "What the hell is the point of any of this if we aren't gonna get the girl or the loot?!"

"Wait, what?" I was even more confused, "What girl?"

"Exactly!" She smiled. "Which is why I *had* to get the loot!" I was about to snap at her again, but there was a knock at the door.

Zora had left the door cracked. I saw it was Rollo and waved him in.

Rollo was short for a man, though not by much. Maybe five-foot-eight or so. At my six-one, he also came up to my nose. Even then, it was difficult to look down on him. He was as wide as I was, and hid all that muscle under a layer of fat just thick enough to make you wanna underestimate him.

He wore a trenchcoat, even in this spring heat. Hell, he always wore it, even in the middle of summer. It was tan leather and specially made to hold a shotgun inside. He also wore his shoulder holster with a nine-millimeter Baretta on each side, and had a Taser, pepper spray, and a rosary at his waist. I knew he would also have at least three pairs of handcuffs somewhere, and one or more of my flame potions.

Rollo had slick black hair, starting to go gray. His eyes were like mine: dark brown above sunken cheeks and a face that had been through more than a few beatings.

Zora squealed and stood up, throwing her arms out for a hug. "Rollo! How's my favorite country-fried piglet?"

Oh, forgot to mention, Rollo's a cop. Maybe it was my upbringing, urban living, or just all the rap music, but cops make me nervous. This one more than any other. I sat back down at my desk and resumed my relaxed position, but the relaxed feeling was gone.

I gripped my burn potion, not because I would need it, but because I knew I wasn't going to like whatever was about to happen.

He made no move to hug Zora, shake hands, or approach her at all. You didn't need to be a career detective to spot a woman covered in a gallon of fresh blood.

He smirked and eyed her up and down like someone would

look at a misbehaving toddler caked in mud. "Why Zora you look as... as ever. Something I need to know?" Rollo's slow speaking southern accent was right out of an old movie. Even though we were in North Carolina, you didn't hear it all that often in a city the size of Raleigh.

"Yeah, I got a new part-time job at a slaughterhouse." She grinned. "We specialize in hard-to-find meats."

"So, none of that is human blood then?"

"What blood? Maker, do you see any blood?"

I had my feet up on my desk enjoying the last of the afternoon sunlight through eyes that were mostly closed. "I don't even see you two having this conversation."

"See?" She was still grinning at Rollo. "Besides, it's good honest work, making the world a better place, blah, blah, blah. How many guilty until proven innocents have you harassed today?"

"Why Zora, I take offense to that. I haven't violated anyone's civil rights since..." he rubbed his chin in mock thought, "yesterday."

They both huffed a laugh and Zora went to grab her bag from the corner. Rollo nodded over to me. "You get a permit for that weapon yet?"

It was my turn to scoff at him. Shithead. He knew this was a touchy subject.

"And put what! Name! On it?! Maker the Wizard? Abracadabra the Magnificent? No, wait, I know—Finn-2187! You're the detective, go detect shit! And if you ever find out what my last name is, come tell me, and I'll be happy to *not* put it on a permit."

Zora thought it was funny. She slung the duffle bag over her shoulder and made to leave.

Rollo grabbed her arm as she tried to walk past.

"What's in the bag?"

"Personal property and no business of any law enforcement personnel not currently in possession of a warrant," she said.

That was the trouble with cops. Even if I did want to be Rollo's friend, and I can't imagine why I would, he would always be a cop first and my friend second. At best that made him unreliable and reliability was the number-one thing I looked for in a person.

Zora seemed to see it the same way. Rollo was good for banter, and a tool if she needed something, but not much more than that. She gave his hand on her arm a pointed look and met his eyes. Her other hand flipped out a few inches of sword. "You're not going to try and haul me in are you detective? Cause that's not gonna end well for anybody."

"Y'all can't act any way you want 'cause you're wizards." He was looking at her just as fiercely. Technically, Zora was threatening a police officer, but he'd never make that stick.

She smiled back at me. "Lay garlands atop the iron chains that weigh them down and let them love their slavery by turning them into something called civilized people." She seasoned the last two words with liberal doses of contempt.

I smiled back. "Hmm… definitely French. Rousseau? 1769? Good year. This will no doubt taste nutty—with legs—and go great with pâté and baguettes."

Zora and I both giggled. The joke didn't make any real sense, but it had the effect of confusing Rollo. That made it funny enough. I didn't even know what pâté was.

"And what the hell is that supposed to mean?" Rollo obviously had no head for 18th century French philosophers. Shame, too. Rousseau was a great read.

Zora snatched her arm away with a growl. "It means we don't act any way we want because we're wizards. We act any way we want because we're criminals."

"She's got you there," I said with a laugh. Zora and I did whatever it took to survive. Unfortunately, most of it just happened to be illegal.

I blinked and missed Zora leaving. There was a rustle of air and a blur as she left. Except for a few drops of blood, there was nothing to show she'd been there at all. Rollo just stared out the open door after her.

"Will you knock it off?!" I said. "You can't find her if she doesn't want to be found. Unless I help you, and spoiler alert: I'm not going to help you. Even if you somehow managed it on your own, you couldn't catch her. If you got that done, you couldn't hold her. And if by some miracle she was exceedingly bored, or in a coma, and let all that happen anyway, your forensics team would tell you that most of that blood came from something that doesn't exist. Now, what do you want?"

Rollo stared out the door for another moment before refocusing on why he was here and closing it.

"Got a case."

"What does that have to do with me?"

He answered by tossing a small cloth pouch on my desk. I picked it up. It was simple black cotton, closed with a drawstring. Inside were small chips of glass. I had designed and created a prism for Rollo that glowed in the presence of magical energies and intense radiation. Worked pretty well too. If I'd known at the time that he only wanted it so he could ensnare me into investigating magical happenings, I would've told him it was impossible.

"I walked into a crime scene, and the damn thing turned into a hot potato. By the time I got it out of my pocket, it had shattered. I need you to come take a look."

"No."

There were a few hundred things in the world that were strong enough to shatter that prism, and I didn't want to meet any of them.

I could use magic. I could make potions that did all the things I told Blan they could do. That didn't make me a real wizard. In the arena of magical brute force, I was in the kiddie division. That made casting powerful spells a draining activity or a flat-out impossibility. No way I wanted to go wherever Rollo had just been. Whatever it was would kill me for sport and eat me as an afterthought.

Rollo nodded when I spoke and kept talking.

"Took some photos of the place. Some kind of satanic ritual maybe?" The glossy eight-by-tens were portraits of two kids. The others had blood but no corpse in sight. I recognized the summoning circle in one of them. Rollo was still waiting when I finally succeeded in tearing my eyes away.

"From what I know, the prince of darkness is in a very deep hole with some very bad things and isn't coming out anytime soon. If you wanna know more, see a priest."

Rollo ignored me again. "There's two children missing. The blood types on the walls don't match either of theirs. Go take a look and let me know what I'm dealing with."

I stayed silent as my eyes flashed back to the pictures. I just shook my head. Rollo must've noticed the fear on my face. I wasn't about to go near that place, wherever it was.

"Dammit Maker. How far do I have to push this?" I knew what he meant.

I ran across a lot of things while hunting monsters. Some monsters had immaculate taste, but I couldn't eat a Rolex. Sadly, the process of turning a dead vampire's jewelry into groceries was illegal and Rollo knew it. He had me dead to rights on enough money laundering to put me in jail for a few years—and that was the least of my felonies.

"Answer's still no. Jail's better than dead."

"Why're you being a coward about this?"

"Why do you walk in my lab once a year and say, 'Hey Maker I have another meat grinder for you to walk into?' Get out!" I realized I was on my feet. I realized I was yelling. I also realized I didn't care.

Normally people accused me of being stoic. I certainly tried to be. If only they could see me now. One deep breath later, Rollo dropped a piece of paper on my desk and went to the door. The paper had an address on it for a street I didn't know. "I can keep the place empty and the press in the dark for another day or two. A full-on badass wizard shouldn't have any trouble sneaking into one little crime scene."

"No trouble at all, since I'm not going," I said

"His name is Ryan; eight years old, likes baseball. Theresa's twelve; good at math, wants to be a teacher." With that Rollo closed the door behind him.

The Bastard.

Chapter: 2

I sat down and brushed everything in the trash. Damn him. The paper went too, but that didn't matter—the address was burned into my memory the moment I saw it.

I told myself I had a choice, but I didn't; not if I wanted to continue my endeavor of one day becoming a decent human being. I was frustrated he'd backed me into a corner, but I suppose that was part of his job. Sometimes it seemed like being backed into a corner was mine.

I looked at the trash where the shattered prism lay. I'd only made four. It was a simple design, and therefore resilient. No one had ever come back with a broken one before. How much residual magic did it have to absorb to heat up like that?

It didn't feel good knowing there was something within a few miles of where I stood that could do that. Whatever it was had to be beastly as far as magical force. The prism hadn't just shattered; it had shattered a day or more after the spell had been cast.

I dropped my head in my hands. Two kids missing and I was thinking about myself. There was no place for children in the supernatural world. The woman who taught me about magic was named Tema Rion. She had tortured me since I was six. She'd called it training, which just proves how gullible I was as a child.

She'd cut me open more times than I could count, used me as a guinea pig for magical experiments, and I was certain she was the reason I couldn't remember two-thirds of my life. She was dead now, but her memory held enough sway to get my pulse racing with a familiar amalgamation of anger and fear.

I took a deep breath and let it out. Then again. Then a third time.

"Dammit." I huffed in frustration at my neurochemistry. I wasn't going to get far if I let my fears run wild. Meditation to calm myself down was a skill I picked up early in life. Just how early I couldn't say. Up until about six years ago, most of my childhood was a blur of suffering, hunger, confusion, and screaming.

I put my hands together on the desk and spread them apart to about six inches. "*Light,*" I said. There was a chill in the air as I cast. A thin beam of illumination traveled from one hand to the other and back again with a slight hum.

This was the spell I'd used to train as a kid. Despite the associated memories, it was relaxing and helped me focus. The light moved slowly enough to govern my breathing. Left to right, inhale. Right to left, exhale.

When I felt the fear rise again, I watched the light and did what I always did when meditating; I thought about elementary particles.

All wizards get a physics education, whether it's formal training or a crash course in the school of hard knocks. Even magic must yield to the almighty study of everything. Unlike most wizards, I fell in love with the subject.

Every mage I'd met saw the universe as something holding them back; most even going so far as to dismiss science entirely and subscribe to long outdated ways of thinking about the world.

There are indeed four fundamental forces that shape the earth, and they are not concoctions of nitrogen and oxygen or mixtures of silica, alumina, and iron. Not the universal solvent, and certainly not the rapid oxidation of a material in an exothermic chemical process of combustion. Don't get me wrong, I like throwing fire around as much as the next wizard, but there's nothing mythical about it.

Only when you let go of all the mysticism garbage can you see the world for its breathtaking beauty.

The cosmos is a giant clock made of anarchy that's always on time.

It runs on laws. Infallible, unbreakable, no exception laws. No excuses, no passes, and no uncertainty.

That was part of the reason I didn't relate to most people. They were always adding needless complications to straightforward concepts. When someone chafes at the idea of a law that applies under all circumstances, it's certain they are only looking for a reason why it shouldn't apply to them.

I hear it when they whine about things not being fair. Absurd. The playing field is now, and has always been, perfectly level. If it isn't a law of the universe then it's something they made up, or worse—society made it up, and they're just following along.

I break Rollo's laws whenever it's advantageous. Because I *can*.

But no one can plead insanity to escape entropy. I'd love to hear someone build a case for why they shouldn't yield to conservation of momentum. The universe doesn't allow for sympathy, doesn't deal in favoritism, and anytime anyone crosses a line, they die.

Simple. Beautiful.

It can seem like a brutal taskmaster, but no. It's an uncaring overlord presiding over a rigid system that leaves no doubt where you stand, what's required, and what will not be tolerated. It's a wonder that I was the only person I knew who found comfort in that.

For example, any mortal is permitted to move energy from one place to another. That could be something as straightforward as throwing a rock, or as complicated as making a potion that bursts into flame.

The energy of the universe, most often expressed as heat, can be put into anything. It was why old things made by expert hands—and handled often with focus or intent—had power.

The Sistine Chapel is magical. Men and women working on it for years, getting everything just right. The Great Pyramid at Giza is like that. Thousands of people working for decades. Each one imparting a little magic, each day, into each stone. Not to mention the billions looking upon it in wonder over the millennia. As a result, it was hands down the greatest single source of magic on the planet.

As far as the universe is concerned, wizards are just advanced humans. No normal human can gather the energy needed to light a candle all on their own. A few dozen together could have enough power, but they'd have no way to harness it and make it do anything.

Wizards are humans born with a harness. We can reach out to all those electrons, quarks and bosons, take a little power from each and direct the energy elsewhere. The difference being that wizards do it on purpose and not unconsciously like normal humans; but the universe is immune to such trifles.

That's why it gets cold when most spells are cast. The energy is literally being sucked out of the room.

I have a hypothesis that is why wizards are almost always depicted wearing thick, elaborate robes. This life is a chilly one.

Throwing fireballs like an Italian plumber is nice and all, but enough cold would kill you. Without taking the time to recover, I could die of hypothermia, or have some of the blood in my body freeze at just the wrong moment. All the fuzzy bunny slippers in the world couldn't save me from a potent incantation making sno-cones in my brain

I could cast a spell to destroy the world, standing in the center of a volcano, wearing a heating blanket, with a steaming cup of cocoa and I'd still freeze to death long before it went off.

Mages trained long and hard to gather energy from outside their body. The better their focus, the more power they can wield and the further out they can get it from. But no matter how much training we do, a spell will always chill someone down to their bone marrow, and it never becomes something that could be construed as safe.

The power out in the world is practically infinite, but the power inside my body is easier to get. It's the classic question of speed vs. power.

Speed is riskier, but I've always been weak. If I had to cast a spell and couldn't get it done in time, I was probably gonna die anyway.

Tema had been in the majority of those who saw physics as a hindrance. Horrid bitch that she was; she leaned far the other way on the speed vs. power debate, and no wonder—she had been one of the strongest wizards on the planet.

It hadn't been the cold that killed her, but the mental strain… and I helped a little.

Mental exhaustion was a part of casting, and that could be fatal too. Gathering energy and releasing it wasn't like flexing a muscle. It was like an emotionally draining day after an all-nighter, raised to the power of a relationship conversation that starts with "It's not me, it's you."

I could cast ten spells and run a mile with ease. Cast ten spells and sit down for a math test and I was screwed.

That's what the spells were for. Wizards need some way to keep all that energy in check. If it's uncontrolled, even for an instant, bad things happen. The incantation for a spell is a tool to hone intent and focus all that power.

It was the reason I couldn't just copy someone's words and gestures and get the same result. "Abracadabra" might let me pull a rabbit out of a hat, but it could incinerate the next wizard who tried it.

There are dangers, but they seldom come up as long as you were careful and don't start thinking you were special enough to put one over on the universe.

Tema's final scream echoed in my mind. Her last cry as the universe ripped her from existence. I shivered a bit and reminded myself how happy I was that she was dead. All my hatred and anger aside, she had been something special—but not special enough.

Reliving her last moments threw off my focused deep breathing. The light spell in my hands shattered, and I flinched. I checked my pulse and didn't have to wait the full fifteen seconds to know it was through the roof.

Meditation… Fail.

Chapter: 3

I sighed, getting lost in my own head again. "Only the present," I said out loud to an empty room. It was a rule I had and almost never followed. Only the present moment mattered. Reliving the past was destructive. That didn't stop me from doing it, but I could at least remind myself that the goal was to stop eventually.

By now the sun had sunk below the horizon, and that left me sitting in the dark alternately growling at Rollo and trying not to think about it. I didn't know what time it was and didn't bother to pull my phone out of my pocket to check. It was dark, and my day was done. I also didn't bother to lock the door. I wanted people to come in when I wasn't around to return bottles and see that I kept nothing of value in my labs.

Sighing, I grabbed my black leather backpack and headed down the stairs. I didn't know what I wanted to do, which sucked for someone who usually knew what they wanted to do.

The first floor of all of my labs were homeless shelters; one giant concrete room with about thirty cots set up on the far wall. There was a table near the stairs that went up to my office, and on it was a large pot, some dirty plastic bowls, spoons, a water cooler and an overflowing trashcan with more of the same.

The cots were all empty, which was odd, but not unheard of this time of year. If it were winter they would all be full, with folks on the floor beside them. This time of year, people mostly came for the free food.

Only one person was around. I'd never seen her before, but that wasn't odd. People came, stayed for a while, and left; she was new. She was also hunched over filling a cheap plastic bowl with Miles' stew from last night. I finished the stairs and headed past her towards the back door.

"You must be Maker," she said as I passed.

"That was a nasty rumor for a while. Most folks are decent enough not to repeat it."

Her nose had been broken, and her shining blonde hair hid most of a nasty bruise on her forehead. When she smiled, she showed a mouth that was missing a couple teeth. Life had been hard lately. She was young though, younger than me. Still had time to recover and make something of herself. We should all be so lucky.

"What's your real name? It can't be Maker, can it?"

"No, that isn't my real name, and I'm not gonna tell you what my real name is. To know something's name is to know its nature. Gives you the power to get its attention." She nodded like she understood.

Everyone here knew I was a wizard, though most thought I did kid parties and card tricks. That, or they thought I was a few blades short of a massacre.

"If someone knew your full name, they could do all sorts of nasty things to you, and I've only got one. No last name, no middle name, no hyphened-on additions. Most people have at least three. It's horribly unfair." That wasn't entirely true. I knew I had a full name because most people did, but hell if I knew what it was.

I didn't teach magic 101 to the masses or anything. It's just the people that came here were far more likely than average to have a brush with something big, mean, and supernatural in a dark alley. It certainly didn't hurt to spread a little knowledge.

"Do you know Myer?"

"Met him once in passing. I know a couple of Merlin's crew. Wait, how do you know Myer?"

There are moments in life when your brain suddenly registers a million facts at once. This girl was wearing jeans and a t-shirt. The jeans were ripped but not worn. The shirt wasn't threadbare, in fact, there wasn't a loose thread to be seen. Her hair was white, which meant she bleached it. Not impossible to do in a gas station sink, but highly unlikely it would look that good. Lastly, she was clean. Her broken nose and scars no longer convinced me she belonged here, as she had likely showered more recently than I had.

"*Raken Symtam Tiala,*" she yelled and grabbed my arm. I felt the chill of the magic in the air just before I screamed. I've been hit by a Taser before; compared to that, this wasn't that bad. High voltage. Low amperage. Still hurt though… a lot.

"*Breezy,*" I grunted. Pretty sure it was just a grunt. No one listening would've known I spoke, but my pack always knew what I meant. The tiny vial would've come to my hand except my hand was clenched in pain. Instead, it fell between us and shattered. The gust was enough to blow her back to the wall. A few dozen cubic feet of air, violently expanding in the presence of suspended gravity, will tend to do that. I was blown the opposite direction, but I knew it was coming so I landed on my feet, more or less.

She was rising. I had a million questions, but I'm not the type of man that can bet on winning a fair fight. I can light candles with magic, and I can make a gust of wind that would make Marilyn Monroe blush, but not much more than that. My magical abilities are minimal, but fighting for my life—I knew how to do that.

"*Expelliamus!*" The spell made my blood feel like it was being served on the rocks. Trillions of photons gathered at the command.

I cocked two fingers on both hands and fired from the hip like I was in an old western. The good ones that are black & white and feature six-shooters with infinite bullets. The shots hit her and did nothing; it was just bright light and nothing more. Theoretically, she would be fine—even if I hit her a million times. That was before she opened her eyes. A scream tore from her throat as her retinas burned and the light sent her into permanent darkness.

Wizards were not supposed to kill with magic; it was frowned upon to kill at all. Any wizard that used magic to kill a human would wake up facing down one of the Martinet. Or worse, never see the Martinet and not wake up at all. I had never broken that law on purpose, but Merlin and his crew didn't care much for the 'it was an accident' excuse or 'he's just a child.' Amazing they let me live this long.

Because I tried hard to follow that rule, I pulled out of my jacket the one thing no wizard should ever go without: a pistol.

I took aim at her chest and was about to fire when she screamed.

You don't need words or gestures to work a spell; they just insulate your mind from the forces ripping through it and help shape all that energy into the form you want. She didn't use any words this time, she just screamed.

Whips of fire lashed out from her in every direction. There were enough that I didn't bother to shoot, I just dove to the floor and started scrambling away towards the back door. The fire licked the walls behind her and triggered one of my traps.

Plastic tubes sprung from the wall and tore into her. There were more than fifty, and each had a low gauge needle that stabbed into her body. They wrapped her up and burrowed beneath her skin. I designed it to drain someone of blood but not kill them; the trap would even put blood back if that's what it took to keep her alive.

It didn't work well. In fact, it had killed everyone that had ever tripped it. Nothing I made worked well—except potions.

The fire stopped almost instantly, but I wasn't taking chances today. I couldn't channel that level of evocation on my best day, she'd panicked and done it by reflex. My pistol barked twice, but she was already gone. That level of mental strain was fatal.

Maybe I could tell the Martinet that she'd died from mental strain. I'd already talked them into letting me slide on traps.

"As I was saying, I know Myer," I said getting up from the floor. I kept the gun on her and searched for any movement as I crossed the room. "I know a few of the Martinet, and while Myer and I have only met in passing, we seem to have one thing in common, but I digress."

I looked down at the lump of flesh that used to be a living breathing woman. That had been one of the more obvious magical traps I'd set around my lab. I guess she couldn't feel it coming. The tubes and needles unwound and disappeared back into the wall. They could only respond to something alive. I sighed. It had been an all-around crappy day.

I turned her over in the growing pool of blood. Death was always so messy. Blood has a metallic smell, with all the minerals in the human bloodstream. It stunk, but at least she hadn't let go of her bowels yet.

She wasn't blonde anymore. Her hair was stained with streaks of red already oozing onto the floor. Normally blood would gush from the body with two shots in the chest, but not if it's mostly frozen. I could feel the cold standing over her and see patches of frost on her skin. Even if there were no mental strain, she would've died from the cold. Amateur.

I holstered my pistol and sat down against a wall to rest for a minute. If she activated a trap, that meant my wards were down. My wards appeared formidable, but they were quite weak—just like anything else I did. Instead of being a defense that could fry anyone that walked in, they held back the power that flowed to my traps.

I made them like that so they could only be triggered by wizards who knew enough to tear down someone's wards before they attacked. No one that knew of this place—and had a reason to be here—would take down my wards. She must've ripped them apart and got all confident, not knowing she was arming all my traps in the process.

I worked hard to make the mistakes of my enemies fatal, since I could never rely on overpowering them. Half of that was setting things up in advance, and the other half was figuring out ways to do maximum damage at minimal power. Good strategy was the only reason I was still alive. I ambushed, set traps, and ran like hell the moment things stopped going my way. I was a student of Sun Tzu, and I like to think he'd be proud.

This particular wizard wasn't big on tactics; that's why she lay dead on the floor. I would never come for a wizard's life alone—unless I had blood, hair, true name or some other overwhelming advantage. Even then, I'd rather shoot them from as far away as possible. Then again, I had no proof that she'd come alone.

I wanted to search her body, but I wanted to get the hell out of there even more, so I got to my feet.

"*Coroner.*" Summoning something from my pack was never cold like a powerful spell. It was more like someone with cold hands rubbing a few hairs on the back of your neck.

A perfectly plain, impossibly white sheet appeared in my hand. I laid it over her and spoke the word, "*Disappear.*" Space was not an easy thing to manipulate; it greatly resisted folding in on itself. Any spell that created an extra dimensional space was exceedingly complicated, but it wasn't impossible with a little finesse.

The shroud collapsed. I picked it up and began to fold it. The body was gone, and there was not even a drop of blood to say that it had been there at all.

I couldn't do much about the scorch marks, but homeless

people tended not to ask questions when they had a warm bed and a hot meal.

I would've liked to put the sheet back in my pack, but that would take a few hours I didn't have. I shoved it in the pocket of my black canvas jacket, and headed for the back door. I wanted to be out of here. It was too dangerous to stay until my wards restored themselves, and that would take a few days.

"*Staff.*" Most wizards used made-up words or dead languages for their spells. I didn't know why; something to do with proper visualization. English had always worked fine for me.

My staff appeared in my hand. It was a collapsible kevlar stick almost six feet long and a couple inches thick. Right now, it was folded up to be the size of a small baton, but that could change with a thought. I could fight with it as a staff even if I didn't have magic. I practiced with Zora for the day when I'd need to. I left through the back door hoping that wasn't today.

The alley outside was dark, and I rushed out. I got to the end of the alley and into the pale, dead glow of streetlights. I slowed to a walk, which occasionally trespassed into the realm of slow jog. The street was curiously empty, even for evening, and that put me on edge. This wasn't a busy street by any means, but there was normally the occasional car or pedestrian to be seen. I started moving towards a main thoroughfare a few blocks over.

I'd figured out years ago that everyone wanted my pack, but not necessarily my life. I have five laboratories. When warlocks attack, they normally come in at night, ransack the place, tip over some furniture and hopefully trigger a trap or two.

This was one of the few times one attacked when I was actually there. I couldn't say I approved of that turn of events. I was more than happy to walk in once a year and find bodies rather than having to make them myself.

For the time being, I had to find a safe place to hole up.

Running into a single warlock is the same as running into a single ant.

Going home was out. I'd only lead whoever else was coming for me straight to my safest space. No warlocks know where I live, and I'd like to keep it that way. If there has to be a fight, I'd rather it be on my terms; in a setting of my choice. Some out of the way place. Somewhere no one who wasn't directly involved would get hurt.

Chapel Hill was the next city over and after that was nothing but large tracts of open land, with thick forest in places. I decided to spend the night there, and hope that blonde troll-faced gunman was acting alone.

Two blocks over and I was on a busier road. Busy enough for me to wave down a cab at least. The driver was nice enough, although she turned a pair of wary green eyes to my strained face. Still, I was asking her to take me to Chapel Hill, which ought to make her night as far as paychecks go. She nodded once, and I crawled in the back. Cabbies are often talkative, but she didn't say much. I was glad for the rest and a chance to think.

Most people think I'm insane and don't speak to me anyway. I vocalize most of my thoughts as low muttering and everyone just assumes that anyone thinking out loud must be crazy. Anyone crazy must also be dangerous, and that pretty much sums up all my social interactions.

As we drove, I kept an eye on the traffic around us. I didn't see any cars following us, though that meant little. We were already on I-40 heading north like a bat out of hell, and I wasn't about to tell her to slow down.

I held my staff, felt it, and focused on it. It was more than half full. My staff didn't help me focus magical energy or help me do something I wasn't good at on my own, like most wizard's staffs. It was actually the magical equivalent of a battery. While I slept, it siphoned off my magic to store, and it took me more than a month to fill it up completely. The stored-up magical energy was what allowed me to power any spell I chose.

"UUUUUND!!!" The sound was like a bass drum and a clap of thunder happening *inside* my skull. I managed not to scream, but just barely. I think my stifled grunts worried the taxi driver even more and had her reconsidering if the fare was worth it.

There are ancient beings in the universe. Some were there at the beginning of it, and I just-so-happened to have one in my head. Tema put it there, and I killed her for it. It was actually the backlash of all the power in the spell, but my anger always demanded the credit.

Tema Rion was not a nice person. If she were still alive today, I'd kill her again, and be doing the world a favor. I didn't know anything about the spirit, beyond that it was some minor god of knowledge and wisdom. Like Athena with a lot less power.

Whatever its name was, I didn't know it; I couldn't interact with it at all. I surmised that it moved through time differently than I did. A day for me might be ten thousand years to it, or vice versa. Imagine a creature whose whole life lasted all of a half-second; no matter how fast you talked, you could never have any meaningful contact with it. So, I couldn't speak to it and it couldn't speak to me.

Despite the communication barrier, I had to wonder if it was the reason I was so gifted with magical theory. Sometimes a spell just comes to me, then I find that I don't have the power to actually cast it. Normally that results in me constructing some tool to cast it for me that doesn't work.

I cradled my ringing head, staring at my staff and wishing to god that it was full. I pulled out my phone. There were only about five numbers in it. Zora, Miles, and a couple places where I knew I could get a decent pizza. I only briefly considered calling for help. The only other wizard I knew in the area was Zora, but she was only slightly stronger than me, currently injured, and I didn't know everything I was dealing with. The other wizards I knew could be contacted easily, but none of them would be able to get here today.

The Martinet had their hands full. The war with the vampires was on the upswing since vampire numbers were rising. They were also at war with the werewolves, the fae legions, and of course, evil wizards. "War" was a misnomer; it wasn't like they ever got together for pitched battles or anything. It was just the most succinct way to say "we don't like you and we're going to exterminate you." "The Genocides" would be a better appellation.

The Martinet in North America were particularly strained. Martinet Wizard Christian Gomez was on the West coast, and probably had more important matters than dealing with a warlock or two. Myer might still be up in Canada, but he would just as soon kill me right along with whoever was hunting me.

I was on my own, like always. It'd sure be nice to have a little help once in a while though. I started texting Zora.

Sitrep: A lock hit me at the lab and I'm heading north in a cab to hide out. Think she was alone but I'm gonna spend the night in the woods to make sure. If you haven't heard from me by tomorrow night feel free to go hunting.

It only took a moment before the response came:

Ackd

I reached into my backpack to grab a potion. I hadn't slept well the past few nights, and I was already feeling the fight with Blondie. I muttered "*Wakey wakey*" under my breath to avoid spooking the cabbie any further. I downed the blue liquid in one gulp, dropped the bottle in my cargo pocket, and sat back to let it take effect. It was my Wake-up Special. I sold these too, though not as often. This was like five shots of espresso, two Adderall and a full night's sleep. If someone sawed off my leg I would barely notice.

The formula was flawed. It woke me up, but it also wouldn't let me sleep. After a few days with no sleep and constant activity, the human body goes into revolt. I had to heavily dilute every batch, which is no easy feat for potions. The benefit was that I could throw spells a little longer before it caught up to me. I would pay for it in the morning.

We were past Chapel Hill, heading west on I-40 when a semi sped past and jack knifed right in front of us, blocking three of the four lanes. Luckily, the cabbie had the reflexes of a cat and swerved to avoid it. Not so luckily, the taxi spun out, and we slammed into the ditch going eighty miles per hour. We slid to a stop before hitting anything more significant.

I had the seat in a death grip as the smell of overheating brakes and burnt rubber wafted into the car. I slowed my breathing down and shook my head. I must've hit it on something because I was a bit foggy. The adrenaline locked me up, and it took a few breaths to release my death grip on the seat and regain control of my faculties.

I fumbled with the seat belt, finally got it to release and stumbled out of the car. My head was still foggy and I was and dizzy. The crash had taken us past the truck. The driver and I were mostly unharmed, if somewhat shaken, but the car was trashed. I could tell when she tried to restart it.

I ducked back in, collected my pack, tossed a fifty on the front seat and climbed out again, leaving the cabbie to her frustrated muttering. It was bizarrely quiet and dark on the road. No traffic was making it past the wrecked rig. I sniffed the air; nothing smelled dangerous, and I didn't hear anything that sounded like I should be running from it. I walked cautiously up the embankment, towards the truck. Shaking my head in a vain effort to clear it.

A small crowd was already gathering; a number of cars had pulled off to the shoulder or simply stopped in the middle of the road, and people were milling around. I hung back, wanting to have some idea what the situation was before deciding to get involved or not. I saw a couple people with cell phones to their ears, but couldn't make out any of the conversation.

I looked further back up the road. There were a handful of vehicles parked in a row across the freeway at the exit we'd just passed. All of them had their hazard lights flashing. The drivers seemed to be directing oncoming traffic to the off-ramp. My attention wandered back to the people closer to me, but something was bothering me. I couldn't quite put my finger on it, but something wasn't right about this.

I checked my phone. I'd obviously hit my head and blacked out in the cab, but it couldn't have been more than a couple minutes. How had everyone reacted so fast?

My eyes flicked back to the people on the off-ramp. It was more than a little strange for innocuous bystanders to be this… organized. Not to mention, calm, and so soon after such a big accident. Even stranger—I didn't hear a single siren, and the only flashing lights I could see were ordinary car blinkers. For this stretch of highway not to have a single emergency responder within five miles yet was simply unheard of.

I frowned. My head was clearing and my suspicions sharpening. Was this an accident or a poorly executed ambush?

A warlock just tried to kill me, so it was entirely possible I was just paranoid. Then again, it would only be paranoia if I was wrong. I started to back away from the milling crowd, trying to look inconspicuous. Glancing around, I took stock of my options and decided to head for the woods on the far side of the freeway.

Beyond the semi-truck, the freeway was dark and quiet. It was easy enough to slink over the median unnoticed once I'd put some distance between myself and the wrecked rig. The eastbound side of the freeway was a different story; traffic had slowed due to the rubberneckers, and no one was paying attention to the road. I nearly got hit twice, and it seemed like it took an eternity, but I finally got across. Shaken, but unscathed.

My little game of Frogger was accompanied by car horns and screamed curses. The noise surely alerted any interested parties in the crowd at the accident to both my location and my intended destination, so I didn't dawdle.

I snapped my staff, sharply extending it to its full six-foot length as I dashed across the shoulder and stepped into the forest beyond. I could already hear the bastards behind me.

Chapter: 4

I trailed my staff along the ground behind me, allowing a trickle of power to flow from the tip. Living things grew if you gave them power; it was that simple. Although some plants were more responsive than others.

Weeds, for example, grew faster than trees given the same amount of energy—even when the plants themselves were the same size. I channeled the energy out in a four-meter spread behind me. The weeds and brambles sprung up, growing nearly twice their height in moments.

I was pretty fit. I could jog forever if I wanted, but I couldn't keep up that pace on this terrain for more than a mile or two. My boots would probably give me another couple miles. They enhanced my speed and gave me sure footing even mountain goats would envy. I wanted to know who was after me and why, but I sure as hell wasn't going to stop and ask them about it.

I heard a howl in the distance, and two others answered. I prayed that they were just hunting dogs. If werewolves had gotten my scent, there would be no hiding until they were dead. There would also be no point in running. I'd make it a few miles only to die tired.

I heard an answering call from something a few hundred yards in front of me, and my stomach dropped. Similar voices to the left and right told me I was surrounded. "Damn," I muttered. How the hell did I walk into this?

I raised the hood on my jacket and pulled the black mesh attached to it over my face. I really hoped this didn't turn bad.

I pressed myself as hard as I could into a thick tree, jerked my pistol out, and punched my staff an inch into the ground. Long grasses and brambles flew up the tree and over me. Hopefully they would conceal me entirely, scent and all.

I couldn't do an illusion, or an invisibility spell large enough to hide me, even if my life depended on it. I have proof of that statement since my life currently depended on it, and I couldn't. I wasn't the greatest in power, but I was adept at using what magical energy I did have to great effect—and being outgunned while doing it. I could create a gust of wind, split it into five parts and use them to blow out candles on a few dozen birthday cakes… well, probably. I mean, I've never tried that exactly, but it's the sort of solution I'd come up with.

I huddled back into the weeds, took a deep breath, and held it. The hunting party came in sight; mostly cultists with rifles and hoodies, one visible warlock and three feral men in chains. They looked like large hairy men, but they acted just like wolves at times. I called them "wilds" or "wildmen." They were people who'd had their humanity wiped away and now lived exclusively catering to their baser instincts. Behind them were five ordinary looking men and women, all dressed in jeans and black hoodies. One of them was holding the leashes, and each one had a rifle. The warlock was a gnarled old woman in red robes who seemed to glide along the ground rather than walk. I felt the power in my staff and on my lips.

They were headed right for me, and they'd pass me not more than ten feet away. If I got lucky, I'd go unnoticed and be able to slip away once they were beyond my hiding spot. I wasn't counting on being that lucky.

They were moving closer, but I could barely see through all the foliage. All I could hear was my heart pounding in my ears. It was so loud I was sure it would give me away. I grabbed my fear by the scruff of the neck, and gave it a savage kick to the back of my mind. "And stay there!" I thought. I had to stay calm if I wanted to live through this.

I was starting to wonder if I should've bought a lottery ticket when the howl of the lead wildman went up, just before I would've been able to slip away too. I tore myself out of the brambles and made a mad dash in the other direction.

I hadn't made it two steps when I heard, "*Flancanio Sano Ithc Forn Ignus!*" The flame shot towards me. I brought up my staff and swung. The gust of wind from my staff was minuscule in comparison. I had time to be shocked, yet again, at the power some wizards could wield.

There was no way I could stop that fire; but stopping things was never an option for me. Moving something a few inches to the right or left so it didn't kill me was much easier. I parry, I dodge; I never block.

Any wizard can toss a flame, but creating a ball of solid air that suffocates your enemy if they cast a spell? That's not taught at the prim and proper spell-casting academies. That's a street fighter move.

The wind at the end of my staff captured the fire and swirled it around me. It was enough to feel the heat, even at that distance. I spun, bringing it back around to smash into the face of the first wildman. It screamed at the burn and reeled away as its head caught fire.

The second was right behind him, snarling. I ducked, and the hairy beast went sailing right over me. I yanked on my pistol and took a shot at the fire-wielding hag before I was back up and running. The bullet went wide and harmlessly took a chunk out of a tree near her face. The second wildman had landed, spun around, and was heading back to face me.

"*Steam*," I whispered, and the water molecules in his eyes evaporated. He screamed and clawed at his face, but I was already on to the next assailant. A third wildman swiped at me. The dirt and filth caked around his infected nails were probably as dangerous as the claws themselves. I dodged as he drew his arm back to swing again, noticing another bonfire headed straight for my face.

"*Kelvin!*" The potion dropped into my hand just in time for me to fling it at the fire. The bottle exploded, and the liquid helium inside turned the flame into a large benign puff of smoke. Good thing too; I could use as much obfuscation as I could get. It would stop anyone far away from targeting me, but that wasn't gonna work on the wildman coming for my throat.

"*Solid*." A marble-sized drop of blood in his neck became a hard, jagged, blood-colored chunk instead. His swipe turned into a stumble, shaking his head and coughing. It would only last a minute or two. I wasn't near strong enough for permanent transmutation in a living thing, but he wouldn't bother me again.

My attention moved to the five hoodie-clad people who were coming at me now, and the fire-slinging woman who was preparing another spell—something bigger and more involved this time. "*Puppet!*" Strands of invisible stiff air pushed and pulled at her arms and legs, jerking them in random directions.

It wouldn't stop her from casting technically, but casting is mental; it requires focus. For many wizards, the technically nonessential movements are just as important as the technically nonessential words. She was no exception, snarling and shrieking in frustration. It wasn't a win, but I'd bought enough time to deal with the others.

I heard the automatic gunfire before I saw the guns. I wasn't paying attention when the hoodies aimed those rifles, but each one pointed at me and went full auto.

My canvas jacket and pants were laced with spells that made me bulletproof, fireproof, and every other proof I could think of; however, there was no way to completely steal the momentum from a bullet. After all, magic must still yield to physics. What my spell-stitched clothing could do was spread the momentum out over a larger area and greater time; converting the energy into heat. Same principle as a bulletproof vest.

Even with the magic helping, it felt like getting hit in the chest with baseballs thrown by a major league pitcher. One bullet hit my mesh facemask and sent me spinning to the ground. I screamed, but pain and I are drinking buddies, and like any good friend he handed me a beer and reminded me I was still alive. So, I clutched my staff, gathered power, and turned my whole world into a freezer.

"*Tetanus!*" This time I screamed the word. I was well into the realm of panic. I had to end this, and soon. About ten old rusty nails dropped into my hand and I flung them in the general direction of the gunshots. They weren't big, but they didn't have to be. The hoodies went down screaming, reaching for their bloodied shoulders, knees and other non-vitals. The nails were designed to find a joint, dig in and shatter. All the hoodies went down, and the bullets stopped pummeling me. Now if only I had time to celebrate.

The wizard woman had regained her focus and was already halfway through a spell. "*Shut up!*" I screamed, and she went bug-eyed as a fist-sized ball of invisible solid air was suddenly holding her jaw agape. Her hands flew to her mouth to try and force it out.

I could try and kill her, but my hands were shaking, I was already starting to feel the frost lingering in my blood, and my vision was blurry from the head shot I'd just taken. It was all too much to guarantee a hit—even at this close range. I didn't dare get closer. I couldn't even line up my sights. I didn't want to fumble my gun and waste more time, and I wasn't willing to break Merlin's rules… again. I was out of options. I left the flame-throwing bitch with her invisible gag and stumbled away.

It wasn't long before my head cleared and the stumble turned into a flat-out run. I heard more people behind me. I tapped my staff on the ground and did my weeds-and-brambles trick again. This time I sent the trail of plants off to the north while I went south. A simple trick; I didn't expect it to divert them all and they'd figure it out in short order, but it should buy me enough time to figure out… whatever I would think of next.

I came to a road and crossed it at a dead run. I didn't look to see what road it was, but I knew if I could make it another mile or so I would be in downtown Chapel Hill—and relative safety. They've proven they could find me too easy in these woods and towns had hiding places. I put up more brambles behind me, hoping that would make them think I'd taken the road.

Something grabbed my calf with sharp teeth, and I tripped. I hadn't heard a thing. The first signal I got, other than the stabbing pain, was a threatening growl behind me. I flipped on my back to see a dark grey wolf the size of Detroit. Something about it was off—it didn't immediately register as a werewolf, but I was in no position to study it.

"*Boingy!*" I don't know if it was coming for my throat so I cast a spell, or if I casted a spell, so it came for my throat. What I did know was that it wasn't gonna get far trying to crush my arm with rubber teeth.

"*Solid!*" I slammed my hand into its chest and its blood solidified, but far more than I wanted. It seized up and fell, making wheezing sounds. I grabbed my staff where it fell, got to my feet and stumbled. I had to use a tree to get my balance, and shook my head to clear the cobwebs that were forming.

The werewolf lay there twitching. No way it was going to

survive. I put too much power into that spell. Dammit, I could almost feel one of the Martinet over my shoulder.

Living things resisted being transmuted into other things. Whatever was altered always changed back, unless there was some power keeping it that way. None of the living transmutations I cast ever lasted more than a minute or two. Normally I didn't need that long to make someone rethink attacking me, but these guys weren't giving up.

What the hell was going on?! Warlocks were glorified scavengers. They rarely put in this much effort, and they were never this organized.

I concentrated for a moment. I was breathing hard. My breath was white vapor in front of me as the energy in the air was pulled in. The bone-deep chill felt as familiar and natural as the breathing, but even after casting spells for most of my life it had never gotten comfortable.

"*I want eyes on everything*," I said in my best Nick Fury impersonation. Behind my closed eyes there were eight screens; each was a little blurry and lacked any depth perception.

I knew that eight floating, translucent eyeballs exactly like my own appeared in front of me. They hovered for a moment, then shot off into the night.

The screens all showed different scenes and the eyes found my pursuers easily enough. There were around twenty of them. One was a giant black wolf, and three were robe clad warlocks, the rest where men and women with Ak-47's at the ready. They were striding through the woods at a brisk pace, with the wolf in the lead, not one of them was even looking around. A small glowing eye, hovering in a tree thirty feet above you, was hard to miss if you were paranoid. The reason they weren't looking for anything is because they knew exactly where they were going.

They were confident, I could use that, but no way I could take on three 'locks when one was a challenge. Where the hell had all these people even come from?

I couldn't take this into town now. If they tried to take me out on an interstate, a few late-night roaming college kids looking for various combinations of sex, beer, and pizza, wouldn't stop them. Had there been a few cult followers I could've lost them easily in a town. There were too many now, and none had fallen for my brambles. Not with a werewolf in tow. That wolf could smell me from two states away, see me move in the dark of a new moon, and hear my heartbeat while standing between the Superbowl and a Carnegie Hall performance. That was an exaggeration, but not by much.

I opened my eyes and the screens in my mind disappeared. I was shivering and breathing even harder—that was one of the most demanding spells I had. You couldn't just tell an octillion atoms to drop whatever they were doing, rearrange themselves into a completely new configuration and do some scouting for you without consequence. At best, my staff was an eighth full by now.

"*Recluse.*" I threw the bottle down and died a little inside. Getting a hundred brown recluse spiders into a jar wasn't easily done, nor was speeding up the reaction of their venom, nor getting them sit quietly long enough to bite the person you wanted. I wasn't entirely sure I could reproduce it, and it was gonna take months to figure it out if I wanted any more.

"*Oz,*" I said, repeating it twice. Three small apples appeared in my hand and I tossed them up into three nearby trees. None of them were apple trees, but it made no difference. "Kill the werewolf first, then everyone else." I commanded, and ran on.

The trees would only be able to move for a few seconds, but now they had my intelligence, sans my pesky sense of self-preservation. Add some poisonous spiders, determined to bite any human in sight, that equation equaled deadly. If that plan succeeded, I could shake these douchebags and go home.

The trouble with having plans, is that they almost never worked out precisely how I planned. The cure for that is having lots of plans. I never set just one trap or just one ambush. I'd set ten traps with each one being fatal and I couldn't care less which one finished the job. The trouble at the moment was the cold seeping into my flesh. It was a warning, but for the time being I had to ignore it.

I came to a large puddle and reached for my pack again. "*On the rocks.*" A penny appeared in my hand, and I tossed it in. Hopefully, that would catch a few of them. Stepping on or near the penny would cause the mini lake to freeze solid.

I strung some burning lines of p-quinone between two trees. I didn't know what p-quinone was two years ago, but David Attenborough was happy to tell me all about it. Now it was the tool of myself and bombardier beetles, used for the express purpose of convincing predators to reconsider their life choices.

There were lots of chemicals in nature that were barely held together and dying to release their bond energy in a symphony of exothermic chemical reactions. Getting them not to explode until they were touched was the trick.

The lines looked like yellow spider webs, and therefore almost impossible to see at night. The strings would burn hot enough to leave a mark on anyone that touched them. They were an annoyance at best, but their point was to get my pursuers to be cautious. Caution would slow them down, which provided a greater chance for more of them to be in the water when it froze solid.

I ran another few steps and set a pile of leaves to explode when they were kicked or stepped on.

I was setting up a stump to shatter in a hail of splinters and thinking up the next trap, when I heard the trees crash behind me. There was a loud yelp, gunshots, and a lot of screaming. Plans hardly ever worked the way I intended, guess this was one of the "hardlys."

There wasn't much you could do to stop a moving sentient tree from doing whatever it wanted. No wolf would be expecting a tree to come to life, no human either for that matter.

With a growl, I turned around. Whoever these warlocks were they had almost killed me several times, chased me from one end of town to the another, and for what? I still didn't know for sure. It was time to beat some answers out of someone.

"*Kitty Pride*." A potion appeared in my hand and I drank it. It had to have been ten minutes already; so much had happened.

After a few moments, the world became brighter—almost like daylight. Odd that it was the way it looked to me. To anyone looking on, shadows would be gathering around me like waves of heat. I ran back towards where the screams had been; they weren't getting away now. Despite my speed, all was serene; the potion made all my movements silent.

I was back in no time and found a dead wolf, a dead warlock, several cultists, and a partridge under the two trees that had fallen over. The third tree was scorched and leaning at a severe angle; one of the warlocks must've gotten a spell off.

By the time I made it to the road, the rest of the cultists were piling into an old brown van and driving off. "*Peel*," I whispered with malice. I started running; with the potion, the spell, and my magically enchanted boots I was making about eighty miles an hour. This would probably leave me half dead the moment everything wore off. I caught the van easily; it wasn't like they could see me.

"*Nail*." The gravel under the tires shot straight up. I didn't think any went through the bottom of the van. The two front tires popped like over eager party balloons.

"*Lance!*" Funny how you start screaming when you don't have much left. The air in front of the van solidified into an eight-foot tall invisible road block. Like some giant had stabbed a sword up through the ground at an acute angle. With no front tires, they didn't have a chance in hell of stopping in time.

Non-living things were much easier when it came to transmutation. If it was living, or even touching something living, the effect tended to be a lot smaller, not last long, or both. I could make a roadblock this big, but only because it wasn't living… and it only had to last a fraction of a second.

It wasn't enough to flip the van over like I'd hoped. It didn't even last the full half-second I'd been hoping for, but it was enough to send the van flying out of control. It plowed right through the roadblock and only stopped when it t-boned on a telephone pole.

I walked up slowly, which was a little tricky with a spell, a potion, and magical boots all affecting my speed. I didn't sense any movement, and I didn't want to reach out with my magical senses. If someone was alive in there and doing the same, they would feel me coming.

My staff was empty, so I sent it back to baton form and shoved it in a cargo pocket. I stumbled towards the van. I was openly shivering now. It was too dangerous to cast much more until I warmed up. I grabbed my pistol and held it in both shaky hands.

I took aim on the van and started to circle around to the front. I saw the driver was halfway through the windshield. That made this easy, "*Last Call,*" I said. He wasn't alive, so this would last for hours, maybe even days. The police would find his blood alcohol level through the roof. Take blood, turn it into alcohol. It was a spell I thought up for use in interrogations, but it had other more obvious uses. Better living through chemistry.

The van was full of people, everyone was unconscious and covered in blood. I noticed a few swollen legs and hands turning black with necrotic venom already. They had obviously tried to begin first aid once they were in the van. They couldn't all be dead, but their superior numbers, even in this state, talked me right out of the grand interrogation schemes I'd thought up minutes earlier.

I'd won, more importantly I was alive. That was all that mattered.

I turned and ran off towards Chapel Hill, feeling the wind whip my face as I went faster than a car on the freeway. I sighed. Physically and mentally leaving the van behind, I relaxed—that was my mistake.

"*Danken Shambla Haren Ulsa Aarithan Dabilto!*"

Normally when someone is moving at a mile a minute, that's sixty miles an hour for those not savvy with arithmetic, they tend to have something that keeps them from being killed if they stop suddenly. Seat belts, airbags, a perfectly placed pillow, or something made by Acme. I had enough time to realize that my legs had locked up somehow, and enough time to wish I had some kind of helmet in case my hood and mask weren't enough. The thought of solidifying the air around my head occurred to me, and then there was pavement.

Lots of pavement.

I don't remember the tumble, but I must've hit the grass quickly because I was still alive when I woke up to midnight in a ditch. I was being dragged along by my arm, in far more pain than anyone dead could claim.

I didn't open my eyes. Everything ached. There was talking, but I couldn't make it out. I stopped myself from shaking my head at the last moment, and instead focused on keeping every muscle placid. Especially the ones in my face.

I didn't know what was going on, but my head was starting to clear. First, I wasn't dead. Second, judging by the way my body was already complaining, by morning I would wish that I was. Lastly, I still had my pack strapped to my back. All good news.

I cracked my eyes and could barely make out stars in a cloudless sky. I could see the Hag fire lady, a handsome hawknose man, and five of their followers. The one dragging me along in the procession was a large scruffy looking man with reddish-brown hair. I couldn't see the other faces since they all were wearing black hoodies. As far as I could tell, everyone was limping or injured to some degree. They probably left behind anyone who couldn't walk. Firehag was speaking, and it was clear she was upset.

"…losses on this debacle of yours," she hissed.

"Brian is no great loss. Did you see the way those trees came to life? This one is worth two morphs and a dozen normals." I assumed it was Hawknose talking. He was the only other one wearing a long heavy coat in spring. It was always nice to hear respect and fear of your enormous powers from your enemies. Especially when they were wrong.

"At best, all we've done is replace Brian with this one. That's not a victory. We'll be lucky if we aren't killed for your *initiative*," she infested the last word with scorn. "More like incompetence. Can't believe I let you talk me into this."

There was a pregnant pause, and I took that to mean the conversation was over… but I was wrong. Hawknose was quick on the uptake. He felt it before she did.

"Do you hear—" he began. That was as far as he got.

"Leroy Jenkins!" It was Zora with the best battle cry ever. She came in from the right so fast that she was only a blur. The man holding me only had time to turn and face her, taking the strike full on. He didn't even have time to scream, before his head toppled to the ground. I heard spells being prepared and weapons being cocked, but there was no target for them to hit. She was gone.

"Breezy, Owl." I said. Sunglasses appeared in my left hand and a clear bottle in my right. I slammed the bottle down just as Hawknose let loose. Roots sprung up where I had been and grabbed the body of the dead man who'd been dragging me. The breeze blew his severed head toward the others and blew me into the sky. Those roots would've crushed me and dragged me down with him had I stuck around.

"*Fa anthom!*" Firehag screamed. I was yanked backward a bit. She hadn't put enough power into the spell to overcome both the force of the expanding air and the enchantment on my jacket. I was thrown out and away, almost to the height of the tallest trees.

Zora thought my jacket gave me the ability to fly, which was ridiculous. It was more like falling without the inconvenience of dying at the end. Still, it was great for escapes. Literally suspending gravity at varying frequencies depending on the height. Gravity still won. Gravity always wins, but if you could delay that victory then you were Tinkerbell.

If they had a werewolf they could have tracked me, but I was betting they didn't. I only remembered two wolves, and Hawknose had mentioned "two morphs."

I put on my nearly black sunglasses before my feet touched the ground, and the world became bright as daylight cast in pale shades of blue. Compared to most of the things I made, giving myself night-vision was pretty straightforward, just had to pay more attention to the infrared spectrum instead of visible light.

I landed fifty meters away and got down behind a tree. The night was dark, and this was a thicker part of the forest. Zora couldn't have picked a better spot for her ambush.

I pulled my pistol, peeked around the tree and took three shots. None of them hit. The warlocks were on the move, tearing off through the forest faster than even I thought safe.

Zora appeared next to me with her back to mine and her sword out.

"Your timing is ridiculous," I said.

"You're welcome," she laughed.

"I told you to hang back til tomorrow."

"Not as ridiculous as your lack of gratitude." She said. "Besides that's not what you said. You said I could go hunting tomorrow night. I wanted to get a jump on the other hunters, so I came early." Even without the glasses I would've seen that grin.

"Come on. They're running, and so are we."

"Cool I'll take Pinocchio, and you—"

"The other way." I said.

"What?! You just said—"

"Rule 1," I said. "Surprise round is over. We're done here."

She bared her teeth at me and stared after the warlocks like she was about to go anyway. Then she growled and sheathed her sword. We didn't make it ten strides before she forgot all about it and started teasing me instead.

"I'm not kidding. It's literally painful to move this slow," she laughed.

"There are lethargic sloths in Africa that would be happy to have this speed. You'll run at my pace and you'll like it." I'd known that using the potion and peel at the same time would leave me trashed. My legs and back ached in a way that had nothing to do with the tumble, and I was so tired I could hardly maintain a slow jog without tripping over my own feet.

Zora bounced on the balls of her feet, skipping around me in circles and grinning as we ran through the night. I did get worried about the pace though. We'd spooked them, and they ran, but that didn't mean they weren't regrouping and coming back.

I was beyond tired. With all the varied aches and pains, I wouldn't've objected to passing out right there. It was likely they weren't following us and cutting their losses. It was also possible they were making a new plan. It was that possibility that made me decide on a little more distance before getting comfortable.

"*Kitty Pride.*" I waited only half a second before I panicked. That was much too long for something to appear in my hand. Most things appeared before the words were fully out of my mouth.

I reached for my pack and found only a few loose threads on my shoulder—that must've been the spell Firehag cast. I looked up, and the sky seemed to be laughing. Suddenly, the night felt a lot colder, and I wasn't even casting a spell.

"Damn!"

Chapter: 5

Zora appeared back from her scouting mission.
"No dice. They tore up the ground pretty good, but the trail got to a road and ends there."

"Dammit," I spat. Seemed like that was the only word I was capable of speaking at the moment. That or some other curse word. The time was just after midnight, and my phone had sprouted a few more cracks. "See you back at base. I'm gonna look around."

She nodded grimly and tore off into the night heading south.

I made my way back to the road. The cops and fire department were already on the van. Once I saw the flashing red and blue lights through the trees I turned around. I had thought there was a chance someone had survived to interrogate, but it was a long shot. I didn't even bother getting closer. I could see all the white sheets laid out on the pavement from here.

I went back into the woods and retrieved the penny I'd thrown in the puddle. With no pack, I could use all the weapons I could get. The apples were one-use items, so I didn't go looking for them.

I had my staff, my clothes, an old penny, some potions and my first aid kit back at the house. Not enough.

My leg and back hurt like hell, but the injuries weren't fatal.

A few fractured vertebrae, ribs, and what felt like a broken femur. Hurt just enough to be annoying. The spells on my shirt, jacket, and pants didn't just stop bullets and knives after all. I was quite happy for that.

I tried using my boots to run and quickly stopped. They could take me from average human running speed well into average horse territory, but moving that fast only aggravated my leg.

I limped southwest. It took nearly an hour before I got to Chapel Hill and found a busy street, and another twenty minutes for the cab I called to show up.

The ride was uneventful, outside my head at least. The cabbie this time was some brunette guy, with a shaved head, who didn't talk, thankfully. Despite that, I couldn't slow down my thoughts enough to be of any use. You could never be sure what you'd get from mixing thinking and panic, but the result was never anything tasty.

I had three days—five if I were lucky—before they found a way past all the traps and into my pack.

Another run in with whatever warlock had smacked me tonight was not high on my list of fun family activities, but there wasn't much of a choice. I'd stolen things so powerful I didn't dare touch them, and things so mysterious that I didn't comprehend them fully. Not only was my pack dangerous in the wrong hands, but I was practically defenseless without it.

I still had a few days. I kept repeating that during the cab ride. It wasn't as calming as it should've been.

The security measures on my pack were considerable. They were far from infallible though, and with enough time and study any competent wizard could find a way in. There were horrible things in my pack. At least it wasn't the vamps that had taken it.

Raleigh was the seat of power for the vampires in the region. It was central on the east coast; between the deep south and the New England states. I didn't know what made Raleigh special, but it probably had something to do with the ports at Wilmington, Charleston, and DC. Everything the vampires brought across the ocean came through here at some point. I had some people paid off at the harbors to keep me informed. Vampires didn't bother with new-fangled, unproven devices like airplanes.

I had a complicated relationship with the local vamps I guess. They all lived in a mansion on an expansive estate on the north side of town. The place was called The Vermillion Falls Manor. I thought it was ironic for a bunch of vampires to live in a place essentially named "arterial bleeding." Apparently, their leader Duke thought so too.

Duke, knew me, disliked me, but didn't want to kill me. He had once called me "useful," which was "the highest praise prey can receive." I knew what prey meant, but I had no clue what he meant by useful. I was quite certain I'd never done anything that wasn't antagonistic, but apparently he thought differently.

The vamps didn't know about me robbing them… for the most part. They just knew there was someone hitting their shipments. I had invented a persona called the Phantom Lorde to throw them off.

When I hit their shipments, I destroyed everything I couldn't carry. Most times it was mundane stuff. Occasionally there were magical tools included.

Destroying anything magical wasn't something lightly done. So, I held onto most of the items so I'd have something to trade to the Martinet for points, or when I needed a favor like "please don't kill me." I had been robbing monsters since I was in my mid-teens, and I couldn't let some two-bit warlock get their hands on any of it.

I was staring out the window, three hairs from panic with a side order of gloomy. Back to my place, whatever sleep I could salvage, and an uncomfortable phone call. I decided I could procrastinate on the phone call, and I was way too wired to sleep.

It was 0200 by the time I got home. It wasn't the best neighborhood, but wasn't the worst.

I walked right by my place and into a diner two blocks down. The hanging wood sign out front read "Miles." A chef named Miles owned the place. He was probably the oldest person I knew; well, the oldest human anyway. He was a dark skinned, formerly muscular man with a head and face full of gray stubble.

Walking into Miles' made you feel like your grandfather was there to take care of you, give advice, and generally make you feel better about being you. Whether you wanted it or not.

Miles had been in the Marines for over twenty-five years, but he never talked about it. Then he'd become a state or federal officer—some kind of law enforcement—but he never talked about that either. He did that, and somehow ran a a restaurant for most of those years. He'd invested his money well, and now ran a bar and grill in a four-story hole in the wall. You could tell when his day had started based on how many white spots were left on his apron. There was no one there this time of night. In fact, there was almost never anyone there.

Miles' was closed at random hours—mainly whenever he got tired and decided to sleep. Otherwise, it was open and he was behind the bar, talking to his single patron, cooking, or entertaining one of his thousand grandchildren. I could count on one hand the number of times I'd seen the place full. There were six tables all along one wall and the bar was on the other. There were eight stools. I went to my usual spot; three down from the end.

Most people had a friend or therapist they could tell everything to; a few had their parents or some family member they trusted that much. I had a cook named Miles, and he'd give any therapist a run for their money.

He saw me limp in and plop down on the stool. He didn't miss a beat. A cold beer was at my normal stool by the time I got there. Finally able to relax, I nearly broke down. It felt like the world was over. I was safe for now… but I sure didn't *feel* safe.

"Rough night eh son?" I nodded and took a twelve-ounce pull on the bottle. "Where's your pack?"

"Stolen," I said, slamming down the empty with a clunk and a pathetic sounding belch.

"Finally. They've sure been trying long enough."

"Seven years," I nodded.

"Who was it? That new warlock guy?" He asked.

"I don't know, probably."

"Well whoever it is will be on their way to kill you with it soon enough. You can find out then."

"You want me to sit here and wait til they walk in and ghost me?!" I was on my feet now. Funny how a little adrenaline made everything feel better. I didn't even notice the leg. Miles wasn't fazed, of course. Nothing. Fazed. Miles. His face split in a grin that seemed far too big.

"Unless you got a better idea," he said.

I did. Start stepping on necks until someone told me where my damn arsenal was… and that was the moment I realized I'd been manipulated into feeling something a bit more useful. Anger could be acted upon; anger will get shit done. Despair? Not so much.

I sat back down, still mad, but there was another beer so I kinda had to forgive him.

"Bastards were well armed. Soaka seems like a good place to start, but it doesn't matter if I find them. I can't beat a full-on wizard. These guys were strong enough to be Martinet maybe. I can't beat the head honcho when I just got my ass handed to me by three of their lackeys."

"What happened?"

I told him. Everything from the blonde girl hitting my traps to me heading out of town. By the end, Miles was laughing. "There's four directions on the compass you know? And you always go west. You always pick rock too, don't ya?"

I did always pick rock. Rock was reliable, solid, and steady. But, what I said was, "I don't need this shit old man!" He handed me a broom and turned to toss some chopped beef on the pristine flat top grill. I started sweeping angrily. By the time I was done, there was an open-faced sweet n sour beef something and a third beer waiting for me. Ah, forgiveness, thy name is microbrew.

"I agree, sounds sloppy. I'd have taken you out in the cab, if I'm gonna go that high-profile," he said, leaning back and wiping out a mug that didn't need it. "Doesn't sound like they only wanted your pack. Why not just take it and leave you in a ditch?"

"Because they don't know how it works."

"Pssh, got all the time in the world to figure that out once you're dead. No way I'm gonna leave an enemy alive to threaten whatever I got planned."

"They had to want my pack. I mean… of course they wanted my pack." I didn't sound sure. "What else could they've wanted?" I hadn't even considered that they were after something else.

It must've shown on my face.

"Son, if someone tries to kill you, or has an opportunity to kill you—and you're still alive to ask questions—then the first one should be, 'How am I still alive?' Or even better, 'Why did they miss?'"

"Zora saved my ass." I said, but I still didn't sound certain.

"Not good enough. Sounds like she only showed up after they were dragging you along for a while. What do you think they were talking about? Because it sure as hell wasn't where to put the bullet."

"Well, they might've—"

He cut me off. "And just to spoil it for ya, the answer is never 'I got lucky.'"

I shoved some more food in my mouth to keep from having to answer. Surrogate grandfathers were there to help and nurture.

Sometimes that help came in the form of making you feel like an idiot. "If I had to guess, I'd say Mr. Martinet Warlock is calling you out."

"What?! What for?"

Miles just shrugged "Get up, go ask him… Hard."

I finished my beer and headed out. I didn't feel much better. I was also sleepy, my leg hurt, and I still had to limp three blocks down to the phone booth to make a call I wasn't looking forward to.

* * *

"Gomez," said the voice of a Latin man on the other end.

"Hey Christian, it's Maker." I tried to keep the nervous tone out of my voice. I didn't have to report. I wasn't Martinet or anything, not even close. I just thought it was a good idea to let the nearest Martinet know what was going on before they had to learn the facts on their own. I wasn't willing to risk them getting one or more of those facts wrong and coming to kill me. I'd only ever met three Martinet, and Gomez was by far the most reasonable.

The others were too trigger happy for my tastes. All too ready to stamp out someone for being a *potential* threat. Sometimes they were willing to wait until after the crime to kill you, but that was reserved for special occasions.

The most reasonable I'd ever met didn't mean reasonable. Gomez might've been a friend, except that I couldn't afford to trust him for the same reason I couldn't trust Rollo. He would kill me if the job required it and sleep well that night. That was why I'd only ever called him from pay phones and landlines in motels located in other cities.

"Hey man, what's up?" He said. "How's the East Coast enforcer doing?" I'd have laughed if I weren't so nervous. At least I think I would've.

"It doesn't count if you're just getting lucky," I said.

"Six warlocks in two years? It counts man. That's six I didn't have to take out myself—and that means something with the whole world coming apart."

"Eight, as of tonight." I said it and almost flinched. I didn't *technically* kill any of them with magic. The wildmen had their minds wiped so they may as well have been dead already and of course, werewolves didn't count. "I blew up some trees, they died in the confusion another was in one of my traps and we already talked about how that doesn't quite break the law so when you find out the—"

"Whoa, slow down dude. Start at the beginning," he said.

I spent the next ten minutes telling him everything that had happened that day. He only had to tell me to slow down one other time. When I was finished, there was silence on the other end, then some paper shuffling. I was getting angry; I hadn't done anything wrong… well, mostly, and here I was waiting for Gomez to come kill me.

I sighed; add him to the list I guess.

"Dammit!" He said, back on the line. "I can't get out there for at least a month. You need to get your gear back. Can't have your pack in anyone's hands we don't trust. I'm texting Myer to see if he can make it."

My stomach dropped. If he sent Myer to handle this I was leaving the state until it was done. I bet a mile beneath the most isolated swamp in Georgia was nice this time of year.

"I can get my pack, I think." I hoped I could anyway. "I can't deal with these guys though; you said yourself that sometimes Martinet defect, right?"

"That's the rumor—nothing official." He said. He was lying, but I didn't call him on it.

"Right." I said. "So, I can't do anything about most of them. After I take back my gear, they're gonna be after me. Someone is gonna have to—"

"No, you are." He interrupted

"What?"

"Just texted Myer." He said. "No one can get there before next month and it'll be too late by then."

"But—"

"Listen, dude. I don't like it either," he said. "But you know what's going on. We're swamped. That attack on Giza last month, Great Wall of China a few weeks ago… and Tuesday night a clan of leopard morphs just fricken decided that Chichen Itza should be theirs. Victor is still out there hunting down the last of them. We do what we can, but it's not enough. We're all on our own. Listen, I'll be there as soon as I can, but I think you'll have it handled by then. If I could, I'd send you the number one warlock killer in the U.S., but as of tonight, that's you. Understand?"

"Yeah," I said, dejected. "I understand."

"Dude, you're smart. You got magical theory out the wazoo. So out-think him and keep me posted."

"I will," I said. "Maker out." Well that didn't help. I hung up a bit harder than I wanted to and stood there in the phone booth feeling disappointed.

It was unrealistic to think that the Martinet taking care of the whole damn continent would drop everything to come save me. Guess I got my hopes up. At least he's not coming to kill me… I think.

As for being the number one warlock killer, the judges will take the trophy away once they learn that five had died in traps I wasn't even in the room for, two in car accidents, one was completely unintentional, and the last had essentially killed herself.

Never a face to face battle. That was a good way to get dead. Never pitting my magic skill against theirs as the Martinet did. I snuck around in dark corners, waiting for them to do something stupid and capitalizing on it.

Sure, I got results—there was no arguing that, but I wasn't a hero like Gomez or Merlin. I left the phone booth and looked up. I had about five hours of dark left; there was nothing more I could get done tonight. As tired as I was, sleep was the most productive thing I could be doing. Warlocks tended to be active at night, so I'd find and break into their place tomorrow.

Zora was waiting outside the booth, standing tall with a giant smile that tugged at her scar, as always. She was cleaner at least. Showered and powdered, she no longer looked like the female protagonist at the end of a low budget horror flick. She was wearing a blue tank top this time, and like the tan cargo pants, it was baggy enough to hide the curves she had. The shoes she wore were simple and brand new. Zora went through a lot of shoes, for obvious reasons.

I nodded to her and started limping home. She fell in beside me. "Heard you're going hunting," she said.

"Nope," I replied. "Where'd you hear that."

"From you," she smiled. "I was upstairs lifting when you were talking to Miles, and I was listening to your convo with Gomez. What's he like?" Zora lived in an apartment above Miles' diner. There was also a boxing gym up there. Miles never got around to getting anyone to use it, so Zora rented the whole thing. There were also three other empty apartments and one empty floor that served as Zora's lab. Must be nice living above the best food for a square mile, two blocks away wasn't bad either.

"Didn't anyone ever tell you it's rude to eavesdrop?" I said.

"Sounds like something somebody would've said at some point. Now, tell me—what's Gomez like?"

"He's a hot Latin dream," I sighed. "Like Enrique Iglesias, only sexier." I said it in as flat and dry a tone as I could manage.

"Ooooh, citation needed," she sighed. She said that a lot. My time on the internet was limited to research. I didn't find it any better than books, but I still knew what she meant. I spent a lot of time on Wikipedia, clicking the random article button. I probably knew more about obscure European royalty than anyone.

"No matter what you heard, I'm going to bed, and whatever comes after that I'll handle by myself."

She just shrugged and kept walking beside me.

"You aren't going," I said.

She nodded, not turning to look at me.

"I mean it this time."

"Where else am I supposed to get my adrenaline fix?" She whined.

"Head downtown and kill some vamps or something," I said.

"Without you to make sure I get out alive? Me thinks not. I'll go lift some more."

I sighed. She didn't sound sarcastic or patronizing, but one could never tell with Zora. "This is dangerous. I'm only going to steal back my gear. Hell, after I find Rollo's kids I'm thinking of bailing off the grid until Gomez or someone else can get here and take care of things."

"Rollo's kids?" She asked.

"Yeah," I sighed. "There are two kids missing."

"Aren't there always two kids missing?" She asked.

"Technically, yes, but Rollo wants these two found," I said.

"Why?"

"He got assigned the case," I said. "You know they send him all the weird shit. Whoever got to the scene first probably saw the circle drawn in blood and passed the buck."

"No, I meant why are you bothering?" She said.

"What? Uhh… because there are two defenseless children who—"

"Maker," she interrupted. "We don't do rescues. We kill monsters. One could argue that it's the only thing we do well. I believe we have a rule about playing to our strengths." You know you've taught your student well when they start quoting you, *to* you.

"I'm not gonna let two kids twist in the wind just because," I said.

"Why not?!" She said incredulously. "If it was Andre, or Nakeisha or another one of Miles' kids, then of course. If it were Rollo's *actual* children, I'd make the time, just so I could hold it over his head forever, but whoever these kids are, we don't know them. We can't save everyone, and we'll get killed trying. They may as well be a cat in a tree."

"Seriously, this shit again?" I said. It wasn't the first time we'd had this conversation, or one just like it, and it wouldn't be the last. "We aren't doing crap to save starving children in India. We aren't curing cancer. We are not out to save every cat in every tree, but when life sticks a tree right in front of us and there happens to be a cat in it, we'd be assholes if we didn't climb up and get it."

She smiled, "And we'd be smarter assholes if we just killed the dog at the bottom of the tree."

I sighed. She wasn't exactly wrong, but I didn't have the mental capacity to explain everything I was feeling after the shitty day I'd had. If I were more articulate at the moment, I might've won this debate. Instead, I got annoyed.

"Don't expand my metaphors; you know how that annoys me." I said

"In this case it's apt," she replied. "If we kill every warlock, vampire, ghost, fairy, werewolf, and whatever for a thousand miles those kids don't have a problem, no matter what tree they're in, so why aren't we doing what we do best?"

"We're branching out," I smiled.

"Did you just make a pun? I'll cut you." No one I knew did a deadpan expression better than Zora. Probably because she's so animated at other times. I laughed a bit and kept walking.

"I'm gonna find them, and you're going to help." I sighed. "If nothing else it'll score some points with Rollo."

"We can't *spend* points with Rollo!" She said, looking outraged.

"Hey goody two shoes, can you look the other way for a few days of felonies?"

"Fine. You're helping because it'll give me a warm, fuzzy, feeling."

"Whatever," she shrugged. "Here," She tossed me a small clear jewel, on a chain made of the same material. Whatever it was, it was heavy, and it cooled off slowly as it lay in my hand. Weird. "Pretty sure that's what Blueboy was after," she said. "Makes dead goblins into undead goblins. Pretty useful if you wanted to rule all of Outland or Faerie. Works too. After I ate, I went back to the warehouse and had them all doing the electric slide. Then I had them all march into a furnace, I dropped the loot at Micheal's, and Blueboy's body got sucked back to Faerie… so that's case closed, I think."

"Good enough for me," I said. I'd just add this to the long list of things in my pack that someone would be coming to kill me for. Once I got it back, that is. Realistically, Blueboy wasn't nearly powerful enough to have this. It took some serious mojo to punch a hole in the universe. Whoever he was running errands for—or being manipulated by—would show up eventually.

I didn't realize we were at my house already. I waved and headed in.

"Oh, and Maker, one more thing," I stopped. "If ever we find an orange tabby in a tree, or a toyger, you won't have to twist my arm so much." I just exhaled audibly at the joke, but she thought it was funny enough to walk away giggling and talking to herself. "OOOooo or an abyssinian, nah savannah. Angora's are pretty too. Maybe go simple and we can rescue an American longhair. Bengal? Hmm… Nope savannah, definitely savannah. There's gotta be a savannah in a tree around here somewhere. I'm gonna…" Her voice trailed off as she walked away.

I just sighed again and limped inside, wrapped a bandage around my midsection, downed four aspirin, elevated a thigh that had swollen to the size of a basketball on a couple pillows, and went straight to sleep. Didn't even brush my teeth.

Chapter: 6

I did brush them when I woke up.

Converting an attic into an apartment gave it the appearance of a studio. The sink, toilet, and shower were all in one corner. My workstation was in the opposite corner, next to my bed.

To reach my toothbrush I had to make my way past all my notes, failed experiments, stacks of books, lots of plants, and a refrigerator full of potions, chemicals, and magical components, that had never even heard of food. It was still a bit before sunrise; the sky was dark but getting lighter, and there didn't seem to be a cloud in it. My only window up here was an air vent, and it was quite tiny.

I had only slept a few hours, but I slept like a rock. Sleep was always peaceful in my apartment. Occasionally an attacker tries to surprise me elsewhere, but not at home. No one ever attacked me here. My apartment was strong enough to stop a rogue angel.

I lived in an old Victorian house that had been built sometime after the Civil War. I stayed in the attic apartment upstairs with a family downstairs that had six children and one more on the way. The house had remained in that family since it was built. All devout Roman Catholics—generations of them.

The family alone made for a formidable threshold. Add in my magic wards, and it was highly unlikely anything would be getting in anytime soon.

Why would the Masons let a heathen wizard live in their attic? Well… they don't know I'm a wizard of course. One of my wards renders me kinda invisible. Everything I do merely fades into the background.

I'm essentially stepping over a threshold that isn't mine; but because I'm mortal and I never meant them any harm, I get to keep my meager magical abilities. Might also have something to do with paying rent. Thresholds had never been made entirely clear to me. The universe ran on rules, but it was under no obligation to tell you what they were.

The wards only work when I'm home, though. That's another reason it works so well. The same power, the same magic of that family powers the wards. My spells channel it into powering them.

That was how I did everything. Using one thing to power another. It's the reason I lived where I did; it's why I never left. Four hundred years ago or so, someone planted a seed from the first tree in what is now western North Carolina. It was unremarkable forest at the time.

Now that seed is a tree of massive strength. Once every couple years or so, I went to tend it in a long ritual spell that helped maintain its growth. I wasn't entirely benevolent—I got a wand out of the deal.

I turned from the sink and sighed. The walls were piled high with boxes. Everywhere on the floor were open books and papers dotted with things I'd been working on. My table in the far corner held my laptop, an old spectrometer, some of those empty small glass bottles and a few other things. There were more on the shelf above that were full; fourteen to be exact.

I could take things out of my pack with a thought. Putting

things in took time and effort—time and effort I hadn't taken in the last few weeks.

Last week I felt like a procrastinating, unproductive, douchebag. Now I was a little glad for it.

There were a few other things in the clutter strewn about the room.

A pair of slippers that let me walk on walls, but didn't always work. A small spring that worked quite well, just not the way it was supposed to; it let me put a minuscule force on something at a distance. I wanted high force at a short distance. What I got was almost no force at distances I couldn't even see.

There was my pen that never ran out of ink; it was one of the first things I'd made. The ink also disappeared and reappeared whenever I wanted. A plastic fork that could stab through almost anything. A balloon made of solid lead that could provide enough lift to get me off the ground for a few minutes. Unfortunately, after it did, it spent the next few days being immovable. A concrete block with the consistency of clay that was heavier than a cinder block should be. That was just a dismal failure.

There was a compass that I would always know the direction of, but could not tell direction. The soup bowl that dehydrated everything down to a powder—except for milk and coke. There was a pot with a plant in it that worked perfectly, watering and feeding whatever was put into it. I'd made lots of those for my dozens of plants. I spied the sugar cube that made everything bitter. A prototype of my pack that transformed whatever I put in it into more packs. At least it wasn't the wooden goose I'd enchanted to lay golden eggs. It laid regular eggs on demand for almost a year before it failed. Miles was happy with it at least.

People call me a genius of magical theory. What they don't realize is most of the things I make are failures. If I make something that's crap, and just so happen to find a use for it, it's still crap. Like fertilizer. Ha! Some of the things in my armory are downright nasty, but *I* didn't make any of them.

Even the best things I made had limits. Anything could burn out after a few uses, and I'd have to make it again. I often had to carry copies of things. A real wizard only had to make something once and it lasted forever.

I sighed again. Time to suit up. I threw on the same clothes from yesterday. They were clean, pressed, and a slightly darker shade of black after a night on the floor. All the rips and tears from last night had been mended; even the bullet hole I put in my jacket had repaired itself. That was a useful enhancement. My pistol went into its holster under my arm.

I had an old satchel and shoved in the potions from the shelf, the spring, the pen, the sugar cube, bowl, compass, and my staff which had somehow made it into my pants cargo pocket. I didn't remember putting it there, but between the tumble, the fatigue, and getting shot in the face, a lot of fine details from last night were foggy, or downright missing. Last, I packed the sheet with the blonde cadaver in it.

All the potions were the real pain. Without my pack, there was no way to keep them organized. Some of them were the same thing at least. I never cooked just one potion—that was inefficient.

The only other things I had to help me reclaim my pack were what I was wearing. Everything I wore was a magical tool, even my socks. I'd had some problems with foot fungus in the past.

At the moment I was most happy with the sports bandage wrapped around my midsection. It had done its job well while I slept; taking the power from the air and using it to repair cells and nerves. I didn't feel like I was dying anymore, so the internal bleeding had to have been repaired. I had four more smaller bandages in my pack. Sure wish I had them now. Even though those were single-use items, like potions. I had a dozen scrapes and pains that were more than simply annoying.

It was still dark, about an hour before dawn. I already wasn't limping as bad as I had been, but I popped two more aspirin anyway. The swelling on my leg had gone down a lot—now there was just a dull ache when I walked rather than a sharp twinge on every other step. Hairline fracture at worst; I guess someone up there still likes me.

I unwrapped the ace bandage and wrapped it around my leg since that was the second biggest injury of last night.

I told myself I wasn't hungry, but ended up walking into Miles' place anyway. There was no sign of the old man, nor anyone else, but I knew the drill by now. I threw on an apron, a pot of coffee and a flat of bacon. As it fried, I swept the place even though it didn't need sweeping. By the time I was done the bacon and coffee were making the place smell like a lower level of heaven.

Zora came down with hair standing up everywhere from the rat's nest of a braid she sported. She looked red-eyed and groggy and went straight to the coffee. She was scrambling eggs by the time I put the broom away.

"Toast?" I said, barely audible.

She just grunted in a way that said no. She'd likely say something about carbs or some such.

"Carbs," it was raspy, tired and right on time.

I had eggs, bacon, and toast with some-berry jam. Coffee with enough cream and sugar that you couldn't taste the vile, bitter brew beneath. I drank coffee to wake up; to keep me sharp. The taste had never grown on me, so I piled on the cream and sugar and drank twice as much.

Zora and I sat silently, staring at our phones. I was reading a pdf of an old book on witches and theriomorph tigers in 1960's India. The woman who wrote it was obviously a wacko, but it was also obvious that she had experienced something supernatural. Whatever it was drove her insane, and her ramblings were recorded in a medical journal.

I looked over Zora's shoulder and saw her staring at a schematic for what looked to be a linear accelerator.

"Send me that." I said.

"Mmmph," she grunted back. I got the link after another moment or two and added it to my already ridiculously long reading list.

"Vamps have been quiet. See what you can find out today. Also, try and scout out that north side haunting we heard about. No risks. Take a peek and get out."

"Mmmph," she responded. "I'll get someone to do it…got a date tonight."

"Grant?" I asked. It was hard to keep all her men straight at times.

"Brian. New guy," she said with a yawn. "Grant and Tyrone are history. Being great in bed gets old quick if you have the IQ of a garden slug, and Tyrone asked about the scars." Sometimes it sucked being a wizard. You could never get too close to anyone. Sooner or later you'd have to tell them what you did for a living.

I knocked a few articles off my reading list while we ate and caught up on all my web comics. I was procrastinating and I knew it. That was the worst kind of procrastinating.

Miles appeared after about an hour and grunted towards us both on his way to the coffee. By the time he'd plated up breakfast for himself, I was done eating.

"Maker, almost forgot," Zora didn't look up from her phone "Rania called last night. Said she needs to see you today. Sounded panicked." I nodded, dropped a few bills on the counter, and walked out.

I stood just outside the door taking deep breaths and trying to think about quarks and muons to relax. It was going to be a hard day, but at least there would be lots of sunshine.

I could hear Miles and Zora strike up a conversation the moment I stepped out.

"Well, if you'd read the last FDA study I sent you, or even

bothered with the internet…" I tuned out. It was clear they were going at it about nutrition. The fundamentals of milk this time. Or should I say, again.

Two seven-year-old boys and a girl not much younger came running around the corner of the block and ran past me into the diner, all tossing me a "Hi Maker," along the way. Marcus, Anthony, and his little sister Natalia screamed "PANCAAAAAAAAAKES!" in unison. You could tell they had practiced this.

I smiled, and listened to Zora yelling about noise in the morning, and Miles asking them all about school. I didn't know exactly how many grandchildren he had, but it was easily over twenty. Must be nice having so much family you could barely keep track of them all.

Kids.

"Damn you, Rollo," I growled. Rollo didn't know about Tema—at least I'd never mentioned her—but the idea of leaving two children to the whims of whatever horrors the supernatural could conjure hit home hard.

I rationalized that this aligned with my interests, but I still felt forced into going. They were either taken by vampires or the new warlock cult. Theoretically, I guess, it could be anything, but those were the usual suspects. I caught a cab to the north side of town, once again lamenting my truck being in the shop.

The cab took me out of downtown, past NC State College and towards the northwest end. When we finally started getting close, I handed off a couple of twenties, got out, and walked the last three blocks. Trying to look inconspicuous and likely failing.

The house was straight out of a suburban fairy tale, right down to the white picket fence. Rollo had done exactly as he'd promised and kept everyone out. There was a patrol car out front with no one in it. That meant there were two cops around somewhere. Didn't take long to spot them. One was walking the perimeter of the house and the other was standing near a side door. I shrugged. If I wanted to sneak around, I should've come last night.

I rooted around for the right potion and found it after a few moments. Felt like forever.

I felt the charmer potion start working instantly. There was a warm humming sensation in my throat, and it slowly spread to every joint in my body. It was uncomfortable to be suddenly aware of every place in you where bone met bone.

I ignored it and walked right up to the house. I nodded to the officer and said something in greeting. He nodded back and asked if I was sure I wanted to go in. Of course I wasn't sure, but I didn't say that—just walked right past him, looking grim. I shut the door behind me and waited. The officer didn't follow me in.

I took a deep breath of stale, dead air and let it out. I felt it immediately. The magical equivalent of a mouth full of sludge. It was coming from the right, and it took great effort not to look. It felt like a threat. The worst filth in the world and it felt like it was on the verge of consuming me.

All the shades were closed. I waited for my eyes to adjust to the dimness. The stairs went up in front of me; the living room was on my right. Straight past the stairs were a kitchen, dining room, and a door out to the manicured backyard.

The field of magical energy that surrounds every mortal home settled on me tight and clingy as I crossed the threshold—like walking into a giant bubble and feeling the residue on your skin. I was human; a threshold wouldn't inhibit my magic, but I was also a wizard, so I could still feel it. Some supernatural beings could cross, but they left their powers at the door. Others, like vampires, couldn't cross unless invited, and still others couldn't cross at all.

I went upstairs first. I could feel the magic still flowing in the place. I knew what Rollo wanted me to see was in the living room. I also knew I didn't want to see it.

Heading upstairs was like getting a breath of fresh air,

magically speaking. It was more innocent up here, more wholesome. The air certainly didn't clog up in my lungs with the wrongness from downstairs. I looked around and saw four rooms. One was a nursery and craft room that appeared to not be in use.

One was obviously the girl's room, Theresa's. The right wall was pink slashed with purple. She did like math; there was a whiteboard on the wall filled with numbers and equations. Basic algebra, and elementary calculus. At twelve, that was rather impressive.

There was some cartoon character I didn't recognize on the perfectly made bed. The desk had little on it to interest me, but was cluttered with all the things one would expect of a young girl slowly putting away the regalia of a child and moving into adolescence.

I saw a hairbrush of hers and pulled out all the hair still on it. Those went in my pocket. If there was a fresh enough one, I could make short work of all this. I wasn't strong enough for a tracking spell, but I had voodoo doll in my pack that could do the job. It was especially easy with blood or a fresh enough hair; you just had to tell the universe "find the largest concentration of deoxyribonucleic acid that looks like this."

Now, I just needed my pack to track down the kids and get Rollo off my case. Not to mention reclaim dominion over my conscience.

The next room was the parents'. It was immaculate. Everything in its place. I didn't go in. I took a long look from the hallway and wondered where they were. Rollo hadn't said anything about what happened to them. I assumed they were dead, painted all over the walls downstairs; or worse.

Ryan's room was in similar order. Filled with baseball everything. The bedspread was baseball, as were the posters on the wall. On the desk, there was a baseball pencil holder with pencils shaped like baseball bats.

On the wall were quotes by what I assumed were famous

baseball players. Baseball wasn't my sport, so I only recognized two names.

"Every strike brings me closer to the next home run."

—*Babe Ruth*

"The more I pitch, the stronger my arm will get."

—*Satchel Paige*

I took one last look and walked out. I was getting angry and that was good—anger killed fear and self-preservation. At least it did with me. I cared less about my safety and more about whatever was happening to those children. Whether I was angry or not didn't change what I would do, but at least I'd feel better about doing it.

I didn't want to look in the living room as I came down the stairs, so I didn't. Whatever ritual, blood rite, or spell that had been done had no business in my head. It was a horrible, twisted thing, whatever it was.

The thought occurred to me that it would be better to burn the place. Fire worked in every dimension; it was a force of destruction, and therefore, renewal. Nothing touched by a hot enough flame could ever be the same again. It would wipe away any trace of whatever that was. I stood there feeling it slither up my senses, leaving that foulness feeling behind. Didn't take me long to decide.

"*Fire.*" The flame shot from my palm and caught the carpet. It was a special type of flame. I was crap with evocation. Fire, lightning, and all the "go boom" magics. I'd invented this spell to make a flame that sought to consume magical energies. In addition to wood, paint and drywall for fuel, it sought out anything unnatural—that included all things magic.

I wasn't strong enough for it to make a good offensive spell, but for non-living things it did ok. I had another that was just difficult to extinguish, but that primarily went into potions.

The fire ignited and spread across the floor like a liquid. When the officer outside ran in, it was licking up walls that were covered in blood, feces, and the entrails of small animals.

"What happened?" The officer demanded. I hadn't looked at him on the way in, and I didn't do so now. I ran past him before the fire came after me. Not only was I a wizard, but I was under the influence of the charmer potion.

"Some kind of booby trap," I yelled back. "Get the fire department out here now." The officer ran back to the patrol car, screaming for his partner to get away from the house.

The thought occurred to me that I had done this family another small favor. Insurance would actually cover this. The panic rose quickly as neighbors left their homes to watch the action.

I melted away in the confusion. I wasn't a part of that nicer world where something burning down or blowing up was a fascinating spectacle to be watched. Besides, I had one more favor to do.

Chapter: 7

Rania was an upscale psychic, but her office looked like that of an average therapist. It had a solid oak desk and book shelves on every wall with titles like *Neurochemistry 5th edition*, *Handbook of Dichotic Listening*, and *Cognitive Behavioral Therapy for Chronic Anxiety*… not to mention, dozens of other titles on human thought and behavior that even their authors couldn't pronounce.

She actually did have a degree in social work, and psychology—along a few other things, most likely. That made her a good person to know. People needed to hear that they weren't crazy when they saw a werewolf or a ghost.

She had the gift of being able to make all that go away. Talk to her for an hour once a week and the world would be a safe and reasonable place again. Of course, she couldn't help me; I knew better.

Rania was a little tall if you included the professional black pumps she wore. Her business suit had a cream blouse under a black jacket, tucked into a black skirt that stopped just short of her knees. Her curly blond hair was shoulder length and always looked wild. She was more handsome than pretty; a beauty that had aged well as she hit her late thirties.

Her handshake was firm as always, and I felt the soft buzz that you always feel when touching another mage. She was probably much stronger than I was, but so was everyone.

"Thanks for coming so quickly," she said. There was an edge to her voice that was normally absent and she smoothed out her clothes as if trying to gain some composure. Made me wonder what was going on.

"I was around," I replied—which was true. The house hadn't been far from here. If her window faced the right way, we could see the smoke.

"I have an appointment in fifteen minutes, so I'll come to the point. I had a dream about you."

"You know that screwing with prophecy is forbidden by Merlin's laws. I wish you would get that and stop telling me things." I said.

"You always say that, you know." She sighed.

"Because you never listen."

"I listen just fine. 'Divination is frowned upon,' you said."

"No one frowns like the Martinet. They'll kill you if they even *think* you did something wrong. Better if you just never do anything suspect."

"Nice to meet you pot, I'm kettle. Did you forget that almost thirty percent of my patients are referrals from you?"

"I did not forget. I do what I have to."

"And so do I. Even if I were to stop helping people—and I won't—I can't help having dreams." She could be right. I had no idea if it could be controlled or not. I offered to look into it once, and she politely refused saying that she'd be scared not to get them now. This was an old conversation.

I sighed. "Fine. What was the dream?" I asked while imagining Merlin or one of the Martinet standing over my corpse.

"It was two days ago, the night we had that storm. A month or so from now, you and I will be sitting here. I don't know what we'll talk about, but you'll get up to leave. You transform into an ox and charge into a black wall with Zora on your back, along with some man I've never met and a vampire. You all go into the darkness and then there's nothing."

"What do you mean there's nothing?"

"I mean just that. There is nothing after that. The dream itself wasn't scary. It was actually sort of peaceful. I didn't call Zora until I did Henry's reading and got nothing after two months. Before him, I did myself and a few others; no one has a future that goes beyond two months." Henry was her husband. He was a nice guy, former military. We got along the few times we met.

"So what are you saying? A bomb is gonna go off and kill everyone in town?" I said, sitting forward.

"One of my patients wanted her fortune told before she left on a trip. She will be in Malaysia for the next two months; she'll meet a man she wants to marry there, and after that, nothing."

I whistled. It felt like getting punched in the stomach. The future wasn't set. It couldn't be. Certain beings had free will—humans more than any others. Having a choice changed everything. Divination worked on probability; whatever was the most likely outcome was what Rania would see.

When she looked, she gained knowledge, and having that knowledge changed things. Even if she made the same choice she made in a reading, she made it with foreknowledge of the outcome. That was enough to make things turn out different.

The fact that she looked and then looked again should've changed things.

"But you had the dream, and then you looked at it. Twice." I said. Maybe there was something in the way things changed that I could use.

"Actually, I looked seven times," she said grimly. "It was supposed to change. It's changed every time before now." She sounded afraid. I couldn't blame her. Her eyes were frightened too, reliving something unpleasant. "This one didn't change at all Maker. It…

It didn't change." She sniffed and went to her desk for a tissue. I was feeling taken aback myself. I walked over and gave her a hug. It seemed like the right thing to do.

"I don't know what to do about this. According to you I've already done it, but I know I'm not ready to die in two months. I'll tell the Martinet and get some help to try and stop whatever the black wall is."

"I could try to read you again, or Zora. Maybe… I don't know. Maybe it'll be different," she said. She had tried to read me three years ago and failed. She couldn't explain it. All she said was that I was "wild in time" while babbling like a mad woman. I figured it didn't work because of an overload caused by the being in my head and we never did it again.

"No. Try not to worry and let me know if you learn anything else. I'll handle this somehow."

She just nodded. I got up to leave, and she grabbed my sleeve. I turned to look at her, but she'd already let go. I could hear her breathing hard, and the pulse in her neck was running wild. She kept her face placid—no doubt the mark of a great psychologist—but she couldn't stop the slight tremble going through the rest of her body. Zora was right; she was panicked, but then again, so was I.

* * *

I needed to go somewhere, find someone, and ask some pointed questions with threats attached. I hated asking questions; where I'm from it made you look like a cop. Fortunately, I knew where to go and just what to ask. That and as far as he was concerned, I was a cop. Murder and shape-shifting would get you killed but, letting someone assume you were Martinet, when you weren't, was perfectly legal. Merlin's rules had never made sense to me.

His name was Soaka, and he was a toad—a beautiful toad, but a toad nonetheless. He was a halfling who dealt in arms, and he moved around a lot. He'd been supplying the vampires in the area since the war with the Martinet started ramping up however long ago.

To his credit, he'd sold me information about large shipments of arms they'd paid for in advance, and I was able to destroy them. He got them to pay in advance as much as possible. Most of the time I'd been able to trash everything after they'd taken possession. A few times I did it before—just so they didn't look too hard at my informant.

Any magical tools I collected were interned in my pack until they could be destroyed or turned in. I didn't wanna touch anything vampires would use in a fight. He always said it was a favor to me, but I knew the real reason was so that I'd owe him and he could order up more and charge them again. Maybe that just made it good for business all around.

He was easy to find as he was living on the north side—the nice part of town. The type of place where people stared long and hard at a black guy in cargo pants, a canvas jacket and satchel slung over one shoulder. I was wearing black today; I always wore black. It wasn't that I had a Johnny Cash streak or anything, it was because I couldn't do laundry to save my life. Black clothes were the only ones that consistently came out clean, and after I figured out how to enchant my clothing, I didn't do laundry at all. At least the t-shirt was white.

The building had a doorman and everything. I walked in, took a deep breath and reminded myself that I owned the place. I didn't own it of course, but you'd be surprised the number of places you could get into with a snotty enough attitude. I walked past the front desk and straight to the elevators.

Security just missed asking me a question. Eye contact is permission to speak. I didn't make eye contact, not even when the elevator doors closed on his face. The place I was going was on the top floor. Soaka wouldn't live anywhere without a penthouse.

When I got off there were two doors. I didn't know who stayed in the left one. Maybe I'd have a look one day, but the noises from the right told me where I was going. Screams, squeals and laughter. I knocked hard on the door, and the noise died instantly—I didn't have to wait long. A vision in red lingerie that didn't cover much slid the door open. Her short sandy blonde hair framed an angelic face with a pointy nose, below her blue eyes. Despite the slender frame not being my preference, it was an effort to keep my eyes on hers.

"Soaka please." I walked right in, not waiting for a response. Most beings of power were careful about thresholds. Being invited in was the only known way to avoid a supposedly massive power decrease. I didn't know *why* it worked; only that it did. Some old law of home and hearth being sacred. I liked walking over them with impunity. It put people off guard.

Magic wasn't science; like everything else it just had to obey science. Zora and I were both good at science. Two plus two equals four in science. If you did it a million times, it would always equal four. Add in a little magic, and it could equal 4.1, 4.3, 3.9. Maybe it would eventually average out to four, but there was no guarantee that a certain magic effect wouldn't change slightly with repeated castings.

Since it didn't violate anything we knew about quantum theory, Zora had come up with some way to flesh it out. A hypothesis that magic has something to do with manipulation of quark states, though the last time I checked her math, it didn't look all that promising.

The security guard showed up just as the woman in red closed the door behind me. I couldn't have timed it better if I'd tried.

There were more women and men inside. Three of each, all in various stages of undress. My eyes lingered on a brunette so lovely that I tripped over a stool. She was a larger woman that carried her weight in all the places men dreamed about. She was lying naked on a fancy looking couch with her thick black curly locks draped over her breasts and making a pile on the floor.

Apparently, everyone else was only there to pleasure her. I could almost be convinced to join them if it weren't a trap.

My escort looked back at me and I shook my head and muttered about needing to get out more as she led me into the back room. I smirked to myself as I followed. I was using one beautiful woman to distract me from another.

I didn't stare at her legs exactly. It was more a detached appreciation. These women were either fairies or thralls of a fairy. Nothing good would come of mixing with them.

I took a deep breath and let it out. My lust faded to background noise where it belonged; like all my other emotions.

Soaka was a halfling. Not the Baggins kind. A halfling was someone who was part fey and part mortal. Normally they chose between the two at some point, but they didn't have to. While they were choosing, they just so happened to get the otherworldly beauty and grace that was characteristic of most fairies and wildlings. Not to mention the immortality.

This particular halfling had been putting off that decision for centuries. No one knew how he'd done it; least of all me. Soaka appeared to be my age. Late teens, early twenties or so. His light brown hair was neatly slicked back with just enough out of place to be intentional. The rest looked right out of a catalog.

He was sitting back in a chair with his hands behind his head, staring at the ceiling. He was wearing a shirt that was unbuttoned, and his chiseled pecs and abs had just enough sweat to glisten in the afternoon light. Female fey were gorgeous, breathtaking, and no real woman looked like that. It was like seeing a perfectly photoshopped Instagram come to life. Male fey just looked ridiculous to me. Not only did no man look like that, but even pictures of men didn't look that good. It was like watching a perfectly formed work of art come to life and start trying to sell you a car—hard to take it seriously. He glanced at me with impossibly green eyes.

"I'm busy," he said as the blonde smiled and walked out of the room.

"Get unbusy." I snapped back. It was still early afternoon, and despite the bandage, my leg was hurting again after tripping over whatever that was in the outer room. I didn't get angry; as far as I could tell, I felt practically nothing in comparison to most people. I was just having a crappy couple of days. To the fey thing's credit, he picked up on it.

Soaka smirked and didn't speak further. He gestured to a seat, and I waved it off. "Food? Drink?" I shook my head no. Stupid formalities, but I'd have to be crazy to accept food or drink from a fey—even half of one. Might as well start smoking crack and quit at life—it was that good—probably better. There was an entire population of humans in outland that got there because they had sampled that food or wine and felt such elation at first taste that they never left.

"What can I do for you?" He asked.

"I got hit by some warlocks last night."

"You look good for a dead man."

"Who was it?" I growled.

"What makes you think I—"

"They had automatic rifles." I snapped. "If you didn't import them, then you know who did." The smirk on his face told me nothing. I was supposed to take it as an admission of guilt, but with a being this old there was no assurance that his face would tell me the truth. His body, on the other hand, never moved. Since he didn't shift positions, that meant he was still comfortable—which suggested that it was an act.

"Maker, I'm flattered that you think so highly of me."

"Save it." I said leaning forward on his desk. "Playing coy doesn't work when men do it. Those bastards nearly killed me."

"I feel the need to remind you that our agreement doesn't include information on any of my contacts outside the dominion of Vermillion Falls. You wanted to help the Martinet in their war. I have no obligation—"

"AKs!" I interrupted again. "They had AKs when they hit me last night. I'll find them with or without you, but if you choose not to help and if I trace them back to you, then I'll have recourse for a summon. Merlin will forgive me if I sell it as self-defense. I can't kill you, I can't even put you out of business, but we both know trolls work cheap. I'll have you kidnapped and thrown into some goblin dungeon for a few hundred years. Not even Titania could get you out of there, that's if you could get her to give a shit in the first place."

Titania and Oberon had been at war forever, but they were also married. They would feud, their armies would slaughter each other for a few decades, then they'd forgive and forget until the next time. Here I thought my relationships were complicated.

The queen of the night and the king of all fairies separated their whole plane of existence into Outland and Faerie—the borders of which were fluid and changed with each of their powers. Every fairy wanted the strength to impress Oberon and the grace to attract Titania's attention, even if it was only for a moment.

They would talk endlessly to friends, neighbors and complete strangers about the time Titania glanced in their general direction, or whispered to them a secret in a time of need. There were worse insults among fairies than implying they weren't worth Titania's attention, but not many.

To prove this, Soaka's face grew darker by the word. The odds of me actually doing any of that were slim at best. Besides, I liked Soaka… well, maybe not "like," but we did have a good working relationship.

"I don't currently have an order for any warlocks," he said. He narrowed his eyes slightly, and his jaw was clenched tight. No doubt he was deliberating on what would be the most satisfying way to kill me.

"You're lying." I said.

"I can't lie. You know that," he said.

"Bull, I don't care what name they put on their order or what they told you the weapons were for. I want a copy." Fey were predictable. They couldn't tell direct lies, but they could talk their way around the truth better than a southern belle politician. It never seemed to fool me. The ways around the truth were all predictable. Besides, not knowing when someone was lying could get you killed. I knew that from bitter experience.

"And how do I know this will satisfy you? How soon until you are back in my office making threats and demands?"

"I don't know," I said. "My pride is bruised. I'm out for blood, and until I get it, expect threats and demands." Soaka sat back again and sighed.

"Banter and posturing aside, I suppose I understand your anger. Three commissions."

"None, and I'm still getting your full cooperation. Everything you know now or learn in the next year about any warlocks."

"Two then. I know quite a lot about my clients."

"None." I snapped. "I don't have to give you shit!"

"Actually, you do." He growled. "I'm not going to yield to blackmail, so piss on your threats. I won't give anything away for free. Ever! One commission or get the hell out."

I liked anger. Whenever you could get someone emotionally involved it always felt like they were being more genuine. It wasn't true in every case of course, but as a general rule, the more emotional someone got, the less time they spent thinking.

It was a mistake to fall into any assumptions about a being that was hundreds of years old, but I felt like I knew Soaka well enough to believe this outburst. Fairies couldn't give anything away. The concept of a gift was abhorrent and did something terrible to them I couldn't understand. Suffice it to say giving or getting anything without reciprocation was akin to spitting in their face. Soaka was a halfling, so it shouldn't have mattered… but he was an unusual halfling.

From what I could gather, the rules of the fey held him more tightly than most. He'd never elaborated on what those were, and I didn't ask because I knew he wouldn't tell me.

"One it is," I said. "No more than three months of work. I'm not gonna be slaving away for another year on whatever you can dream up." He nodded and shuffled through the papers on his desk and handed me one of them.

"Warlocks 101 will have to wait, as I suddenly find myself in need of relaxation."

"There's a brunette out front that's to die for." I said. "I'd start there." With that, I turned and left.

The brunette that I tripped over the stool for was the reason I could treat Soaka like a second-class citizen. Often, halflings that chose to be human did so for love. They would fall in love with a human and not want to watch that person grow old and die. As a commission for him, I'd pulled a Dr. Frankenstein and created a vessel that could hold a human consciousness. It wasn't hard per se, but it took me over six months, drained my staff from full to zero several times, and left me unconscious or lethargic for weeks on end. He'd since shaped that vessel into the form she wanted. It was almost four years old, and in twenty or thirty years or so, she'd need another.

I wondered what he'd want made this time.

I didn't look at anything on my way out. Keeping my eyes on the marble floor was great for my balance. Stupid orgy-having fey.

I was in the elevator before I took the sheet out and looked at it. A boat had arrived in Wilmington last night, and the shipment was due for pickup this evening. Good timing. The address was a parking garage downtown, and I had all the time in the world to get there.

Still, no reason to dally.

I dodged security again and hailed a cab. The fatigue of the last couple days was piling up and I submitted to my biology's demand for a nap. I was startled whenever a semi-truck sped by. It was gonna take a while to get over that.

The occasionally interrupted nap had the advantage of making the trip seem shorter, and I could certainly use the rest. The cabbie dropped me off outside the parking garage. I handed over a few bills and thought longingly of my truck, which was in the shop for repairs.

Careful to avoid any cameras, I walked into the garage. Reaching out with my magical senses was just a form of concentration; a way of noticing large pockets of energy or areas devoid of it. The stronger the magical thing was, the easier it was to detect. I found the van pretty quick: a white panel van, simple in the extreme.

I felt for enchantments, and there was one. "Not taking any chances today," I sighed. I crawled under a truck a couple spaces down just in case someone came along. From there I was able to study the spell. Took me almost an hour before I fully understood it. Not only was the van forgettable; it also cast a spell on anyone who touched it. "Stupid fey magic." I sighed. I hated mind magic. There wasn't much chance of my getting in. I could probe all day and not find a way around. Besides, there was no telling when these people would come to pick it up. I went down to a mom and pop hardware store to pick up a few things.

When I got back, the truck was still there. That was a relief.

I laid some copper wire down in a circle around the truck as best I could. Circles were the preferred tool for blocking or manipulating magic. The more perfect the circle and pure the material, the better it worked. Magic was like electricity in that it liked to gather at pointy places. A perfect circle made from an atomically precise material could theoretically dissipate an infinite amount of magical energy.

Unfortunately, a perfect circle was physically impossible. This material was cheap copper wire from a hardware store, so I wasn't holding out much hope for the purity either.

I bit down hard on my thumb and pressed the pooling drop of blood to the copper ring. It amplified my meager magical abilities into… something slightly less meager. I wanted all the help I could get.

Have you ever tried to bite yourself so hard that you broke the skin? It's difficult; there's a trick to it, one that I'd learned at the tender age of twelve. I shook off the memory. I did that a lot with my childhood.

With an exhale I gathered my power and closed the circle to magical energies. Someone could physically walk across, but any magic discharged inside would stay there… theoretically.

I took out the pad I bought and scribbled something down, then put the pad in my pocket. Next, I took a handful of washers and threw them at the truck. Not to damage it, but to trigger the spell. Nothing happened. I was afraid of that. The spell was designed to be triggered only by a living thing.

If two people had come to pick up the truck, one could trigger the spell and the other could get in and drive once the spell was gone. Pretty clever actually. The washers landed randomly inside the circle under the truck. That would help to disperse some of the energy as well.

Not much, but every little bit helps. I took a deep breath and reached for the handle, the spell discharged, and I was knocked on my ass.

"Dammit," I sighed. This wasn't working. It was futile trying to get in at all. How many times have I told people—reminded myself—that these guys could be Martinet? They were strong enough to be one of Merlin's personal crew of wizard assassins. I was way out of my league for this. Screw it; they could have the pack. I'm done.

I was five steps away when a sharp metal something stabbed me in the leg. Reaching down, I pulled out a wire ring notepad that I didn't remember having. The words "Don't Panic" were printed in large, friendly letters on the yellow cover. I didn't laugh. I was low. I was gonna go curl up in a ball somewhere and sleep for a week. I flipped it open as I walked. The first page was the only one with writing.

Dear Maker,

ROB THE DAMN TRUCK!

Love,

Maker

The spell shattered and tried to take a few pieces of my mind with it. The pain sent me to my knees, but was gone by the time I got there. I would've screamed, but there was no time. Not even a throb to say that the white-hot knife in my skull had just been ripped out. I grunted after the fact, but that was more for the shock than anything.

It took me a minute, but I was able to catch my breath and stumble back to the truck. It was easy to see now that the spell was broken. The copper wire was burned black in a conspicuous oval shape. I looked in the window. The keys were on the seat.

I moved the truck to a different spot a few spaces down. Whoever came for it wouldn't pass the burned black circle on the way in now. Maybe it wouldn't've raised suspicion, but no sense taking chances. Checking the back, I found three wooden boxes. I pulled the white sheet out of my pocket. After dispatching the body yesterday, it would still have plenty of room in it. I threw it over the wood boxes. Funny how useful a kid's party trick could be.

"*Disappear.*" The last item I had bought at the hardware store was a can of green spray paint. I spray painted "Phantom Lorde" on the inside of the truck and got out, feeling like a badass. I placed my compass in the cab behind the seat. With that I went home; it was gonna be a busy night.

Chapter: 8

"Reappear." I spoke the word, bringing the power forth with an effort filled with grunts and funny faces. Forcing the universe to behave was tough at times , especially when I was low on sleep. Taking the metal and wooden boxes out of the sheet and leaving the body in it was the effort. I was in one of the Forcing the universe to behave was tough at times, especially when I was low on sleep. Taking the metal and wooden boxes out of the sheet and leaving the body in it was the effort.

I was in one of the empty apartments above Miles' diner. It was lightly furnished and only a little dusty. When I asked Miles if I could use it for a week, he just tossed the keys, not even bothering to put down his paper.

There was an old couch, a dining room table with two chairs, and a queen-sized mattress set in the bedroom. It was nicer than my place. I sighed, every place was nicer than my place.

The wooden boxes needed to be pried, so I went downstairs to borrow something. When I got back from the basement with crowbar in hand, I found one of the three already open. Zora was standing there holding one of the ten AK-47's that had been in the box.

She was wearing her standard khakis and colored wife beater. She called them camis, but I didn't know why. This one was green; not camouflage.

She was posed as if someone were taking a picture. I rolled my eyes and tossed her the pry bar. She tossed me the rifle and I caught it, taking a seat and staring in wonder. It had been more than two years since I'd held one. I went through the motions, clearing it and checking the slide and sights. I had never had a brand new one before. Zora was excited, bouncing from one foot to the other.

"Where'd you get all these?" She said, getting down to pry open the next box.

"Stolen from the new warlock crew. They ordered through Soaka."

"Well, there aren't any traps or auras." She said, looking through the other two boxes. Damn. I hadn't thought of that. Though it didn't make sense for anyone to spend that kind of money just to lay a trap for me. I was still wondering why Soaka had bothered to have someone put a trap on the truck, but it wasn't wise to linger long on the logic of fairies.

The real treasure was in the third, slightly smaller box. Grenades. Twenty of them. The last crate was filled with metal boxes. Each one had enough ammo for the apocalypse. Even if I hadn't been trying to tweak warlock crew's nose, I was ecstatic I'd found ten Kalashnikovs before they could be used for whatever they had planned.

Dammit. I had been avoiding these guys quite successfully until yesterday. Now, I'd have to find out what Firehag and her people were up to before anyone got hurt. Then try to delay them a month until Gomez or someone else could get here and handle them. Might be nice if they were as crippled as possible before that happened.

Gomez would certainly appreciate not having a warlock at full power with a full-on crew to deal with. I couldn't let them run around unchecked anymore. Shit! Find the kids and get the hell out of dodge. I watched in helpless agony as that plan died.

"I'm going to have to go to work for a while," I said. Suddenly, even a brand new shiny Kalashnikov couldn't make me feel better.

Zora was serious when I looked up. Her eyes said she had put it together as well.

"What was he gonna do with these?"

"Nothing good, I imagine. I have to keep him crippled until Gomez can get here, or until he sends someone."

"How soon before he realizes you took them?" She asked.

"Not long. The truck was delivered this morning. It should get picked up before dark. So far, these guys fall into the 'warlocks are more active at night' stereotype. I'd say I have a few hours, maybe."

"You'll have to do whatever you're gonna do tonight then. His hackles will be up once he sees his truck is full of gunless air."

"Yeah." I sighed. "That's what's bothering me. Nothing for it really. Guess I need to quit being a baby, go hit em, and hope that my pack is around somewhere. I may not be able to hit again before they get into it."

"Do you want me to go?" She asked.

I was a little shocked. She had never asked before. Maybe she should go—technically, Zora was my apprentice. I say technically because it didn't take longer than a couple years to teach her everything I knew since our fields of magic didn't overlap. She had no gift for making anything. Getting any spell to go much farther than her skin was a serious challenge.

Mostly we talked magical theory. What was possible, what wasn't. Then one of us would go out, try it, and report back. I felt protective of her. I certainly couldn't take seeing her hurt.

I sighed. "I'm walking into the lion's den. Someone's gonna have to be here to explain things to whatever Martinet shows up.

Even if this goes as well as possible, I won't be able to show my face for a few weeks. Can't risk them tracking me down."

She kept her head down. "I'll… stay here for a while." she murmured. There was a sniffle as I got up to go.

I wasn't good at dealing with crying women. Zora wasn't good at crying in front of anyone, so I pretended it wasn't happening.

I loaded up five of the grenades and took an ammo box with me as I went downstairs. Miles was there. The flattop grill wasn't on, and there was nothing cooking in preparation for dinner. Whatever ended up at my five soup kitchen labs would be cooked and out the door later on. Miles didn't put down his paper. He read one I didn't recognize, probably from wherever he was before this.

"I should be back in a few weeks or so," I said

"Mmhmm," he said, going back to his paper. I walked out, cursing inside. Sure wish I had some resolve to go with all these catch-twenty-two decisions. I crouched outside the door to load magazines and think about my life.

"Where's my diamond stone?" I heard Zora yell from inside. "I know you've been using it on that German crap." They argued about knives too.

"You been crying girl?"

"Crocodile tears. Now hand it over." Zora was sharpening her sword. I heard the sound of stone scraping on metal. "Strawberry pancakes and steak in the morning, old man. I'm working up a sweat tonight." I heard her steps thumping back up the stairs.

I got to my feet and stretched a few minutes later. That woman was insufferable. Like I wasn't going to a place that could get us both killed. She had been with me through the worst scrapes I'd ever been in, and seldom had I planned for her to be there.

She would probably say that somewhere deep down all my plans had her showing up at some point. Not sure I would go that far. I walked back upstairs and caught her in the middle of strapping grenades to a belt. She looked like a kid caught filching cookies before dinner.

"This…" she began with a smile. "Ah screw it. This is exactly what it looks like."

"It looks like lying to me." I said.

"Pretending to cry isn't lying. It's strategy." She grinned.

"It's manipulation," I said.

"Ya know, I'm fine with sarcasm, I'm cool with scorn, but I'm calling bullshit on the surprise in your voice." She said.

"Alright," I sighed, "Wait for an opening, take out anything moving, then regroup with me. This is an ambush; hit and away. Don't move until I do. If there's a chance to get this done quietly, I'm taking it."

She nodded, going back to what she was doing while muttering. "Like you could raid a geriatric bingo tournament without me." I assumed I wasn't supposed to hear that part and went back downstairs.

I took the rifle apart and shoved the parts into various pockets and my satchel. The barrel went under my jacket and peeked out in a way I hoped no one would notice. Miles was still engrossed in his paper, so I didn't speak, just walked out once again cursing the need for taxis.

It took me half an hour and almost ten blocks of walking to hail down a cab. I got in and took stock. I told the cabbie there would be a few stops—just in case—and gave him a twenty in advance. He looked at me through the mirror with a wary eye as I put the rifle back together with deft movements.

I told him that I'd just come from the Personal Defense and Handgun Safety Center. I explained that there was a range there. It was a range that only allowed pistols, but I didn't explain that part.

He relaxed and told me about his adventures being a marksman in the military. Marksman was actually the lowest score you could get, but I didn't tell him I knew that. I just let the words wash over me while we made small talk, and I thought about what I had on me.

I had a sheet with a body in it, a few potions of shadow, few that made me mostly immune to electricity, and two charmers. I sold most of those to people on first dates. Even though they made everything you said or did cast in the best light possible, it didn't matter much. Punching someone in the face or shooting them could only be viewed one way.

Five wake up specials though I'd never need that many. I had four that made me physically stronger and faster, but those left me wasted afterward. I'd had them for two years and never used them.

Lastly, I had everything I was wearing and a few of my misfits.

The cabbie pulled up to the parking garage where the truck had been, and I started giving him directions.

The stream of shimmering pink particles only I could see went up the street and around the corner out of sight. We left downtown going north; my place was west of downtown. I was relieved when we hopped on I-40 going off towards Durham.

Durham had been a tobacco town. I didn't have the whole story, but the industry had dried up and left more than a few old empty buildings. The city had an ongoing effort to keep them from getting too rundown.

We passed the world-famous Carolina Theatre on our way to the worst part of the city. There I saw the trail of sparkles go inside an old warehouse that had two large men in suits out front smoking and looking intimidating. I directed the cabbie to a random house a couple blocks away.

I overpaid and got out thanking him. He drove away, and I jogged back towards the warehouse. A block away I drank a charmer potion and said a small prayer. I only had the two of them, but it was much better than a shadow potion if I had to interact with anyone.

I walked towards the front door. The same two men were still guarding it. I'm pretty big, but they were bigger. Much bigger. I reminded myself that I owned the place. "Sorry I'm late," I offered in a voice that implied I was no such thing. The lantern jaw on the right waved me in.

"You're not late, friend. We are getting underway soon." It was like listening to a bass guitar speak.

The truck was inside the door to the left. It had been backed into the warehouse through a large bay. It didn't look like it had been opened. Of course, there was no way to know that for certain. Between the crowd of people milling around, the six or seven sets of work lights on stands, and the truck, this place was quite full. There were fifty chairs arranged in five rows of ten and a wooden stage in front of them.

I suspected there were more in the back. This room was two stories and pretty big, but it was still smaller than the building—I suspected there were more rooms

Metal walkways and scaffolding crisscrossed the ceiling at right angles. I noticed a few people up there walking around with rifles at the ready. First thing I had to do was get my compass out of the truck where I'd left it.

I shook it violently to stop the sparkles and tossed it in my satchel, took my rifle, and walked up the stairs. If the shooting started, I wanted to be up high, and I certainly didn't want gunman above me.

Once I got upstairs, I pretty much had the run of the place. On the ground floor were about the fifty people needed to match the chairs. I couldn't tell who the warlocks were, but I could tell that this was the inner circle.

Everyone up top had a rifle. Everyone down below was wearing a black scarf around their left arm. I didn't know what the difference was, but I knew that you didn't bother to give uniforms no matter how slight to disposable personnel.

You wouldn't want them leading back to you. Though these

'locks were pretty brazen already, they may think they're powerful enough by now to not care who finds them. They may even have a point. After all, the Martinet was currently engaged elsewhere—wherever that was.

I saw doors at the back on both floors that led to what probably used to be offices. I started to head that way. I kept my head down as I passed the first man. He was a skinny guy and for some reason was wearing sunglasses indoors at night. I murmured gibberish as I passed too low to be heard clearly. He took it as a greeting, and responded "Hail Blackstar."

Charmer potion FTW! Whenever I passed anyone now, I could just say that. I had a chance to try it a couple times as I made my way to the back. It was taken as a greeting, and I thanked my lucky stars each time that the potion was working. I looked away from anyone who looked at me and kept my face deep in my hood.

My initial surveillance suggested that I was right. I was focused pretty hard on not dying at the time, but I saw a few people I recognized from last night.

"Friends," said a man in a dark robe standing on the stage with three others. The four of them had appeared from nowhere. Nice trick. The crowd rushed around; there was some push to the front as everyone tried to get the seat closest to the stage.

I looked more closely at the people on stage. The one on the right was an ugly woman with sparse black hair on her head. I could see more of her boiled scalp than not. Her face was also covered in open sores. Firehag. Her robe was black this time, like the other three.

The man on the left was short and had a belly that had seen way more beers than mine. His hair was salt and pepper and he was balding on top. The hair on the sides of his head was combed over.

The woman on the far left was blindingly beautiful with flowing yellow hair. Even in the loose robes you could tell she had the type of curves men lost sleep drooling over. She was a bombshell, posed up on the stage like a model. I didn't let my eyes linger.

The man in the middle raised his arms as everyone finally got to their seats. Up on the walkways, everyone had stopped what they were doing and were leaning on the railing.

The two hulks came in, slamming the sliding metal doors and throwing a large plank across it. So much for that way out.

I was standing just above the doors at the far end from the stage. I moved to the center and discreetly looked around. I was the only one on this section of walkway; everyone else seemed to be closer. Now I could do more than just look around quickly and hide my face in an attempt to be invisible. I recognized a few faces. More telling, I recognized injuries. There were about ten or so in the room that I had tangled with last night.

Everyone was looking enraptured with the speaker. Even those on the walkway who had obvious places they should be standing edged closer or leaned over the railing. Mimicking them, I leaned over as well. Charmer potion or not I wanted to be inconspicuous.

Everyone was seated and looking up at the stage. There was a door at the end of the walkway to my right, and it was slightly ajar. I didn't dare risk a peek to see what was in there. I was directly in the line of sight of the four on the stage, though none seemed to be paying attention to the second floor at all. With every light in the building pointed at the stage, they probably couldn't even see me, but I was unwilling to take that chance.

"Friends." He repeated.

"***OOOOOAAA***" the rogue god said in my head. It was an instant migraine. I managed to make it through only by clenching my teeth. It had never happened two days in a row before. Normally, I went months without hearing from it. This would have to be researched.

Not now though. I realized that the man was still talking. I'd missed it. They'd brought a person up to the stage.

"…into our fold. Comrades, I give you our newest ally." The bombshell took a large syringe obviously filled with blood and stabbed it into the neck of a waiting young woman who had stood from the chairs and approached the stage.

"We have all taken lives," he continued, as the young woman began to scream. Someone took a cloth and held it in her mouth as the man continued.

"We have all given the blood of another to the Lord of Shapes. Those who have given the most are authorized to receive his gifts. The Lord of Shapes speaks through me. I take his wisdom into me, and when all the world is his, its rulers shall be his faithful." He raised his arms at the last. Everyone hooted, and cheered. Some stomped their feet.

The woman on the floor was growing fur, or feathers. I couldn't tell from where I was. There were shouts of "Hail Blackstar," and "For the Constellation."

That was all I needed to hear—this was the crew I was looking for all right. I made a few low hoots while reaching into my pockets. I pulled out four grenades and then pulled out the pins. I took a deep breath and set my resolve.

"Hail Blackstar."

Chapter: 9

You know those news stories you sometimes see that report a gunman cutting loose in a crowded theater or something? There's always one dead, seven dead, etc. I've rarely heard any number over twenty. My question is always the same; how many bullets did they have?

The reason is because killing another person is difficult. I learned that skill early, but I still sometimes felt the pangs of how hard it should be.

The theatre gunman is often someone who doesn't use guns often. They unload too quickly, pouring several bullets into one target. Or just spraying the place without picking any specific targets. Inevitably, someone gets hit.

In most cases, that's the first time that man or woman has ever heard someone screaming until their voice broke, knowing they were the cause. The effect is instantaneous—the next round goes wide, as does the one after that. The next is a hit, but not the place they were aiming. They start to pull to the left or right at the last moment. It's as if their body refuses to let them commit another murder.

At that point, the gunman is committed. They know they are

going to jail or going to die. They can't just stop shooting. The crowd thins, the smell, the screams, the adrenaline… it's all too much for any human being. You have to train; it has to be beaten out of you. The idea that you must strike first is a philosophy of the weak, and I was weak.

The grenades dropped from my hands. I ran for the door at the end of the walkway, hoping I wasn't seen. But of course, I was.

The thought had occurred to me to wait a few seconds to cook off the grenades. To pull the pin and let the spoon fly, waiting two seconds before throwing them. That had the possibility of accomplishing two things. First, an air detonation would, in theory, give the shrapnel a few extra yards of range. Second, the enemy wouldn't have enough time to throw it back.

I had never tested either of these theories. Giving a grenade a few extra feet of range meant it also had a better chance of reaching me. Things exploded in 360 degrees, after all.

Most grenades had a five-second fuse, but there was never any way to be certain, and I didn't know about these. Trying to get a few extra seconds wasn't a good idea anyway. You're holding a *live* grenade after all. Five seconds isn't a long time, and it's an eternity.

I ran through the door at the end of the walkway, rifle at the ready. There was only one person in the room: a man in a lab coat standing over a bloody table. I didn't hesitate; one shot to the head and he collapsed with a look of shock on his face.

I heard a cry of "grenade!" a moment after I hit the door. One gunshot, a cry of grenade and the cheers had stopped dead. Even for the ones who did hear the yell, there would be heavy casualties. Knowing there was a live grenade in the room didn't tell you what to do about it. Only a few would react in time. Bullets came through the door. I wasn't in their line of sight. Some tried to shoot through the concrete wall.

I heard some ricochet. The building was large, but it was still an enclosed space. With them outnumbering me fifty to one, they had a lot more to lose from wayward bullets than I did. They were already panicked. Good.

Then came the booms.

Four of them; right on top of each other. It wasn't deafening. Explosions never are, but then again, I had never been in the same room as one when it went off either. From the other side of the wall, it was just enough to hurt my ears and set my guts to rumbling.

I heard screams and curses, commands to find the intruder, and someone crying; well, more like wailing. They were screaming at the top of their lungs because there was nothing else they could do. Gunshots and confusion; pain and despair. I couldn't help but smile in a euphoric wave of relief. There was an odd peace to be gathered in the sounds of your enemies dying.

Despite the enjoyment, I couldn't stay in here. I didn't know how many had survived, but I had done my damage and my pack was nowhere obvious. Peace was quickly being replaced by fear. I already wanted to start running. The fact that I was winning was irrelevant. I made a beeline for the only window in the room when I heard a man scream in pain and another voice as loud as the grenades.

"My name is Zora Wade Theresa Kenpatchi! Which one of you is the strongest?!"

I rushed to the door and the sound of the main guy from the stage screaming. "Retreat! Get out! Now!" I threw up my hood, pulled my mask over my face and ran back through the door, firing at everyone on the catwalks who were firing down at Zora. I got two before I had duck back in the room for cover.

There was one left, but she was splitting her attention firing at me and covering her allies on the ground. She paid for that mistake in the next second. They were heavily armed with superior numbers, but they didn't know anything about fighting. They weren't off making life and death decisions as often as Zora and

I. The moves I saw were reflexive and defensive. Experience was everything in a fight. These guys didn't seem to have any.

I moved out onto the platforms as I was firing. I dropped one man who was fumbling with a pistol trying to reload. My rifle wasn't on full auto like theirs were. I almost never went full auto; I was picking shots. There were six left on the floor and a wild-haired goddess of death in the center.

Zora had one other power besides the insane speed: the ability to set up a sphere around her body. This took an even greater toll on her, but in a situation like this, she had to use it. Six people were sending bullets her way and it was all she could do to dodge them. Inside her sphere, she had what essentially amounted to clairvoyance. If a bullet, fist, or over-eager insect came inside that sphere, she knew. From the outside, it looked as if she reacted to things with a couple seconds head start—which was everything in a fight. She'd been training to make the sphere bigger. I haven't checked with her lately on how successful she'd been, but the last time we talked about it she wasn't dodging bullets with this much ease.

I took out two by the time she'd dropped the other four. The stage was empty, save for someone's severed arm. Everything was suddenly eerily quiet. Without the yelling, gunshots or explosions, only the moans of the dying broke the tranquility.

I heard my heart pounding in my ears and Zora's breathing. The wall behind the stage exploded inward. Zora moved with a speed that was hard to describe. An instant before I heard the explosion, she was up on the platform and had me turned around to shield herself from the blast. The pebbles from the wall hit like boulders. Without my magically enhanced clothing, they would've torn right through me. I grunted through blow after blow as Zora picked me up a couple inches and ran along the platform back into the room at the end.

"Good meat shield," Zora said, patting my head and looking

up with a half-smile. I narrowed my eyes and growled in answer before I realized that was playing right into her joke. The smile got much bigger.

I looked out into the main room for targets and saw none. Everyone out there that had been dying was now dead. The exploding wall had made short work of the injured. Dammit. I should've been aiming for the warlocks.

"The window," I said. Zora climbed up and smashed it with the butt of her sword. She cried out and jumped clear just as a gout of flame came through the window, blowing what was left of it inside. Zora hit the table with the bloody sheet and knocked it over. A large man fell to the floor and groaned loudly.

"He's alive," she said with two fingers on his neck. Of course he was alive. This was obviously their infirmary, given the table of medical supplies and a trashcan full of used bloody bandages. Zora sliced through the cuffs as if they were paper.

"That's more than I can say for us if they regroup." I handed her the rifle to hold and she looked at me like I'd grown horns.

"You're kidding, right?" She said. "That's just like a sword, only slower, clumsier, and less efficient."

"Fine," I said slinging it on my back, "just watch the door." She went over and stood by it, leaning casually against the wall. I dug through my satchel and rummaged around for the fork. It took too long. Way too long. God, I missed my pack.

"Please don't fail," I whispered, digging at the wall.

The concrete turned the consistency of pudding when it was in contact with the fork. It became the density of concrete again as I flung it to the floor. I heard myself begging the damn thing not to fail. "Just a little more; please don't fail."

I was through!

I grabbed the big stocky man and pushed him through the hole first—just in case someone on the other side had seen me and had something nasty prepared. Next, I crawled through as cautiously as I could. This room was dark. The fires from the door in the far corner said this was the upstairs office I'd been looking at before.

I grabbed a flare. An ordinary, average, everyday few bucks at any auto parts store type of flare. With a trickle of power, it ignited, and I threw it across the room.

In the center of the room was a feral vampire inside an open cage. Its pasty, lifeless white skin was dry and it groaned with a need for feeding. Two smaller shapes were there as well, placed in smaller cages on opposite ends of a summoning circle that took up the whole room. I saw a wisp of sandy brown hair on one.

There were four small things in layers and layers of dark robes standing around the circle, chanting. I didn't know what they were. I leveled my rifle at one on instinct, but they didn't immediately register to my senses as human. With all those robes, they looked like waist-high piles of dirty laundry. They didn't react to the sounds of gunfire or acknowledge my presence at all. They could stay here and burn, for all I cared. I smelled smoke. Zora came up behind me putting her back to mine.

"What the hell is this?" She said.

"I don't know," I whispered, "but they lit the building. We gotta peel." I gestured to the two smaller cages. "Get them out; I'll cover you." I walked up to the circle and stabbed it with the fork, taking a small chunk out of the floor. Circles were a great way to build up power. Feeling the power that had built up inside this one as it released was shocking. I jumped back, even though there was little reason to—the massive burst of power discharged into the ground. So much for that spell, whatever it was.

The all-black layered things still didn't register my presence. They didn't alter their motions at all, even though I'd disrupted the spell. They must've been homunculi of some type. Automatons made to do some simple task. Like, "sit here, provide a living presence for this circle to feed on, and never move." The vampire didn't react either. It sat in the cage and groaned in pain. It didn't even react when Zora sliced it—and the cage—in half.

Homunculi were hard to make. Not complicated, though. They required raw power; the more, the better. At my best, I could make one the size of a flea. These were child-sized, and there were four of them?!

That was concerning, to say the least. Still, it was no more concerning than standing in a burning building with enemies on all sides.

I glanced out the door and still didn't see any obvious movement in the main room. Zora soon joined me. She had the big man up on her shoulders and a child under each arm. I took the larger child, which turned out to be Theresa.

It was hard to know what to feel at that moment. I didn't think they would be here, of all places. In hindsight, it made perfect sense. Stupid hindsight.

Mostly, I was relieved. There was a tension in my shoulders that left when I saw it was her; tension I hadn't realized was there. Now that I had her and she was alive, all I had to do was keep her that way. No easy feat at the moment.

The tension returned.

There had to be another room below us. Shifting Theresa onto my hip, I went to the door again and looked out. I was looking out on the main area again.

The first thing to catch my eye was one of the hulk-sized doormen dragging his stabbed, bloody form towards the truck. I didn't know what he was trying to do, but I assumed I wouldn't like it and tried to aim. I shot at him twice and missed. I'd never practiced shooting bad guys while carrying children. One of my bullets punctured the gas tank, and with the worst of luck, a tracer round ignited the fuel. Now the place was on fire inside as well, and the only stairs down were covered in flames. On the bright side that also took care of the doorman.

I jumped over the railing holding Zora, the big man, and both kids. It strained my coat and we landed hard, but all five of us were ok. My brain was working overtime thinking of how to get five people out of here alive. I handed Theresa off to Zora. She moaned every time she was jostled, but didn't wake up.

The room under the summoning room was actually five smaller rooms. Obviously, it was the administrative offices of whatever used to be here. One of the rooms still had a cubicle in the corner. I counted three dead bodies before we came across a room with a man still alive.

He was wearing jeans and the same dark cotton hoodie all the guards on the ramparts were wearing. He was trying to put pressure on a bloody mess that used to be his left leg. He saw us enter and his eyes went wide. "No please. I surrender—"

Zora smiled. "Aww how cute. He surrenders." She dropped all three people she'd been holding, stabbed him in the throat, and was back in time to catch them. The scream he took a breath for came out as a pathetic sounding gurgle instead.

Zora was a surgeon with her katana. She'd pierced his trachea, esophagus, and carotid artery—and I knew she'd done it just the right way on purpose. The only question was whether he would drown in his own blood as it filled his lungs, or bleed out, desperately trying to swallow it all. A shot to the heart would kill someone in about ten seconds. It would take him two or three minutes to die.

"That's just cruel. Finish him."

"What? Why?!" Zora said scrunching up her face and tilting her head to one side. Honestly, I wondered the same thing. The priority was getting the hell out of the burning building, not being nice to the people who would happily kill us.

"I said finish him." The confused look never left her face, but after a stab through the heart, he was gone.

We moved on to the last room where we found the blonde bombshell trying to roll an old refrigerator that looked like it was from the fifties. She wouldn't be in a burning building screwing around unless that fridge was important. There was *something* in it.

She screamed something and threw fire at my head. I rolled. The room wasn't big. I felt the heat of the flames as they sailed over me. I came up on my feet not far from her and threw a handful of dust at her face. It didn't stop her, it just bought me a second.

She coughed right before my fist hit her and ruined those supermodel features. Her head went back to the wall and I put more effort in it, smashing her skull between my fist and the concrete. I felt bone crack under the blow. Wizards often made the mistake of being so dependent on magic that they couldn't fight a lick without it. Bombshell had made that mistake; I hadn't. There was shock on her face as she fell.

I grabbed her head, twisting up with a violent jerk, and snapped her neck. I let the twitching body drop and went to the fridge with my fork. I could only hope she'd been guarding something important.

Zora came in with her back to me, sword raised in one hand and watching the door. She'd somehow managed to get both children under one arm and the man in a fireman's carry. It looked precarious.

"So warm-blooded; you should unfinish her," she giggled.

"Yes," I said, inspecting the fridge. "That's the proper thing rather than leaving enemies alive to come back and trouble us."

"Well, you aren't gonna win any feminist points that way," she said with a smirk.

"I treated her as an equal. What more do you want?" The fridge had a simple padlock on it with a wire running from it into the fridge. I suspected someone had rigged it to explode if anyone opened the door. I knelt down to one side and started digging at the metal. "Please don't fail." I chanted as the fork dug a hole in the side.

"Maker." Zora coughed. That was the great thing about fire.

It didn't have to burn you to kill you. We could suffocate as the fire stole away oxygen or by breathing poisons released into the air from things that were never meant to be burned.

I decided the best course was to waste even more oxygen. "Please don't fail. Please don't fail." I carefully moved the big hole of the refrigerator to the floor and saw my pack inside. I heard a scream of joy that probably came from me as I grabbed it.

I saw papers underneath. I grabbed those too. There was also some money, a small blue figure, more papers, a weird looking small disk, and several bags of what looked like blood. Everything in the safe went into my mundane satchel. The only things that didn't were the four sticks of dynamite and blasting cap duct taped to the inside of the door.

Glad I'd stopped to look.

"Maker!" Zora screamed. I looked up to see the fire getting to the door. Slightly more alarming was the short, balding man who now had only one arm. His sleeve was mostly gone as well, and he was covered in blood up to the shoulder. The stump had a strip of cloth cinched down tight, forming a tourniquet.

And here I had kinda hoped he was off somewhere bleeding to death. Instead, he was walking cautiously towards us through the flames. He looked like a predator searching for an opening.

Zora had her sword raised in a defensive stance. Not much offense to be done when carrying three people. Despite the fact that she'd taken off his arm, we were all sitting ducks.

Suddenly, I realized these guys had no idea how weak I was. They didn't know a thing about me except that I had made an extra dimensional space—which I admit is pretty complicated. Like long division, there are a lot of easy steps, but they had to be done in the right order, or you ended up with nonsense. They might not know that either.

Sure, I'd used grenades and not magic, but that could be chalked up to not wanting to break one of Merlin's laws. Also, they know that many of their people got hurt when they hit me last night. Bombshell was still twitching behind me as her body came to grips with brain signals that made no sense. He had sized up the situation and was being wary. I would do the same in his position.

That hesitation was all I needed. "*Digger,*" I growled, and threw the satchel in the air. A wand appeared in my hand: a simple gnarled root, slightly thicker than a finger, and about a foot long. It was a simple looking wand, yet it was the most powerful thing in my pack that I ever dared to use.

I pointed it at the wall behind us, and an eight by eight section of concrete imploded and went into the tiny stick. In the same fluid motion, I brought it forward. Zora was already blurring past me at unnatural speed—even while carrying a man twice her weight and two kids—she made vampires look slow. She caught the pack, slung it over a shoulder without the slightest sign of slowing down.

That left me with the bald man. We were standing in a burning building; he was on the other side of the room and I still felt the cold from his spell. It dwarfed anything I could do. "*Ignus Sayunto Fausto!*" the man screamed. At the same time, I yelled

"*Expel!*" A ton of stone and rocks and dirt flew at him as fire the size and ferocity of a demon tiger came for me. They met somewhere on his half of the room, and I saw him get blown back just before I was.

The whole world went white.

* * *

"That sucked," I groaned when I came to. I was outside, face down on some grass. Zora was kicking my leg. I shook my head a few times and got up to my knees. The tall figure that had been on the center of the stage doing all the talking was at the far corner of the building and stalking towards us. This one was not being cautious.

He had a brisk, confident stride. He wasn't sizing us up; he was coming to kill us.

I was on my feet so fast I had to shake off a little dizziness.

"*OOOOOO*," Bellowed the trapped god in my head. Dammit, I didn't have time to be dealing with headaches.

I gripped my wand in one hand and the fork in the other. I must've looked like an idiot. Facing down a crew of 'locks with an old plastic fork and a twig.

"Go," I whispered.

"I'm not leaving you," she fired back.

"This isn't a movie! I'm not fighting. I'm running away." I said, pretending to dig in the satchel. "*Kitty Pride. Kitty Pride.*" I said. The two bottles of black liquid appeared in my hand in less than a second. Man that felt good. I handed her one, and she drank. The man had stopped moving closer. Instead, he stood not far away looking like he was confused. "If I get caught, you can rescue me. If we both get caught, we're screwed. Now, go!"

Zora was a rare person. When things got emotionally charged, she had the ability to listen to reason. In my experience, that was a rare thing. She sheathed her sword with a man on one shoulder and two kids under the other.

"Hit and away," she whispered. And then she was gone. Not even a rustle of wind to show her passing. The shadow potions were literally made for her; I'd come up with them when I was experimenting ways to make her even faster. That was before she came into her own as a mage and started getting insanely fast on her own. One shot of shadow potion turned her from kinetomancer into the flash. She was forced to have her bubble up, otherwise she couldn't see things and process them in time.

I drank mine and shoved the glass bottle into a cargo pocket. "Dr. Blackstar, I presume. Where's my pack?" The man smiled and lowered the hood. His hair was salt-n-pepper at the wings. His moustache grew down into a neatly trimmed goatee, which was also starting in on the grey. He reminded me of Ras Al'gol from the Batman cartoons.

"I'm assuming she's your apprentice. Very talented—you must be proud."

"Where's. My. Pack," I growled. The anger was real, and the fear was real. I just had to keep him talking long enough to find an opening to escape.

"I'm afraid, my new friend, that it is there," he said, gesturing to the building. The wand was drawing in rocks and dirt as we circled each other. I'd crush him under a ton of rubble, throw some spells on the run, and bail. It could be done. "Do not worry. You will join me. I will take you and give you all you need to make another, and all it contained. We will rule, you and I."

"I can't rule with anyone with a name like a comic book villain." I said.

He just shrugged "A wizard by any other name…" I had no idea where that accent was from; maybe somewhere in Europe. "A Joker is a clown on a playing card. Lex Luthor is a man of business. These things are not intimidating. We could be called Happy the Peanut and it would make little difference. Not a name, but only the fear, that matters." I found myself unsettled by that. According to the hero's book of banter, chapter five, verse three, I was supposed to win that one. It was advantageous since I was stalling, but still disturbing.

"What makes you think I'd join you?"

"How could you not?" He shrugged his shoulders and smiled. The crow's feet at his eyes said he didn't give out many genuine smiles, but this was one of them. "You killed a few of mine. I would overlook this should you join us. There are other forces in the world. I will make you aware of them. You are a minor power, magically speaking. I will mold you into something grand. Your other choice, run around ignorant and disruptive until something takes notice and kills you."

Say what you want about Blackstar; he saw things pretty clearly. Most minor talents didn't know about the Martinet, fey, demons, goblins, lycanthropes, vampires, ghosts, angels, dragons, and I didn't know nearly as much as I could. The last sentence was a pretty accurate description of my future.

I realized with a rush that through all that, the charmer potion was still working. Another advantage, but how to capitalize on it? I lowered my wand and relaxed my stance.

"We should be called the Beatles," I said. "They were the greatest."

He shrugged again, "I've always enjoyed the Rolling Stones. Perhaps the Rolling Beatles? There is time to discuss it."

"Of course, I certainly don't want to clash with you over a misunderstanding," I said with a smile I wasn't feeling. Making faces was easy for me, even when I wasn't feeling it. The recipe for a smile was to wrinkle my forehead a bit, squint ever so slightly, keep both sides of my mouth even and don't show any teeth. It fooled practically everyone. Maybe I missed my calling and actually belonged in Hollywood. "What are we summoning?"

"Ahh, that is a fine surprise, one I think you will…" He looked at the burning building, then back to me with a furrowed brow. There was rage in his eyes and a gust of foul wind suddenly rose. So much for the charmer potion.

The breeze smelled like hatred feels. Like a swamp full of dead and dying things mixed with fire, burned flesh, and a dash of screaming. I threw my wand up before me.

"*Fire!*" A single stone flew from the end at blinding speed. It bounced off a shield of solidified air and took a chunk out of a tree. There were sirens in the distance, and I heard them getting closer. Small favors.

Firehag came out of nowhere, screeching like bird of prey after a kill. She'd burst from the flaming rubble and charged. One arm was covered in blood and hung limp at her side. She was in a rage and came at me with the fingernails of her good arm aiming for my throat. This was the reason I worked so hard to control my emotions. Had she stayed back and thrown spells, they could've taken me, easy.

This attack was a distraction for Blackstar who, assuming he cared, now had to worry if he'd hit her. It was worse for her. Thirty feet apart, we were a weak wizard versus a strong wizard throwing spells to the death. Three feet apart, and we were a strong young man versus an injured old woman.

I dodged the physical attack, which was laughably slow and raked the fork down her face on reflex. I didn't expect it would work on something living, but it did. Her flesh melted and reformed as the fork trailed through it. It ended with taking a small piece of her jaw. She screamed and grabbed her face with her good hand; the nails were long, and the pink fluid leaking from them sprayed me as she retreated a few steps.

I noted the pink stuff was corrosive as a few drops burned straight through my jacket. She splattered droplets on herself when she went to cover her face and screamed again as the acid from her nails burned her skin.

My fork was dead. I could feel it. Changing something living required lots of power, and that was a permanent change. It was as worthless now as, well… as a plastic fork.

I advanced, hoping to finish her and was just in time to walk into a hammer of air swung by Blackstar. It was like getting hit by a semi-solid missile. I flew through the air for about thirty feet and rolled with the impact of the landing. Add to that my pants, shirt, coat, and the fact that I was scared out of my mind, and even slamming into the concrete wall of the building didn't keep me down. I was up again before the pain fully registered. Pain was easier to manage when you were standing.

I thanked my lucky stars I'd put my hood up earlier, or my

skull would likely have split like a melon. As it was, I was shaking off a torrent of dizziness.

Blackstar was smiling and stalking nearer. I couldn't hear anything since he had the air around him solidified into that pesky shield, but I could tell from his lips moving rapidly and the grandiose arm gestures that something nasty was coming. This was gonna get ugly. Well... uglier. The smell from the building was something toxic that made me cough.

Then I felt a heave from my stomach, and my eyes began to burn. Blackstar was finished casting and crossed his arms with a smile, and then I got it.

Tear gas, or something like it—and it covered the whole place. I could hold my breath, but the damage was done. A flame shot from his hand and barely missed me. I dodged and rolled away, looking for a place to hide.

When I looked up the wall had a six-foot hole burned through it and Blackstar was holding a ball of glowing concrete over his head like a second sun. He was still smiling, waiting for me to get to me feet before he threw it.

It was lava, but lava was still rock, so I held up my wand and absorbed it as it came in. I screamed from the heat. Enchanted jacket or not, this was too much. I grabbed the wand in my right hand and coughed as the tear gas made my vision worse. Blackstar clapped and appeared to be laughing, as if he was enjoying a performance.

I knew when I was being toyed with. The attacks that only came after I was ready and the amount of power being casually thrown around made that abundantly clear. It was insulting, but it was also good news. It meant he wouldn't kill me if I kept providing a sufficient level of entertainment and didn't prove to be a genuine threat. At least the second part would be easy.

I held my wand near the wall, shut my eyes, and ran. Blackstar was after me in that long stride, and I saw with dismay that Firehag was back up and right behind him. Unfortunately, she seemed unaffected by the gas.

My wand cut a wide furrow in the stone work as I ran. I didn't stop until I felt fresh air hit my eyes at the corner of the building. I exhaled and gulped the air—which was blessedly free of pain.

My eyes were still blurry as my tears tried to clear them, but I could see well enough to know that Blackstar was stalking closer with Firehag behind.

I held up my hands as if I wanted to talk.

They didn't believe me, but they hesitated a moment, and that was all I needed. The wall I'd weakened creaked and fell. With the fire raging inside there was no way it could stay up. Blackstar caught on first. He raised his hand and a large section of the falling wall shattered into smaller rocks that all came straight for me.

I dodged most of them and interned a few more in my wand. The last was the size of a beach ball and moved like a bullet. I didn't have time to get my wand up. I dodged and it hit me in the left side. My burned arm lit up with a blinding agony again. I heard ribs crack and felt my body crumble. How long was this damn shadow potion going to take?! Fire department, shadow potion, divine intervention; I'd take anything at this point.

I got back to my knees, and the lurching motion made me nauseous. Hag was standing next to Blackstar and both were smirking.

I had to do something. I couldn't afford to let either of them think this fight was over. They'd finish it.

"*Fire.*" I croaked. It didn't sound like a word, but my wand knew what I meant. A rock the size of my fist flew at Firehag. She saw it coming and stepped aside, putting Blackstar between us so I couldn't see her.

I got back to my feet in time to see her arms wrap around Blackstar and turn into flamethrowers.

"*Hydrate!*" I screamed. The grass at my feet withered as every molecule of water came to my call. I sent it through the flames and all the way to her hands, but there was no way I could extinguish that fire completely. The cloud of steam blocked any sight of them. This was the chance I'd been looking for.

The art of tactics is the art of deception. It's figuring out the one thing your enemy would never expect and then doing it. I knew what they wouldn't expect, so I charged. I saw Firehag first and swung my broken limp arm as hard as I could. My whole left side turned into a mass of screaming pain sprinkled with numbness, but it was worth it.

I hit her square in the face and she fell in a lump, unconscious. At the same time, I aimed my wand at where Blackstar had been and screamed, "*Fire!*" I heard the thunk and figured I'd hit his shield. That was as much cover as the steam gave me.

Blackstar became clear. He was standing casually with his arms folded, still looking at me with that superior smirk.

Then I saw a trail of steam move through his cheek. A mote of dust—more than one—floated into his arm. An illusion!

I whirled the wand in a circle above my head just as the world grew brighter. Finally.

"*Expel!*" Rock, dirt and metal rushed out in every direction as the chill of the spell rushed in. Not more than six feet to my right the real Blackstar was now visible, and flat on his back. He was up again right away, gasping for breath and choking on dust in the night air. At least that's what I assume.

I wasn't there to see it.

Chapter: 10

We had to drop off the children, but first I had to be certain that Happy the Peanut wasn't pursuing them.

I regrouped with Zora, and after a long session of first aid, we spent the night jumping from place to place and doubling back. We couldn't find any sign of being followed. That was good. It was pointless to drop the kids off with Rollo if Blackstar could just walk right in and take them back. It was near dawn by the time I was finally willing to risk it.

Rollo got to work early; I knew that. Sometimes he never left. With two missing children on his watch, I was sure he would be awake and out looking for leads. That or sitting in his office with an IV full of coffee.

The police station downtown was open all the time, but it wasn't safe. These kids needed to be someplace out of the way. A bunch of cops with guns would only slow Blackstar down a few minutes—if they slowed him down at all.

My only choice was Rollo's house, which was dangerous because I could lead Blackstar there. Same story with every other place I knew of. In the end, I picked the police station. I could stay for a while if needed.

I walked in and left Zora hiding in a nearby parking garage with the kids; somewhere on the roof where she could see things coming. She had my jacket, and if needed it could get her a swift exit off the roof so she could run. We'd left the big man at my lab on the east side, mixed in with the homeless. Once I'd slowed down and had time to think, I wasn't sure why we'd pulled him out of there at all, but I was glad we did. I had questions, lots of them, who was he? Why was he there handcuffed to a bed? I certainly wasn't going to ask Happy the Peanut. Another time, whoever he was it was clear he wouldn't be getting up anytime soon.

Zora had been asking the children questions and making small talk as we moved. They weren't all that coherent. They were awake, but still under the influence of whatever Blackstar and company had done to them. I kept my distance, keeping a lookout.

I walked into the station looking around for each camera and alternate ways out. The place was a nightmare in that regard. The lobby was a desk, a metal detector and a door you had to be buzzed through.

The only obvious way out was the way I came in, and that was a giant glass wall of entryway doors that were just dying to be blown up. Architects seemed to have a fetish for glass, sometimes I could swear that had it in for humanity. Windows explode inward, you morons.

The cop at the front desk looked me up and down in a way that made me think he was cataloging details. Like he'd need to pick me out of a line up later. Tall, black, shaved head, young kid with black cargo pants, white t-shirt, black backpack, and an arm covered in bandages. Survey says: petty criminal, drug dealer, undesirable. I guess that wasn't too far off.

The officer had seen one too many doughnuts, and was old enough to not care. He had a full head of gray hair and a sparkling uniform. He was likely just waiting the few extra years he'd need to retire. I sighed. Retiring would be nice. If only there were no monsters.

"Is Detective Rollo available? I have a tip on a missing person he said he was looking for." I said that to allay any suspicion. It didn't work.

The officer said nothing, just got on the phone and called Rollo. He must've dealt with informants before. I was certainly looking over my shoulder enough to be one. He knew if he asked to take a message I would refuse to say anything. That was normally the way it went anyway. Or maybe he just didn't care.

Rollo appeared after about ten minutes. This was his station, but as I expected, he was out in dark alleys getting answers. When the door opened, I heard a car horn and jumped, reaching for a pistol I wasn't wearing before realizing it was Rollo standing there.

"Damn son, you alright?" he said, moving his hand away from his gun. The desk cop was doing the same. Maybe he wasn't the fat useless type after all.

"No. But I'll be all right." With a deep breath, I put my fear back in check, but it didn't go away. That particular neurochemical cocktail didn't fade quickly when I was exhausted.

I walked out, and he followed. We were outside and moving at a brisk pace before he spoke.

"Got a lead on the kids I assume?"

"Stop talking. Monsters have great ears." I said. Talking out in the open and not behind a threshold before the sun was up was practically inviting a vampire to listen in. I didn't think there were any around, but I hadn't lived this long by taking stupid chances.

I was looking around as I made for the once-empty parking garage. It was starting to fill up as a line of cars were already queueing to get in. I checked my phone and it said 0458. It was downtown and people were already starting to arrive for the workday. The janitors, sanitation people, and bus drivers—all the people who made things run smoothly.

Rollo followed me to the elevator and we went up to the top floor. There weren't enough people around yet for there to be more than a few cars up here.

I whistled and got a hoot back. I whistled again twice and waited. Zora stayed hidden just in case Rollo wasn't Rollo, but I'm pretty sure he was. Monsters felt different. It was hard to explain, but the better you knew someone, the harder you were to fool.

The children came forward hesitantly. They were still drowsy and lethargic. They were holding hands, dragging their feet and looking like they might fall at any moment. I wasn't good with children. People said I was, but I didn't think so. They did seem to make much more sense to me than the average adult. Maybe that was it. I couldn't even look at or say a word to these kids. I hadn't looked much at Rollo either.

Rollo rushed over and scooped them up like they were his own. Ryan passed out on his shoulder almost instantly, while Theresa just stared in bewilderment at him like she had done with everything since she'd woken up.

"Get them into witness protection or something and keep them there. A month at minimum. Someplace with lots of families, and never invite anyone in. Treat everything that comes to the door like a vampire, and never go anywhere that isn't well populated."

Rollo nodded. "How did you—"

"No time for that story. Suffice to say you owe me a few beers," I said, walking off to where Zora would be. No way I was gonna tell Rollo I had committed arson, murder, attempted murder, destruction of property, criminal trespassing, and disturbing the peace just to get them back. Those were just the broken laws I could think of. The list would be ten times as long once the District Attorney got a hold of me. Hell, they'd probably charge me with terrorism. That was popular these days.

Dawn was at hand, and I could already hear traffic starting to pick up. It was time to quit.

I ran off with Zora into the early morning, wondering why I didn't feel better. The answer wasn't difficult to find. I had just painted a giant target on my back and Zora's. Those kids were fine. They could go to the nearest rooftop and let off fireworks. Blackstar would be coming after me. Taking that premise as a gospel truth left me with few options; none of them good.

* * *

As exhausted as I was, sleep had been elusive. Instead, I wrapped my burned, shattered arm in my ace bandage and a few hours later we were sitting back at Miles' having breakfast. There were stories about the fire in Durham on the news and all over the net. The fire department was able to contain it before it spread to any other buildings. The fire was said to have started by a random spark setting off grease in an abandoned car repair facility. The man who owned it blamed transients and so did the fire department.

"Thankfully no one was injured," said the newscaster, an older distinguished looking brunette woman.

"No one injured?!" Zora laughed pounding the counter with her fist and spitting pancake crumbs everywhere. "Do they realize what an insult that is to my professionalism?!"

If they decided to investigate thoroughly, they would find a gross number of inconsistencies—but they wouldn't do that. That wasn't the way the world worked.

I sighed. My breakfast had long since gotten cold. Scrambled eggs, bacon, grits and coffee. I wasn't hungry. Zora was though. Miles was flipping her fourth serving of strawberry pancakes. So much for the carbs; she always ate like that after a fight.

"Should've known that was you. They been talking about it all night." Miles said, slapping down another T-bone and pouring on another half dozen scrambled eggs for Zora. Telling the universe how to behave took a lot out of you. Had to have some way to put it back. Kinectomancy burned a lot of energy. Zora ate like a whale even when there wasn't a fight. I, on the other hand, couldn't have less of an appetite—despite how many spells I'd cast.

Only a part of it was all the carnage. Bodies ripped up and broken apart. It was difficult to maintain a respect for life when you could end them with a few chemicals mixed in just the right proportions. Maybe it was terrible. Maybe I was used to it. That was actually the thing bugging me the least.

At the top of the list was a ritual summoning involving two children, a Vermillion Falls vampire and enough dark magic to raise the Titanic. I'd disrupted the circle, and even if I hadn't, the fire would've probably taken care of it.

It would be dumb to think that they would cut their losses and not try again. Now I needed to find out what they were summoning and stop them. If they needed two children, at least I would have a few days warning. Not that a few days would be much help looking for two needles in a city-sized haystack. As ruthless as it was, it would be far more advantageous if they needed those two specific children.

I desperately hoped this had nothing to do with Rania's prediction.

Had I known the kids were there I would've rigged the entire building to blow, snuck in, gotten them out, grabbed my pack, blew the building, and put a bullet in any survivors from a hundred yards away. Too late for that now. It was a good plan for the information I had at the time, but hindsight always made me feel like a blind idiot.

Next up was a man held hostage. Blackstar and The Constellation obviously weren't above torture. I'd dressed some of his wounds, so I knew from touching him that he had power. Was he a member of Blackstar's crew? Some supernatural creature that looked human? Why was he strapped to a table being tortured? Was it torture at all?

It was possible that I was holding a Martinet level wizard who was going to wake up at any moment and rip me to shreds. It was not outside the realm of possibility that he was being punished in some way. He may wake up and find that delivering my head would put him back in The Constellation's good graces.

That was unlikely, but a small chance wasn't zero chance. I could also be deluding myself about how unlikely it was. He was locked up behind the strongest threshold I had access to, which just so happened to be twenty feet above where I sat. He was chained to a bed, gagged, hooded and inside the most powerful circle I knew how to draw. All that could hold nearly anyone.

He wasn't awake and showed no signs of waking anytime soon. At the moment he was getting nutrition through a vein. Zora was keeping tabs on him since he was tied up in the apartment across from hers.

The phone rang, and Miles picked it up. It was a brief conversation. He grunted, hung up, and went right back to flipping eggs, steak, and pancakes.

"Maker, your truck is ready, and when you gonna start using your phone?"

"Never," I said at the same time Zora chimed in,

"You know we can't use our phones, old man. Besides, why bother, we have a secretary."

Phone calls could be tracked. A lot of things could be tracked. In a world that was becoming more and more connected, hiding was becoming more and more difficult. Rumor had it that vampires had heads of state on the payroll. Finding one little ol' wizard wouldn't be difficult at all. Anonymity was one of the greatest advantages Zora and I had. Using our phones as phones all the time would be like painting a giant neon sign above our heads. I only used mine to read and tell time.

Zora was an electronic wiz kid before her magic began to manifest. She was still pretty good at it, but she hadn't found a way to make a cell phone secure yet. I was waiting for that. It was always nice to have one less thing to worry about.

"Still the first good news I've had all day," I said, shoving some eggs and bacon into my mouth. It tasted terrible, but it had everything to do with my mood and nothing to do with the cooking. "I need to think; I'm going shopping. Then I'll walk over and grab my wheels. Standby here and watch our mystery man, got a lot of questions for him."

Zora grunted something that resembled acknowledgment while shoveling more food in her mouth.

I decided to walk and not bother with a taxi. The mystery man wasn't getting up today. I kept my mind empty, thinking about philosophy or the motions of elementary particles. Any subject was preferable to the mess I was in. It was nearly an hour before I got to where I was going.

The place was a hole in the wall; at least the door was. It was a door in between two buildings. There could be an alley there just as easily. Most folks walked by without even a glance at the simple gold lettering of "Graced Antiques."

I walked right in, even though there was no open sign on the outside. The place was dark—there were no windows in the large room. There were tables along the front wall filled with all sorts of knick-knacks. Anything and everything, so long as it was old.

Everything was sparkling clean and beautifully restored. At the back of the store were shelves filled with books; more books than you could read in a lifetime. Not because you couldn't turn that many pages, but because they were mostly written in dead and ancient languages you'd have to learn and correctly interpret first. The place was a library of old arcane scrolls and texts.

Grace was the grandmother of the woman who sat on a stool behind a small table polishing something brass. It could've been a spittoon or chamber pot of some type, but Jayne polished it gently, and almost lovingly—like it was the most precious thing in the world. She had brown hair that touched her shoulders and brown eyes. A face so remarkably plain that she was beautiful if you could keep your eyes on her without them simply sliding away to something more interesting. Despite the heat, she wore a sleeveless turtleneck sweater and a flowing white skirt that went to her ankles.

"Hey Maker," she said without looking up. I waved but didn't speak, already passing my hand over the objects on every table. There weren't many new items this week. There was just enough to keep me busy and take my mind off my life for a bit.

"How's business?" I asked, though I didn't need to. Even one different thing on the tables meant business was going quite well.

"Very good. Everyone seems to want a talisman or something to protect them lately. Apparently some asshole out there is stirring up the locals."

"That hurts. I'm an innocent bystander in… whatever it is you're talking about."

She looked up just long enough to let me know she didn't buy a word of it. I smiled to say I hadn't meant a word of it.

"It's cool. Wiccans come in, I tell them whatever they've picked out is probably useless, and they buy it anyway. Not sure what it is that makes folks think everything old has power. Maybe the fact that a certain someone has been seen shopping here."

That was a shock. Sure, there were practitioners everywhere, but to hear there was a "Maker following" was a little jarring. I'd ask why, but that was a stupid question. Everyone knew about Vermillion Falls and Duke, and I had worked hard never to confirm or deny any of Duke's suspicions. I was way less powerful than he thought.

There was a thorn in his side, and he didn't want to act until he could prove it was me that put it there. I didn't know why.

Duke could squash me like a bug at will, even if I was a Martinet reject like he thought.

My hand passed over a small wooden box and I felt the faint hum of more photons being emitted than anything else on the table. Sensing magic this way was always a faint impression. Waves of energy coming off of things brushed against my senses in a way that felt like someone breathing close to my skin. That was why I called it whispering.

All magical tools, I've found or made, either radiated power or sucked it in—both stuck out like a sore thumb if you knew what to look for. The top of the box was all edges and fit together perfectly. I didn't know what wood it was; I knew little about antiques.

What I did know was that some things were made with exceptional quality and skill. Old things made by master craftsmen; things made precisely and carefully. Those things had magic infused in them from their making or from being a part of people's lives for so long.

Just from touching it I knew that this box could be made into something magical. If I laid down the right spells, any box could be made magical, but "any box" would have to be powered by me. This one, if done well, could power itself in full or in part. That took the burden off of me, and it would last a lot longer before failing.

Grace traveled all over the world, bringing back any antiques she fell in love with. She and Jayne restored them, and then they were sold. Some antiques could cost a hefty sum.

"Got anything that's not obvious?" I asked, gesturing to the tables. The answer was almost always no, but I asked anyway.

Jayne just shook her head. I walked through the rest of the store browsing. I found a few books that looked sufficiently old, but nothing else that had power. I paid two hundred dollars for the small box and left the store wondering what I could do with it.

I walked out onto an empty street—no cars, no people. That was...

"**OOOOUUNNNNN,**" the voice in my skull was a roar, and it didn't go away this time. It was so painful I fell backwards into a building and stumbled down an alley. Fat lot of good it did trying to run from a voice in my mind. I wanted to will it away. Tried and failed. Gritting my teeth through this assault wasn't helping either.

I started to run, stumbling down an alley and knocking over a trashcan, only to see a woman in front of me. I didn't have time to register her features before I was hit in the face with a bat. I didn't remember hitting the ground, but I was down and surrounded by three figures.

There were punches, kicks, more one on one time with the bat, and a crowbar that made gravel out of my once pristine ribs. I kept trying to speak. A potion—any potion, my wand... nothing would come to my hand.

Each time a spell formed on my lips a scream left my mouth. The word or phrase itself had never mattered before. Then again, I'd never had a fallen god bellowing in my head before. I was thankful for the darkness when it finally arrived to engulf me.

"Took ya long enough."

Chapter: 11

I woke up—that was a surprise. Pro tip: if ever you're captured and you wake up, the best thing to do is keep your eyes closed.

The fact that I was alive meant that whoever was standing over me while I was unconscious didn't want me dead. If they didn't want me dead—at least, not right away—then odds are good I could learn something useful while they thought I was still passed out.

The room was warm and the air smelled stale. I could feel the straps that held me down, and the bed I was on felt more like a recliner since my head and knees were elevated.

I tested the straps and found they were quite secure. I decided it would be best to sneak out before anyone noticed I was awake. Just as I was ready to burn through my bonds, a screaming pain ripped through my head.

I stole a glance down and saw that the bonds on my right wrist were large grey, heavy manacles. They appeared translucent. It was like having shackles made of smoke and the weight of lead. Wraith shackles—specifically designed to capture wizards. Tema had a pair that I was locked in almost nightly. Any photons I attempted to gather would be absorbed by the shackles and used to trigger every pain receptor I had. Well, this was unfortunate.

Unfortunate there were wraith shackles on my wrist, and even more unfortunate that Blackstar was powerful enough to have somehow procured a pair.

The other end of the shackles was attached to the chair. My left hand and feet were done up in plain duct tape. With even more pressed tightly across my body. They weren't being lax with the restraints, at least.

I could eventually pick or chew my way through it, but it wouldn't matter in the slightest unless I wanted to carry the chair out of here.

The air was beyond gross. It was humid and smelled of mildew and rot. If I didn't know better, I'd say I was outside in a swamp somewhere.

I didn't hear any movement or breathing, so I cracked open my right eye again to have a look around. I was in a stone room, alone; the only other furniture, besides me, was a table with some rather nasty looking implements on it.

The fact that they were covered in my blood should've registered somehow, but it didn't. There were several candles burning in sconces around the room, giving it a dull light.

I also noticed they'd placed my pack on the table. That would be useful... if I could reach it. My wand was inside, as well as potions galore. I'd never tried using a wand while wearing wraith shackles of course, but the wand was a gnarled root from the first tree. It had its own power—lots of it. More than enough to get me out of here, but I had to get to it first.

A door opened behind me. I snapped my eyes closed. Whoever walked in was heavy-footed. I heard them cross the room to the table. I stayed still, suddenly realizing I was scared out of my mind.

I managed to keep my breathing under control, but my heart was racing and that's probably what gave me away.

"Come on then; I know you're awake." I heard the voice say. It wasn't Blackstar, or anyone else I'd overheard back at the garage. The voice was familiar. The accent was… French? It was becoming clear that none of these Constellation goons were from around here.

I didn't open my eyes. In fact, I squeezed them shut even tighter because the pain in my head this time was like nothing I'd ever felt before. Every nerve ending in my body fired at once. I could've screamed. If I had air, I would have.

You hear stories about people who last through torture, who refuse to talk or capitulate. Like everything, there's a trick to it.

One of the differences between human consciousness and instinct is that you can think about what you're thinking. I started thinking about the pain. Analyzing it. Wasn't easy, but I reached for it. Focused on it, embraced it.

It was a spectacular amount. It was already starting to hurt less, but maybe that was my imagination. I heard myself scream. Heard it die as my lungs emptied, and start again almost immediately. It was high pitched; animal-like. I didn't know I could make a noise like that.

Like a drop off a cliff, the pain stopped and was replaced with a pleasure I have never known. I felt old aches lessen and muscles release, but it was only for an instant and then there was more screaming. The pleasing sensations caught me off guard and destroyed my focus. I wasn't prepared until the third time it came. Was it a hair longer this time? Maybe I was imagining things.

"Pleasure is harder to fight than pain," I thought, dispassionately. Objectively, I noticed that pleasure destroyed my objectivity. That brought a laugh. Whoever was behind me took it as an insult.

My throat burned on the next scream, every muscle contracted and my back arched up from the bed ripping a few strands of duct tape.

I blacked out again.

* * *

When I woke up I was standing in a room made of light. The restraints were gone, along with everything else. Beyond the thirty-foot circle of illumination, there was nothing but black. I looked up, but couldn't see a light source. The floor was transparent, with nothing but darkness stretching out below. About thirty feet up the blackness started, down too.

There was a woman standing across the circle from me. She was skeletal, her back hunched and her skin pulled tight across her face and body, but she didn't look old. Somehow I knew that she was my age or even younger. Wisps of brown hair dotted her scalp in patches and her skin was decorated with bruises and other discolorations.

I had every nasty spell I knew ready to launch, but she spoke before I did. "Good to see you Maker." Her voice was strong and hard. There was nothing in it that reflected the weak, emaciated creature I saw before me.

"Yeah…" I responded slowly. "And you are?" Some distant part of my mind noticed my voice was calm and held none of the fear I was feeling at the moment.

"You may call me Arta." I got the feeling the woman was lying, so I did what I always did in that situation.

I told her so.

She laughed; deep, and throaty. It was totally at odds with her appearance. "No, not a lie. I simply have many names. While I wouldn't mind telling my true name to a mortal, it would take five of your minutes to speak it properly, and hearing it would kill you. That would be more than a little inconvenient for me."

"I can understand that," I responded. "It would be a shame to kill your boss' prize right after you'd captured me."

Her eyes flashed with anger and she sneered, "You think I'd work for some petty mortal sorcerer?"

"Prove to me that you don't!" I challenged her. She smiled, and I regretted it right after the words left my mouth.

"Years ago, you were tied up in a basement, inside a summoning circle covered in arcane symbols that you didn't understand. *That* is where this… complicated relationship of ours began." Despite myself, I took a step back. It felt good, so I took another. Before I knew it, I was running.

I only made it a few yards before the blackness outside the circle came to life. Ghostly, shadowy arms reached for me. I couldn't say for certain, but it looked like they were aiming for my throat. I stopped just in time and spun around to come face-to-face with Arta standing just inches away from me.

The laughter and amusement were gone. She was hovering a foot or so off the ground to look me in the eye. If she were standing, the tiny woman would barely reach my lowest chest hair, but I'd never felt smaller than I did at that moment.

"I don't work for mortals. Not then, not now. You and I are going to have a talk, boy."

I was breathing hard, and it had nothing to do with the short run or the torture. I simply nodded, not trusting myself to make words at the moment.

"Good." She said with a smile that appeared genuine. She returned to her position across the circle, but she didn't cross the intervening space. One moment she was an inch from my face, and the next, she stood seven feet away. The center of the circle of light followed her. Turned out *she* was the source.

"Okay, this is bad," I muttered. A table and two chairs appeared. She sat down, moving as an old woman should. I took a hesitant step towards the table and she motioned to the seat across from her. By the time I was seated there was… tea? And some old bread-looking biscuit things.

She gestured for me to pour—which I did. I've never actually sat and had a "proper tea" with anyone before, but I'd seen it on Mary Poppins as a kid and knew to ask, "One lump or two?" The sugar bowl had honey in it. I poured some tea for myself, even though I wasn't drinking.

I was in a state of shock. I know that because before I could think of something polite or diplomatic, what flew out of my mouth was, "Get out of my head!"

She waved a dismissive hand and snorted, "Boy, if it were that simple don't you think I'd have done it already?" I managed to put some thought into the next question, though not much.

"Why can't you just leave?"

"The same circle that kept you in that basement for a week keeps me in your head. Like I said, our relationship is complicated."

"But that was years ago," I replied, "I was twelve!"

She nodded, "And that same circle is etched into your brain, your heart, your liver... all those lumps of meat you mortals are so fond of. Mmmm Sideritis. No other tea can compare." She didn't look at me while she sipped. Somehow the action seemed menacing. Or maybe I was just scared enough to piss myself for the second time today.

"What do you want?" I said. She snapped a glare at me, and I rephrased, "Uhh... I mean, what can I do for you?" That didn't come out any better. I was attempting to rephrase again when she held up a hand for silence.

"You and I are going to be together for quite a while," she said. "Probably until the day you die. Until that day, I think we should do whatever we can to get along." I thought about that. It didn't sound quite right. Suddenly my brain was working again.

"Why now?" I asked.

"Finally!" She responded, "I thought we'd be on our second pot of tea before you got to it. Bringing you here, creating this place. It all takes energy, even though it's only taking place in your head. I certainly can't use yours; you're weak as a kitten, even by mortal standards. Thankfully this Blackstar person was good enough to provide what I needed. Those spells of his aimed at taking over your mind… well, I kind of ate them."

"Wait, what? You *ate* them?" I sputtered.

She sighed, "Try not to be so three-dimensional. Ate, absorbed, used-to-power-this-construct. I'm dumbing this down as much as I can."

"I know a bit about magical theory. You don't need to dumb anything down."

"I can assure you I do," she smiled. She was thirty pounds soaking wet, looked older than dirt, missing most of her teeth and still made me feel like the small, weak one. "We move through time at different rates," she continued. "With you barely conscious, full of adrenaline, and me thinking at the speed of a garden slug, we can actually have a conversation."

"Uhm, okay…" I said. "So now that we're talking…" I trailed off and left the unasked question hanging in the air.

"I'm going to need you to start being a better host," she said.

"What do you mean, host? You're not my guest!" Supernatural beings had all kinds of not-quite-laws regarding the etiquette of guest and host. I didn't know all of them, but they essentially boiled down to, "don't be an asshole."

"An unwilling guest is still a guest. And being a good guest, I didn't just kill you immediately and leave."

"I suppose," I responded. "Why didn't you?"

"Oh, you'll be dead in a hundred years anyway," she waved her hand as if the time were nothing, "and I'm not going to sacrifice everything that I am for a minor inconvenience."

"So, what can I do for you?" I repeated. Turns out it was the right question after all.

"You can start by getting me more to eat. You barely produce enough in magical resources to keep me conscious."

"You mean get attacked?"

She shrugged, "You don't have to be attacked, but it does have to be some spell that is aimed at affecting your mind. If I had my way, I'd have you stay in this Blackstar's torture room for a while. I think you'll be staying for a bit anyway."

Until she smiled, I didn't notice that she had more teeth than she did when we sat down. She was a little lighter in the bruises department, too.

"Am I still being tortured?" I asked, amazed at my comfort with the issue.

"Oh yes," she said. Her face brightened and perked up when she spoke. "You're also screaming like a little girl. They are trying everything they know to break your mind. I'm letting them think they are succeeding. Once they believe you a thrall, they remove the manacles and you walk out of here."

"Wow… uhh, thanks," I said.

"Starting to think it's useful having a spirit in your head, eh?"

I laughed. Things weren't as bad as I thought at least. I even sipped some tea. It was cinnamon flavored. I didn't like tea, but I love cinnamon in all its forms. I realized the opportunity here and suddenly had the radical idea that I might live through the week. "What do you know about Blackstar?" I asked.

"Everything," she responded.

"Great." I said grinning "Tell me everything."

"No," she said taking another sip.

"Why not? Isn't it part of being a good guest if…"

"Maybe, but I don't work for mortals or interfere in the lives of mortals. I won't tell you anything you don't already know."

"Aren't you already interfering?" I asked.

"No."

"I don't know the laws of guest and host, so forgive me if this is rude, but if you're keeping Blackstar from stirring up my brain with a spoon, that strikes me as interfering." Wasn't just having her in my head interfering? I could point that out, but thought better of it.

"It isn't rude, and thank you for asking. I can understand how it seems to you to be interfering. You will simply have to take my word that it isn't."

"What good is that?" I said. "You just said it would be inconvenient if I died."

"No. I said it would be inconvenient if I killed you. I don't care one bit if you die on your own." She smiled.

"And here I thought I was confused before. What good is it to tell me things I know already?"

"Trust me, Maker. What you know would terrify you. I know, I live in your head," she laughed. "I've even stopped you from remembering things that would destroy you. Tell me, did you ever ask why Den'Tema Rion wanted to imprison me inside you?"

"There was no one to ask." I said. "I just assumed she wanted power. Tema wasn't complicated, even as a kid I knew that."

"Her intention was to kill you, or rather wipe your mind away—which is the same as killing you—and use me as a repository for power and knowledge. She didn't know about your artificer abilities at the time."

"How would she have done that?" I asked. "It doesn't make sense to imprison something inside me. Well, it does, but it's ridiculously inefficient. Better to make a homunculus and put a spirit in that."

"In certain circumstances," Arta said, taking another sip of tea. "But maybe she didn't know how to make one. Maybe she planned on me being so weakened by your lack of magical talent that she could walk into your mind and subdue me easily."

"That makes no sense," I said. "First off, when did I ever learn that? Secondly, homunculi are easy, and Tema was a beast. She could've made a construct the size of the Empire State Building if she wanted. Third, why wouldn't a spirit have its own power? Just the fact that you need to summon it means that it's plenty strong. Putting it in me would add to that power, not subtract. Tema wasn't that stupid."

"Your respect for your old master is quite endearing, especially after all she's done to you. Consider this, if you spend your adolescent years being smarter than your peers, then isn't it likely you will find intelligence the solution to everything? It's the same with beauty or fighting prowess, wouldn't you agree?"

"Yeah," I shrugged. "When all you have is a hammer, everything looks like a nail. Makes sense." She nodded as someone would to a fencer who'd just scored a point, but she made no move to speak. "Tema's hammer was her strength," I said, sipping the liquid cinnamon again and earning another nod. "No matter what she got herself into, she could just power her way out of it." Another nod. "So she didn't bother to study up on magical theory like I do because she believed that whatever it was she could power right through. Tema was many things, but short-sighted? Naive? Overconfident?! No. That would be stupid."

"It would only be stupid if she were wrong."

"Was she *that* strong?" I asked. I had seen my master work spells a million times, but I had never seen her go all out. I had no idea just how strong she was. It was the difference between looking at a bodybuilder and actually going to the gym with them.

"Yes, she was," Arta said.

"So, she wanted you to tell her things, use your powers whenever she had something *really* nasty planned, and store information but that would be impossible because you would refuse to tell her anything or lend her your mojo. Only now you're telling me she was smart enough to find you, savvy enough to catch you, ballsy enough to try and hold you captive in the first place, and strong enough to force you to behave?! So why is she dead?"

She smiled large and nodded as if she were talking to a student who just said something right. I started thinking. I didn't know much about Blackstar, but I knew plenty about Tema. What could they have in common?

Tema and Blackstar both wanted power. That had to be why

Blackstar had taken the kids. What was he trying to summon, another minor god? Why take two if Tema only needed one? Is that one of the things that would destroy me to know?

"What went wrong with Tema's ritual to capture you?" I flashed back to that time but it seemed muted somehow. There wasn't the same visceral emotion attached. Her last scream seemed distant, like it was miles away.

"That is a good question," Arta said, "but there is a better one."

"What do I know about Blackstar?" I asked, uncertain. Didn't get a nod for that. She just scoffed.

"Certainly not. Now you're not even trying." I sat and thought for a moment. I realized I'd been trapped in my head figuratively and not just literally. Thinking about Tema always did that. The promise of answers and an outlet for my anger. I shook my head to clear it and started paying attention.

She sipped her tea again, and I realized the cups weren't getting any emptier. She was sitting up straight and most of her bruises were gone now. I shuddered to think of what would be happening to me if she were not here, but she *was* here—that had to be interfering.

Gods couldn't technically interfere in this universe, or any universe from what I gathered. However, since they existed outside any form of causality, any move they *could* make had already *been* made. It was always confusing thinking about systems that didn't include time.

I was sure I knew only a fraction of the rules, but I knew mortals were the wildcard. They could increase or decrease the power of a god through worship, prayer, and focus. Just like giving their energy to an object.

In order to affect things, gods sent their proxies to this universe. Angels, demons, ghosts, fairies and the like. Having the ability to die made them technically mortal, and that meant they could affect anything in the universe they pleased.

That brought up the question as to whether Arta was an actual god stuck in my head or some attendant that Tema had overpowered. If Arta was some form of proxy, then she could interfere at her whim—but then what did she have to gain by lying and saying she wasn't interfering?

Blackstar, or whoever, is pelting me with spells that she's eating and she admitted to not telling me some things that I "knew." She had to be one of the few supernatural creatures able to lie. The only other way this made sense is if the spells wouldn't affect me or if the things she was keeping from me were things I would never know.

Suddenly I got a sinking feeling. The words tumbled out of my mouth, but I didn't register speaking. I was watching a train speeding towards me at a million miles per hour, and I was too numb to move.

"How did Tema's spells affect me?"

She laughed and clapped her hands. The tea cup was back on the plate on the table. It was disconcerting to have everything teleporting everywhere, but that was the least of my worries.

Arta steepled her strong fingers just below a handsome, ageless face, with flawless skin framed by a full head of chin length chestnut hair.

"Excellent."

Chapter: 12

I was back in the stone room, screaming. The pain died and was replaced by the most amazing feeling. I wanted to cry, it was so beautiful. A man stood by my bed. He had on a white lab coat. His hands were in his pockets. I'd seen him once before—Hawknose from the ambush a few nights ago. He was young, with long black hair past his shoulders and angular features. He was beautiful; the whole world was beautiful, wonderful. The straps were loose, and the duct tape was all torn. That was nice.

I threw my legs up and got them around his shoulders. I quickly adjusted to his neck faster than he could move away. His brown eyes were surprised as I squeezed his neck with my calves. It felt so amazing.

He gurgled and wheezed as he slowly choked to death. I felt his larynx beneath my calves and moaned at the pleasure of it pressing against my leg. I squeezed harder, and the feeling against my calves was literally breathtaking.

He spoke, but my ears were far too overcome with the pleasure of the sound to make out any words. His voice was euphoric. The ice from the spell he cast along my skin caused the most delightful chill. I shivered and locked my legs together even tighter.

The pain started again, I screamed and my body jerked hard. I managed to keep my legs tight as I jerked and took him with me. He lost consciousness. The pain left as quickly as it came. All the sensation was gone. I felt dead; felt tired. So. Tired.

I realized there was a mouth guard in my mouth like boxers wear and let it fall from my teeth. Where had that come from? I wasn't wearing it before. The chair was stained with urine and feces. So were my pants. That was embarrassing, to say the least.

I got up off the chair and realized I could barely stand. The dizziness hit as I got up, and I bent over to puke though there was nothing in my stomach. Every muscle suddenly ached, and each protested in a new and interesting way about my demands for more action.

The bastard groaned, and I found the motivation to reach for my pack. It took some mostly futile yanking on the chair, but I managed to reach out to it. "*Digg…*" My throat was raw and the pain shot through my mind, but compared to before when I'd tried to use magic, it was muted somehow. I was already in so much pain it simply didn't register as much as it might've. My pack had its own power; it didn't need mine. My wand appeared in my hand, and that had its own power too.

A light coat of dust covered everything on the table. Were all the medical tools just for show? I remembered my blood being on everything. I couldn't summon the knowledge that told me why that seemed important. My thoughts were moving through a fog as thick as mayonnaise. I couldn't fathom why everything was suddenly dusty or why I was obsessed with the thought.

I tried zapping the manacles, but it didn't work. The wand had its own power, but it took a small amount of mine to summon it. My pack worked. The wand should've worked as well? Maybe? I wasn't thinking clearly. Between the fatigue and the pain, it was a miracle I was even on my feet.

If anything, it all made me want to scream again. I started

kicking the man, slapping him back and forth. He woke up to my wand in his face.

"Take them off or die," I growled. It was a hoarse, raspy sound. I couldn't even be certain he understood me. It was supposed to be an idle threat, but at this range, I realized I could shove the sharp stick into his eye and into his brain. The nose would work too; it was a large crooked nose. He moved slowly unsnapping the cuffs with a twist and loud click.

"Now which way is out?" I asked, as my mind flooded with images, being taken to a cell, drug out of the van that brought me here. Hawknose's name was Gerod Rosenthal; he told me while he was torturing me—while he was cutting me open with red-hot knives.

I remembered being taken away from this room to a cell and sleeping four times. There were three men and one woman who had tortured me. I knew them from the garage in Durham. Turns out I hadn't killed Firehag, but she was mighty sore about her new scars. She took it out on me, which I didn't understand. She was plenty ugly already.

Blackstar did the same a few times. He was angry about a limp and some busted ribs. I tried to explain that when you mix large rocks and gravity there can be unfortunate results that have entirely nothing to do with me. I failed in getting him to see it my way.

The Executive was named Steven Mendon. He even had a name like someone in middle management. I got a visit from him more than once. I cracked jokes about him being "disarmed," or "disarming." Some people have no sense of humor.

The memories flooded in. I felt myself stumble with the cascade in my mind. The moment of holding my head was when Hawknose attacked.

"*Desenree Fot Impethnum*!" I don't know what he did, but it must've been mind magic, because I didn't feel a thing. Tema, you bitch. The look of shock on his face didn't last as long as I might've wished.

He recovered long before I did. There was a knife in his hand, and I watched as it came towards me. I was supposed to do something. I needed to move, but my arms and legs felt like they had a building attached to them. The knife went into my side. It heated up like an iron, cauterizing the wound as it burned deeper into me. He came in under my lowest rib and up, going for my lungs. I screamed, which was a good sign actually.

I brought my teeth together and grabbed him by the back of the head. We were about the same height, and I saw the determination to live in his eyes. He probably saw the same fire in mine. Mine was stronger. I brought my wand up beneath his chin and screamed again as he stabbed deeper into me.

"*Fire.*" I knew I was dead. I wasn't scared; I was angry. Cold anger. I don't have a temper. I've never had one. When I get angry I don't want to fly off the handle screaming and yelling. I want to sit back with a nice cigar and watch your opened throat bleed all over my shoes. "Die you piece of shit."

The body that fell to the ground didn't have much of a head left. I could've cared, but I decided against it. I wanted even more. I wanted to tear this place to the ground. Unfortunately, that was the anger talking, and despite how strong it was at the moment, I couldn't afford to be thinking with my killer instinct... well, not anymore.

I took a deep breath, which was hard, and yanked the knife out. Bad move. He'd been going for my lungs and must've made it on that last push. I couldn't breathe. I fought for air and nothing came.

Dammit, I wouldn't die like this. Not like this! Covered in shit and struggling for breath. Pathetic! Useless! Not me! "No!" The scream came out as a gurgling noise.

"*Gau...Ga...*" I croaked out. The large gauze bandage

appeared in my hand and I ripped open the package, pressing it to my side. The blood, dirt, and grime would interfere with the spell. The wound had to be clean for it to work best. It wouldn't be full strength, but maybe it would be enough to keep me alive.

I didn't remember falling, but I was sitting on the floor with my back against the chair. Still struggling to breathe. It was slightly easier each time. It took twenty-three breaths before the stabbing pain subsided to a dull ache. Breathing was merely painful; not an excruciating exercise in futility.

Not sure why I counted. I guess I didn't have the energy for anything else. I had to get moving. If someone walked in right now…

The thought didn't bear finishing.

Hawknose didn't have much on him, but it was more than me. I took the forty-seven dollars out of his wallet, his iron knife, and dropped one of the candles on his body. I could only hope it was symbolic of where he ended up.

I put on my pack and looked over the table. My phone was smashed to hell and the box I'd bought at Grace's was just sitting there. I hadn't had anything else in my pockets. At least I couldn't remember if I did.

I gathered up everything, including the shackles, and made my way out. I didn't see anyone in the narrow passages. There were never people in the halls when I was moved from the torture room to the cell with the cot, but just in case, I kept my wand out in front of me as I stumbled along, leaning against the wall for support while I walked.

I was leaving blood everywhere. That wasn't good. Not to mention the puddle Rosenthal was laying in. Only most of it was his.

There were at least four warlocks left. The salt and pepper haired Blackstar, Firehag, The One-armed Executive, and one whose face I couldn't remember, covered in a black shroud. That one didn't seem to notice me. Whoever they were they seemed far more concerned with physically beating the hell out of Blackstar, but I swore to myself I was going to watch them all die.

Anyone of them could track me or kill me with a fresh enough sample of my blood. I only needed everyone to stay out of here for a day or so, and it would be useless, but for all I knew I was going to come round the next corner and find them all seated playing a nice game of Arkham Horror.

The way out was a long spiraling passage going mostly up. I'm not sure how I got so lucky, but when I got to the top the moon was near full and Blackstar's hideout was behind me. An underground warren of caves and tunnels, no doubt dug by an elephant-sized badger with no sense of direction.

I pointed my wand at the entrance and let loose with a rage I'd never felt. All my pain, anger, and fear. At its core, the wand was an amplifier. I caved the whole damn place in. That takes care of the blood and had the added benefit of feeling good. Weak or not Blackstar, I'm coming to kill you.

* * *

I camped by an empty field, under a stand of trees more than three miles away from the now-buried warren. Camped is just a nice way of saying that's where I collapsed when I couldn't walk any further and fainted. It was sunny and warm when I woke up, at least. I didn't mind passing out until after I woke up. It was unlikely I'd run into any vampires or warlocks in the middle of nowhere, but unlikely was far from impossible.

Sleeping on the ground had taken all the warmth from me, and I was worried until I realized it was going to be a scorcher today.

I got up and started walking, shivering from cold flesh and blood loss. The sunlight was a blessing. My wand was nearly spent. I could tell from the dryness and cracks along its length. After a display like that, it could've exploded.

I sighed. Replacing it was a three-week long ritual that almost killed me each time. It was powerful, even though it only did one thing. The idea of facing Blackstar without it did not appeal to me one bit. Even with it, I'd have to be three moves ahead. I could outsmart some jumped up cartoon villain wannabe; just didn't know how yet.

It turned out I was west of Raleigh past Jordan Lake in the middle of nowhere. The lake was like any other—dirty brown water—but if it was good enough for baboons and my hunter-gatherer ancestors, it was good enough for me. I gulped until my stomach hurt and then sat under a tree. I passed out again. Can't say for how long… more than a minute, less than a day.

I got to 64 and hitchhiked into Apex, which is to say I walked. No one picks up hitchhikers in this day and age. Especially not ones limping along, shivering, covered in dirt and blood. At least I was wearing black.

It was late afternoon by the time I got into town. I hobbled up to a gas station that was mostly empty. The cashier was a middle-aged man. Tall and thin, with brown hair and eyes that looked me over and were not impressed.

"Hello," I said, trying to sound as lucid as possible. "Can you call me a taxi, please? Any taxi'll do. Thanks." I walked out before he could answer or complain about the smell. People were fine with helping, as long as you didn't need much.

I looked back and watched through the window as he called either a taxi or the cops.

At this point either would suffice.

It was a hot day, and I was still shivering. I sat at the corner of the building outside wondering why they didn't they teach important things in school, like when you're bleeding internally it's exceedingly hard to get warm.

A woman walked out of the gas station and unceremoniously dropped a few coins on me.

"Thanks," I said, reflexively. I sounded scared, but there was a smile on my face and I felt a rush of excitement. Old habits I guess. I huffed a laugh and got a stabbing pain in my chest. I picked up the change. It wasn't much, seventy cents.

"One... two... three... five... seven... eleven... thirteen..." I sat there huddled in pain, calculating the prime numbers up to seventy while the suburbanites all around me filled up their tanks and headed home.

I calculated the Fibonacci sequence next, but it was too easy and it didn't take long to get to seventy.

Calculating pi out to seventy places was working well for keeping my mind occupied. I kept losing my place and having to start over. Got up to twenty places or so before the cab came.

I snuck up from the back and got in. My pants were dry, but they still stunk like a sewer. I rolled down the back windows first thing, and answered the cabbie's protests with forty-seven dollars, seventy cents and promises of extra money if he could just get me home.

I wasn't used to cabs. Raleigh is not like New York with cabs everywhere. There are enough downtown, and you can always catch one at the airport, but in this city, you needed a car.

The money I took off Hawknose wasn't enough to cover the fare and the upholstery cleaning that was undoubtedly needed. I walked into Miles' with the cabbie waiting and aimed for upstairs.

It was a quaint scene. Miles was behind the bar, cooking as always. Almost every stool was filled with a small black child, and each was spinning to one degree or another. I waved through six iterations of "Hi Maker" before Miles turned around, serving up six plates of something fish that looked fancy.

"Damn boy! You look like hell. Where you been?"

"Had a really rough night," I said. I wasn't gonna say I just escaped a torture chamber in front of the kids. I hoped none of them noticed the bloody footprints.

"Well, at least you're back. That girl's been ornery. Even more than usual." I didn't have time to address Miles' comment. He turned back to the grill and one of the kids squealed.

"Whoa! Maker did you get in a fight?!" It was Andre. He wasn't the youngest, wasn't the oldest, he was on the closest stool though. I didn't have the full attention of every child in the room when I walked in. One of them screaming "fight" changed all that.

"Yup," I said and limped towards the stairs. I was trying to get out of the room before I had to provide any more details.

"Maker got his butt kicked." Marissa chimed in that teasing, sing-song, tone that seems exclusive to children under twelve.

I looked over my shoulder and smiled at the teasing children. "You should see the other guy."

How I was able to summon a smile at that moment is beyond me. Maybe it was all the hoots that followed me up the stairs.

"No way Maker would lose."

"Yeah Marissa, you're cray?!"

"I saw Maker kill fifty Draculas all by himself!" I certainly didn't remember that, but I guess some stories are so good they don't have to be true.

I made it up the stairs out of breath and almost out of whatever the hell was keeping me going at the moment. Zora's apartment was always clean, with everything in its place. Zora was even less materialistic than I was. It was easy to keep a place clean when you didn't have anything to put in it.

Today the place was dirty. The couch was tipped over, and the table was on its side. There were clothes all over the floor and a few were bloody, burned in places, or dirty. There was blood smattered on the wall in one place and holes where the drywall had been punched through. This couldn't be Zora's apartment.

I still wasn't in full control of my faculties. I stood in front of the sink staring down at a few empty potion bottles trying to figure out what they were doing there.

"What do you want, Neka?" I heard someone call from the

back. The voice was raspy; it didn't sound like Zora. Whoever it was obviously wasn't speaking to me, but no one else lived up here. Did Miles get a new tenant? Had I walked into the right apartment? Who the hell was Neka?

The blade of a sword was against the side of my neck before I could figure out an answer to any of those questions, and I felt the disturbingly familiar feeling of blood trickling down my skin.

"Turn around. Slowly." Well that voice at least was unmistakable, as was the sword that I could easily shave with.

"Put it down, Zora; it's me."

"Me who?" She growled. "You could be Maker. You could also be some vamp that Miles invited in using a glamor to fuck with me in my hour of distraughtness. As we both know, I've had an unconventional week, which has impaired my normally warm and inviting sense of humor. The question is not whether I'm going to kill you, it's how slowly. If you cooperate I may find better things to spend my time on than cutting you into little pieces. Now, turn around."

There was something seriously wrong here. The sword trembled at my neck, making a tiny cut into something less tiny. It dug in a few millimeters, up one, down a few. Zora could hold her sword at arm's length and split a hair with the point. I'd seen her do it. This woman was accusing me of not being Maker, but I wasn't sure this woman was Zora.

"First," I said, moving around slowly, "I'm not pretty enough to be a vampire. Second, I'm broke. Third, Broc is the only one who would be stupid enough to come here wanting to kill you, and he would see using a glamor as beneath him. Now, put it down."

The woman before me didn't look like Zora. Her hair was in a braid with so many frizzy, loose hairs it almost wasn't a braid anymore. Her face was frail like she hadn't eaten, and her normally cappuccino skin was pale and filthy. Her clothes were ripped and bloody in a couple places. That was a little familiar, at least. The determined, violent eyes were the only thing I recognized.

I only saw her face for a moment before it was buried in my chest and I was a lifted a few inches in the air. I grunted with a dozen protesting wounds and fractured bones, but she didn't put me down. She screamed in what sounded like triumph or excitement—maybe it was relief—or some combination of feelings that didn't lend itself well to words. I was feeling something similar.

She finally broke the hug after far too long. I was still low on blood and was starting to get dizzy from all the stationary uprightness. "Been looking all over for you. You look like hell." She said, sounding like she was holding back some tears. I rocked back and forth and held off dropping a few of my own. The laughter started on the next inhale.

"You smell like a skunk and cow manure love child." She sniffed again, wiped at her watery eyes, and giggled. "You smell like a Nascar stadium full of roadkill and hillbilly turkey vultures next door to a turbo charged rotten spinach factory. You smell like an infected dung beetle penis with a side order of sadness." I smiled. It was good to be back. "No Maker, this is really bad, I need you to light a match… then set this place on fire. I mean, you smell like a barn full of lovingly cultivated animal puke."

"I don't discuss my barnyard activities with anyone. There's a cab downstairs if you wouldn't mind," and with that, I began the slow process of limping towards her shower.

"Shower! Great idea," she said, making her way around me to the door. "Because you smell like a rancid seaweed salad, with butthole dressing and whale shit croutons. Hell, you smell like…" her voice faded away as she left the apartment. I leaned back against a wall just to breathe. Didn't remember this place having that many stairs.

"Which one of you munchkins let a stinky Maker in my apartment?!" I heard Zora yell from downstairs. I didn't hear the children respond, but I could clearly hear her. "Well, which one of you is in charge of sniffing his butt?!"

Butt humor. It always worked with small children. I finally got to the bathroom and the mirror confirmed that I did indeed look like hell. I smiled and saw a few missing teeth. Zora must've done all that so they didn't worry, or she did it because it helped her get over whatever the hell that rant was about. Probably both.

I was covered in dried blood; you could see it even through the black clothing. The white shirt underneath was stained brown with dried blood in so many places I could barely see the white. My eyes were bloodshot, and my cheeks were sunken in.

I started the shower and cranked up the heat as hot as I could stand it. I didn't disrobe and didn't bother to wash, just curled up in the tub and let the water run over me. Dammit.

After the water warmed me up a bit, I stripped down slowly and painfully. I found an impressive number of bruises, scrapes, and places where I had been cut deep and stitched up again with some downright sloppy needlework. I remembered being stripped out of my clothes for the Executive and the Hag. Hawknose and Blackstar mostly used spells. It shouldn't have fazed me. I'd been cut open by Tema more times than I could count.

I didn't remember everything; only flashes. That was probably for the best. The fastest way I knew to get past anything was to keep putting myself through it.

The fetal position was nice. I could ease the pain, relive it, and watch it be washed away—all at the same time. Time to heal. A more detached part of me noted that I would never fully heal from this.

I wanted to scream, but all that came out were sobs and soft moaning. Shaking off the memories of things I only vaguely remembered. Flashes of Blackstar's goon squad ran through my head and I flinched at each one.

I spread my hands apart. "*Light.*" The slight chill was welcome as I cast. My pocket of light began its slow procession back and forth between my hands, flickering as the water from the shower interfered. Left to right, inhale. Right to left, exhale.

I replayed what I remembered again and again. "Just another thing to have nightmares about. Just another thing to have nightmares about." I chanted. I would have scars from this—lots of them.

I found more cuts that had been stitched as the hot water hit them. More bruises that were black and deep purple. More cracked and broken bones. I didn't realize how much everything hurt until now. Until I stopped, until I wasn't full of adrenaline from looking over my shoulder. I always felt safe in this building. I wanted to sleep, but instead just lay there letting the hot water run over me. Thinking, feeling, and wincing as I relived everything in as much vivid detail as I could summon.

At some point, I did fall asleep.

* * *

I didn't wake up until long after the water ran cold. I finally washed and shut off the shower. I didn't know how long it'd been. More than an hour, less than a week. I didn't remember any dreams, but that meant little. I would be having nightmares for the rest of my life. I had made peace with that a long time ago.

I got up and stepped out of the tub. I was bleeding again, but nowhere near as much. I had three bandages left in my pack and I used all of them. The most serious wounds were deep. Zora had gone to my place, gotten my ace bandage and left it on the sink, so I wrapped up my chest. It was still harder to breathe than it should be.

She also left me a towel and folded my clothes for me. My socks and boots were sitting there also. They'd had all night to clean and repair themselves.

It was just past noon the next day when I stepped out of the bathroom, and she was sitting there on the bed with her sword across her lap and my AK beside her. She opened her eyes as I came out. The place was in order again. Everything had been wiped down, and all the trash was gone.

Zora's hair had been combed through and rebraided, and she'd found a place to shower and change into a non-ripped up set of clothes.

"I'm out of bandages, or I'd give them up," she said. I only nodded. It occurred to me that if she were out, she'd had some trouble of her own. "Where we going?" She had a grim look to her, like Blackstar had taken as much from her as he had from me. Must've been a lot of trouble. I shook my head to clear it. My thoughts were still slow, and I felt even weaker if that were possible.

"We're back to square one." It had been a rough few days. Even if I didn't remember most of it, my body did, and it was not going to let me off easy. "Can't raid if we don't know where they are."

"Why not lay traps wherever you just were?" She asked.

"That's a really good idea, actually. Wish I thought of it before I trashed the place." No one was stupid enough to use the same hideout. I killed Hawknose, and there was no way to hide the fact that I was no longer there. If I escaped and I knew about the place, Blackstar wouldn't go back there. I'd left blood everywhere on my way out and they'd track me down or kill me with it in an instant. That's why I caved it in. Well, that and I was mad enough to spit nails at the time.

"Well, while you were slacking off, I got a lead on where they might show up."

"Oh really," I said. "Share then please, oh industrious one."

"First there's someone you should meet." She got up, casually tossing me my rifle, which I didn't catch or even see coming in time. It smacked me in the head and I gave her a dirty look as I bent to pick it up. A wave of dizziness and nausea told me that wasn't a good idea and I went down to one knee breathing hard.

"This sucks," I said. Zora didn't say anything or offer to help. I grabbed the rifle and got to my feet. Recovery was going to take a while.

She waited until I nodded and led me out of her apartment and into the one across the hall. There was nothing inside, save the standard furnishings that Miles provides. Refrigerator, stove, couch, bed, small wooden table, two chairs, and an air conditioner. I couldn't see the bedroom from here, but I knew there would be a bed in it.

Sitting on the floor was a young, impossibly muscular man. He rose as Zora and I walked in. He was pretty big. I looked straight ahead into his shoulder and I wasn't half as wide. He had shoulder-length black hair in tiny braids tied behind his head and harsh green eyes the color of new grass. His skin was reddish. Obviously American Indian descent. He had on a white shirt and a pair of blue jeans. They were tight around legs that were nearly twice the size of mine.

"Maker this is Neka." The big man put a hand out. I took it and it buried mine in a solid grip.

"I am also called Dakota by some, Ohanko by others. Indiana. Nava. Ohanzee. Whichever you prefer." I was a little sore about all the names. Only a little—I promise.

"It's nice to meet you. I wasn't sure you'd wake up after we pulled you out."

"Yes, I owe you a great debt," he said.

"He's been helping me look for you. He's *mildly* reliable." Zora smiled. Neka made a show of rolling his eyes but smiled at the praise.

I shook my head to dispel the image of Firehag cutting open my arm. "Don't sweat it," I said. "Why were you there?" We all sat down. Zora and I on the couch; Neka on the floor where he had been.

"They wanted my blood. I do not know why." I knew why.

"You're a shapeshifter, right?" He hesitated a moment, then nodded. "They were making their cult members into shapeshifters with it. I saw them inject a woman and she started growing fur or feathers or something. I couldn't tell." He nodded again.

"I have never heard of that," he said, "but I suppose it's possible. If that is the case, I am more certain than ever they must be stopped." They must be dismembered was more what I had in mind, but I sent my anger back into its cage. Neka was looking at Zora, she was looking at me with a dumb grin, and I was looking at the floor—banishing more thoughts of torture.

"I'll buy it. I killed a were-salmon at your western lab two days ago." Zora said.

"Were-salmon?!" I said, incredulously.

"No one was more surprised than me." Zora laughed. "They don't seem to have control over what they turn into. It's like theriomorph roulette. They get excited and become animals. There was a bear there too. We ended up running."

"Ok," I sighed. "Start at the beginning." Zora poked me and I looked at her in confusion.

"You're back; it's hard to believe. I'm just gonna poke you every once in a while for the next few days, make sure you're really here." She grinned and I sighed.

"Story time please," I said.

"Well," she said after another poke. "I went to Grace's looking for you when you didn't come back. Jayne said you'd stopped by and left. I asked around, and some kid said he saw you getting pummeled and thrown in the back of a van. Whoever took you had a day head start at that point, so I didn't bother asking around about the nondescript white van. I called Rollo and told him you were missing and to ask around quietly. No leads, so I headed back to Durham that night. The place was a ruin, and there was no one there. The circle had been trashed completely. The fire wiped out even a trace of it." That was a positive at least. Redrawing it would take them time. How much time was the question.

"On the way back to Raleigh I stopped by Vermillion Falls. I didn't know who took you, but since it was daylight, I was betting against the vamps. I caught one heading off to feed and spent the night downtown politely asking it where you were. Took all night, but I was finally satisfied that it didn't know anything. After that, it was lots of patrols and hoping to get lucky. Did that for two nights before Neka woke up."

"Wait. Two nights? How long was I gone?"

"Grace's was ten days ago," she said. Blackstar and crew had held me for nine days. NINE! DAYS! I must've pulled a face because Neka looked at me funny. Zora wasn't fazed.

"What happened after?" I asked, once again shutting down my anger—though I failed to keep it from my voice.

"I came back here and found Neka awake," she said, gesturing to the man.

"I woke up and my wounds were dressed so I knew I was not being held by… umm Blackstar, you said?" We both nodded. "I was waiting all day before she came back." He shut his eyes and went back to meditating. I guessed that's what he was doing anyway.

"It was another night by then and I spent it getting caught up on my Neka history. It was nice. It's rare I have a man tied to my bed all fifty shades style. I did weird, twisted, kinky things to him for a few hours. He'll deny it, of course." Actually, he just looked confused, turning his head to the side and blinking.

"Can we please stay on topic?" I sighed.

"Right! So after fun time with Neka I headed out to the northern lab on a hunch. The guy that came to pick up the soup reported 'something weird.' When I got there the wards were down, and three traps had been sprung. I went in looking for a fight and found two bodies instead. There had obviously been more people in there."

Blackstar's flunkies had gotten those locations out of me. I was angry again that it put Zora in danger, and once again, this was not the time or place for my anger. I was starting to get angry with my anger. Ha!

"Neka turned into a giant dog,"

"Wolf." He said, without opening his eyes.

"Right! So giant dog. We didn't find where the rest had gone that night, but I reset the traps and left the bodies just in case. The next night we checked out each lab. Got a hit on the east shelter about 0300.

"There were five of them and they were being a lot more careful about the traps. Still killed one of them though. Whatever they were looking for, they didn't find it, and we followed them back to a little house in Garner. I peeped in the windows and didn't see you; just a whole bunch of them laid out and not looking well. Stayed there watching it for a day and no one came or left. On the second day, I was getting restless and was going to go in and knock some heads around. Still hadn't seen any of the heavy hitters so I was pretty sure I could get it done."

"I stopped her. She doesn't seem to understand the virtue of patience," Neka said, closing his eyes again.

"I would tend to agree," I said

"Who's telling the damn story?" Zora said. Neka flinched like he'd been slapped. "I was about to go in when most of them left again. I left Neka there to watch the house and followed. They went to the central lab this time, and two more of them died. I helped," she grinned. "They went in looking for traps this time. Disarmed them all before they started rooting around. I was on the roof. I sent vibes down through the building to rearm the traps manually. Never knew what hit them," she laughed.

"Anything happen on your end?" I said to Neka.

"Nothing out of the ordinary for the two days we were there. They occasionally woke up and moved around the house. No one came or left that I saw."

"Hmm… weird. What next?" I asked.

"Well since I had ghosted two more, I was feeling pretty good about myself. I rearmed all the traps and followed them. I was getting excited when the car they were in got on I-440, but they just took the long way around the beltline to get back to Garner, and I burned a lot of juice keeping up. I left Neka there and came back to update Miles and eat. When I got back to relieve Neka, all I found was a big flying mouse."

"Bat." Neka sighed.

"Maker, have you ever seen a five-foot bat with a fourteen-foot wingspan?"

"Uhh… No. What does that have to do with—"

"Right! So, big flying mouse." She said, looking at Neka who just sighed again. "There wasn't any more activity until two days ago. I still don't know how they were getting their orders. I stuck a sensor in the house while they were all asleep. The place had a threshold, and it wasn't the best sound but…"

"Wait, it had a threshold?"

"Monsters don't get a threshold. Yes, Maker, I know the rules. These were just people. Transients, probably, and I already checked out the house. It belongs to Marian Rogan LLC. Marian is a nice lady in Cincinnati who has a son named Robert who attends college at NC State. I checked the county tax records, called her, and stalked her on Facebook; she doesn't even know he's dead. I assume the business is something she set up just to gain some tax advantage in buying the house her son lived in for college. There were a couple of other college age kids in the pack too, so I'm assuming more than one of them lived there. There was a strong enough threshold even after I cut his lungs open. Nothing for it." She shrugged.

"Damn! I was hoping there would be a lead there." It also meant the shapeshifters I'd killed were technically humans. Gomez tended to overlook warlocks, but I wasn't gonna risk my life by telling him this.

"So did I. No dice. Sensors were worthless too. They hardly even spoke, just laid around on cots groaning all day. Nothing happened then but waiting and legwork. Checked out the house and all the license plates. Rollo helped with that bit; still got nowhere. The next time they left was two days ago. There were only nine people left in the house. This time they went out in force. I followed them and left Neka to scout the place."

"I went in and took another look." The big man said, without missing a beat. "Found nothing. The house didn't have power. There were a few flashlights and burned down candles. No phone, not even a phone charger," and the eyes closed again.

"When Neka caught up, I decided to take as many alive as we could and interrogate them. We were in the middle of making that happen when the old bitch from the garage showed up."

"I named her Firehag," I said.

"Ha! Apt. She was swimming in evocation. What'd you name the others?" She asked.

"Executive, Bombshell, Hawknose, Firehag, Shroud, and Happy the Peanut." They both raised their eyebrows at the last. "It's a long story," I added. I wished Neka would open his eyes more often. For some reason, I was finding it a little unnerving to talk to someone who had their eyes closed.

"I'd just filleted the giant fish girl and the rest weren't looking on their game. They aren't fanatics, Maker. Not like those guys last year. They may have even given up. I was about to offer when Firehag came out of nowhere. One of them turned into a bear and went at it with Neka. Hagbitch threw lightning, fire, mud, shattered a concrete wall and sent that at me. More lightning, acid, wind, ice, and wind with ice in it. Not to mention the oil, needles, wooden shards, and the cotton from her robe which turned into a blade, blocking the only strike I got close enough to get. The fucking bitch didn't even break a sweat." Zora did not enjoy being weaker than the monsters. She growled and stared at the floor as if she could somehow will her way back into that fight. Neka took this as his cue.

"While all that was going on, I was busy with the others. The bear and the wolf were fairly strong. The other six changed when the… Firehag appeared, but they didn't do much besides cower and nip at me when my back was turned. We kept getting hit with things from Zora's fight. It was a small space. Firehag kept throwing mental attacks at me. I assume that's why she didn't use those spells on Zora. Also, since Zora was really—"

"Shut up." Zora growled. The big man stopped like someone had shut off a faucet. His eyes stayed open this time; fixed on Zora like he was waiting for her to attack. "Anyway, Neka thought Firehag was gonna mop the floor with us and yelled for me to open a wall. After I sliced a hole he grabbed me and jumped through. He turned into some giant flying thing with feathers—"

"Eagle," he offered weakly.

"…and we flew away. We went back after a bit of arguing."

"She said she was going back and threatened to kill me in my sleep if I didn't go with her," he said, pointing at Zora as if I didn't know who he was talking about. He took a deep breath, and his shoulders dropped a bit. I was well versed in taking a deep breath to relax and recognized it right away.

"I was having a bad day." She smiled in a predatory way at the man. I was trying to hold in a laugh. Neka looked moderately cowed.

"We went back because I value my life," he continued. "There was no trail to follow. They used magic to wipe out the scent. The home in Garner was deserted after that. They didn't hit the labs again. Then you returned."

I was not relishing cleaning up my labs after all this. I was glad of the spring weather. Transients would happily sleep somewhere else for a while.

"I left a sensor on the front door of the house and the next two nights we hunted. I checked in a few of our favorite dark alleys again. What people know about Blackstar won't fill a thimble. Everyone is too scared to know anything. They just go hide behind a threshold before sundown. As if that would help against a warlock."

I sat back and exhaled. Nine days, almost eleven now. They'd kept Blackstar busy for that long. Gomez would be here with backup in a couple weeks.

As angry as I was, I knew I couldn't win. I could run a few more sabotage missions, but I knew if I found Blackstar in a ditch tomorrow I would be far more relieved that he was dead than upset I didn't get to do it myself. Emotions demanded one thing; logic suggested another. I had a rule in this situation. Do the logical thing. Emotions are background noise, no matter how loud they get.

"All that doesn't change much." I said. "I think we've at least set them back a week. They'll have to recruit some new people, and the summoning circle is still trashed. New plan is the same as the old plan. Lay low, locate their latest hidey hole, and point at it with a bright neon sign once the cavalry shows up."

"That's a great plan Maker. Really. I mean, absolutely top-notch strategy. Now the bad news." I groaned as she spoke.

"I didn't authorize any bad news." I said.

"Yeah, I'm not sure the world cares." She smiled.

"Fine." I said. " Gimmie the good news first."

"There isn't any." She laughed.

"Then I shall leave it to you to make some up," I said, putting my face in my hands. Damn, I was on edge.

"Fine, you're alive, awake, and two days early to engage in

our time honored tradition of robbing vampires. They have a large shipment coming. I don't know everything in it, but I think Blackstar does. He's planning to rob it."

I groaned again. "Must be what the guns were for—to outfit his non-magical people." I said. It made sense at least.

"And I have another surprise for you." She said.

"I'm assuming it's not that the Vamps are on to Blackstar, know he's coming and have laid a trap that's sure to kill him?"

"That would be convenient, but no." She smiled. "Behind door number two, Brendan from the docks called the other night. The shipment has ritual artifacts. There's an ankh that's supposed to be the real deal; a tooth from a dragon. Smaug's I think, some other powerful things I've never heard of, a new car, and lovely edition of our home game. Seriously, I have no idea how they've kept it quiet this long."

"Oh, great!" I said. This backed me into yet another corner.

Neka looked from me to Zora with a squinted brow and a slightly slack jaw. I didn't trust him, of course, but Zora did. He'd proven himself to her. While I was the slightly paranoid type, the reality was if he fooled Zora, he would certainly fool me. Zora trusted Miles and I. Everyone else was suspect.

I was far too trusting at times. Still entertaining some ludicrous faith that people would start making sense one day. I was young by most standards, yet already thought like a jaded old man. A man had to know himself—know his biases—so he can know when they're leading him astray. I suspected my inability to trust most people was doing that now.

"An ankh is a religious artifact from ancient Egypt," I explained. "They are said to have trapped in them the first angels that came to earth. I don't know exactly how many there are, but it's not many. Apparently, angels can repent, and if they do, maybe they get let out of the ankh. Think of it as a portable high-security prison for the supernatural. Even if there is no angel in it, any creature can be imprisoned and left to whatever unspeakable horrors that entails." What I didn't tell him is that I suspected the vamps wouldn't bother with an ankh that didn't have an angel in it.

They were rare enough to deal in, but as the foremost authority in having powerful things that make you a target, I would have to call it a bad idea. I had things that made me a target for evil wizards. An ankh made you a target for gods, angels, demons, fairy queens, and elder things. All the worst things that go bump in the night, and not one of them would hesitate to go straight through any mortal that thought of opposing them with it. There was no reason to risk all that for one that didn't have an angel in it.

"Smaug is the dragon from The Hobbit. We call her that instead of her real name so we never risk getting her attention. Right now, she's asleep. As far as I know, she's been asleep for several hundred years. As dragons go, she's not all that bad, but no one on Earth would be happy if she woke up tomorrow. Having a piece of her allows you to call upon her power. Dragon teeth and scales shed like any other hair or skin. Just happens far less often in dragons than it does for say, you and I. Even so, it's like having your blood in a way. How much power has dissipated depends on how long it's been away from the dragon. It's probably been gone for a long time. On the other hand, that's a lot of power to dissipate. It could be away from Smaug for a century and still be formidable. Even if it's completely lost that power, it has another in being one of the strongest materials on the planet."

"Dragon teeth and scales make diamonds look like bread dough," Zora added.

Neka nodded. It was clear the big man had more questions. I wish I had answers.

Blackstar hitting the Vamps didn't matter to me in itself. I wouldn't care if they were having it out over a stick of gum. I couldn't let either of them get their hands on an ankh. Gomez, Myer, and half the Martinet would show up just in time to be slaughtered. Not only would that plunge the magical world into chaos, but it would also have the relatively unpleasant consequence of killing me.

The vamps were busy elsewhere, so Vermillion Falls was everything they had in the region. In a war for the world the Carolinas were of no great strategic importance. Vermillion Falls could smuggle things in, but Duke, the lord in the area, was actively staying out of it.

He wasn't playing both sides, exactly. He was probably using the upswing in the war to take out his rivals and waiting for the day when the activity would abate and his standing would increase. Apparently, he was small enough that none of the higher-ups in vampire politics noticed or cared, but big enough for the plan to work without someone crushing him.

Duke was the worst thing a murderous demonic sociopath could be. He was patient, he was smart, and he wasn't prone to the bouts of rash, senseless, emotion that immortality and near-limitless power normally inspired. He was the successful man who hadn't yet forsaken the tenets that made him successful. Worse, he didn't mind making more vampires, or killing them.

Most vampires were selective about who they turned. The majority of day-old vampires couldn't handle the sudden lust for blood, and in short order, they ended up little more than feral beasts consumed by their hunger. Most vamps understood how quickly that could get out of hand and they had to have normal humans to kill and eat after all.

Duke didn't care as much. He'd make ten vampires, order them to do a job, keeping his inner circle secure and well fed. If that didn't work, he'd send a hundred. Any that survived the job were killed, unless they showed real skill.

Duke was dangerous. I avoided him as much as possible. Whenever disappearances increased, I knew he'd be up to something soon. After I'd disrupted his plans a couple times he started taking a certain number a day and harvesting from elsewhere.

He didn't come to kill me. Not one attempt. I didn't know why, but it scared me how fast he learned. I also had to wonder if I knew about this only because he wanted me to. To my knowledge, I hadn't vexed him lately. The last time was about seven months ago. That was nothing in the life of an immortal, so it was entirely possible he was still upset.

Blackstar couldn't possibly know that I knew, but he might know that I took his arms shipment. I would kick myself for spray painting inside the truck if it hadn't burned down to the engine block. Though, given the fact that I just killed half his people and destroyed two of his hideouts, it was a silly thought. Since he knew I existed and had it out for him, he'd be on guard generally rather than specifically. On guard and waiting.

Another thing that bothered me was sitting in Zora's bedroom. My pack. I still had it. Why kidnap me, torture me and not ask one question about it? I didn't remember everything. I didn't have enough memories to account for one day, let alone nine.

I knew that they hadn't asked. If they had, I would've had to say something eventually and they'd have access to ten years' worth of stolen gear, with me screaming on a table, begging to tell them how to use everything.

Blackstar also had three other warlocks left to help him. Not to mention a small clan of shapeshifters and any number of normals with delusions of grandeur. I had one small-time talent and one mystery man. I was becoming more and more certain that I couldn't take them on. Of course, proper surveillance on them would be nice. Then I could…

"Wait, Zora, what makes you think Blackstar knows about the shipment?" She smacked her palm to her forehead and walked out grumbling. I looked at Neka who shrugged and closed his eyes again. He dropped in and out of that meditation whenever someone started or stopped speaking. It was kind of eerie. As if there was nothing going on here worth his full attention. Zora returned about two minutes later. I was still thinking—brooding mostly.

She had the satchel in one hand and tossed it to me. The other hand held the stack of papers from Blackstar's refrigerator divided into three folders. She handed me one and set the other two on the couch between us.

"That's where I think they'll turn up. I was planning on following them back to you if I hadn't found you by then."

She folded up her legs and took deep breaths, staring intently at Neka then closing her eyes. He smiled as she did, but his eyes didn't open. I felt the cold come off of them and shivered a bit. I would have to ask them to explain this later; it looked like the mental attacks Zora and I had forsaken years ago.

The folder was full of shipping manifests. There were a lot of them, and while the one Zora wanted me to read was clearly marked with a sticky note, I sat and read them all. By the end of the first few pages I was lagging. Too little sleep, too much torture and nowhere near enough food. It was only then I realized the last time I'd eaten I was here, and that was more than a week ago.

I got up, tucking the remaining folders back in the satchel. As I walked between Zora and Neka, she flinched back as if I'd struck her.

"Dammit, Maker move! I'm winning!" She snapped. The urgent tone in her voice was alarming, so I moved and a stab of pain went through my leg, chest, and stomach. I grunted and kept my teeth together.

"What are you doing anyway?" I asked, looking between them. Sweat was starting to form on Zora's forehead.

"Training. Explain later," she said, with the effort of straining against something. The big man still wore a smirk. They had obviously done whatever this was a lot in the week they'd been together. I limped out of the room and downstairs to where Miles was just finishing sweeping the latest pile of dust out the door.

"Just in time," I sighed, and went to sit at the bar. There was no one there, so I took my normal stool. Third from the end. I opened the folder again and read. I smelled something with grilled chicken and onions, and it made my stomach ache all the more. A salad appeared with lots of greens, chicken, tomatoes, carrots, cheese, and avocado. I started shoving food in my mouth like I'd forgotten forks existed. Miles grunted and I picked up the fork. I was getting dressing on my hands anyway.

I resumed shoveling and finished off the salad in no time. Back to reading manifests. It wasn't weird that Blackstar was attacking the Vamps. It was weird that Duke appeared to either not know, or know and be doing nothing about it. Zora would have heard if he were in a lather about Blackstar.

Some deranged vampire would've shown up for my head thinking it was me by now. Trying to score some points with their boss and hopefully not be disemboweled for their trouble.

The blue statue and the disk were there also. Apparently, the disk had been stolen from Vermillion Falls itself. The manifest didn't say what they were for, but nothing good was a safe enough assumption.

The folder had future manifests as well, though none were marked as the attacked ones were. There was also nothing of interest that I could see. Smuggled goods are notorious for not showing up on the loading documents.

Though often enough, things were labeled as other things for the purposes of customs and passed through by crooked agents. I suppose that was easier than all the lies you'd need for a boat that had a hundred crates on paper when it actually had a hundred five. I was done with the first folder, and put my head down on the bar. I sat up slowly as the lacerations on my chest complained. Hurry up. Stupid bandage.

Miles uncapped a beer and set it in front of me, along with the second course of chicken stew. I didn't speak, but grunted something he took as thank you. I picked at the stew and sipped at the beer. Wasn't easy, but gorging after a long period of starvation could be deadly. I went back to the papers in front of me.

There was something I was missing. I could feel it. Zora saw the manifest and realized Blackstar was hitting the Vamps. An informant at the docks corroborates the story. Both groups are tracking this shipment and I'm running around as a loose end.

That partially explains the attacks on my labs at least. Since the fridge died in the fire, Blackstar may not know I have this anyway. I have… "Yes!" I said. It was a plan, it could work, and there was just enough time to get it done. I hobbled outside to my apartment to grab a few things. A deep cut on my bad leg opened on the way and stained my pants in blood again.

I sat down on the stairs for a while. This was going to take a long time to get over. Months. Years maybe. The physical would heal. It was the mental scars that were going to take forever. I wanted to run off, challenge Blackstar and company to a duel and win. That wasn't realistic. I wouldn't live past the second spell.

I limped up the stairs outside the house up to my attic apartment and collapsed on my cot meditating, concentrating on staying calm, keeping my emotions in check, not thinking about being tortured, largely failing, and running through my plan for anything that would violate the evil overlord's list.

I was doing that right up until I passed out.

* * *

I woke up feeling a little better, and wandered over to my shower. The water was cold. I liked cold showers. I was a hard sleeper. Waking up wasn't an event—it was a process.

I brushed my teeth and headed down the stairs, avoiding looking in any windows that would show me the Masons. I lived above a family that could be a black and white sixties sitcom.

Sometimes seeing that the world could be a nice place was annoying. Sometimes it was inspirational. Sometimes nothing.

I got to the street and felt for my magic. I took a deep breath and felt the power in the air come to my call. I didn't do anything with it; it was just a relief to know it was still there. It was evening, already starting to get dark. I was too hungry to have slept for five hours. It must be the next day. Monday maybe? I realized I had no idea. I had no phone.

That explained why I was well rested. Thirty-one hours of sleep would do that.

I stopped to eat. Miles was making soup in a ridiculously large pot for one of my shelters or another. He stopped for just a moment to slide a bowl down the bar without spilling a drop. Toast followed soon after. It was beef and vegetable, and it was delicious. As always.

The neighborhood's surrogate grandfather went back to reading a paper that confirmed the fact that I'd slept an entire day.

I ate quickly and was still hungry, but I didn't get seconds. There wasn't much time to prepare if we were gonna hit Vermillion Falls today.

I limped upstairs. Zora's door was cracked. I stopped when I heard the talking.

"...planning anything now that Maker's back," Zora said.

"He was obviously tortured, and quite horribly I suspect," Neka responded. "He may have been bewitched by The Constellation and sent back to kill us. Even if his mind is unaffected—and I don't see how that could be. He won't be planning anything for weeks." Neka had a good point actually. I was about to burst in and explain that I was fine when Zora interrupted, sounding angry.

"You don't know Maker," she snapped. "He's strong. He plans better than me, he's more versatile than you, and when the plan inevitably goes to hell like all plans do, no one improvises better.

He'll come up with some way to face off with Blackstar, get the ankh, get us out, and do it with so many contingencies even he won't remember them all."

"We should at least have a plan of our own for if he's… well, if things go bad."

"Do what you want. I'm not gonna bother. I follow Maker. I'll step up if I have to, but if he's around then I'm right back where I wanna be. Second in command."

"Second?" He asked, incredulously.

"Second. All the power; none of the responsibility. All the reckless and no worries."

"That's crazy," Neka said. "You have to take responsibility for yourself. You can't just gamble your life on someone else's decisions."

Zora let out a hearty laugh. "I assure you I can. Besides, it's smart to gamble if their dice are hotter than mine. I do it, you do it, and so does everyone else."

"I don't let other people live my life," Neka snapped.

Zora scoffed. "Then you're just willfully ignorant of the way power works and the ways people use it to control you. I'll put it another way—in a few months we're going to have an election and twenty pleasantly scented, piles of shit, are going to try and convince us why they should be president. Think about that: twenty, out of a few hundred million! If leadership were so fucking great it'd be twenty *percent*. The reason no one applies for the job is because deep down no one wants it—and why would they?

"Why would I want to spend my life catering to a few hundred fat, old men constantly whining about their own interests that are almost certainly in perpetual conflict so they can stay in power? Not to mention, while I'm juggling all their bullshit so I can keep my power, I get to be constantly looking over my shoulder for political rivals of my own trying to steal it? I'm getting an ulcer just thinking about it.

"We could all go off alone in the wilderness and make *all* our own decisions, but the best answer is to give up our authority to someone who we think isn't going to screw us and find a new leader if they do. Everyone has this romantic idea that we should all be leaders, and it's remarkably stupid. I found someone who's going where I wanna go, so I follow them. It's not rocket surgery."

That woman read a lot of philosophy. Most people would hear that and think she was soft in the head, but it took courage to call things the way you saw them. We had both resolved to live our lives with the reality of a naked emperor and refused to believe he was fully dressed.

Neka was no doubt taking this all in, because when I heard him speak again, he didn't sound so confident. "So… you're like… in love with Maker?"

Zora sighed, and I choked down a laugh. Pretty soon she'd start hitting him. "Either you've still got fur in your ears or you weren't listening. I'll assume the former."

"No, it's just that I don't get what happened to you that you could trust someone so—"

"The human condition happened to me." She said in an exasperated tone. "You either have to trust someone or do everything yourself. Most *people* are followers; I'm just a follower who's not ashamed to admit it. Leadership is not a sun-drenched picnic, it's my idea of hell. I don't want that job. No one wants that job, except Maker. He's the only person in the world I've found stupid enough to do it, and you're giving me shit because I'm smart enough to let him?"

Neka didn't answer. There was a long silence. I had the image of them staring daggers at each other, so I burst in.

"Zora, let's go!" I said, throwing open the door. Other than being in a different apartment, they were both almost exactly as I'd left them. Zora was sitting on the couch Indian style with her sword across her lap. Neka was sitting the same way on the floor. They both looked up as I busted in. "Were you winning?" I smiled.

Neka looked at me, placid as a glass lake. Whatever his game, he seemed to be loyal to Zora at least.

"Of course I was winning," she said as she got up. "Where we going?"

I smiled. "You aren't gonna like it."

Chapter: 13

"I don't like it," Zora growled.

"Told ya so." We were walking up the beach in the middle of the night near Wilmington, North Carolina.

I was striding along with Zora beside me and Neka bringing up the rear. Zora stared in horror at the ocean—no doubt wishing she could kill it.

"Not kidding. This has all the intelligence of forty-grit toilet paper," she said.

Neka's dam finally broke. He was stumbling along behind us laughing, holding his sides, tripping over himself, and generally failing to keep quiet.

"That's actually a good idea," I said in mock contemplation, stroking my chin. "Just has some minor marketing issues."

Wilmington was a three-hour drive from Raleigh. With no way to tell time, I would say about four hours ago we had been in Raleigh preparing for this coastal adventure.

I had never gone to pick up my truck, so we walked downtown and stole one. Zora broke the window on a big black Chevy and climbed in. The alarm went off for only a few moments before she got it started.

Next, we drove around to all my labs and I collected all the bodies in my white sheet. None of them had been touched, which was a little odd. Transients knew to stay out if the place was locked, but you'd think the smell of rotting humans lying in stagnant pools of their own blood and excrement would have alerted someone. I could almost wish they had, given the noisome smell. By the time we were done, I felt like I had somehow been poisoned by all the stench in my lungs.

From there we were off. I climbed in the back hoping the wind would get the smell out of my clothes and out of my memory. We made a pit stop for dinner and I suddenly felt like I'd been stabbed in the back. One of my many wounds had ripped open again. Zora asked Neka to drive so she could patch me up, and he said he didn't know how. Zora and I both stared for a moment while he hung his head and shuffled his feet.

I hadn't wanted Neka to come on this trip at all—I would've left him behind. Hell, he didn't even know how to drive. Zora had advocated bringing him along though, and you can't lead people while ignoring their advice.

While she drove, I wolfed down some pizza in the back and tried not to think of all the dead people stuffed in my coat pocket. Thankfully, the smell of bodies was washed away by the time we hit the freeway to the coast. I was still sore and still out of bandages—the magical variety at least.

I wasn't profusely bleeding anymore, and I could walk, talk and breathe without random sharp stabbing pains, so that was something. Neka redressed all the wounds I couldn't reach while Zora drove in as reckless and speedy a manner, as she did everything else.

I realized at some point—while he solemnly went about the task—that we had something in common being held by those misfits.

"They aren't too nice, are they?" He said into the wind of a hundred twenty miles per hour. The wind was always a roar in the back of a pick-up, so I assumed I wasn't meant to hear it. I guess we were both remembering things we never wanted to.

The rest of the drive had been silent, with me huddled up in the back. Occasionally Neka's gaze would cross mine. He didn't look at me too suspiciously; I couldn't blame him, since I didn't trust him either.

I didn't bother to try and explain that I wasn't under Blackstar's control. He already believed I was, so denying it would only make him more suspicious and lead to more mistrust. On the other hand, if I let him see for himself, then he'd buy it. People would buy into anything as long as you could get them to think it was their idea.

You could never trust people to act rationally, say what they mean, or believe anything you say. They had to be manipulated into it if you were ever going to get anything done. Sometimes you'd meet a crazy bastard like me or Zora where that wasn't the case, but as far as I knew, we were rare.

It was the middle of the night by the time we got to Wilmington. It was small, but still a city. Because there was a port and plenty of beach front, the place didn't sleep. I didn't have reason to come here much. The coolest thing about the place was where I-40 ran into the Atlantic. There was a sign somewhere that read, "Barstow, Calif 2554 mi." Presumably, at the other end would be the Pacific and another sign guiding you back. I told myself I'd drive it one day, just to see everything. Hadn't happened yet.

Since Gerod Hawknose Rosenthal had trashed my phone, I had to guess at the time. I shivered and shook off the image of him slicing open the webs of my fingers with a dirty razor blade and reminded myself he was dead. You never realize how much you miss having a phone until you don't have one. I looked at the sky and guessed it was about 0200.

I've stolen a lot of things in my life, and in my professional opinion the middle of the night was the best time for stealing anything—or in this case, borrowing without permission.

Wasn't long before we'd gotten to the docks, stolen a boat none of us knew how to drive, and got out to sea. A pirate's life for me; but no one felt like singing.

I gave them the plan once we were about twenty minutes out. Zora was already starting to get seasick. Apparently Neka had never driven anything in his life. I'd never driven a boat, but the one we took was small enough to not be much trouble; only a steering wheel and a motor at the back.

There wasn't much room in front of the wheel, but Zora and Neka crowded in so they could hear the plan. I remember hearing somewhere that sound carried better over water, which made sense because there is nothing for the sound waves to hit.

I cut back the engine so they could hear me, and had to glance down at the compass embedded in the dash to make sure we were on the right track. I got a sinking feeling when I realized I wasn't sure. Like, at all.

I'd never navigated over water before; you'd think I'd've considered that before stealing a damn boat! There wasn't anything out here that told me where I was, let alone where I was going. All this thing had mounted near the steering wheel was that compass and something to tell me how deep the water was. What good does it do to know the water is exactly eighty-three feet deep?! Stupid boat.

"If there's an ankh on that ship, the probability of the Vamps leaving it unguarded are… what's the number Zora?"

"Zero," she said, looking at Neka. We were both looking at Neka; this was mostly for him anyway. Zora had undoubtedly guessed the plan by now, and so far looked as irritated with it as I felt.

"Really? Lemme calculate the exact number," I said in mock contemplation. "Yup, zero. We don't know exactly what Blackstar is planning, but we're going to hit the boat before we have to find out. We get in, get the ankh and anything else that has a magical aura, and get out. We leave the bodies of Blackstar's people on the boat. When it comes into the harbor, maybe Blackstar and Duke mix it up at the docks and this plan goes off without a hitch. If they don't, then the he'll still find all his stuff gone; the stink of half human wannabe theriomorphs all over his boat and fifty or so dead vamps. It won't take much asking around before he finds out 'who dun it.' We'll need to leave a sensor on the boat for a few nights." Zora nodded. The sensors were her invention after all.

"After that, it's up to the Vamps, but I can't imagine Duke—even stoic as he is—will let this slide. He'll have to kill Blackstar, or at least try. Meanwhile, before Blackstar realizes he's being hunted, we string him out as much as possible."

"Fifty?" Neka said. There was a bit of tremble in his voice that I tried to ignore.

"Not certain of course," I said. "But the way I see it, this can only go two ways. The boat is filled with vamps and enough humans in the hold for them to make the trip; or the humans are the crew and there are a couple of powerful vamps on board taking sips from a couple. With cargo like this, they don't have many options."

"What if Blackstar shows up first and sees the bodies? He'll figure it was us," Zora said.

Probably." I said. "In the least, I don't think he'll believe that his people ran off on their own. I'm counting on the vamps being around. Duke isn't going to let a shipment like this come in without someone he can rely on being there. If it's that important, Broc will come pick it up." Zora's eyes flashed at the mention of Broc. I wanted to facepalm for letting the name slip out. Too much history there, and I certainly didn't want it getting in the way tonight.

I kept talking, hoping I could gloss over the whole thing. "What's Blackstar gonna say if Duke comes out himself? What would he say to any vampire? 'Hi, I was here to rob you but someone beat me to it. Goodbye?' Duke will rip his heart out on general principle."

Neka looked confused, but thankfully he picked up on Zora tensing and didn't ask who Broc was. "What if Blackstar has the same idea as you and attacks tonight? What if he's already been and it's all gone when we get there?" He squinted slightly in what I suspect was suspicion.

Couldn't blame him. If I *were* under a compulsion it would be excellent strategy to be leading them into a trap right now.

"Why would he come out on the water?" I said at the same time Zora spoke over me.

"Stat Mech 101. Large bodies of water absorb any power they can find. The larger and colder, the better. You're essentially gathering heat and trying to release it right next to a giant cold reservoir. It's the first law of thermodynamics."

"Thermo what?" Neka said.

"Oh, for fuck's sake!" Zora threw up her hands. The water must've been getting to her. "Water sucks the power out of anything you try to cast. That's all you need to know. Blackstar would be weaker out here. A lot weaker. With something this important, he won't take chances. There's no reason any wizard would be stupid enough to come out on the ocean. Right Maker?!" She said with a pointed look.

"Weren't you busy puking?" I asked.

"Yeah," Neka said, "I remember hearing that from a wizard. Long ago now."

"Doesn't it affect you?" I asked.

"I've never had an issue in the water," he shrugged. That was odd. I filed it away for later. Neka was weird in a lot of ways, and every single one got my hackles up. With that said, Zora and I couldn't handle a whole ship full of vampires by ourselves.

"So, we're looking for a container ship named Indioc. From

the manifest, it arrives tomorrow evening at around dusk. I want to get into the shipping lane and wait for it to pass by. Zora's phone won't have enough signal out here for the GPS to work." She checked and shook her head. "Yeah, didn't think so. That means all we've got is our speed and the time we've been moving to tell the distance. We only have one chance, so I want ideas on how to find it; I assumed this thing would at least have a map."

Zora glared at me with wide eyes. "A map with what on it?!" she snapped, throwing her arm out over the ocean. Large bodies of water tended to make all wizards a little grumpy. I supported that theory by snapping back at her.

"Quit your bitching and search this thing for a map." The boat was about twenty feet long, and was basically a giant oblong bowl. There was nothing in it anywhere, save several coils of rope, a couple flares, and a first aid kit with chains in it. Everything else in it, we brought with us.

Zora made a show of crossing her arms and swinging her head to the front and rear of the boat, then saying in a jovial tone:

"Hey Maker, about that map. Yeah, I uhh… I didn't find it."

Neka was quite entertained by all this; chuckling in a way that sounded like far off boulders tumbling downhill.

"You gonna help or laugh?" I said, rounding on him.

"Peace man," he said. "I'll find your boat for you." He grabbed a long rope and tied it to the front of the boat with some knot I didn't know. It looked nautical, at least. He put the other end in his mouth and dove overboard.

I looked over the rail at the same time as Zora, when suddenly the boat lurched into motion. There was a whale about six feet under the water. It was dark, so I couldn't tell what kind; I assumed a humpback, since it started singing almost immediately.

"We can't get there before daybreak," I said. "The vamps can see in the dark." The whale made a noise that sounded suspiciously like "duh," but I let it slide as the boat changed course to go south.

"He turned into a whale." Zora said beside me, her voice far off and full of wonder.

"I only dog paddle," I said, in my best André the Giant. I'm a nerd when all is said and done—of course that meant that "The Princess Bride" was in my top ten list of greatest movies.

"I am not in the mood," she growled.

"Inconceivable!"

"NOT in the mood," she growled again. I laughed and called her to the back of the boat. Everything had been moving so fast, I didn't have time to have this talk.

I pulled out everything from the satchel and emptied my pockets. The files, my white sheet, the disk, the statue, the necklace from Blueboy, the dagger from hawknose… everything. Taking things out of my pack was simple; I could do it with a thought. The trade-off was that putting things in took hours.

The enchantment had to be reversed—which was simple, but laborious. Like digging a ditch with a spoon, it wasn't complicated. If you knew your way around a spoon it wasn't even hard; there was just no way to get it done without taking a long time.

These were the terrible spells. Whenever someone says the word wizard, people think of long flowing purple robes covered in stars, moons, and everything else on the Lucky Charms box. Those robes are not to look cool. I suspect it's for the times when a spell takes longer than a few seconds and the chill has you feeling like a damn penguin.

If ever you see someone strolling down the beach in summer wearing a trench coat or fluffy down jacket, you can bet they're a wizard. I sat and got as comfortable as the intense chill would allow. I didn't speak until Zora was seated across from me and looking as comfortable as the swell would allow.

"Tell me a story," I said, nodding towards the front of the boat.

"Not much to tell. He's human, even though he appears not to be. I think the big Indian is his actual form. Not that big though.

Sometimes when he changes in a fight, he goes back to that for a split second before going to something else. I don't think his voice is that deep either. He's younger than he seems—maybe a lot younger."

"What makes you say that?" I asked.

"He's strong, but he intimidates easy. He's logical to a fault. When he does have an emotion, he has to deal with it right then."

"No wonder you guys get along." It wasn't meant as a jibe, and she didn't take it as such.

"No. Not like me. I'm a hedonist, but I know how to put things away until later, I just never have to do it. I don't think he knows how. He reminds me of talking to Andre. I don't know, can't explain it well," she said, shaking her head. "Also, he laughs at all my poop jokes."

"That's hardly conclusive," I laughed.

"Not conclusive, but it's weird," she continued. "I'm beginning to be able to tell when he's putting in effort to maintain a form. He has a limit to how often he can change, but he doesn't hit it quickly. He could probably go at it all day. Smallest thing I've seen him do is a sparrow; the biggest was a grizzly with massively oversized jaws. He nearly bit the entire head off a wolf man that was gonna rip me in half."

"Anything else?" I asked.

"Not really. Like I said, he's good in a fight. Turns into different things by the time you're done blinking. I've seen him do a grizzly, a wolf, a small horse, sparrow, rat, crow, fox, bat, giant eagle, and a few other things. He doesn't have to stay true to form either, and that's the useful part. He could probably do a flying pig if he wanted. Never seen him do anything this big though." She thumbed at the front of the boat. I nodded.

"What is the training thing?"

"Blackstar's people tried to recruit him first. He didn't say how he got caught exactly. Apparently it was bloody, and obviously he lost. Seven months later we found him. Blackstar was keeping him weak by stealing his blood. At first it was probably just to keep him toasted, but I guess they found a use for it." I nodded again. "Since Blackstar knows a lot of mind magic, they tried to break into his mind and couldn't. So, since I can't practice defense with you, I've been practicing breaking into his mind, and vice versa."

At least now I had a hypothesis on why that was the case. I knew that mind magic existed and had taught Zora about it, but every time she tried to defend against one of my mental attacks she claimed she couldn't feel anything. Never what a man wants to hear.

When she attacked me, she said it was like climbing a massive wall that kept getting taller. If you ever got hold of someone's mind, you could make them do whatever you wanted. Jump off a bridge, kill the president, learn to cha cha, eat pickles… even listen to pop music. That person would be trying to break free the entire time of course. Needless to say, learning to defend against those kinds of attacks was important. Breaking free was much easier if you knew how.

"He says he can't attack well, but he still kicks my ass. It's not even close. Attacking him is like running naked screaming through the front gate of Fort Bragg and expecting to win. James Bond couldn't beat him. Attacking and defending are kinda the same. With you, it's like wrestling a boulder—it doesn't budge no matter what you do. With him, it's like punching a river that's fighting back. I attack, and he's never there when the punch gets there; but somehow, he has plenty of time to grab my arm and drag me under. Not pleasant, and if you lose track of the tiniest thing then… well, then it sucks." I didn't say anything. Just sat processing everything I'd heard.

She shook off whatever she was thinking and continued. "Now that I know what a mental battle feels like, I know that Blackstar threw an attack at me when I bailed in Durham. I'm thinking the only reason I got away was because my first few steps carried me out of range. You should start training too."

"Yeah," I replied, though I wasn't sure how Arta would feel about that. "I don't think that'll be necessary. Long story; tell you later. Why'd he stick around? He could've bailed any time."

"Oh, that one's easy. He's pissed. He wants Blackstar dead. Way more than me; probably more than you. What I didn't tell you was back when I was planning to take the morphs alive, he'd decided that they weren't ever going to lead him to Blackstar and wanted to kill them all. 'Abominations,' he said, and a few other less flattering things. I was holding him back when Firehag showed up. He's solid, Maker. I'm sure of it. At least, so far as our current goals are aligned."

I was about to say the same thing. Still, if he wanted Blackstar and company even half as bad as I did, he was useful. I had been held for nine days; I couldn't imagine seven months.

"Here. Loot," I said, handing over the dagger from Rosenthal. "It heats up when it touches flesh. Let me know if it does anything else."

Her eyes brightened. "I love a man that brings me weapons," she laughed. We had rules about loot. Like any other dictator, everything was mine, and it was my job to make sure she got her cut—whether that was cash or magic items that I deemed safe enough after researching them.

As a leader, you had to make sure your people were taken care of. If Zora ever had to get a job at McDonald's to make ends meet, then she wouldn't be there when I needed her. That meant I always had to be out making money and getting loot so she would never have that excuse to leave. I kept Zora well paid, but there was always a knot of anxiety in the pit of my stomach when I handed over a magical tool.

After that, it was quiet and cold. Reversing the enchantment on my pack was tedious, but it had to be done. There were a few hours of silence, broken only by Zora occasionally puking over the side. I watched the sun come up as I finished my work.

The sea was calm. I never sailed on the ocean. Zora was right; for a wizard it was akin to madness, but I could see why people did it. The sky was somehow bigger and the colors more vibrant as the sun rose. The wake of the boat stretched out behind us, and the waves moved off to the left and right as if going off into infinity. The sky lightened in the east and gently painted the whispy, cirrus clouds purple and red, then every conceivable shade of pinks and oranges.

By the time the sky was becoming its long-forgotten blue, I spotted a boat. We were gaining on it fast too.

Without warning, there was a loud splash and Neka was at the back of the boat, soaking wet and out of breath. "Found it. About time too. Sorry it was so chaotic."

"Looked pretty seamless to me," Zora said.

"You didn't see the other ones? This is the fifth one, but the name on back is the same this time.

"I was busy," I said, smiling at Zora.

Neka looked back and forth between us with an expression somewhere between disappointment and incredulity. "Well, I feel appreciated. What's the plan?"

"Thanks don't even begin to cover it. How much you got left?"

"I got enough for a few vampires. Just need a breather." He said through the panting.

"In that case, we need to tie this boat to that boat without being seen. If you can turn into a seagull or something to get a view of the ship, then we can board once we know the deck is empty." He nodded.

Zora took that moment to dry heave over the side. She was completely empty, but that didn't stop her from retching up bile every half hour.

"*Burn*," I said. The watery orange potion appeared in my hand. "Drop this somewhere in the front; nowhere near any cargo."

I handed it over. It wasn't a grenade or anything. It just made a fire that was notoriously difficult to extinguish. "Once we're on board, I should be able to sense the ankh. I'll grab it and dump the bodies while we sit and wait for Zora to do what she does best."

"Which is?" Zora said.

"Showing up somewhere you have no business being, and making lots of noise." I smiled. She'd walked right into it.

Her face tightened and her eyes narrowed. I blamed the water for my snarkiness. "If we're lucky then we avoid any human crewmembers. As I understand it, fire on a boat is a big deal. Anyone they can spare will be up on deck dealing with it. If you do get seen, scream out 'Blackstar' or 'For The Constellation.' I heard their lackeys saying that. Then get unseen as quick as possible. Worst case, we'll have to pay them off or threaten them. A description of any of us getting back to Duke will blow the whole thing, so you need to trash all the vamps while they're sleeping."

"That way is not very sportsman like," Zora said in a deep dry voice. I thought my André the Giant impression was much better.

"Knock that off; it's game time," I said.

Neka put the rope in his mouth, jumped over the side and we were off. There was a monstrous shark where the man had once been, and we lurched into an incredible speed. We caught up to the boat in a couple minutes. Neka turned into a bird, flew up to the railing, shifted form to a small unrecognizable monkey to tie off the boat to the back railing and was back in bird form before I took two breaths.

"That was quick," I said.

"Told ya so," Zora responded

The seagull looked big and kinda spiky, but I knew as much about birds as I knew about boats. It circled back and cawed twice. Do seagulls caw? Is that the right word?

Zora and I shimmied up the rope in short order and silently jumped over the railing. This was in the style of one of those big container ships you see in the movies; only this one wasn't the size of a football field. I moved among the containers with Zora on my heels. I didn't sense anything yet. I looked back at her with a question on my face, and she shook her head. She didn't feel anything either.

We kept moving among the containers, zig-zagging our way slowly to the front of the boat so we'd pass by each one. We were past the huge smokestack in the middle of the boat when Zora grabbed my arm. She felt it a moment before I did. It was almost straight down.

I suddenly realized it would probably be easier just to sink the boat, but I didn't get where I am in life by second-guessing my plans at the last minute. I signaled Neka and saw the seagull drop the potion. I waited a few minutes for some kind of fire alarm, but heard nothing. That was odd, but a few minutes was enough time for crew to get to the fire and start trying to put it out.

There was a door just under the wheelhouse, which was a big glass thing two stories up. I waved at Neka, moving towards the door, thinking it would lead below-decks. Zora and I slipped through the door and waited. A minute later, Neka joined us.

"Go up and kill the radios," I whispered. Neka nodded and proceeded up the steps, more silent than either of us could have managed. Zora drew her sword, and we started downstairs.

I'd seen it before in movies, but I'd never experienced just how tiny the spaces inside ships are. I could touch both walls in this hallway without even spreading one arm fully. Once we got to the bottom, I smelled it.

Death has a specific smell. Blood has a vaguely metallic odor. The smell of a human being who died so afraid they lost control of their bowels is something you never forget. Add it all together and you've got a recipe for something that could make me as sick as Zora.

The trouble was that I smelled plenty of the second and none of the first. Sure there was rotting corpse and feces, but there was no blood I could smell adding to the bouquet.

"This is bad," I whispered. I pulled up my hood and mask just in case and gave Zora the nod to take point.

We moved forward, checking the rooms on either side. There was nothing of consequence, unless you count a dozen bodies. That explains the apparent lack of a crew. If the vamps got hungry, even one losing control of their hunger could've incited the others.

Silent as two more dead men, we entered what we thought was the cargo hold. The room was big, two or three stories high, spanning the width of the entire ship. It was loaded with crates, containers and boxes of every size.

There was no smell in here. One could take that to mean there were no vampires or decomposing humans. I pointed to Zora, then pointed back out the door. She smiled, with that look of bloodlust in her eye that she sometimes gets. She ran from the room, just a bit too eager for me to be comfortable with.

I put my mind back to the task at hand. The sooner I had the artifacts out of this room, the sooner I could go rescue her from whatever the hell she was getting herself into.

I circled the place, slowly running my hand over every crate. There was a large crate on the right side of the boat—the port side, I think. It was roughly the shape of a coffin, only bigger. "*Crowbar*," I whispered, and one appeared in my hand. No, just an ordinary, everyday, run-of-the-mill, ten-dollars-at-the-hardware-store kinda crowbar. I pulled the nails out of the crate quickly and put each in my pocket, not wanting to risk any noise if I dropped them. Vamps had great ears.

There was a full-on Egyptian sarcophagus inside. It had the standard mace and shepherd's crook, but down by its feet and looking positively innocuous was an ankh that appeared to be made of onyx. You'd never know it was anything out of the ordinary.

If you weren't a magic-user, you probably never would. Most

humans would be able to touch it with maybe a funny tingling, a vague sense of awe, or a feeling that it was important. For a wizard—even a weak one—the thing pulsed with energy. Being near it was experiencing a heartbeat with all your senses at once.

Touching it directly would be something like the non-lethal equivalent of grabbing a live wire. So I didn't. I carefully wrapped it in a scarf and stashed it in a cargo pocket. The next aura was in a crate two rows down. The thing buzzed with power; it was almost overwhelming.

I opened the crate to find a five-foot length of yellowish ivory looking material. Flat and wide at one end and as sharp as a needle at the other. It sure looked like a giant tooth. There was a sling on it, which made life simple. Whoever put it in the box probably didn't wanna touch it either. I slung it over a shoulder and reached out with my magical senses to the rest of the bay. It was an effort, given the two things I already held. It was like trying to get a glimpse of the stars in daylight. I knew they were there, but that didn't help me see them.

I walked by every crate. I found a ring—a simple gold band that went in a pocket. That was it for this one. If Zora had done what was needed, we could search the next hold and be done. I walked out of the door—hatch? Whatever—and into the scene from a bad slasher flick.

Zora had left bodies everywhere. The vampires were half out of the rooms on either side of the hall. Each one was either beheaded or gutted, which was the way to kill vampires. Once again, all that was missing was the blood.

Vampires kept the blood of their victims in a special bladder behind their stomach. Piercing it drained them of their reserve of power. It didn't kill them right away, but without feeding, they were as good as dead. Once they were controlled by their hunger they would never be intelligent again. All these vampires were far past that point.

Apparently, they hadn't brought enough blood to make the trip. That was weird. I got that sinking feeling in my stomach reserved for those moments when I've been caught with my pants down. I was sure there would be masses of vamps with humans to feed them, or masses of humans with a few vamps that could be trusted. This skeleton crew scenario made no sense.

There were four vampires just in this section; each with its head and torso in the hall so I knew Zora cleared the room. She was a much better vamp killer than me. Vamps saw a human and instantly assumed that the human wasn't faster than they were. Then she was, and it got them every time.

I made my way to the next hold and found Zora surrounded by six vamps. She was limping and I could see her head bleeding from here. She had her sword on her hip and was dodging every slash, bite and grapple attempt from all six of them faster than I could follow. The dagger was in her hand and I saw fingers, ears and teeth flying out of that circle of madness.

The vamps were skeletons with skin pulled tight over their bones. They had no blood to feed flesh or muscle so it all died. Even their skin was pale and rotting away in places. At this point an infusion of blood wouldn't save them, but that wouldn't keep them from a frantic attack.

A desperate need to end their famine blinded them to Zora smiling. I saw it, but this was just the kind of hallmark reckless behavior I always tried to talk her out of.

"*Air is not soft,*" I whispered. I was up on the balcony looking down into this cargo bay. It wasn't as full as the last one. A long pistol appeared in my hands. It took almost two seconds. Stupid ocean. Before I'd modified it, it shot small plastic pellets. Now it only shot air. Highly compressed air that cut like a razor and expanded violently on impact. It was better than real bullets for supernatural things. The entry wound was smaller, but the exit wound was much larger.

Another advantage over bullets was that I had as much ammo as I wanted and never had to stop and reload. Unlike bullets, the range was only about seventy-five yards—or less, given that I was sitting in the middle of the Atlantic. The air didn't move faster than sound so a powerful enough vampire could hear it coming and move.

These six were just feral animals whose hunger had gotten the better of them. Their pale, rubbery skin shone in the dim light. I fired, taking out one in no time. I had dropped the second by the time they noticed and turned towards me screaming. That was a fatal mistake. I shot another one and Zora took out the other three with a single stroke, screaming out "Blackstar," and "My name is Inigo Montoya." Sigh.

I hurried down the metal stairs, keeping my eyes peeled for more vamps. Zora wiped at her head when I got to her. She was breathing hard like she'd just run… or like a normal person had just run ten miles. She was hopping up and down with a gleeful smile, and there was nothing wrong with her arm. Vamps aren't the only ones who can savor a kill.

"None of them would hiding if these were that hungry, so that's all of them." She said. "Fifty eh?" She wasn't limping either. She'd done that to get cornered by six vampires. Double sigh.

"Yes, I was way off on the number. Did it ever occur to you that's a reason to be *more* careful, not less?"

"Ummm… no. Can't say that it did," she said with a grin. "I was on a 'Yay, Maker's wrong, I can have some fun,' kick."

"Fun's over." I said.

I started searching the room, promising myself that next time I'd watch Zora and we'd clear together. The plan wasn't to kill every vampire; it was to kill every vampire while they were sleeping. I had a feeling she made sure all of them saw her on purpose. Probably knocked on their door, "Hi, can you please wake up?

I'm here to kill you." I slapped down my annoyance. Now wasn't the time.

"Help me search." Zora was still smiling like a loon, running from crate to crate. She got way too excited when things went bad. Killing monsters just seemed to make everything right in her world. The thought never even crossed her mind that the monsters could win if she wasn't careful. Whenever I pointed out that fact, or something like it, she'd smile and say that's what she had me for.

I figured this would be a good place to dump the bodies, so I thought up a scenario that seemed realistic and placed them all accordingly. I saved one to dump in the hall on the way back. Now there was blood everywhere. It looked enough like a war zone to fool me.

Going over the bay turned up a few more things, like an old Egyptian shepherd's crook. Unlike a pharaoh's, this one was wooden with bands of chipped gold and faded indigo lacquer. It was strong, though nothing on the order of the ankh or the tooth.

There was a torch, which seemed an odd thing to enchant, a fresh cut flower that looked like a white and pink lily, and a heavy blue blanket with feathers attached that was quite powerful. I thought it was some kind of cape at first, but it was perfectly square. There was no way to tell what their function was at the moment. That would take a few weeks of careful experiment and research on each item. Zora carried those things and the tooth. I still had the ankh shoved in a cargo pocket, just in case something happened separating the two was a good idea.

There wasn't another cargo hold, so we made our way back upstairs. I decided to lead this time. Zora was still smiling and looking hopeful. It was a bad sign; I didn't need her doing anything rash. We got to the landing where we'd come in and found Neka waiting.

Well, there was a large wolf licking a gash on its shoulder

anyway. I blinked and there he was. Zora said it was fast, but it was still shocking just how fast.

"How many?"

"There *were* two," he responded with a groan.

"Who's driving this thing?" I asked.

Neka shrugged. "No one now. The vamps had gone mad; even came into the sunlight to attack me."

I nodded. "That confirms one hypothesis. Let's get moving."

It didn't take long to check the front of the boat. I wanted a look at the control room before we left, something here was fishy.

Having vamps guarding the important treasure was good and all, but you don't send feral vamps into enclosed spaces with humans for exactly this reason. Insane vampires couldn't escort or protect anything.

Duke never shied away from ferals because all his plans had a place for cannon fodder. This, though, was just sloppy. With artifacts this important, it was ridiculous; very unlike Duke.

The captain's logbook held nothing of interest. It wasn't until I looked at two other logs that I saw all the inconsistencies.

The fire was still smoldering near the front. It had been a good plan, but hindsight rendered it pointless. I found the throttle and pulled it back to something called "dead slow," and we were gone.

Neka needed a rest and I was thinking, so we untied the rope and drifted away. There was only silence as the boat got smaller and smaller on the horizon. The plume of black smoke from the fire Neka set was leaving a trail in the air. It added to the ominous feel of the silence.

We drifted for nearly twenty minutes while I stood and watched the boat. "You alright?" Zora asked after a while.

"It took Christopher Columbus like, what, two months to cross the Atlantic? These guys shattered that record. Not sure why, but they've been out here for three years. Those vamps must've been going nuts after the first month."

"That can't be right," Zora said. "They could just drive the ship to shore and wait until nightfall or signal for help and eat whoever came."

"And why would the manifest say that it arrives tonight?" Neka added.

"Good questions all. You can add the number of guards to that list. A few really powerful vamps makes sense. A hundred ferals makes sense. This doesn't." I said. I was staring at the boat as it finally made its way to land, like I could figure out what was going on if I stared hard enough.

"Duke made a mistake?" Zora offered. She didn't sound like she believed it any more than I did.

"Think about this now. You just said the words 'Duke' and 'mistake' in the same sentence," I said.

"Touché," she replied. "But if Duke didn't drop the ball, then what's going on?"

"No idea. This all smells fishy," I said.

"That's the shrieking eels," she squealed.

"I'm thinking," I growled at Zora, my patience running thin. Again, I blamed the water.

"Am I going mad or did the word 'think' escape your lips. You were not hired for—"

"If she's annoying you, I can take her to Florin and throw her in the pit of despair," Neka said, smiling at me.

"No more quoting, I mean it!" I realized my mistake a moment too late.

Chapter: 14

This isn't a huge secret, but I hate golf. Growing up I was told that it was a game for overly affluent white men; made popular so they could have at least one day where they didn't have to wear a suit and take crap from their wives. I never learned the game. I didn't have to.

If I had a family, I'd be at home with them, making sure they knew the world was full of monsters and protecting them. These idiots came out here to generally conduct business as usual.

Only without the suit.

There were more important things—even without the supernatural getting involved. "Just another thing to have nightmares about," I sighed.

Despite my contempt for all things golf and yuppie, I was nevertheless standing on the 6th hole at the North Ridge Country Club. Today this place was packed with people. Among them were a mayor, city councilmen; there might even be a senator or two. Some big lunch thing. Still, I couldn't have felt more out of place if I'd started slinging spells around. I had my pack with me, of course, so that was actually possible.

Folks think that black people don't play golf and Tiger Woods did nothing to change that. I suppose it's mostly true. I wasn't the only black person around today; by my count, there were five. One more and we'd have a black hole. Ha!

It had been three days since a flaming cargo ship—that I knew nothing about—ran aground in Wilmington. The news made a frenzy over the boat. Unless you were under a rock, you had heard about it. The next day everyone's news feed was onto something else. The only people who cared after that were the port people and the police. Unfortunately, I just so happened to be golfing with police.

My own personal detective on the Raleigh police force had been called by another from the Wilmington area, and all three of us were royally pissed at me. Everyone was growling and smacking the ball to take out their frustrations. Ironically, we were all playing better than normal.

Rollo started the game whining about being a man short. Apparently, this stupid game was most often played with four people. All of his protests about preserving the sanctity of golf only served to piss me off even more.

It had never occurred to me that neither Duke's people nor Blackstar's would be there to greet the boat. Its slow speed minimized the damage to its hull, but it was still a burned-up wreck. Despite this, someone sent out a tug boat

They found all the charred skeletons when that happened. Some cop on the investigation leaked word to the press, and by the time they got the boat into the harbor, everyone knew about it.

Whoever Duke or Blackstar sent wouldn't risk it with sirens and cameras everywhere.

Rollo said they'd managed to keep the vampire bodies quiet. I scoffed. He said it as if that were some great feat. No one wanted to believe in vampires, ghosts, werewolves or anything else that implied they weren't at the top of the food chain. The ability of human beings to explain away the obvious never ceased to amaze me.

Then again, the ability of human beings to gather in large numbers and hunt down anything different with torches and pitchforks never ceased to amaze me either.

"You should've brought me in on this," Rollo said for the seventh time. Short, stocky, and irritated described Rollo today. He hadn't shaved; I suspected it was in rebellion to all the politics flying around.

I found myself thinking about the first time I'd helped Rollo out. He'd come to me about a haunting; a ghost had been scaring his kids. I didn't know he was a cop at the time. I got rid of the shade easy enough. It was just his wife's grandmother saying goodbye. He'd seen things he didn't want to see, and he came to me for advice. I'd never brought him in on anything I was doing; I wasn't sure why he always thought I should start.

"Did you really wanna step onto a boat filled with hungry vampires? No, not hungry. Vampires so starving they'd eaten every human, rat, bug, and then gone insane from thirst."

He swallowed. So did the Wilmington guy Lane, but only Rollo answered. "If it means saving lives, son, then yeah. I wouldn't have been happy about it, but I would've gone. Just like you," he said, looking me in the eyes. He had brown eyes. Nothing remarkable or noteworthy, but I still looked away first.

He sighed. "Listen, I know we're giving you shit. To be honest, I'm not sure I wanna know what happened out there, but this is my home too. I know when something's coming, and if I were like everybody else I wouldn't wanna know, but I'm not. Neither are you. It's better to know. It's better to have a team. I'm on your side—we both are. Don't toss us in a shit pile cause you're trying to keep us outta the mud. Yeah?"

I nodded. I still wasn't going to tell him anything, but I think he knew that deep down. "Can you tell us what you took off the boat?"

"Nothing," I said. Rollo chuckled as he got down on the green, lining up a shot.

"You're a good man, Maker, I really believe that. Now, anytime you wanna stop assuming I'm an idiot I'd appreciate it." He stood to line up his putt and missed by a couple inches. He was ready to sink it with the next shot and was being overly careful.

"Now, can you tell us what you took off the boat?" He asked again.

"Not without tossing you into a cow pie," I said.

He nodded. Lane wasn't standing for it though. Lane was blonde and he looked older than his age. He'd made detective incredibly fast because of what he knew.

His mom and sister had fallen victim to vampires when he was a teenager. He'd joined the police force to fight them, only to find out that no one in government believed in vampires. He'd uncovered a vamp nest and raided the place. Using mirrors and taking down a wall, he cleared out a nest of six on his own. The building caught fire and he was able to get the people out. It went down as a bust on a human trafficking ring, and he got promoted in practically no time less than a year out of the academy. "I don't care. I'd arrest you if I could. There were thirteen people on that ship."

"I didn't kill them," I said to Lane's flat stare. It was a lie, but I was a good liar.

"Stop," Rollo snapped. "We are all on the same side. I can work with not knowing everything and you will too. There are some things we don't wanna know, and the day that changes we won't need him," he said, pointing a thumb at me. Rollo had a firm grip on reality.

Lane backed down with a growl and stalked off to make his putt. By the time he was back for the next one, he didn't look as angry.

"I wanna know. Now, why can't you tell us what it is?" he said.

"Because there are things in the world that would kill you just for knowing it exists." I sighed. "Imagine if every criminal in the world had never seen a gun. Hadn't even heard the word before."

"Ha," Rollo scoffed. "Sounds like a world I'd like to live in."

"Now you find out that one of them has found a gun. They know what it is, and what it can be used for, but they don't know how it works yet. You think that might be enough to convince a cop or two to do something unethical?"

Rollo whistled. Lane grunted. He certainly didn't want to hear a good reason. As if he was hoping I'd say something stupid like, "because I said so."

Lane sounded like he was thinking aloud, "So the police in this hypothetical are…?"

"Angels, demons, minor gods." I shrugged. "The vast majority of them would consider you a threat for just knowing what a gun was called; just for knowing that what it could do was even possible."

"So, what keeps you so safe?" Lane asked. He didn't look angry, but it was still coming through in his voice.

"I'm not safe," I snapped. "I'm pissed I even have it, but I can't drop it off at a pawn shop, can I? Have to find the right people to give it to. The real question is, what were the vamps doing with it? And I don't have an answer for that."

"There's something else brewing, what is it?" Rollo said.

I sighed again. "There's a wizard. Goes by Blackstar. He's into arms, mind control, and making people into were-things. Been leaving bodies everywhere. I thought he was going to rob the ship, so I wanted to get there first. If he'd won that race then we wouldn't be having this pleasant conversation." I filled the last two words with scorn and gave Lane a pointed look, but he was still lining up a shot that—in my amateur opinion—couldn't possibly benefit from any more lining up.

Rollo nodded and ran a hand over an old shoulder injury.

Sometimes he did that when he was thinking. "I assume you're going to handle this Blackstar character? What can we do to help?"

I shrugged. I wouldn't raid a paint drying competition with these two, but I wasn't going to tell them that. Fortunately, in this case, the truth would do. "I don't know right now. I'm in wait and see mode too. Until someone pokes their head up, there's nothing *to* do."

Of course, Gomez or someone would be here soon to settle matters. The Martinet didn't take kindly to the non-magically inclined knowing anything about them, so I didn't mention that either.

"I kept a unit from searching Michael's Pizza two nights ago." Rollo said, changing the subject. "Their warrants weren't right anyway. I'm not gonna call them off again. Settle him up, or I'll have to."

"I'll talk to him," I said. "What'd he do?"

"Running drugs out the place. An undercover went in and bought a calzone with a bag of cocaine in it." I must've looked furious. Rollo squared up as a reflex. I took a deep breath and let it out. It took three more before I trusted myself to talk.

"He's yours." I said.

Rollo nodded again with a faint smile. Don't know what for—that probably meant a load of paperwork for him. "Pay up, Lane," he said. Lane putted and missed his shot by inches, tapping it in with a second stroke. He growled and reached in his wallet and handed over a dollar. Not sure what that was about, but they were always passing singles back and forth.

Michael, that bastard. I found money and valuable things all the time. Vampires had affluent tastes after all. Materials to make magical implements weren't cheap. The higher the quality of the material, the better things performed. I could fence things easy. I could even invest. I had a bank account and everything. Getting the money into a taxable form was important. I couldn't keep telling the government that I found hundreds of dollars in the street.

Also, I wasn't going to be telling them that I lifted everything off a dead warlock.

Unfortunately, in order to get that important task done, money had to be laundered. Laundering money wasn't actually difficult. Just get a business that ran on lots of cash transactions. When people come in to buy five dollars in stuff, take their five bucks and put an extra two in the register. The IRS got their cut of seven bucks instead of five. I got to keep the change from an otherwise illegal venture. Everyone was happy.

Michael was the man who ran a pizza place downtown. He kept half of everything he laundered for me, on the condition that he not do anything stupid that would get us caught—or anything else illegal.

This wasn't the first time. I'd already told him if I found out he was dealing drugs again, we were done. At the moment he was endangering everyone. In hindsight, he's a short-sighted, drug dealing, short-sighted, idiotic, short-sighted, moron. Did I mention he was short-sighted?

I'd need someone else to change dollars for me. Rollo had me by the balls, which was the only reason I ever agreed to these meetings where I got badgered the entire time.

Rollo stared at me for a long moment. I made my putt and missed. It didn't matter. "*Move,*" I growled, and felt the universe obey. The ball rolled past the hole by six inches, turned on a dime and went back in. Stupid game.

There were reasons wizards never played sports. No one was keeping score for me. It was kind of understood that I didn't wanna be here and was going to cheat so I could leave quicker.

"Maker, there's something I think I can do for ya." Rollo said

"What is it?" I asked.

Lane sniffed, grabbed his clubs and looked ready to head back. "I'm done," he said. "Maker, you ever leave a dozen bodies on my doorstep again, I'll bury you. I don't know what it takes to kill a wizard, but I'll find a way. Keep me in the loop from now on, and we don't have a problem. Otherwise..." He let the threat hang in the air and met my eyes. I realized he was serious. It was like looking into a mirror. I also realized maybe I was being insensitive.

I don't often think about what ordinary humans must go through when confronted with things from the supernatural. These two hadn't tried to explain it away or convince themselves of a lie. It probably felt like being a kid banging on the invisible wall of a summoning circle, screaming as flesh was torn from you by shadowy demons you could barely see. There had been no way for me to fight back, but these two had found a weapon—such as it was; they had found me. I dropped my gaze from Lane's.

"Sorry," I said. To his credit, Lane just nodded and walked away.

"Come on son, walk with me," Rollo said after a moment. "Blackstar is bringing in arms shipments—"

"Pretty sure I just said that. What do you know about it?" I said. Rollo rolled his eyes and continued.

"I'm assuming you took one of them. I managed to make that one disappear from the records. We've seized three more. Two cops have been injured so far in animal attacks that have been attributed to some kinda cult. I didn't know he made uhh… were-things, until you said something."

"Were-things are actually called theriomorphs," I said, "A human that turns into an animal. It doesn't have to be a wolf—it can be any animal. Everyone just likes predators, for obvious reasons."

"And here I was hoping werewolves didn't exist. How do I kill a werewolf?" He sighed.

"You don't. You run, and you hope like hell it loses interest. If you can't run, then you're going to die screaming unless you have inherited silver, massive amounts of blunt force trauma, or an aircraft carrier filled with luck. Blackstar's people aren't real theriomorphs though, they're made some other way. Makes them a lot weaker. A head shot will kill them, but I wouldn't stop at one."

"I think it was Blackstar that made a mess at the docks then too," he said. "Some man was there just screaming. They had to sedate him. Didn't help the poor bastard. He died from whatever was done to him. Two other random people are in a similar state. I got them admitted to Holly Hill. I want you to look at them, and I want you to meet with me once every two weeks from now on. If you agree to all that, you can have this." He pulled a business card from his wallet and held it out. I went to take it, but he didn't let go.

"I already apologized for the damn boat. What more do you want?"

"This isn't about the past, son. It's about the future and making sure my children actually have one. I'm trusting you." The weight of those words fell on me with the weight of the average Cadillac.

I didn't trust so easily either—or maybe I was just quick to take it away. "Go see him today and tell him you want to retire. Then give him this and do what he says. After that, you get over to the hospital and look at those people. Do that and we're square." He let go of the card and left me to read it. The card was for a lawyer. Why would I need a lawyer? I was about to ask, but when I looked up Rollo was walking away, taking both our burdens with him.

Chapter: 15

That's how I wound up in the office of Ronald Graid. Mr. Graid, whoever he was, had an office downtown a few blocks from the courthouse.

His office was in a basement, and you had to go into an alley and down some stairs to get there. The door was heavy and had standard gold lettering. Past it, I was greeted by a tiny simply furnished room that held only a single chair, a large plant, and a wall full of seven filing cabinets. A redhead of impossible proportions sat behind a large desk that was so clean it was clearly just as much for show as she was. The nameplate on the desk read Helen C. Collins. She looked up with blazing green eyes that seemed to glow. She radiated contempt. The look she gave me was the look I would give a cockroach.

There are no words to adequately describe the feeling you get when a predator is nearby—the moment you realize you're about to be eaten. There was something about the way she moved, the way she breathed; her eyes made it clear that she would kill me, exert no effort doing it and forget I existed the next moment. The spell to call for a potion or two died on my lips as she smiled and the look disappeared. I kept my eyes on her shoulders—and not for the ridiculous amounts of cleavage. If she was gonna move from behind that desk, I wanted to know in advance.

"Hello, I'm here to see Mr. Graid. I'm afraid I don't have an appointment."

"Of course, Mr. Maker. Go right in."

I didn't stop to ask how she knew my name. Rollo must've called ahead. It was obvious this place didn't do many walk-ins. There were doors on either side of her desk; she motioned to the one on my right. I took my first step and she mentally dismissed me. Suddenly it was like I wasn't there at all. She was entirely focused on reading her desktop screen and filing long, curved, nails painted bright red and ending in points. She'd be a caricature if I weren't so afraid of her. I walked through the door, but I didn't take my eyes off her until it closed behind me. That didn't help me feel safe. Now I wouldn't be able to see it when she came to kill me.

The office was cavernous. I stood on a rise three steps up from a floor covered in long grass and larger plants. In order to get to the man's desk, I had to descend into a jungle.

Downtown, and not only did Mr. Graid have twenty-foot ceilings, he also had the whole floor for his office. That screamed affluence, even if it was the basement.

Everything was wood, oak I think. The man was obviously a hunter. There were rifles in a rack on one wall that looked well kept. Clearly they weren't just show pieces. There was a large stuffed bear in one corner and a bighorn sheep to my right past the first screen of foliage. It was on a five-foot tall block of marble and topped with polished granite—all made to look like one seamless crag of rock. I assumed it cost a small fortune. It looked ready to come alive and start headbutting things at any moment.

The grizzly bear looked every bit as lifelike. Through the plants, I could see a glimpse of another animal. A rhino I think, but all the plants couldn't let me be sure.

Every place I looked, there was something green, or a wild

colored flower often with its own sun lamp above it. Vines crawled up the walls and hung from the ceiling. Others crawled up trees and across to other plants. I couldn't see the far wall.

Luckily, I didn't need to. The nearest wall had Mr. Graid's desk against it and behind it was Mr. Graid. Anyone sitting facing his desk would be sitting with their back to the jungle. With the soundtrack for an actual jungle playing over speakers somewhere, it would be quite unnerving.

Graid was a dark was a dark-haired man. He obviously worked out and had good taste in suits. I offered my hand and he took it in a firm grip. He had mastered the politician's trick of looking you in the eyes without actually doing so. We both sat without saying a single word. He smiled at me over steepled fingers, thinking. Finally, he spoke.

"The infamous Maker. I'm honored. Rollo sent you huh? Guess it's finally time for me to pay up," he said, in a baritone voice.

"I'm not a cop, if that's what you're worried about, and what do you mean infamous?" I said.

"Number one, that's a myth," he said. "Cops are allowed, and in fact, encouraged to lie about being cops. Otherwise, undercover cops would not be a threat. Entrapment is far more nuanced. Never believe Hollywood. Second, it wouldn't matter if you were. Since you are attempting to form an attorney-client relationship, I wouldn't be able to testify since that's such a grey area. Instant mistrial. No one would waste their time."

"Ok," I said, pretending I understood all of that. I bought the "never believe Hollywood" bit. Almost everything about wizards was nonsense. Miles' grandkids had spent the last few years begging me to teach them how to be Harry Potter. I can't imagine how he must feel going to lawyer movies. "Now what do you mean infamous?"

He laughed a deep belly laugh that echoed through the large office. "Rollo was right about you. Son, you can't make as much noise as you do without anybody noticing. I'm sure you believe that you have a good handle on things, but the world is a very big place. The local community of minor powers has gotten much smaller over the past several years, but all of them still know you. Maybe not by sight, elusive as you are, but I've never heard anyone say, 'which Maker are you talking about?'"

"I'm not trying to be popular." I scoffed.

"No. You're too busy trying to save the world. It will likely get you killed one day, feel free to prove me wrong on that. Until then, how can I help you?"

"Rollo said to tell you that I wanted to retire," I said, handing over the card.

"So, you want to retire in style? I can do that. Tell me about your income stream and why we're talking now." I hesitated and his smile grew. "An attorney represents you. For the purposes of the law, I practically am you. That being the case, I can never be called upon to testify against you. It's called the attorney-client privilege. Would you like to go Google it and come back later?" There was the tone in his voice that said he gave this speech a lot; that and his wry smile.

"No, it's fine. I know all about that, but you aren't my lawyer."

"Ahh, good point. This is a consultation. It falls under the same umbrella. I work for you more than Officer Rollo at the moment." He thought that was funny enough for a chuckle.

"Alright." I said. "I find things, sell them sometimes. Sometimes I find money. Just need to make sure that it gets properly invested." He nodded.

"So every time you dust one of Duke's people, you take their stuff, make it liquid, and save. Smart." I sometimes wondered what other wizards did with their money. It had to be something similar. I didn't think it was all that smart. If it were, then I wouldn't need to partner up with an idiot like Michael.

"You're up on current events, aren't you?" I said

"Like I said, you make a lot of noise."

"I don't like the sound of that." I said "I never wanna draw more attention, but—"

"But when someone's in trouble, someone else has to act."

"Yeah," I said simply.

"In my experience, attention comes with the territory in that line of work. Feel free to prove me wrong. What do you have in total assets now?"

"About forty thousand, little less maybe," I responded. He didn't even blink. Instead, he sighed and rubbed the bridge of his nose. I thought I heard him say "Rollo, you slimy bastard," but I couldn't be sure.

His smile didn't return, and he sighed again. "I apologize. Most of the clients I manage money for are well past the ten million mark." My eyes widened. "It's fine," he said, holding up a hand. "I owe Lieutenant Rollo a favor, but after this, I'd say he owes me one. I charge ten percent on deposits and one percent on gains. If you are fine with that, I can start right away."

"That works. It's a lot less than I'm paying now."

"How much are you paying now?"

"Fifty percent; plus, I have to pay informants for tips and my apprentice." This time his eyes widened. "Well, it's a pizza place," I explained, as if that made fifty percent ok, "but I'm not doing business there anymore."

"Ahh, I see. Well, I'll have Helen stop by and make your last pickup then. What do you want to be done with your old partner?"

"I don't understand," I said.

"Well, if he's trustworthy, then we need do nothing. If he isn't, then there are easy ways to end his existence quietly so as not to compromise your financial position."

"No, if it comes to that, I'll take care of it," I said. I couldn't believe I hadn't thought of that. What the hell was I going to do about Michael? He didn't know I was a wizard, but I certainly couldn't afford to have him rolling over for points and getting me thrown in jail with him. I wouldn't stay in jail, of course. I could waltz out of the most secure prisons without much trouble, but it would still make life more complicated.

"Keep it in mind. I've always found it's better to be proactive in these situations." I nodded, still thinking. Graid must've seen something in my face because he went on. "It's a tried and true laundering strategy, so don't feel bad about that. Your issue is that you don't own the business. If you bought a pizza place, for example, you could do it yourself and cut out the middle man. With forty thousand, your best bet would be vending machines. They're cheap to set up and run on cash. ATM machines work well, and billboards are also an option."

"Billboards?" I asked. He just smiled.

"Anything that has little to no setup cost and is largely a cash business will work. As your money gets bigger, you can move up to hotels, night clubs, bars, college housing, online retail, junkyards… any and all of a few dozen other things."

"That makes sense." I hadn't even thought of vending machines before.

"Keep all those things in mind for the future. I send out quarterly statements with all your information and everything you need to know. The pages to be burned will be marked. Burn them, do not shred them. I'll pay all taxes due on all your accounts, any needed maintenance and generally keep you out of trouble. You will be able to go into your bank at any time and withdraw funds."

"That's convenient," I said.

"We are a full-service law firm, Mr. Maker. I've made it my life to make sure your life goes smoothly." He smiled.

"My life can get pretty complicated."

"That's true for all of us, but we can never afford to have the non-gifted aware of us, so someone has to make it their job to ease relations between supernatural powers whenever possible. If not for someone like me, vampires, fairies, werewolves, and Merlin would've either torn the world apart or gotten us all burned at the stake by now. Everyone tends to keep a low profile whenever possible, and it's part of my job to keep it that way."

"That sounds far too grand for a lawyer." I smiled.

"I'm only a lawyer in America," he laughed. "A more correct term would be consigliere or counselor."

I laughed. "That would make me Marlon Brando."

"Indeed." He smiled. "Speaking comprehensively, I provide advice and services to make sure none of your extracurricular activities run afoul of any supernatural agendas or the non-gifted's legal system."

"Rollo doesn't know any of this, does he?" I asked.

"He suspects, which is probably why he sent you to me, but he doesn't know anything beyond my financial services—which he couldn't prove in court if I gave him a hundred years. Which brings me to my final point. What to do if you get arrested. This is important. It's the difference between you sitting here in my office and you sitting in a cell. If you ever get arrested for anything, say nothing—not a single word. The only thing you say is, 'I want my lawyer.' Call me, and keep saying nothing until I get there."

I giggled. This was common knowledge in my world, but I nodded my head.

"I'm serious. I have a client now in jail for eight years and half her wealth gone because of three words. She could melt the bars and walk right out, but that would get us all killed. So she's stuck there."

"Sucks to be her," I said. "Not sure how you screw that one up. The cops even tell you that anything you say can be used against you, and in my experience, they don't care what that thing is or whether you said it before they read your rights."

Graid nodded after a moment. He closed his eyes and exhaled slowly. Helen burst through the door, striding like she wasn't wearing four-inch heels at all. There was a grace and strength to her that was only made more clear by her striding through the grass up to Graid's desk. She smiled at him, but didn't acknowledge me at all. I realized I was a little grateful for that. I hadn't seen the warm smiling woman that greeted him while she was sitting at a desk.

"Beloved, Mr. Maker is our newest client. Please have him sign all the necessary paperwork. Also, I think we are owed a hunt, please schedule it." Her smile broadened at the mention of hunting. Maybe she could shoot too.

Becoming a client gave me a promotion in Helen's eyes. I was no longer beneath her notice. I said goodbye to Mr. Graid and returned to the front office. I signed some papers. Well, I made the same scribble I always make when asked to sign something. Not like I actually knew my last name.

Helen moved about the office handling everything deftly, knew where everything was, and answered my few remaining questions before they were fully out of my mouth. All done with a smile meant to melt hearts and put children at ease. The monster that showed itself in the first half-second of meeting was gone.

When someone wants to kill you, there was always some hint, no matter how slight. A squinting of the eyes, a slightly lowered chin… something. That feeling of malice meant I had a chance of predicting behavior; a chance to see an attack coming. Malice isn't necessary to step on an ant—you just do it. All the smiles in the world wouldn't make me forget the beast I saw in that first impression.

Damn, she frightened me.

I was so on edge that it wasn't until I left that I realized Rollo no longer had me over a barrel. As far as the city police were concerned, I was untouchable—unless it was for a parking ticket. To celebrate I even did a little jaywalking.

Rollo had earned more than a few notches of respect from me. Not enough that I would take him on a Blackstar hunt, but if he were willing to help I'd have to think about what he could actually do that wouldn't have him dying on my watch. I had enough on my conscience already.

* * *

Dorthea Dix was probably the biggest hospital in the Raleigh area. I never measured it of course, but the place was huge. It sat on a corner inside the beltline and up a few blocks. There were also clinics lined up and down the street on either side for doctors specializing in one thing or another. Holly Hill was one of those.

I certainly wasn't going in the front, so I found a drug store parking lot and started walking the few blocks to the building. I didn't like cameras. Avoiding them completely was impossible, but I could certainly increase my odds.

I was looking for a back door and wondering why hospitals didn't have a threshold. Vampires and other supernatural baddies could come and go as they pleased. It didn't make sense. There were residents that lived here, and patients that died here. People hoped, prayed, were overjoyed when a relative lived and destroyed when they died. A lot of life happened here, and living done by mortals was what created a threshold.

It was a reminder that I was still a rookie, and I didn't know nearly as much as I could about all things magic.

"*Charmer*," I said, and downed the potion. It started working before I got to the loading dock in the back. I shivered at that humming sensation in all my joints at once. I pulled up my hood and walked in, keeping my head down.

The charmer was a precaution. If nothing happened and there was no interaction with anyone, I would be quite satisfied with that.

There was no one around, and the place only had one door for trucks to unload things. I hesitated. I told Rollo I would, and he had technically paid me by giving me Graid's card. "Nothing for it," I sighed. If I didn't wanna do this then I shouldn't have taken the money.

My rule about not being hungry made me do it. I had another rule about not getting myself killed, and I had a feeling Graid would help a lot on both fronts.

I went in and found a locker room in short order. It had a lock on the door. One of those that you had to have a card for.

"*Master card.*" An old credit card appeared in my hand, and I held it to the card reader. I felt the ice down my spine as I sent some of my power into the card, hoping it wasn't the time for this thing to poop out on me. These things were virtually worthless.

They could get me into any door, but after two or three uses they were back to being cheap pieces of plastic. If only there were such a thing as a well-made, antique, plastic card fashioned by a professional with care and expertise. I almost laughed at the thought.

After a moment, the light on the card reader flashed green and I opened the door to an empty hallway. On the right was the men's locker room, and I went in. Finding an unlocked locker wasn't difficult; I changed into nurse's scrubs and tossed on a lab coat. Whoever this guy was, he was a size or two smaller than me, and certainly didn't have my shoulders.

Also, he seemed to have a thing for Scooby-doo. The scrubs were covered in the gang from the old cartoon and depictions of the mystery machine from different angles. I looked doctor-y enough I guess.

I found a paper mask and left the locker room, heading for the mental health wing. I didn't hear any screaming, but I could probably puzzle out who was who when I got there. I said hello to anyone I passed, but otherwise said nothing to no one.

The mental health wing was far more quiet than the rest of the place. In the middle of the day I would've expected more activity. Then again, I was heading to the section for people that were far gone; folks that no one knew how to help. I didn't think hospitals did padded cells anymore, but if they did, this is where they would be.

The nurse at the front desk was a short thing with touches of grey in her brunette hair. She wore glasses, was reading a textbook, and looked up with a smile when she saw me.

"Good afternoon nurse," I said with what I hoped was a jovial tone. Of course, thanks to the charmer potion it didn't matter what I said. "Can you point me towards the two that were brought in from Wilmington a few nights ago? I'm supposed to have a look."

"Room 1054. Shame too. Do you need their charts?" I didn't know what that would accomplish—there was no way 'attacked by warlock with mind-altering spell' would be on that chart.

"Lemme have a look first and then I'll see what the chart can tell me," I said. She smiled again and went back to her book, hopefully forgetting all about me.

The room was down on the left. It had four beds, with a television over each, mounted to the ceiling. All the curtains were pushed back so I could see that only three of the four beds were occupied.

One of them cradled an old man who was restrained to the bed.

"Are you here for the bus?" he asked. I ignored him. He was obviously not who I was here to see. As insane as he might be, he could still talk.

The other two were sedated, but not sleeping: a man and a woman. Both were restrained to their beds with leather cuffs around their ankles, wrists, and across their chest. They both twitched violently, constantly, and their eyes were fluttering. I looked at the IV drips and wondered how much sedative it had taken to put them down. Even if I was able to help, would the sedative do damage?

If Blackstar's spell and the sedative were pulling in opposite directions what would happen if I broke the spell? It was enough to get me worrying.

I laid one hand on each of their foreheads and felt the hum associated with magic users. They were wizards? That could be coincidence with just one of them, but both? That was more than a little weird.

The spell in effect was obvious to any wizard who was looking. A persistent spell was a difficult thing. Another in a long list of spell types I would never do because they required more power than I could wield in a month. If my staff were full, I could maybe perform the spell I was feeling, but this had been done twice… in the same night.

I got ahold of it after probing around for a few minutes. It wasn't complicated. The power in the air was being channeled into their minds and creating as much fear and pain as they could handle. The spell would kill them, but that would happen slowly. The amount of power being channeled in was slowly increasing. Every time their minds adapted to a new level of pain it ramped up. Eventually, the level of adrenaline their bodies produced would kill them or they would break their own back or neck struggling.

Rollo had asked me to look at two dead people. There was nothing I could do about this. I had a BB gun that could take down any bird in sight. I was worthless if an elephant showed up—and this was a whale. It'd be like pushing against the ocean or putting my finger in a dike that had just exploded.

Dammit. I sat down in one of the chairs. I didn't need to be touching them now that I knew what the spell did and where it was. So I just studied it, looking for some weakness, some way in, or some way to dissipate it.

This spell was made better than anything I'd ever felt. There were no ways in, no way to counter it. My heart started beating faster. I could practically see Blackstar smiling.

I was there so long I felt the charmer potion dying. That was my last one, so I was thinking about getting out of there. The only thing I'd come up with wouldn't work.

The spell was indiscriminate. It was not specific to these two people, probably because there was no reason to make it so. Most spells were indiscriminate. The ones that weren't—that I knew of—were what the modern world would call curses or voodoo. Voodoo almost always had a specific target; the spell by its nature couldn't affect anyone else.

I could make this spell switch targets, but that was it. I could make it target the ceiling and call it a day, but in this case, the target had to be someone's mind. There was no point in putting the spell on someone else to save these two.

"…a spell designed to affect your mind," Arta had told me. This would be a smorgasbord of magical noms noms for her. That is, if she could use it, if she was paying attention right now, and if she were telling the truth about everything to begin with.

I often said Tema Rion was the scum of the earth. It would be foolish to take the spirit of whatever she'd tried to summon at its word. Most supernatural beings either couldn't lie or didn't lie, but my list of the ones that did was far from complete.

There was no way to be sure. Even if I could summon Arta right now and ask her, there was no way I could believe her. I let out a deep breath and got up to leave. I got to the door before I stalled.

"Dammit!" I bit through my thumb and pressed them together. A little blood wouldn't hurt, given the power this was going to take.

"*Staff.*" I didn't look at how full it was, or I was certain I would lose my nerve. I went back over to the hospital beds and laid my hands on the afflicted magic users, smearing a drop of blood on each forehead. I had to move both spells at once. This would either be slightly tricky or wonderfully straightforward—I didn't know which because I'd never done anything like this before.

My power flowed into them both. The spells eased out of their minds like a needle gently being removed. I felt the spells trying to go back into their victims, but spells followed the flow of power like water downhill. Currently, the power was flowing from me into them and then "downhill" back into my mind.

Turned out redirecting persistent spells was simplicity itself. Then I had bigger problems.

Imagine the strongest person you've ever seen. Imagine them pounding on a tree with a sledgehammer. Not repeatedly, just one shot as hard as they can. Now imagine the tree is your head.

That's what it felt like as both spells slammed into me. Every nerve in my head lit up, and my skull was suddenly five sizes too small. I screamed—or at least I think I did. There was nothing but the pain.

"*MMMMMAAAAAAKERRR!*" The bellow inside my head sounded pleased. It was even worse than the spell, but at least the bellow ended. I stumbled and fell. I couldn't get to my feet. Did I scream again? I wasn't sure. I had to get out of there before nurse bookworm came to check on the commotion. There was a lot of power flying around—it shorted out the TVs, and the lights had gone off.

I got up and stumbled out. I wasn't the one screaming; the third patient was. Poor old guy, I could've given him a heart attack. There was no one in the hallway, but with the old man yelling that wouldn't keep. I ducked around a corner and into another room. This one had only one old woman in it, and thankfully she was asleep. I shut the door and sat down with my back to it to catch my breath.

I was curled up on the floor breathing like I was in Lamaze class, trying to deal with the all too slowly fading pain.

There are moments in life when you make a choice, and after seeing the results, it skyrockets up the list of stupidest things you've ever done.

This was in the top ten.

* * *

I got back to Miles' in time for dinner. It was salmon with some creamy white stuff on top of a salad. I ate two plates and left a twenty. Miles was mostly engrossed in watching an ultimate fighting match with a teenage grandson. I think his name was Murrey. I didn't know most of the older ones. Not many teenagers came to hang out with their grandfather.

I went upstairs and could hear the music coming through the ceiling. Zora was in the gym, undoubtedly giving herself a beating.

The second floor was one big room. It had been a boxing gym, and still was—though no one ever trained here except Zora. She'd outfitted the place with speakers and televisions everywhere. Three were playing some kind of anime, one had the new Deadpool movie, three others were TEDtalks, and two were nature specials. Over all that, there were speakers blasting at least four kinds of rock and techno music. I only recognized Disturbed and Lindsey Sterling wailing away on a violin.

Since Zora's power was sensing and reacting to incoming vibrations, she trained with as many vibrations in the air as possible. She was separating them all out and would know what each one said, despite them all screaming at once. It was impressive, to say the least.

She was in the ring now, sword fighting with the mannequin I'd enchanted years ago. She wanted something that could test her sword work, and I knew nothing about swords.

She had to feed it energy while she used it, and it learned as she did. Every stroke was like fighting against your own speed, power, and combined knowledge. Nearly two years and it still hadn't failed. The enchantment itself *was* rather simple.

One of the anime characters screamed something, and I looked up at the screen. There weren't any subtitles; she didn't need any. Zora spoke Japanese, Mandarin, French, Italian, Arabic and Swahili. She started on Latin, but the last I heard she had stopped because it was a "boring language."

Neka sat nearby on a cushion, meditating and throwing mental attacks at her. I could recognize them now. She looked tired and excited. She always did in a fight. She was sweating, and her long hair was wet and matted. That was Zora for you; she never relaxed, and never took days off.

She wasn't just cocky, she had the skills to back it up—even if neither of us had the magical muscle. We had intellectual muscle, and that was just as important. I just wish it was always enough.

I didn't want to interrupt, but this was important. I walked up to the ring and waited. The pain from the spells was gone completely, and Arta was presumably feasting. I shivered again, just like I had each time I thought about it over the last couple hours.

I hadn't given a single thought to what would happen had the redirection failed. "Just another thing to *maybe* have nightmares about," I muttered.

"Neka, hold off!" she yelled, jumping back a few feet and blocking a slash to her midsection. She moved to the side of the ring and grabbed a remote. All sound died when she hit the mute button. Well, all of it except for the slight ringing in my ears.

The dummy fell limp into a pile at her feet. She was breathing hard with her hands on her knees and dripping sweat. I wondered how long she'd been at it.

"What's up?" She said, looking over at me. The wooden kendo sticks she used lay forgotten on the ring floor. When she looked at me, I saw she had a large bruise on the side of her face.

"Need a favor," I said simply. "You alright? Your face looks like a side of beef."

"Did you upgrade my dummy?" She asked.

"What? No. Why would you even ask that?"

She took off her shirt and showed me another bruise across her stomach. There were more on her back as she turned. She dropped her baggy yoga pants around her ankles, and I saw her legs were covered in black and purple welts.

"This is why," she said with a smirk, "I haven't scored a hit all day." She pulled up her pants up and looked at the dummy as if she was ready to go another round. I thought I saw a flash of disappointment from Neka. He wasn't dropping into closed eyes meditation now. I held back a laugh. If our relationship ever improved, I'd have to warn him off that path. Zora would eat him alive.

I shrugged. "Then you've learned something profound. I don't know enough about swords to do that to you, so I couldn't've upgraded it."

"Maker, you know I'd never miss an opportunity to stroke my own ego. I'm not this good. I've never been this good."

"She's right. I've been watching," Neka said with a smirk.

"If you turn yourself into a sheep first, is it still bestiality?" Zora snapped at him. Neka scrunched up his face in confusion. Most jokes went over his head. I thought it was worth a chuckle. "Not that I'm complaining, Maker. If you did, it's cool. I've learned more in one day than I have in a year."

"That's good, but I didn't touch it. I could look at it for you and see what went right, I guess?"

"Nope. If you didn't mess with it, then it might be doing that thing that light bulbs do. A surge of power right before it gives out. I'm gonna be here until it does." Light bulbs didn't technically do that—and in my experience neither did magical tools—but I didn't feel the need to point that out.

There had been a lot of sword work the last few weeks. It was far more likely that she had just learned something new and not consciously noticed.

"Ok, just don't trash it. I can re-enchant it if it gives out."

"Yes sir, Captain Obvious." She saluted. "What's the favor?"

I handed over my kevlar baton. I hardly ever let my staff out of my sight. It was always a little difficult. I felt my gun under my coat and felt a little better. "Fill er' up. With premium. As much as you can without killing yourself. I used the last charmer today, we're nearly out of shadows, we're completely out of bandages, and one way or another there's a fight coming."

She just nodded and tucked it in her sports bra. I was going to say the dummy would murder her if she were charging my staff, taking attacks from Neka, and fighting it at the same time, but that was impossible. Despite its fine performance, it still couldn't know more than she did. It probably had more to do with Neka throwing distracting attacks than anything.

Unless Neka was affecting her mind somehow without me knowing. I still didn't trust him completely; I only trusted that he wanted to kill Blackstar. Having complete control of Zora would certainly help with that.

I knew Zora like the back of my hand. If she were being affected mentally I should know instantly just standing here, but I was getting no indication of that. I resolved to give her a closer look when Neka wasn't around.

I went home to rest, suspecting that no rest would actually happen, then took a detour to make a couple calls. Called Gomez again, but he didn't answer. I didn't leave a voicemail. I never left messages because there was no way to tell for certain who would get them. He said someone would be here soon, and so far, nothing. If Rania's prediction was any indication, the world may come apart before they got here.

The second call was to Rollo. I called his cell because I didn't wanna deal with the police department's automated service just to get sent to another voicemail.

"Rollo," said his voice from the other end.

"I got it done," I said, and hung up. Some people might say I just wasted fifty cents, but now that those people didn't have their minds being torn up they would belong in recovery and not the psych ward. Not sure what Rollo could do about that, but I wanted him to know that his trust hadn't been misplaced. That was always important for a mercenary's reputation.

"Still not bringing you in on anything," I grumbled as I left the phone booth.

Once home and in bed, I predictably couldn't sleep. There were still a few hours of daylight left, but that didn't matter in an attic. There was only a vent to the outside that let in a soft light. I didn't need candles in the daytime, but I normally had no trouble sleeping through it either.

There hadn't been much to do but think and study for the last few days. There was a lot to think about, including everything we took off the boat to study. Zora was seeing what she could learn from the tooth and the ring. I had everything else.

So far, only the torch had given up its secrets—and they weren't deep, mysterious or breathtakingly dangerous. Once lit, it would burn for hours, and rather than smoke, it produced a soft flowery scent. I planned to leave it at Grace's on consignment. The non-magically inclined would likely get into a bidding war over what amounted to a big scented candle. I got up thinking about the fork failure. I remembered laying down the symbols for it.

It came through for me in Durham, so I decided to try a good one. I had a few antique tablespoons made of pure silver. I placed one on a small stand on my desk sitting underneath a large lens. That helped a lot with checking all my tiny arcane symbols. I pulled out my soldering iron and all of my micro-etching equipment.

I opened up my laptop and started my imaging software. I also turned on *Philosophize This*, which was one my favorite podcasts. I was a few episodes behind, so I'd have a couple hours of sound while I worked. I measured the spoon with some digital calipers and input the dimensions. One day I'd pop for a 3D imager, but that wouldn't be anytime soon.

I plugged the etcher into my laptop, double and triple checked the spoon's placement and started the program.

Laying down spells was calming… and cold, but mostly calming. Layer upon layer of them. Each symbol was infused with my power and each in itself was a tool to gather more power. The more of them I could fit into each piece, the better. Using my laptop and an automatic etcher, I could fit three times as many onto each piece I made.

The etcher moved quickly, and I had to infuse each symbol with power as it moved along. I had to keep up—if I missed even one then some section would eventually have more or less power than all the others, and the damn thing would fail at probably the worst possible time for me. Or it could shatter and take half my hand with it. That had never happened, and I wanted to keep it that way.

Making magic items is like writing an algorithm. Each symbol is either to gather power, store power, or instructions on how to release it. The better the algorithm, the more elegant, the better it worked. Same thing here.

The symbols had no power on their own. They are meaningless, just like the made-up words of other people's spells—they only meant something to me. It was all about intent. The most central symbol had to be done even more carefully. It was an instruction on how the energy was to be converted and then released.

In this case, increasing or decreasing the electromagnetic force to alter density and suspending gravity on whatever was touching the spoon. Gravity didn't like being suspended or doing anything except being gravity. You could always get electromagnetism and the weak force to cooperate, but the strong force and gravity were assholes.

The last symbols were always as much art as they were science. It took days, sometimes weeks, to get them just right.

Scritch, scritch, scritch, cast spell. Scritch, scritch, scritch, cast spell. It was both relaxing and exhausting. I think most people who build things love it. Not a statistic, I know, but I bet the number is high.

Even though it drains me, it was nice doing it. It was fulfilling watching something take shape. Something I could control that I knew wouldn't overwhelm me, kill me, or immediately go south. It was also good for thinking and taking stock of the three-ring shit show my life had become.

The people in the hospital had been far gone. Blackstar or whoever had not been kind, essentially taking everything they were and sticking it in a blender. I did what I could. It wasn't much, but at least they wouldn't be screaming in pain or constant fear while they put their lives back together.

Rollo would probably think that meant they were cured. I'll have to explain that as minds go, theirs had been ripped apart. They were lucky to be alive.

A minor concern was that they were wizards. If Blackstar were grabbing people at random to vent his rage, the odds of him grabbing two of the few hundred wizards in the world were nil. They had to be his people. Guess he was pissed about the boat, but I didn't know exactly what that meant for the current situation.

In the long run, all it meant was that Rania had two more clients. I just hoped she could help them find some relief. Of course, that would only matter if I could keep the universe from going dark in the next few weeks. It wasn't wise to put too much faith in divination, but it was downright stupid to ignore it. I hadn't forgotten her prediction and the time was getting closer.

I tried to contact Arta every time I slept, to no avail. It was impossible to think of her without flashing back to screaming under the sadistic ministrations of one warlock or another. I never gave much thought to memory; I don't imagine most people do. Some things you remember, and some things you don't.

Other than a few dozen particularly horrible vignettes in vivid detail, I barely remembered my apprenticeship with Tema. Only that it was on a farm in the middle of nowhere and it was harsh. When I tried to summon anything more specific, nothing came.

Arta said the things I knew would scare me. She was likely

right since she was in my head, and I suspected she was holding back all of my worst memories—among many other things. The question now was, why? I wanted to ask even though I was sure I'd get some cryptic riddle answer. She was as bad as any fairy.

Duke hadn't moved on me at all. I expected a bang and didn't even get a whimper. Zora's sensor in Vermillion Falls hadn't picked up anything. The sensor she left on the boat was just as useless. She'd let it go sometime yesterday. It was dangerous having sensors out.

Zora was good with movement, vibration, waves. Everything she could do relied on one of those things. It was by chance that she'd discovered she could detect vibrations even when the drop of blood or piece of skin, was no longer attached to her body. Leaving a few flakes of skin or a drop of blood stuck to the ceiling in your enemy's stronghold was never an entirely safe proposition.

The blood had to be refreshed. Meaning Zora still had to feed it and keep it as a part of her. Whenever the air around it vibrated, whenever someone was talking, she could pick it up.

It was a spell specific to her. I tried it and couldn't pick up a thing; I couldn't even detect the blood without an appropriate spell.

We all had our talents.

Neka and Zora had been watching Duke's place from a distance. Vermillion Falls had been quiet on the outside too. As quiet as an affluent mansion full of vampires ever was, anyway. Duke should be investigating who'd taken the stuff from the boat, but instead, he was sitting in Vermillion Falls Manor doing absolutely nothing as far as I could tell. The sensor wasn't in a well-traveled area of the mansion. Some side hallway or other. Still, I'd expected Zora to tell me about some angry shouting she'd overheard. Something. Anything. The silence was unnerving.

Blackstar should be searching for the boat perpetrator as

well, but there wasn't a peep out of him for the better part of a week now.

There was word that Blackstar was recruiting. That was nothing new. Mostly I was fine with them taking their time as long as they were doing nothing with it—but I'd have to be an idiot to believe that. It sincerely bothered me that I didn't know where The Constellation was and what they were up to. The Martinet would be here soon. I just wanted to hand this mess over and never think about it again.

While Zora and Neka watched Vermillion Falls, I'd gone out looking for Blackstar every night. The plan was to string him out; take out his people one or two at a time and run. That plan couldn't work if I couldn't find him. Seemed like the whole Constellation had vanished into thin air. I'd searched everywhere from Chapel Hill to East Raleigh—and nothing. I'd start on the outskirts of town tonight, but I wasn't optimistic. Blackstar had forgotten about my labs entirely.

Once he discovered that every location they'd gotten from me held a healthy population of traps, he and his people had given up on my labs. That or they realized that I'm not stupid enough to keep anything there in the first place. This "wait and see" nonsense sucked.

It was morning before I was done with the spoon. It could've taken me a couple weeks, but once I started, it just came together. I gave it a thirty percent chance of working at all. I could make a dozen of these pretty quick while I worked out how to do it without me having to power it myself.

I finally called it quits when the sun was coming up and I had to squint for a moment at my laptop screen to read the time. I needed to get another phone. Guess there'd be no Blackstar hunt since I'd gotten so engrossed in my work. On the bright side though, I was freezing and exhausted, so my cot became far more appealing.

I woke up around dusk and went to find Zora. I tucked the spoon into a pocket and headed downstairs to the kitchen using the fold-down attic stairs. I left my "rent money" taped to the fridge. The Mason family was all crowded around the dining room table playing Settlers of Catan. I didn't stick around. Watching them now was only making me sad. They did sometimes serve as a reminder of what I was trying to protect, but that was rare.

Often I was just looking to get out of whatever I was in alive. This situation was one of those. I kept my truck parked down at Miles, and the walk was a nice few blocks of dark thoughts.

I went in to see Zora having dinner—a stew that smelled good. I sat down next to her at the bar to have a bowl. It was more fish. Something spicy. I made good use of the biscuits. Zora looked trashed.

Not a wonder. As she slid my staff over to me, I picked it up and it was nearly a quarter full. That would give us back a few bandages.

We'd both gone almost completely nocturnal the last few days. Most humans simply didn't do well unless the shift was permanent. I was barely keeping it together myself; I couldn't imagine what Zora was going through.

"Dummy give out yet?" I asked.

"Nope, I did." She laughed. "Hurry up with those bandages. I feel like a car wreck." I nodded. "Got a tip from a homeless guy on that haunting by the way," she said. "Said he found a bunch of dead cats near a bridge. We've been so busy I left it. Paid him to look in every few days and not get close. Last night he found a dead deer. Belly ripped out, head gone—just like the cats."

"Oh great!" I said. "This, on top of everything." I put my head in my hands and sighed.

"Aww, knock it off. You've been brooding over Blackstar and Duke for days. One of them will turn up dead sooner or later, and then you'll be feeling dumb for playing whiney, emo wizard for nothing."

I just grunted. I was in no way as certain as Zora's reassurances would have me believe.

"Come on," she smiled. "This will help take your mind off things. Besides, it's been ages since I killed a troll."

Chapter: 16

The north side of town was the nice end. I lived downtown with the dregs and houses that were more than a hundred years old. Here everything was shiny and new—that included the bridge.

It wasn't hard to find. It wasn't in a well-traveled area, either. The road ran north and east, and there were a few subdivisions being built on the near side. Nothing but farmland after that. Lucky thing, too, it made stealing a goat rather easy. In the long run, the farmer would probably thank me.

A troll's favorite food was goat and sheep, after all. We only had a tiny one. If the goat was too big, it would send the troll running for the hills screaming. I sighed at that. Stupid wildlings.

The bridge went over a creek that was currently dry. Zora and I led the goat down and waited. We had enough shadow potions for this, ready to drink at a moment's notice. Now there was nothing to do but wait.

On Zora's recommendation, I had invited Neka along. He made it clear that he was only interested in hunting down Blackstar and went off to do that instead. Can't say I blame him. I wanted

The Constellation found too, though I suspect we had slightly different reasons.

I'm glad he didn't come; it gave me a chance to talk to Zora alone.

"Protocol 1," I said. It was a difficult topic to broach.

"What? I'm not compromised. When would that have even happened?" She said. There wasn't much anger in her voice, but it was there. It was never fun to hear that someone didn't trust you. I sighed.

Protocol 1 was something we came up with years ago that we'd only used twice. This was my first time calling for one.

It was a way to say that one of us thought the other was acting funny or was under some kind of compulsion. When one of us said it, the other had to submit to being looked at. If they didn't, that was admitting guilt. It worked well when it was needed. We just spent so much time together it was never needed.

Of course, answering any questions was right out. If the other person was under some mind control, that may alert the controller to what their mistake had been. It was part of the rules that even if I wanted to tell her I was just being a little paranoid, I couldn't until after I'd had a look.

"I can tell you're tired. Get some sleep," I said. "I'll look while you're out." Zora only nodded. Just the mention of sleep brought on a yawn from us both. We had been up almost every night this week. Her and Neka at Vermillion Falls, and me looking for Blackstar. I'd actually slept today, but I could tell Zora was low on that particular resource.

This was confirmed when she didn't even argue about sleeping. I removed my coat and tossed it to her. She made a pillow of it and was out in minutes. I reached out with my senses and felt for her presence. It was so familiar it practically jumped at me.

I didn't feel anything magical that was different about her. Like I said, we spent so much time together that anything like that would've been obvious. I hesitated a moment. I wasn't sure if I wanted to take this to the next step.

May as well dive in; just hope the pool had water in it.

I hated doing this, so I almost never did it. I took a long exhale and got into a comfortable position. There was no outward change, save for me shivering. There was no cartoonish disembodied spirit rising out of me. No ridiculous eye popping open in the middle of my forehead.

The ethereal plane looked almost exactly like this one. Some would call it the land of spirits. In actuality, it was a barrier between separate planes of existence. It was what you had to cross to get to Faerie or Hell. Probably heaven too. Like any universe, it had its own laws. I never came here because I didn't know any of them. At least there were no vampires.

Crossing to the ethereal plane was difficult. This wasn't punching a hole in another universe. It was more like creating a window, sending energy through it and hoping like hell nothing on the other side noticed. It wasn't impossible—a normal human could get it done in a century or so of meditation, but a wizard just needed the right spell.

Crossing over physically was right out. That required a *powerful* wizard with the right spell and the courage—or stupidity—to ignore things the Martinet had no tolerance for.

In the ethereal plane, you could see the world as a collection of spirits or impressions. I tended to think of myself as a constantly shifting pattern of particles, arranged in just the right order. The ethereal plane showed me the impact of those particles on the world. At least, my mind's interpretation of them.

Everything here glowed slightly, and some more than others. The rocks looked like individual stars compared to Zora the sun lying on top of them.

You could see a thing's true nature in the ethereal plane, but it didn't pay to linger. The ethereal was where many planes of existence met, so it was a violent place and full of spirits from benevolent to pure evil.

Zora appeared to be a light made of steel. She always looked like that; some rigid metal that was strong as diamond wrapped around a core of some dark crystal. No matter that the metal felt strong, it was covered in hair-thin cracks and splattered with blood from so many battles she'd lost count, but she hadn't lost focus. The blood was black, fetid and each drop slowly moved towards the nearest fissure. The metal glowed slightly and pulsed with her heartbeat. It felt good just seeing it. It felt righteous, intense, like battling angels must feel.

The only thing amiss was a sword next to her. At least I think it was a sword. It was a black mass lying next to her katana. Her katana appeared to be perfectly formed and made of that same black blood. The story there was obvious.

The black mass wasn't evil, it wasn't good. It was hungry. Hungry for what I couldn't say but it was the personification of hunger, thirst and the hope of being sated. It was weird for certain, but I knew it had nothing to do with Neka.

I "returned" to my body and let out a breath I didn't know I was holding. At least there was nothing wrong with her. The exertion of opening the way to the spirit realm was considerable.

"I'm done," I said. "No real reason, was just paranoid about Neka." She grunted, yawned again, but didn't say anything.

I looked up into a clear night sky. The glow of the city invaded from the southwest, blotting out the few stars that would be out this early. The goat was walking around sniffing the ground looking for grasses. It would be far more stressed if it knew what was coming.

Trolls didn't like sunlight. They hated it—if they were out in it long enough, they would turn to stone and crumble into dust. They also liked goat, and trolls lived to eat. Even more than humans.

Given those facts the legends made sense. In olden times,

farmers still had to get their livestock from point A to point B. Everyone would use the local bridge, which also functioned as a way to block out the sun. Trolls are stupid, but it probably didn't take them long to figure that one out.

Pretty soon trolls were burying themselves under bridges because it's an easy way to ambush a goat. If a farmer got in the way, then it was a bad day for that farmer. The worst scenario was if a kid who was just taking the sheep out to or from pasture got in the way.

And thus, a legend was born, stories were told, and troll killer became a line on someone's CV. Tonight it was mine. These days livestock was moved around by truck. I'd never heard of a troll jumping in front of a semi trying to get a meal, even though I'd met one big enough.

The danger was that the troll would get hungry—desperately hungry—and some lone jogger would wind up on the menu. There was no way to tell, but I would bet that the industrial revolution saw an increase in that exact thing. Without sheep and goats crossing bridges willy-nilly, and the rise of larger and larger localized farming, trolls would get that desperate level of hungry far more often. It had never happened on my watch.

Relatively speaking, trolls were loud. They left a trail of bodies wherever they went, and that made their hidey holes obvious to anyone who knew what to look for. I could smell all the rotting meat from where I was sitting.

There were a few dead cats and dogs lying around, all with their bellies, chest, and heads missing. Seeing a troll eat was quite disgusting. They tend to grab the front and back legs in each hand and take the midsection in a single bite all the way to the spine. Then they chomp off the head in a single bite and throw the rest away.

Most ate in exactly that order, and wouldn't eat anything that was too big to eat this way… or anything too small to make the process an effort. As a rule of thumb, it was a good way to judge the size, and therefore, power of the thing. Which was why Zora had slept on it for a while. Big enough to take down a small deer was as big as we were willing to risk. Theoretically, there was no limit to the size a troll could get.

I yawned. There was nothing to do but stare at the goat moving around. It had been more than an hour and I was thinking about waking Zora, but decided to let her sleep some more. She went down quick, but she'd been tossing and moaning the whole time. There'd be no point to any of this if I woke her, and she passed out again. If we slept past the goat getting snatched, we'd have to be out here again tomorrow.

That was about the time the ground trembled a bit, followed by another tremble a moment later. It was obviously the sound of our resident menace rising out of the nightly grave it dug for itself.

I stood up and stretched. "Wake up. It's game time." She sat up with far more vigor than she would if she were sleeping peacefully. She got to her feet and tossed me my jacket. "*Kitty Pride. Kitty Pride.*"

She stretched, caught the potion I tossed her, yawned, and pulled her sword. We both drank our shadow potions, though I had the feeling I should've given Zora a wake up special.

"These are the last two," I said. Zora nodded and said nothing. I pulled up my hood and mask and let out a long breath. We were both focused on the bridge.

The underside of the bridge grew black as the troll rose up out of the earth. It was still pulling itself out from under the bridge when Zora charged and sliced across its arm. The pain took a half second to register. Trolls were stupid.

It screamed, which turned into a low moan as it continued to pull itself out. Zora struck again, this time across its back with the same result. She was back next to me in a moment. She was nearly black, with shadows coming off of her like waves of heat. My potion hadn't even activated yet.

"Armored," she said.

"Figures," I growled. Trolls came in a few different types. Armored trolls had thicker and tougher skin that most. Hard as granite in most places. It didn't change the fact that to kill one you need obscene amounts of physical trauma, fire, or sunlight. They weren't the worst type of trolls to run into, but certainly not the best.

The beast rose to its full height. It had to be at least twenty feet tall. Green-skinned from head to toe.

"He's a tall one," Zora yawned.

The troll was covered in lesions and boils with random patches of oily looking black. It was coated in dirt and dust. I could tell it was male, as it was wearing *only* dust. Its face was a mess. The nose looked like it had been broken several times and hadn't healed right once. Its uncharacteristically small mouth was full of a whopping seven teeth which went in every direction, and it was missing an eye. All over it looked so diseased and dirty it was enough to spoil my last meal.

Worse, was the size—it was enormous. Trolls grew more powerful the bigger they got. This one should've been on cows, not deer, but with that mouth it likely couldn't eat things appropriate to its size.

The goat was snatched up and in its teeth with a flash of diseased, mottled, green. It was the only time I'd seen a troll eat all of something. Maybe it just got excited. The goat was screaming in pain and terror, but its volume just didn't compare.

"Half rot." That was the term trolls used for humans, something to do with our smell. The thing thought for a moment looking for a word. "Human! Yes, humans bring goat for Ga. Worship him. You bring more goat and me no eat you," The voice was deep and gravelly. If BB King were a river, this thing was the bottom of the ocean.

It also spoke like a particularly stupid four-year-old. Many a wizard had underestimated a troll for just that reason. They made it hard to remember that stupid could still mean dangerous when you were that strong.

I heard the goat screaming its last. What a shitty way to die. Even razor-edged teeth weren't efficient killing implements when you only had seven of them.

"Aww, it wants to bargain. How sweet." Zora said.

"So, if we bring him a goat every night, we join the church of Ga?" I laughed.

Zora was away. She charged, moving in a flash, and appeared for just a moment where the shallow slash on Ga's ankle started spewing dark, almost black blood on the rocks. The thing didn't even flinch. She ended up standing next to me where she had been.

I smiled over at her. "Now children, what have we learned about the dangers of procrastinating?" She was away again and struck the thing in the same ankle while it chewed on the goat, making pleased mewling noises.

My potion kicked in and the world got brighter. Bright as daylight. I moved to its other ankle, punching it with everything I had. I heard bone crack, but that would take a moment to reach its brain. By the time it did, both Zora and I were gone. The thing roared. Even this time of night and this far out, I was certain someone would hear it. We had maybe ten minutes before the cops showed up.

"If you got something to say you can just come out and say it," Zora said, rushing back in. The troll saw her coming and swiped at her with a large hand. She easily dodged and took off its index and middle fingers.

It looked at its hand in confusion, obviously wondering why it didn't look right. I hit the same ankle again. "*Hydrate*," I growled, and felt every molecule of H_2O surge out of the thing. I had a large ball of water floating around my hand. I couldn't keep it long; maybe a minute before it would disappear and make its way back to the troll. I was fine with giving it back early.

"*On the rocks.*" The old penny appeared in my hand. "*Move!*" I threw it at Ga with enough power behind it that it rivaled a bullet. A large section of his forearm froze solid.

Sometimes magic is so cool!

I was so happy the penny had worked, I let my attention lapse. Ga's arm reversed and headed back for me.

"*Water gun!*" I cried. The water around my hand surged forth and blew a large hole in the troll's forearm, shattering the frozen parts. My boots launched me through the newly made tunnel in its arm and landed in a roll coming up next to Zora. I had hoped that the arm would come off entirely, but I shattered enough of it to slow him down.

"Kill you, half rot!" Ga bellowed. It may have been a shriek, but when you're that far into bass drum range…

"Seriously, how reliable was this info?" I said. "This guy was on deer last year maybe. He's probably chomping on elephants by now." I laughed.

"Yeah, I'm gonna have a long talk with Brian after this. Still, no reason to complain," she said and rushed in again. This time she took off the rest of its left hand. I went in just as the pain registered. Ga roared, holding the bloody stump of its left arm with the half-frozen torn up ruins of its right. I clicked my heels once and jumped high enough to get level with his throat.

"*Solid!*" I screamed. As loud as I yelled, I could barely hear myself over the din. The chill of the universe reclaiming its power was as deep and uncomfortable as ever. I threw as much energy as I dared into the spell. This fight was far from over. The troll's vocal chords seized up and left us all in relative silence. Likely, a lot of its blood had as well. I landed softly thanks to my jacket, and was yards away by the time the Ga's foot made a crater where I'd been standing.

"Thanks," Zora said. "So loud I couldn't hear myself cut things." She ran in, scoring a trivial hit on its leg. I came in on the same side.

"*Salt*," I growled as I passed. The black blood seeping from the wound clotted and turned a lighter shade as the salt in its body collected at the site. Deep cuts hurt. Salt makes them burn and sting and causes even more of a distraction. We couldn't get to its head and end this unless it was distracted.

On the other hand, Ga only had to land two hits, and this fight was over. Shadow potions and Zora's speed were making that difficult.

It tried to roar again and the sound died before it began. Probably would've been "Ga angry," or "Ga smash!" Either way, I assumed I wasn't missing any intelligent commentary.

"Well let's see," I said. "Ga the troll is out here offering us kool-aid so that we can go to goat heaven, and it's more than twice the size we assumed it would be. For what reason should I *not* be complaining?"

"These are fair points." She blurred to the opposite side this time and stabbed Ga in the hip, leaving the sword there. She was back in a flash. "I think you should console yourself with warm thoughts about how much fun I'm having." When the beast went to cover the area in pain, it slammed the sword much deeper into its flesh.

Zora was there again. She grabbed the hilt and savagely ripped it out, taking a chunk of Ga's hip with it. With so much attention on its right side, I went left.

"*Solid*." This was on its thigh. Trolls were essentially built like humans, and I'd just plugged a major artery. Plug up enough of them, and you get a heart attack. Maybe I should've named the spell cholesterol, or triple bypass.

I was back with Zora again. Ga was down on his right knee and spraying blood everywhere from his ruined stump of hand and many cuts. The only thing that smelled worse than human carnage was troll carnage.

We moved at the same time. Zora went between his legs, ignoring the obvious target, and sliced at his spine. It took a moment to register pain, but motor control worked right on time. He jerked around to swipe at her and I heard the scored bone crack like a stick bent too far over my knee. That is, if the stick were the size of an oak tree.

I struck just in time for Ga's vocals to come back. "*Burn*," I said, and the familiar orange potion fell into my hand. "*Breezy.*" I shoved the orange bottle as far as I could up Ga's nose. To that, he reacted immediately, screaming from the pain in his back. He swatted at me. Too late.

I slammed the next bottle just inside his nostril. The air expanded as violently as ever, blowing me backward and away from Ga's strike; blowing Ga backward and bending his back in a way that it couldn't afford to bend. Most of the air went up his nose, slamming the fire potion up and through all the soft flesh in the troll's nasal cavity.

Ga was soon trying to scream from pain he couldn't ease. It was too much, even for his voice. His whole head caught fire almost immediately. All that flesh igniting like tinder. It must suck being flammable.

Ga's final strike snagged on my coat and sent me flying. I hit the ground hard. Not hard enough to break anything, though I couldn't call it comfortable. And that he'd done with just a fingernail.

Zora was there before I stopped tumbling, standing between me and Ga. Her sword was dripping with black, repulsive smelling blood. I took my time getting to my feet, and by the time I did, Ga was dead. We both watched the troll burn for a moment before I spoke.

"So… When does this fun actually start?"

Chapter: 17

Zora practically danced back into Miles' diner. Miles was behind the grill with something in the deep fryer, making the place into a southern food lover's paradise.

"Excuse me, Sir," Zora said knocking on the screen door. "Do you have a few moments to talk about the church of Ga." Miles gave her a confused look as we walked in, but said nothing. He had way too many grandchildren to fall for that.

"If you do have a moment, you'll be sorry you used it," I said. "Lots of hell, bad breath, you'll feel like an idiot working for that idiot, and sporadic court battles since, like Santeria, it requires the occasional goat," I laughed. I walked down to my normal stool and had a beer in front of me before my butt touched it.

"Blasphemer!" Zora yelled.

"The church of Miles has beer," I said, smiling at her and taking a long pull. "Just sayin."

Zora looked between Miles and me. "You're both irredeemable heathens, but that does not relieve you of your obligations, old man. Now feed me or I'll turn into a giant plant and take over the world."

We were eating fried chicken, green beans, and potato salad

so good that it must've been made by Jesus himself. Take that Ga. Zora was hungry as always, finishing off her third plate by the time I was done with one. I went for seconds on chicken and potato salad.

Didn't take more than an hour before I was brooding again. It had been nice to go out, do a job and have everything work out ok. I didn't think I'd get out of this situation with Blackstar as cleanly.

"Hello Sir. Come in and be welcome," Miles proclaimed. I smirked. At least someone was in a good mood. He talked like he was in a Monty Python skit. I turned on my stool and flinched. I prayed it came across as disgust and not the fear I was actually feeling.

The man at the door was wearing black jeans, a shirt the color of blood and had blood still around his mouth from his last feeding. He moved with a kind of grace that was otherworldly, and his eyes weren't quite human. Let's be honest: G.Q. models would have no business in this neighborhood. It was obvious what he was.

The vampire smiled a predatory grin, took a step forward and then stopped dead.

I looked over my shoulder and saw Miles holding a shotgun on the thing.

"I got six guns behind this counter filled with shells dipped in holy water that I pray over every morning. You behave yourself now." Miles had a way of talking to everyone like a misbehaving grandchild. As far he was concerned, most people were exactly that.

He also maintained one of the most formidable thresholds I'd ever seen. That shouldn't have fazed the vamp since Miles had invited it in, but the look on its face said it wouldn't enter even if we'd all slit our wrists and offered it a drink. It backed out of the doorway with a jerk, keeping itself to the far side of the threshold.

I checked my fear. One vamp versus Zora and I? And on our

home turf? With a shotgun-wielding former soldier who hadn't lost a step? We had the advantage here.

I choked down my fear only to have it rise again with the idea that it was Zora, Miles, and I versus one vamp that I could *see*. There was no guarantee that he'd come alone. Best to remain wary then. Overconfidence would kill me as surely as any vampire.

"No thanks," the monster said in a soprano that belied his size. "Your hospitality is appreciated, but I cannot stay. I am only to deliver a message to the one named Maker."

Zora didn't miss a beat. "Leave, leech before I tear out your blood sack and—"

"Zora," I said as polite and stoic as I could manage in the presence of a vampire. "Kill him or don't. There's no cause for rudeness."

Zora backed down. It was an act we'd come up with long ago—done it a million times and it still managed to keep predators off balance. They wondered who the bigger threat was, if they didn't know for certain it was less likely they would attack.

I turned to the vamp and looked through it. I didn't want to meet the eyes of another vampire; one had been quite enough.

"Deliver your message," I said, in a commanding voice. I hoped it sounded commanding, at least. The vampire bowed and fished an envelope out of its pocket. It was red, nice paper, expensive. Like "something someone would use for a wedding" type of expensive.

I fished in my pocket for a pair of gloves as I moved to the door, careful not to get between Miles and the vampire.

I made a show of putting on my leather gloves before taking it, which upset the vamp. I snatched it away, pretending I didn't care, and turned my back so it couldn't see my face as I broke the wax seal.

Showing your back to a vampire was a good way to get your neck broken. I could feel the malice from the creature, but no one in Vermillion Falls knew how weak I was. There was a rumor there that I was estranged from the Martinet. I'd never refuted their assumption.

The red envelope went on the floor. The letter inside was written in a flowing, yet simple script. Bright red on white paper. I didn't want to think about what that ink might contain.

Maker,

I desire a meeting one hour before dawn at the place of your choosing. Safe conduct is assured for the duration of our meeting.

-D

I didn't need to ask who D was. This was interesting. The place of my choosing? Safe conduct?! I'd have to be some kind of moron to think Duke was on the up and up. He'd take the opportunity to kill me if I gave him one, no matter what he said.

The biggest question is, why now? There's no way he could suspect me for the ankh, was there? Refusal would be like sending up a flare, saying that I needed a much closer look.

"Hemlock Bluffs in Cary. It's quite beautiful at sunrise." I said with a dismissive wave. "I'll bring one aide, so he may also bring one." The vampire bowed again, smiling. I wanted to knock out every one of those perfect teeth. "I will offer no safe conduct from here." Judging by the vampire's reaction, that was at least as good as a punch in the gut.

"But—"

"No!" I snapped. Zora completed the threat by producing her sword from nowhere. "If Duke wants a guarantee, that means he has something to say that he knows I'm not going to like. I'm also not stupid enough to believe words on paper." I ripped the invitation in two, and with a surge of power, I got it flaming and threw it at the vamp's feet. He didn't recoil, but the effect it had on him was obvious. He was even more confused about this mortal sorcerer. That was good.

Where Duke was concerned, I was sure I still only had my head because of bluffing, bluster, and luck. If he knew how weak I was, he'd have a field day finding new and inventive ways to kill me.

People tend to give predators a lot of credit. They deserve most of it, since their day job is murder. Vampires were certainly predators, but predators attacked the weak, the slow, and the old. When confronted with a large healthy chunk of prey, they tended to throw it in and go find an easier mark. When that wasn't an option, they would circle and harass, looking for a weakness to exploit.

I'd never shown Duke a weakness. He had no clue what my soft targets were, and like any good water buffalo, I worked hard to keep it that way.

The vamp showed his fangs and growled for a long moment. I returned to my stool and took a bite of food, chewing slowly.

"Unless there's something else?" I asked without looking back.

"I will ensure that my Master receives your reply." It spoke in a voice that communicated with no uncertainty how badly he wanted me dead.

"Good boy. Now run along. Zora, if our guest hasn't left in five seconds, show him on his way."

Zora started walking towards the vampire right away, but he was gone the moment the last word was out of my mouth. It wasn't good to let the bad guy have the last word. I had no proof of this in either direction. It just seemed right.

Once he was gone, Zora was staring daggers.

"Y'all need to learn to be more polite." Miles laughed. Giggle just didn't apply to someone that old.

"Why'd you agree?" She growled. No giggling there.

"Because Duke isn't stupid," I said. "He'd get suspicious if I'd said no. We'd be swimming in ferals then. Even if he isn't suspicious, there's no way to tell how he'd deal with the insult. That may be just what he needs to rationalize killing us. The only reason he hasn't hunted us down already is because we play ball. We can't afford to cross him. Not that blatantly at least."

Zora didn't answer. Rolling over for monsters, even when strategically advantageous, was not her forte.

"Why Hemlock? It's a death trap." Ahh, switching tactics.

"Now you're just being difficult. What's wrong with you lately?!"

"Me?! You're the one who just agreed to meet the oldest vampire we know in the middle of the darkest part of the hundred acre woods. I don't think he's coming to try the honey."

"Well Eeyore, did you forget there's a river right there? We can lie at the bottom for an hour until he gets bored and goes home. Barring that, there's a golf course right across the street. No trees, no shade—we can retreat there if needed and run around in circles until the sun comes up. We're gonna have to agree to safe conduct when we get there to even *have* a meeting in the first place, and that's no laughing matter—even if he does have a way around it. Also, we have Neka now. He'll certainly want to go, since it might have something to do with stopping Blackstar."

"That's not a good plan," she growled.

"No, it isn't," I sighed "but it is the best one." I was frustrated enough to chew rocks over how often in my life the best plan was still well into the realm of incredibly stupid. "Anything interesting on the tooth?" I said, changing the subject. She'd asked for a few days to run experiments on the tooth. She'd had it the entire week.

"Yeah, damn hydra never flossed a day in its life," she said, getting up and stalking upstairs.

Miles was giggling. Maybe it did apply. "What'd you do now?"

"I don't know," I shrugged. "She's been like that all week. Maybe even earlier. She's just been irritable lately."

"Yeah, I noticed too. She's been off. You should talk to her about it." I just glared. Warlocks trying to kill me. A vampire that might know I just stole from him, and no current back up. I was not gonna add hand holding Zora to that mix.

"It'll have to wait. She's a big girl."

"Doesn't matter how big she is," Miles said, sliding the shotgun back in its place behind the bar. "It does bother me that you still don't seem to get it though."

"Get what?" I asked.

Miles sighed. "You're the leader, son. She relies on you, and you don't seem to see that."

"Of course I see that," I said. "She's my apprentice."

Miles smirked. "Nah, I think it goes a little deeper than that. A long time ago I had a guy in my unit. Jensen was his name. Damn bastard didn't have the impulse control god gave a squirrel, but he'd follow orders. When someone's world has been garbage long enough, all their thoughts and behaviors are garbage too. Now, if you're smart, then at some point you start to question everything you think and feel. You start to look at *yourself* with suspicion. Now, that's the beginning of wisdom, but it can also drive ya nuts. Jensen didn't know the right things to do; he just knew that everything *he* wanted to do was garbage. So, at the end of the day, he used the military to sort the healthy things from the unhealthy things."

"Jensen sounds all kind of messed up," I said.

Miles chuckled and shook his head like I'd just said the dumbest thing in the world. "Oh yeah, because you two are the gold standard of mental health."

"Neither of us are doing *that*," I said.

"Only two types of people come out of wars, Maker; emotionally ravaged casualties and corpses. Sorting bodies into those two categories is what wars *do*." He said it in a manner so simple and nonchalant. For me, it was like a kick in the nuts and a slap in the face; all rolled into one. For some reason, I started to feel a little sick.

He leaned back with his arms crossed and smiled wide. Just another emotionally ravaged casualty. "I figure between the two of you I might be able to cobble together a decent human being."

I launched to my feet and seized a few billion electrons to make a spark between my thumb and index finger. "I'll fry your ass, old man!"

Miles laughed so hard he doubled over for a moment. "Go ahead. All the lightning in the world ain't gon' make me wrong." Miles went back to making dinner though, like most times, there was no one here.

"You're lucky you're the only place that won't card me," I grumbled as I sat down. Miles huffed another laugh and produced a beer from the mini fridge behind the bar. I gave him a pointed look on my first sip, though he was still chuckling at my not-quite-idle threat. I drank and tried to think.

He was right that Zora didn't conceal her emotion well. She could be out not killing vamps all day, but she could never hide being mad about it. Second was her need for violence; her propensity to start a fight when monsters were involved was that of the average kindergartener. Maybe a first grader on a good day.

She was reliable. I had bet my life on that several hundred times by now. She would always do what was needed. She would just be angry, bloodthirsty, and snarky while she did it.

As always, Miles was right. Stupid surrogate grandfathers.

That insight didn't tell me what the current problem was though. It was entirely possible that she was still upset about being seasick, kill stealing the vamps that had cornered her on the boat, my asking about the tooth, or the fact that I was nervous about it. To be honest, I had nightmares about her finding dumb things to do with it, each one more reckless and ridiculous than the last. She could also be upset about something that had nothing to do with any of that.

I'm stoic, and I know it. I just don't have a wide array of emotional responses. Angry, happy, sad, scared. Like meat and vegetables. Strictly speaking, you don't need anything else. I had far less than the average man; Zora had more than the average woman. Zora and I had been at war with every kind of monster for the last four years. Emotionally ravaged casualties, indeed.

Know thyself, that was rule one, and I couldn't believe that Zora had abandoned it. Even if she were a puppet to her emotions, like me, she had always worked to see the strings.

"Dammit," I whispered and marched upstairs. Business first.

Neka had rented the apartment right across from Zora's.

"Neka, you here?" I called from the door.

"Back here," he called from the bedroom. I walked in, and he was sitting on the floor, meditating as always.

"One of Duke's vamps just stopped by to set up a meet. I don't know what he wants to talk about, but it's conceivable that it has something to do with Blackstar. When we get there, Duke will demand safe conduct and I'll have to agree if I wanna have the talk. Because of that, I can't tell you what to do because that might make you subject to the agreement."

"So it will or it won't?" He asked, never opening his eyes.

"I don't know." I shrugged. "I never learned all the details, so I can't tell you. What I can tell you is that Zora and I will be meeting with Duke at Hemlock Bluffs in Cary an hour before sunrise. Do what you will with that information." I smiled.

He huffed a laugh and flew out of there—literally. He turned into a giant owl and flew out the window. Odd how quickly I'd gotten used to that.

Zora was across the hall, and I walked into her apartment without knocking. She was sitting on her bed facing away from me. She wiped her face on her shirt, and I pretended not to notice. There was a large long thing wrapped in cloth across her lap.

"You're volatile. What's up?" I said.

"Nightmares about the boat. Tasha. No sleep. Nightmares about you dying. More no sleep. These damn hours." She shook her head. "I'm trapped in the world between expensive caffeine drinks and sleeping pills. All the while being scared out of my mind because this damn tooth has a mind of its own. Finally, to put the frosting on this cake, you're making deals with Vermillion Falls instead of killing them all." It certainly didn't help that she was right. This meeting was a fancy decorated invitation just begging for trouble to RSVP.

"Nightmares are par for the course—we're wizards. Tasha has been avenged as far as we're willing to go. Even if we could exterminate Vermillion Falls, it wouldn't bring her back." She nodded her head at each fact as if she had been saying them to herself. It wasn't the first time we'd done this—or something like it—when one of us was about to lose it. Having to be occasionally reminded of what was important came with being human. Just another reality of life.

"These hours suck. They're temporary," I continued. "You only think you're scared," I laughed. "I'd almost pissed myself when that bastard showed up downstairs, and if we ever decide not to deal with Vermillion Falls, then Duke will have us killed or turned. Now, what do you mean the tooth has a mind of its own?"

"It has a will. It's so weak it's almost imperceptible, but it's persistent. I imagine it's like the one ring, except that instead of doing something useful like turning me invisible, or convincing me to walk into Mordor with a bunch of small hairy people, it just wants to be soaked in blood all the time. See for yourself." She tossed me the cloth, and I fumbled, dropping the thing. It had the thickest part thinned and elongated into a hilt with an intricate pommel. The rest still looked like a long, serrated tooth. I picked it up and felt something faint but undeniable. Like an extra presence in my head that was mute.

Zora pricked her finger on the needle-like point and the presence let out a pleasurable sigh. It was the oddest thing. I'd picked up artifacts on occasion. Sometimes they are so powerful that they have a form of sentience. A will of their own. Their focus was always narrow; always trying to get you to do something that corresponded to their purpose. A demon artifact was always trying to trick you into opening a gateway to hell, for example. This thing didn't care what happened. Apathy was what I felt, and it was coming off the thing in tidal waves.

"What's your phrase?" She asked. It was a research trick we'd worked out to help determine what something was. It worked well for items that had a will of their own because they never seemed to say the same thing to different practitioners.

"Emphatic apathy," I said. She nodded.

"Figures. In that case, I want this as my share of the loot," she said, nodding to it. "My phrase is 'Blood, flesh, and we'll get along fine.'"

"If it has blood, so much the better. If not, then it has a dragon's patience?" I said.

"Oh, but it gets better," Zora said, wiping her bloody finger down the length. The tooth soaked up the blood almost as fast as she wiped. I felt like I just had two cups of coffee. "How's that feel?" I didn't say anything; I was still staring in wonder at the thing.

"It's the perfect vamp killer." Drink blood, gain the blood's power and not exert any credible will otherwise.

"Perfect *anything* killer. I get stronger with each cut. They get weaker. Now, the million-dollar question: why does Duke want it?"

"Good question. Wish I had the answer. None of this makes sense," I said. The tooth made my skin crawl. Maybe it was holding that much power at once. Zora didn't seem entirely comfortable either. "Duke may want it to kill some rival or give it away to another vamp for points. It's a little simple for him, but I could live with that if I had to. What's the ankh for? What would he want to imprison? And why the hell was the ship out there for so long? We also have to consider what Blackstar would do with any of this. This thing makes my skull rattle, and I can't even touch the ankh to study it. Just having it in my pack feels like a knife between my shoulder blades. Why would Blackstar want it?"

"Uhh, powerful?"

"Come on Zora, think. The ankh has a purpose; it does one thing only. I can't imagine anyone who constructed a super-prison would leave it vulnerable to anything that wanted to siphon off its power for something else. This tooth has a will of its own. I doubt it would *let* anyone siphon off power for anything that didn't end with it 'soaked in blood.' These two things at least, have to be used for what they were intended."

"Maybe Blackstar wants to imprison whatever he was trying to summon."

"Maybe," I said, "but if that's the case, why summon it? Why summon something so powerful you need an ankh to control it? That's suicidal. That's like saying you can control a tank and all you need is twenty sticks of lit dynamite. It might work, but either way it ends badly for you. Besides, I've never read anything that makes me think an ankh grants you influence. It's just a holding tank. I can't imagine that it's a revolving door you can just let beings in and out of either. Like any prison, it's probably easy to get things in and hard to get things out. That leaves you in a position trying to blackmail a powerful entity with threats of locking them in it. Don't need Rania to see how that one ends."

"He could've been after something else. The feather rug, the staff thing, or something."

I sighed. "Can't say for certain cause I haven't had time to study anything, but my instincts say no." We both stood there contemplating for nearly a minute. Zora broke the silence.

"Well, I'm drawing a blank," she said, sitting back on the bed. "And since I've slept maybe twenty of the last two hundred hours, you're on your own figuring it out."

I sighed again. I didn't know enough. I kept feeling like I was walking around blind. You'd think I'd be used to it by now.

"Wait, why does it have a pommel?" I asked. The accusation in my voice was mild. I think.

"Because it's forming itself into some weird, twisted, replica of my katana. Shouldn't have left it on the bed when I was asleep. Maybe it saw a few dreams or stray thoughts or something. Maybe that means it likes me."

"You must have a way with dragons," I said. We both grunted a laugh, hoping it wasn't true. "Earlier you said hydra."

"Yeah, the hydra." She yawned, more exhausted than I've ever seen her.

"Who are the hydra?"

"Not the hydra. THE Hydra."

I gasped in horror and threw the thing across the room. I had sudden images of a five-headed beast rearing up and tearing me limb from limb. Zora only smiled a wry smile before laughing.

"Ya know, that's exactly what I said."

Chapter: 18

"That thing is from the Hydra? Greek legend? Founded Athens? Slain by Heracles? THAT Hydra?!"

"You only think you're scared," Zora said, smiling even bigger. "I've been sleeping with it in the same room for days. Now ask me why my dummy's been kicking my ass."

"That may be even more powerful than the ankh."

"Doubt it." She said. "I don't think it's even intelligent as such. I mean, it has a purpose, that's obvious, but it doesn't have the power to influence anything. If the Hydra had its mind somehow imprinted, that would be a different story. This is just a piece of it, and since the thing had so many heads, and by extension teeth, it's not even a very important piece. I was terrified before I started thinking through it. Think about it, what would one of your teeth say if it could talk?"

I thought about that for a moment. "Probably, 'There isn't a meal happening. I'm bored. When is the next meal happening? I'm bored. Why not floss for once in your life?' I guess it would sound like a hungry insistent child or a frustrated dentist."

"Right. I'm not certain, of course, and you'll have to keep an eye on me for a while, but it makes more sense if it's just a tooth from a powerful monster and not the infinity stone of hunger." She shrugged. We were still standing there, staring at the thing where I'd tossed it in the corner, waiting for it to grow a few new heads and kill us.

"Why does that explain why your dummy is so much stronger?" I asked her.

"Because my dummy knows everything in my head. Even things I've forgotten. Even things that *I* don't actually know. How many swordsmen do you think the hydra ate? How much expert swordplay did that tooth have a front row seat for? Because I don't think it was eating many amateurs. If you got to the peak of your sword-slinging back in those days, killing the Hydra would be the next logical step. It'd be like winning the lottery."

I sat and thought through that for a moment. It made sense—which was more than I could say for most of this so far.

"Would it help to talk through the ankh?" She asked.

"No, the ankh is an infinity stone. It started whispering the moment I took it out to look at it. I can't even say for certain if it's empty. Even if it is, there are still impressions of powerful beings left in it. Don't get me started on the splitting headache. The next time I touch that thing, we'll be in Hawaii. It can sit in my pack and rot until then."

"So, drop it in a volcano if you start calling it precious. Got it." She said.

"It'd be nice. With Blueboy's undead goblin generator, the fanatics last year, now this… At this rate we're going to have to make another run next year."

"Maker, as much as I love nude, black sand beaches, it would be really nice if we occasionally kept a few of these uber powerful would be weapons." I looked at her and opened my mouth, but she continued. "Yeah, yeah, hunted down by demons. Minor gods actually giving a shit who we are. Better to just trash things and not ask questions. I get it. Hell, I agree. What I'm saying is one day we're gonna toss the wrong thing in Mauna Loa and really piss something off. *Destroying it* will be what gets us noticed, and we just threw our best hope of defense to a fiery grave." She was right of course. We had made two trips to Hawaii in the last five years. Pretty soon someone would notice. I just shrugged.

"Cross that bridge when we come to it," I sighed. "The tooth needs to go in too. It's way too powerful to be loot."

"Really?" She smiled. She got up and grabbed it from the floor. "What tooth?" The moment her hand touched it, the flow of power from it disappeared.

Magical tools were always taking in energy or radiating it. Absorbing power in one form, converting it to something else and releasing it again was what magical tools *did*. Wizards too. That's why any wizard could pick up on whether something was magical or not.

The tooth was like a heat source. Zora picking it up was like lying on a beach and feeling the sun set in half a second. Walking around with a magical super weapon was a terrible idea. Unless that weapon hid itself when it was being wielded.

"Well, isn't that handy," I said. Zora smiled. "Fine. It's yours." I sighed. I had a feeling I'd regret this. "I'm gonna go off and patrol. Get some sleep, and for now, sleep with that thing a few rooms away."

"Don't think that'll work." She yawned again. "First night I was researching it and fell asleep with the damn thing on the bed. Had a dream I was slaughtering an entire village of people wearing rags and togas. Took ten minutes of brushing to get the taste of blood out of my mouth. Haven't slept since."

"As curses go that doesn't sound too bad," I said.

"Speak for yourself. Miles had to make my steak well done yesterday. He made it rare and I almost puked."

"Maybe more than a few rooms away." I said. "See if it eases any with distance. If not, we'll have to build another circle to keep it in."

"Way ahead of you," she yawned. "Tried the silver ring and it didn't work. Still had a nightmare, so I got together everything I needed for a better one—it's all upstairs now. If that doesn't work, then I'm heading to Hawaii early. Only thing I still need is the gold. Gonna need a buttload of it and all I have now is a few grams of impure slag."

"Dammit," I sighed. "Add it to the list I guess."

"Add it to the top," she said with another yawn. "I can't sleep more than thirty minutes at a time, and it's making me crazy already. Not sure where we're gonna get three kilos of gold, but I have a plan." She grinned. "First, you sell everything you own, then I sell everything I own. We use it to buy a few high-end, designer speedos and you get a job as a stripper. Soon you'll have a bit of notoriety, gained through some high production value web performances. Once that happens, we schedule a show at Ft. Knox for the USO and invite all the female soldiers who guard the gold depository. Then you—"

"We'll figure something out," I interrupted. "Preferably something that doesn't involve massive amounts of attention, stripping, whoring me out, or turning into Jesse James."

Her smile disappeared. "How come you never like my ideas?"

I didn't answer, just laughed and walked out.

Gaining magical power or knowledge was never free. The consequences were always hard on someone. There was no way to tell how it would affect someone before it did. Nightmares, warts and boils, weird birthmarks and hair loss were all pretty common.

I summoned every wake up special I had and left them on her kitchen counter. They would be a bandage on a broken leg—nothing I knew of could entirely replace sleep.

I left, heading down the stairs and once again turning my attention to Constellation matters.

The disk from Blackstar's safe was a twin to the one on the ship. I hadn't made time to fully study them, but my initial inspection suggested they were like magical cell phones. I had Blackstar's when he raided the boat, so he couldn't have known what happened on it that way. At least now I knew why he'd known about the shipment in the first place, but that didn't answer who put the other on the boat or why the boat had been at sea so long.

I was expecting warts any day now.

I shoved down the thought of Blackstar curled in a ball on the floor with Shroud mercilessly kicking him in the face. He took the beating well, then took the frustration out on me when I started cracking jokes about it. The full body ache that went along with remembering was a little harder to dispel. As I reached the kitchen, Miles was reading yesterday's paper for the third or fourth time.

I didn't say anything as I passed. It was time to go to work.

The clock on the dash of my truck read 0126 when I climbed in. My truck was a matte black Toyota Hilux, and it was practically indestructible. Some guys in England dumped one in the ocean, threw it off a twenty story building, set it on fire and it still started with no spare parts.

Once I learned about that I knew it was the truck for me. It lived up to its indestructible reputation—as long as whatever trashed it wasn't supernatural. I had replaced the windows with something bulletproof, geared down the transmission to get off the line like a superbike, installed a remote driving system that Zora and I had designed, but other than that it was dealer specs, and I had put it through hell.

I'd replaced the speakers as well.

Eminem came blaring out as the Hilux roared to life. Damn right I'm phenomenal. I revved the engine a couple times before I peeled out. The agenda for the night was to find Blackstar. Rather, look for Blackstar and make sure he wasn't out looking for me.

We hadn't heard a peep out of the Constellation and that had me nervous enough to brave the possibility of actually finding them.

I drove around to each of my labs, reached out with my magical senses and didn't feel anything out of the ordinary. All that meant was that no one had left me an unpleasant message in the form of a large and conspicuous magical something.

Next, I checked Blackstar's last two hideouts. Nothing. I was heading back from their lake hideout, thinking of a few dark alleys where I could maybe get some answers when a stag ran up to the side of the road.

In rural North Carolina this was not a big deal, but this was a caribou; a reindeer. A little too far south to be put here by mother nature… by about two thousand miles. It was ill-formed; its front legs shorter than its rear ones. One of the rear legs was far thicker than the other. The fur was hard and matted in places, and missing in others. It looked like the deer equivalent of mange.

I stopped the truck and got out. I had my staff in one hand and my pistol in the other. My pack was on the passenger seat close enough to call something if needed. The ankh was safely inside behind every obfuscation and magical trap I could dream up in the past week.

I was on highway 64, heading back into the city. I had walked this road after the nine days of torture, and I was more than a little on edge. There was enough traffic that they couldn't easily hide, yet more than enough to cause a ruckus if I started slinging spells around. Not a good spot for me.

The deer changed back into a human. Now that I had seen Neka do it so many times, the difference was night and day. It jerked and twitched. Its joints popped and its bones cracked. It took nearly a whole minute for the screaming woman to emerge. The longest it ever took Neka was a second or two.

I paid attention to my surroundings while I watched her change. This was either me getting lucky or me walking into a trap—and luck just wasn't in the cards lately. One way or another, I felt sure I was about to find out where Blackstar was.

The woman was crying in pain, and her fingers were crooked like they had been broken and healed wrong. She didn't stand; just laid there whimpering. It took a moment before I realized she was uttering words. I wasn't going to get near her.

"Speak louder. I can't hear you," I said, not wanting to get more than a few steps from my truck.

"P… please… help me." She spoke like she had trouble forming the words.

"Help with what?" I said, still watching the woods. I had several nasty spells ready to delay anyone long enough for me to make it back to my truck. From there I could hit the auto drive and peel out, shooting and throwing spells at whoever had come to spring this trap.

"It hurts. Please, it hurts," her words sounded as jerky and pained as her transformation looked. I was still waiting for the act to be over and the curtain to fall on an ambush.

None of this made sense, and I wanted it to. That need was keeping me here, waiting for an explanation.

"If I agree to help you, do you swear on your power that you will perform no act either word, deed, or omission to cause me harm? Answer all of my questions fully, and ensure my safety for long as you are in my care?" I had dreamed that up in case I ever had to make a deal with someone from Outland or Faerie.

"On my power?" She asked. Her voice wasn't carrying any less pain, but she managed to convey that she had no idea what I meant.

"It means that if you break your word, you lose your magic," I said. That wasn't strictly true, but it wasn't a lie either. Words have power—people give them power. Swearing something on your power was using a bit of that power infused into the words. Break that promise, break that power, and it took forever to come back. If you did it enough times, it would steal away all your magic.

The promise of safe conduct was like that as well, but there were way too many loopholes in that oath for my tastes. She managed to gulp.

"Will you help me?"

"On my power. If you give your word, I will do everything I can within good conscience to help you or release you with no physical harm from me if I cannot." Of course, I could just let Zora harm her, but the oath seemed to cover me and anyone I saw as being under my authority. Those ancient gods had thought of everything.

She completed the vow—word for word, in a jerky pained voice—and I told her to get in the truck. That didn't mean I trusted her. I put my staff back in baton form and kept my gun out. I climbed into the driver's seat and held my pistol in my lap pointed at her. Even with an oath, there was no way I was gonna turn my back on a warlock.

With a trickle of power, my truck lurched into motion and drove itself to my southern lab while I stared and shivered and she huddled up with her knees to her chest. There weren't many cars on the road this late, and the few that were never got close enough to realize I didn't have my hands on the wheel.

I didn't speak on the twenty-minute trek, and neither did she. I held my staff in my other hand and studied her.

She was older than me, mid-thirties, early-forties maybe. She had shoulder length brown hair, brown eyes and hard features. They may have been softer once; she looked like she had missed a few meals recently. Her clothes were rags, and they hung off of her. She shivered as we drove and it had nothing to do with the wind or the night cold. She didn't look at me once, just curled up in a ball and cried. I don't think there were any actual tears, but her body moved as if she were sobbing.

We arrived at my lab, and she wiped her dirty face and climbed out slowly. My wards were up, which was good, but I still had her walk in front of me. Motioning with the gun for her to move along, I grabbed my pack out of the cab.

"If I gave my word, then why do you need the gun?" She asked.

"Yeah," I shrugged. "You gave your word, but that doesn't mean you won't break it. Sure, it will cost you your magic, but there are people I wanna kill bad enough that it would be worth it. Why would you be any different?" She didn't answer, just walked inside. I was expecting a trap. I was expecting Blackstar to be waiting inside on a recliner, stroking a white cat like a James Bond villain.

Like my other labs, this one was a just a large room in an old industrial building. There were only a few people on cots and a hot pot full of a few gallons of soup on a table by the stairs—just like there should be. I holstered my pistol, but I didn't let my guard down. One of those few people had tried to kill me some weeks ago. The scorch marks were still on the walls

The only thing out of place spoke up immediately. A girl about sixteen or so. She had slightly wavy brown hair to the middle of her back and bright blue eyes behind a pair of glasses. Her clothes were baggy. Jeans that were too big, and a t-shirt that would be large on me.

"Are you Maker?" She asked.

"This late, I'm no one. Who are you?" I said. I didn't have any animosity towards her at all, but these meetings tended to go a lot smoother when I got them off guard right away.

"Kristen… Umm… Madeline Taylor told me that I should—"

"Yup. Come upstairs," I said, and nodded to the warlock to move along.

We got up to my office, and I closed the door behind them. It occurred to me then that I was putting Kristen in danger, and I gripped my staff. Best to get this over with quickly.

"What can I do for you, Kristy?" I said, sitting on my desk. The warlock went to the opposite side of the room and sat down on the floor, curled into a ball and watched. She was clearly still in pain, and just as obviously, not as much. Even from the fetal position in the far corner, she made me a little nervous.

Kristen eyed her for a bit before she turned to me and spoke. "Umm… so prom is coming up, and there's a guy I want to ask. He's on the basketball team though and—"

"Ok stop," I said. "You want to ask him to the prom, you just need the nerve right?"

"Yeah," she nodded. "I mean, what if he says no?"

"Why wouldn't he say yes?"

"Umm…" She looked down, "Well, he's out of my league. That's what all my friends say, at least. I'm not very pretty like some of the other girls, and I'm not really, like, all that popular."

"Hmm, well I could give you a potion like the one I gave Maddy that would make you very charismatic for an hour, but that wouldn't work. You would ask, and he would say yes, but the prom is a couple months away right?" She nodded. "You might screw it up and get clingy or something before then. He'll stick your ass right back in the friend zone."

Her face sank. It was downright tragic how pathetic this girl had convinced herself she was. Out of my league is just code for "I'm scared this person is better than me," or "I don't think I'm good enough." In reality, she was quite attractive. A teenage boy could get lost in those eyes, spend hours running his fingers through all that hair. The only reason she wore those baggy clothes was because she was ashamed of a body that most women would kill for. Sigh, teenagers.

Sure, I was only a few years from my teens, but when I was her age I was living on the street killing vampires in hopes they had enough cash on them to feed me that day.

I smiled suddenly. All the masses of problems in the world that she knew nothing about. Maybe that meant I was doing a good job.

"Well Kristen, I think I can still help. I have kind of a makeover potion. It'll take a few weeks to work fully, but it should do the job. You're gonna find that you're smarter in class, and that you work harder for your grades. In a week or two, you're going to be feeling more confident than you ever have. You'll be wearing nicer clothes, reading makeup blogs, practicing your smiles in the mirror, and generally driving every boy around you crazy. I can't promise that Mr. Basketball will say yes when you ask him, but by the end of the month you'll be able to have any guy you want anyway. Sound good?"

She was nodding enthusiastically, like I'd just asked if she wanted a pony for Christmas.

"*Makeover.*" I held out my hand and the small glass bottle appeared in it. The liquid in it was viscous and cloudy. It looked like water mixed with a bit of cornstarch, because that's exactly what it was. It had a few trillion extra photons packed in to make the person feel like something just happened, but there was no spell involved.

There was nothing wrong in Kristen's life that a tiny dose of good ol' fashioned, nose in the air snobbiness wouldn't fix. She pulled the cork and drank it down. People didn't normally get that excited, but I didn't say anything.

"Thank you so much," she said. "How much is it?"

I told her it was a hundred bucks and she stood up and fished in her pocket for it.

"Feel that tingle?" I asked. She nodded. "You're going to be tingly for a day or two. You're going to do some things you've maybe never done before, but that's all part of the magic. You'll still feel a little nervous and weird, but just try to relax and go with it. It'll feel better after doing it a few days in a row. Now, if you'll excuse me, I have some other things to attend to." She smiled again and went to the door, thanking me the whole way.

"Oh yeah, this potion doesn't affect your libido. Do you want that one too? Mostly I sell it to old men who can't get it up anymore. It'll basically turn you into a horndog for a month or two."

"Umm… no." She giggled.

"Alright, so if you start feeling anything sexual, that's you—not the magic," I laughed.

She giggled a bit with me and left. Didn't need her coming back with complaints and prom night regrets for giving her a glass of water. She left and I put my attention back on the mousey-haired dirty warlock crouched on my floor. She was staring daggers at me.

She got up and sat in the chair Kristen had just vacated. I went and sat behind my desk. I felt better having something large between us.

"How could you do that?" She said.

"Do what?" I replied.

"Give her that. Spells are dangerous, and you just gave her the power to control everyone with what—her feminine wiles? She's gonna grow up thinking that she can solve all her problems with her looks or with some magical shortcut. You're no better than The Constellation."

"Said the power-hungry murdering warlock," I laughed. Felt good to have a real laugh. That put me more at ease. "Our good friend Kristen needed confidence. Nothing more. I gave her confidence, nothing more. The placebo effect works wonders because it's one of the rare times when humans focus. If I had given the potion away for free she might suspect something—even if just subconsciously—and that would ruin everything. Besides, people make fortunes giving other people pep talks. The 'power to control everyone' I gave her was water. Would you like some?" I offered with a big smile. She shook her head, cowed for now. "Good. Now, what do I call you?"

"Carol," she answered simply. I almost laughed again. Carol the warlock. All the other soccer moms kneel and tremble in her presence. If she wasn't shivering, suffering from malnutrition, and nursing a dozen hairline fractures, she might have been dangerous.

"Ok, Carol. What can I do for you?"

"I need another shot." She was rocking back and forth, shivering and rubbing herself as if she still couldn't get warm, despite being inside. What the hell was she talking about? I deal in potions not heroin.

"I don't understand. Why don't you start at when you joined Blackstar and tell me everything you know about him." She looked a little surprised that I knew the name. As if I hadn't been paying attention to the people trying to kill me.

"I joined late last year…" she began, and rambled for nearly an hour before she got to the attack in Durham. It was an interesting look into Blackstar history. Unfortunately, she had only been with him for about six months. She went through their old hideouts, activities in the past and all the warlocks, but she didn't mention Shroud—so I brought it up.

"Tell me about Shroud," I said. She looked at me with a confused expression. "Purple robe, face cloaked in shadow, doesn't speak much."

"Oh, The Blackface." She said. I saw the fear on her face dial up a notch or two and she shifted her feet around as if her chair were suddenly uncomfortable. "I don't know his real name; no one does. He's not a member of The Constellation, but we're all scared of him. He hates all of us and beats up anyone that makes him angry. He almost killed Martha just for not getting out of his way fast enough. I don't know how someone could be that cruel. He killed a wizard named Jennifer a few months ago. She was just as bad as the rest of them, but all she did was ask if he wanted tea. She was screaming for the rest of the night. He's… He's just… evil."

"We're all evil. We're humans," I said. "Why do Blackstar and the others put up with it? If no one liked this Jessica person, then she wouldn't've been there in the first place."

"I don't think they have a choice. I'm not supposed to know that Blackstar takes his orders from Blackface, and I'm certainly not supposed to know how hard he beats them all for failing."

"Sounds like a member of The Constellation to me," I said.

"No, because when they tried to catch you in the woods and you got away, he didn't care. He never told anyone to go out and do that, so it didn't matter to him that everyone came back injured. The next day he sent us to rob that big museum downtown, he killed three people because they were too injured to go, and later on…" She fell into a fit of sobs, hugging her knees to her chest.

There was nothing I could do except wait for it to be over. I had a big box of toilet paper in the corner for the bathroom downstairs and I tossed her a roll once she'd pulled herself together enough to use it.

After she blew her nose a few times, there was even more diarrhea of the mouth and I let her ramble on. I've heard the saying, "If you think your subordinates know twice what they should then you don't know the half." Carol certainly knew more than The Constellation would approve of, but she didn't know what Blackstar was summoning, or who Neka was.

"It took me a week to heal from your attack," she said, with the malice I would expect from someone who I'd dropped a grenade on. "A few were that lucky."

"How many of you lottery winners are there?" I asked.

"Nineteen survived the attack. Five more died after." The number killed in attacking my labs since then brought that number down quite a bit more. I nodded for her to continue.

"The blood they brought us was always warm, alive it was… amazing." She looked right through me like she was somewhere else, no doubt reliving pleasures not meant for sane people.

"After you attacked, the blood was… colder. It didn't keep us going as long; changing was even more painful, and healing takes forever now. The Constellation told us that the Lord of Shapes had forsaken us. They said it was because we hadn't been faithful and that we had to capture you." Her tone said that she didn't think much of that idea.

"Everyone went out looking for you," she continued. "But your labs were always guarded, and you were never there. We began following you to catch you in a weak moment. Everyone assumed we were being punished, but I got blood almost twice as often and each time it was less powerful. I never bought that Lord of Shapes nonsense. Eventually I figured out it was you. Why attack the garage if you didn't want something? I would like some more blood… please."

I sat back and whistled. Now it made slightly more sense. Blackstar took blood out of Neka and injected it into people. His strength had been decreased when I took Neka away. He probably didn't even care about the shapeshifters I'd killed, since he could just make more.

If the injections gave them the power to change shape, then it was a real problem if he was out of blood. What was an evil wizard cult without their lackeys, after all. I suspected he'd kidnapped me and hit my labs so hard because he was looking for some secret that would help him open my pack, but he had been looking for Neka.

"What happened after that? You wouldn't be here if you were still working for Blackstar." She looked at me with a fire that said she'd like to kill me, probably because I just ignored her request for the second time.

"I left when they tried to kill us."

"Ahh, the plot thickens," I said dryly. I had no sympathy for this woman. As far as I was concerned, she was scum. She'd spit on the natural order of things, killed people, caused havoc, and done so casually—like getting coffee on a Tuesday. Even now I couldn't detect a speck of remorse. She was the most abhorrent thing a wizard could be.

"They told us to go get something from a ship, and they could fix us. We all went, even Blackface." The ankh was important enough for Shroud to make an appearance, but it made sense that he sent them onto the boat. Shapeshifters and people like Zora whose spells only buffed themselves weren't as affected by the water. "There were eight of us. The ship was run aground near the coast. There had been a fire, but we looked through the ashes anyway and found nothing. When we reported back to shore they were furious and..." she sniffed, holding back some more tears, "there are three of us left."

So Blackstar had tried to board the boat at sea. They must've launched their little expedition before it got pulled into the harbor. This explained why Blackstar hadn't gotten the ankh, but not why he wanted it in the first place. It also confirmed that the people left screaming at the docks were Constellation goons. Now I had to watch them when they woke up.

"What were you supposed to get off the boat?" I asked.

"I don't know," she snapped. "And I'm not going back out there to look for you. I'm done with all this. I hate you people." She was losing patience with this process, but I couldn't let her run off and tell anyone where she'd been.

I smiled inside at the plan suddenly forming in my head. "I don't need you. I can go look myself." I said.

"No, you can't. The police impounded it. They're probably still crawling all over it," she sneered.

"Dammit!" I said. I shot to my feet and threw my hand up as if to hit her. It shouldn't matter since I was on the other side of a desk, but Carol still flinched. I growled and sat down, but inside I was happy about her reaction. Anger was an easy one to paint on my face. I furrowed my brow, squinted slightly, pressed my lips together tight and lowered my chin.

Using a battered woman's past against her for my own personal gain ranked quite high in the realm of shitty things to do to a person, but I kinda wanted to live long enough for the Martinet to come save me, so I got over it pretty quick. For my plan to work, Carol had to be too scared to think clearly.

"Where's The Constellation now?" I asked.

"They operate out of a farmhouse west of Hillsbourgh." That explains the coordination of that first ambush. The place I ran to was a few miles away. Carol was betrayed by a smug smile. The kind you get from a person who believes they know more than you do. Perfect.

"I'll give you some more blood, provided you do exactly what I tell you." She perked up at first, turning into a low growl when uncertainty was introduced. She wasn't scared enough so I took it as a challenge and jumped to my feet again.

"*Burn!*" The potion appeared in my hand, and I raised my arm to throw it. Carol ducked to the floor, already starting to cry.

"I'm sorry," she screamed, repeating it over and over. "Please! Please, just tell me what you want—I'll do it. I swear!"

I walked around and leaned back against my desk. She couldn't see me with her face on the floor, but I was still making my angry expression. "My conditions are as follows, and spoiler alert: you aren't going to like them."

Chapter: 19

Cary is a suburb of Raleigh. It was jokingly called the Containment Area for Relocated Yankees; it was a nice place, and the housing prices were way less than the New England states. Given that and the great weather, the area was experiencing a boom in the number of northern imports.

Hemlock Bluffs was a small park off the center of the city. It was peaceful, lots of trees, with a few simple trails. There was a deep ravine running through the park; it was just about the least expected thing to find in a city. One of the trails ran right up to it, and you could look down. I didn't get vertigo, but walking down near that cliff was foolish for other reasons.

We both had water breathing potions. Vampires couldn't do running water. Lots of water stole away their powers, and since vamps were all stolen life, it could even kill them.

If needed, we'd drink the potions and sit at the bottom of the creek in the ravine until the sun came up. Duke was no doubt powerful enough that sunlight wouldn't kill him, but daylight made all vamps weaker and gave us a much better chance of getting away.

Despite all the pretty nature, Zora and I were in a clearing near the entrance. She was behind me with her sword on her hip; the tooth was back at her apartment above Miles. I was loaded for bear with practically everything that I could use to keep vamps at a distance.

Exactly one hour before dawn, a man stepped into the clearing. The shadows clung to him as he left, as if they were alive and in pain at his leaving. He didn't seem to notice. He was a shorter man—both Zora and I stood head and shoulders over him. His straight hair was long and black, his eyes were black, his fingernails were painted black. The suit he wore was a matte black and likely cost more than most mortgage payments.

A long time ago he was African, but now his skin was pale and waxy. There were none of the subtle signs that told me I was looking at a human. Between steps, he looked like a corpse or a wax sculpture. Positively unnerving.

"Maker." His voice was as nice as his suit. A rich baritone that made you want to fall on your knees and pay homage. I resisted the magic in it; strong, but intermittent, like standing in the surf and having the whole ocean break over you.

"Turn it off," I growled. Meeting a vampire's eyes was a terrible thing to do, so I didn't. Duke could still affect me because I had met his eyes years before. Theoretically, he could bring me to my knees for the rest of my life, even if I only ever stared at his forehead.

The effect was greatly reduced, yet still nearly overwhelming. Meeting a vampire's eyes was an opportunity to see the world as they saw it: the violence of their life made real. In Duke's mind, all things were both predator and prey, and it was no more nuanced than that. It was a terrible truth, and it rushed into my mind and pervaded every thought.

The next "wave" hit. I could hear the screams of victims long dead. I could feel their blood rushing into my mouth. I felt powerful. I felt like a god culling the weak and passing judgment on the living. Who lived. Who died. It was all up to me. It was majestic.

That was the danger. The promise of power—even just a taste of it. Meeting a vampire's eyes often broke someone. It brought the illusion of society crashing down. That power was seductive; it promised all that and more, and all I would have to do is offer Duke my neck.

I didn't break instantly because I already knew that civilization was a lie—a thin veneer over the chaos beneath. We're animals, every single one of us. We strive to be more than animals, that is to our credit, but for the time being, we battle with being savage. This promised acceptance of that savagery. The ability to run and hunt and kill as I was meant to. That primal desire that lives in all of us, but I have long ago made peace with mine.

"Turn. It. Off." I growled again through my teeth. I was grunting with the effort of resisting as much as from anger. Better men than me have been broken with a lot less. The next wave hit, but I didn't look away. Instead, I pulled up the sleeve on my right arm and grabbed my staff in my left, snapping it to its full six-foot length. One way or another, this was about to be over—I couldn't take much more. People were dying in my mind as Duke feasted on them. Entire lives were taken and discarded like trash.

No, not trash. They were precious. Those lives were valuable. They were food.

If you wanted a movie vampire to behave, you needed an advantage. Garlic, a sharp stick, or an article of faith.

Only one of those ever worked in real life. I only had one tattoo. I never saw the point of them until I realized they could be used against vampires.

I raised my right forearm towards Duke. It didn't exactly matter what the article of faith was. It could be anything. If I had faith in a cucumber and I stop the most powerful vamps in the world.

For me, it was a simple equation written in permanent ink on my arm:

$S = K_b Tr\ (p \log(p))$

It was the equation for entropy. Translation: Everything is chaos. Everything burns.

It all stopped with no warning. Duke didn't even lift an eyebrow. It was such a shock that I took a small step forward from the entirely mental effort of pushing against it. I dropped my arm and contemplated how I could kill the bastard before he could move.

An owl hooted twice and my shoulders tensed at the first. There was a short scream as something died. Another hoot came that Neka was able to make sound apologetic. Oops.

I growled, but I wasn't really angry at Neka. I was angry I had to be here at all. Still, if you're gonna go somewhere, turn into an owl and use hoots as code, at least get rid of all the other owls that naturally hang out there.

Zora didn't relax. The owls' hooting started again; eight in total. There were eight vamps out there. I guessed that half were ferals and the other half were serious threats. The most serious of them took that moment to melt in from the shadows, much as Duke had done. Broc's was a mundane entrance. The shadows didn't cling to him; there was no surge of power in the air. Just a large, threatening man out for a stroll in the middle of the night.

Broc was nearly a foot taller than me and twice as wide. The type of guy that played professional football all by himself. He moved in complete silence; not even a twig cracked under his bare feet. His pants were threadbare rags that hung down just past his knees. The only other thing he wore were heavy iron shackles on each wrist with nearly twenty feet of heavy spiked chain looping down from each and wrapping up and around his arms. He was bald and wore no jewels and no finery.

He was an oddity among vampires in that regard, but Zora seemed to understand him. His finery was his body, his strength, and his mental fortitude. Duke was my antithesis in practically every way. Everyone has to have a nemesis.

"Broccoli," Zora growled through her teeth. "So glad you could make it. Did you get my friend request?" I stopped looking at Duke the moment Broc entered. I hoped he took it as me being dismissive. I only did it so he didn't see I was pretending not to be afraid.

Zora was *actually* not afraid. She stared up at Broc and seemed to revel in the fact that his autobiography of death and destruction didn't faze her. Years ago, I made peace with my demons. Zora made friends with hers. She'd never break seeing all of his horrors because deep down, she wanted to know. She wanted to know everything she could about Broc. So she could kill him.

He stopped only a few feet from her, just close enough to look down his nose at her. He wasn't afraid either.

"It's good to see you alive, swordwoman," he boomed. "I feared some other weakling sorcerer had gotten to you before I could hear you scream a last symphony for me."

"Sadly not, and even if I'm roasting in hell next week, I'll be coming back for my sweet widdle side dish." They were both showing their teeth. Made sense. They were both predators.

"Really?" Broc smiled. "I picture a sisterly reunion taking longer than seven days."

"Nah, humans eat quickly." She said. "It's not like we're anemic, debilitated, cowardly ticks that have to sneak around in dark corners sucking our power out of someone else."

That did it.

Broc's face grew darker by the word. A child could tell an attack was coming, and I was still late.

The chain on Broc's left arm unfurled. I didn't see it move, but that was the only way it could've struck the ground where Zora had been standing and leave a crack in solid rock.

As fast as Broc's left arm was, his right was faster, Zora blurred away again. I heard the chain crack like a whip. The crack of a whip was the tip breaking the sound barrier, and he'd done it with a hundred pounds of chain.

Zora moved again. She was inside swiping her sword up at Broc's throat. He came down on her with both hands, as if to crush her into the dirt. His manacles met her sword and there was a ring that hurt my ears.

"You get more predictable every year!" Zora yelled. Broc yelled also—a scream of rage. With Zora standing still for the moment, I had a target.

"*Puppet.*" A hundred threads of air wrapped around Zora. They would pull in random directions without any guidance, but not this time. I yanked them all back towards me as hard as I could.

As fast as I was, I was by far the last one to move.

Before the first syllable was out of my mouth, Duke was seven feet in the air with just the effort of flexing his toes. He turned in the air and kicked Broc in the mouth with such ferocity that I heard the vampire's jaw and skull crack. The big man went flying off of his feet and would've gone into the woods if he hadn't hit a large tree almost instantly. Duke didn't show any emotion, save for his eyes which betrayed a frustrated twinge.

"I requested you to be civil for this meeting, and you sacrifice your composure over a single cattle? I take no pleasure in repeating myself." I don't know if that show of strength was more impressive, or the way Broc took it and lived.

Zora was behind me, struggling against the invisible air wrapping her up. "Let me go, Maker."

"Uhhh… No. I think you can stay there a moment," I said. She looked at me the same way she looked at Broc.

"Let. Me. Go." She growled.

"I won't let you ruin this meeting and you know it."

"Fuck your safe conduct. He attacked me first."

"This isn't the fucking time," I yelled, and quickly started gathering up my anger and shoving it down. This wasn't the time for emotion. If I lost it, we'd both be dead.

She looked me in the eyes, and suddenly her large grin was back.

"Just so I'm clear on this," she whispered. "You are facing your only ally, who you tied up, chastising her about bullshit while the two most powerful vampires you know are behind you."

I released the spell before she was done talking. It was a good point after all.

When I turned around Broc was still getting to his to his feet. His jaw was severely broken and terribly swollen. "I offer safe conduct to the first rays of dawn, should you offer the same," Duke said.

I could nod to his offer of safe conduct, but if I did, then it wouldn't bind him either. I had to offer the same. Glad I had an ace.

"I do so offer," I said formally.

"Flawless," Zora whispered. I turned to look at her and she grinned. "Like I said, predictable." I was still confused. It must've shown on my face. She sighed. "Think hard—you'll figure it out," she said and strode across the clearing.

Broc made a noise that may or may not have been an attempt at words. He was clearly unable to talk. Zora made no attempt to hide her giggles as she walked right up to him again.

"She sells seashells," Zora said slowly enunciating each word. Broc's face grew darker but he made no move toward her. Zora's hand rested on her sword, but she didn't move closer either. "Put, pat, putt," Zora began and stopped due to a fit of giggling.

Next there were things flying out of her mouth in Italian. Broc and Duke were probably old enough to know every language on the planet. I didn't speak anything but English and Math. Still, I could assume they were insults as Broc's face grew steadily darker, but he was stuck. If he attacked again, Duke would probably kill him.

I wasn't the only one who realized it either. Adding salt to the wound in true Zora fashion, was the fact that even if he could talk, he wouldn't be properly enunciating those syllables any time soon.

Then it hit me. Of course *Zora* would know just the right insult to get Broc to attack. Of course, Duke and I were going to break up the fight; it was *our* meeting and no way Duke was gonna tolerate disrespect of his meeting from a lackey. Of course, he wasn't going to miss an opportunity to make an example of Broc in the most brutal way possible. After all, there were other vamps out there; ever watchful for any sign of weakness. Of course, Duke was gonna offer safe conduct, and of course, I was gonna accept, sealing her and Broc into the agreement with us *after* Broc had been chastised.

Of course.

She'd done all that just so she could torment Broc for a few minutes, and I couldn't do a damn thing about it because I needed every scrap of focus just to make small talk with Duke. That could've easily gone some other way that ended with us both dead.

Zora and I were gonna have a long talk later.

"Shall we leave your associate to her spiteful torments?" Duke said, with a gesture down the path. I took about seven steps before I stopped. I didn't wanna be too far from Zora who had moved on to cursing in Mandarin.

There were two hoots from just over my right shoulder. There were two vamps behind me. They must be ferals—the hoots sounded… confident.

"What's this about?" I asked. I couldn't see a reason for the preamble ancient beings always included. Maybe if I lived a few hundred years, I wouldn't care about five minutes either. For the moment, though, I was quite impatient. It would take a madman to stay in Duke's presence willingly.

"What do you know about the container ship run aground off the coast?"

I growled, furrowed my brow slightly and relaxed my jaw muscles. It was an act. Being an exceptional lie detector had the benefit of being an exceptional liar. "That was you? I'll add those lives to your account vamp."

Duke merely waved a hand dismissively. "No. If you're concerned about the fact they are dead, you can lay blame at the feet of our common enemy."

"Common?" I scoffed. "Phantom Lorde is no enemy of mine. He only troubles you." Duke suspected I knew who Phantom Lorde was, but didn't suspect me or Zora anymore. It hadn't occurred to him yet that it was Zora and I working in concert with a few paid off homeless people as decoys.

"I mean The Constellation. " He said. "They are responsible for more on this one debacle than the Phantom could dream of."

"What'd they take?" I asked.

"Did I say they took something?" He said narrowing his eyes just slightly.

My words were lies. My anger was genuine. "Don't be glib and waste my time. It was a cargo ship. Used to move things from one place to another," I said as if I were talking to a dense child. "If they didn't take anything then why are we talking?"

Duke was taking joy from getting me flustered and smiled wide. "Because they took something. Let's not be glib and waste our time."

I said nothing. I wanted to pull out my airsoft and blow his head off. If I thought it would work, I would have—to hell with safe conduct. "What did they take?"

"What they took is of no consequence; it is lost to me. The Patrician himself is angered by this. I'm sure you don't want him to stop in and see to the matter." And that was what it looked like when Duke backed me into a corner. I had never met The Patrician. He was the head vampire in all the world. Even if only ten percent of the stories were true, I didn't want him within a thousand miles of me. Duke smiled again. It had to be a bluff.

"I'm not bleeding for you or your king," I sneered. His eyes tightened slightly and almost immediately went back to normal. I assumed that meant there was no love lost between them, but there was no time to explore it. "I'll stay out of the way. If you want to destroy The Constellation, you have my blessing."

"As if I'd need it," he scoffed. I pretended to lose patience. Duke believed I was a volatile child. It was always good to behave as your enemies expected—at least on the surface.

"State your business, vamp!" Duke grew serious, Zora stopped in the middle of a tongue twister, the owl went quiet, and Broc tensed every muscle, which was quite impressive.

"First, you will remember your place, boy. Second, you will assist me with the *full* destruction of The Constellation. Lastly, when they are all dead, I will remember that when the time came, you chose a side—which would increase rather than omit your utility."

"I still don't see why I should get involved." His face darkened further. I did my best not to notice, but failed miserably. "You have an issue with The Constellation; so do I. My problems do not eschew the idea of seeing them dead, but I had no plans to go out of my way for it, yet. Either of us could handle this. Why should one need the other?" Even I was taken aback by the magnitude of that lie. The idea of me "handling" The Constellation by myself was comical. Dr. Who's psychic paper would show some wavy lines and burst into flames.

"Ahh. Well, imagine you're given a dagger and your wits," he said. "Could you step into an arena with a lion and not respect the challenge of turning it into steak? You're all food to me Maker, nothing more. It would be a mistake for you to doubt that. Luckily for you, I prefer chickens and fish. I'll only take on a rabid bull if it's causing problems. This one is."

"Once again, why do you need me?"

"I don't." Duke shrugged as if I was no matter at all. As if he hadn't called me here. "I simply have a level of losses I am willing to accept, and this will put me over it. I can save up for a few weeks making a few hundred ferals, or you can take their place." I could feel my face darken. Duke saw it too and wasn't fazed.

"Or I could side against you and rip you apart for bringing more ferals in my city." I said.

"You could." Duke looked in my eyes without flinching. He couldn't use that seduction stare on me again so soon. Even if he could, neither of us had changed. I focused hard on his eyebrows. No way I was gonna volunteer for that again. Seeing Duke's true nature once today was enough.

"It's a simple question Maker. Do you want to deal with the devil you know, or fight the mad bull alone? After all, the enemy of my enemy can be my friend. At least, for a time."

I scoffed. "You're obviously not a student of Howard Tayler so I'll enlighten you. The enemy of my enemy is my enemy's enemy. No more. No less."

Duke chuckled at that. "Touche'. However, the fact remains that in the few months we're all waiting for the Constellation to cross you grievously enough, a hundred people will die.

I will be gearing up to kill them; they will be preparing a defense. I happen to know that they are currently... short-handed," he said, showing his fangs. Had they mixed it up already? I desperately wanted to know if anything happened, but showing too much interest might tip my hand. I decided to leave it at a slightly raised eyebrow.

"You wish to preserve human life, so I propose that you take the place of the ferals I would need to make before they've converted enough members for a defense. Afterwards, we can go back to insulting each other."

There are few things in life more frustrating than when the bad guy is right. Maybe it's when they know they are and look at you with a smug grin. I wasn't willing to let Blackstar run wild, killing or converting anyone in sight. I wasn't willing to let Duke do it either. The difference is that Duke gave me a chance to stop it for the low, low, price of throwing my life away. Ruthless efficiency in a tiny, undead package. God, how I wanted him dead.

He was supposed to go off and trash Blackstar, but I didn't wanna be dragged into it. I wanted to sigh, but instead, I barked a laugh. Then, for a few seconds, I couldn't stop it. All my plans to get two giants to clash, and when they finally did, I was gonna be in the middle.

> *"There are only two tragedies in life,*
> *one is not getting what you want, the other is getting it."*
>
> —*Oscar Wilde*

There wasn't a way out, though—not now. My only hope was the Martinet showing up and getting me out of this mess. I calmed my laughter. Duke didn't look confused, concerned, or anything at all. To believe that he wasn't thinking about what that laugh meant would be silly. So I tried to smooth it over.

"Well played sir," I said, and nodded as if he'd won. It wasn't difficult since he had. "There is only a minor issue with your proposal. I don't work for free."

"Your price?" Duke's smile never faltered, but his eyes betrayed a slight twinge I recognized as annoyance. Vamps were still based on humans—all the facial ticks were still the same. This one meant that Duke would kill me if the price were too high, though I couldn't imagine what I could ask for that would enrage him.

"Nothing you should have an issue with. Salvage rights from our enemy and gold up front. Unstamped and untraceable. You must have a giant statue of yourself somewhere you can peel it off of."

"Gold?" He asked. I knew that eye twinge too. It was suspicion.

"Yeah," I said. "Have you seen the price of crucifixes lately?"

The twinge left, and I saw the briefest glimpse of surprise. All the things a human could request from a powerful vampire and I wanted money? He probably thought I'd gone mad.

"Granted," he said.

"Good. Once I'm paid, I'll set up a date," I said, with no small amount of resignation. "Be prepared for a fight. If I even suspect that you came light I'll hamstring you and leave you for Blackstar. We don't want the rabid lion getting lucky now do we?"

"I will commit what I have if you do the same." he said. Zora was worth a few dozen ferals, and he knew it. He also knew Zora hated him with a passion that burned like the sun.

In fact, the only thing Zora hated more than Duke was Broc.

"Agreed. We'll be there." I didn't have to see Zora tense. I felt it.

"If you'll excuse me then, I have preparations to make. I leave you to the dog house I've relegated you to." He smiled at the joke. There was laughter coming from the shadows. My eyes shifted, and in that moment, Duke was gone. The laughter faded to the northeast, back towards Vermillion Falls.

I turned to find Zora glaring at me. She had the presence of mind not to speak. We left the park and walked across the street to the golf course parking lot and waited for daylight. It wasn't long before the first rays peeled over the horizon. As soon as they touched us, she began a tirade that I mostly didn't hear. She was screaming out words so fast that I only caught snippets while I waited for her to fizzle out.

"Common sense like a damn superpower… your prostate if you'd rather… with an elephant seal… sparkling, Mother-in-law!"

I huffed a laugh. "So, what you're saying is that you still haven't slept. Or drank one of the potions I left." As far as volatility went she was just getting worse. At least we could fix it now, since I'd soon find a few kilos of gold lying in a gutter somewhere. Zora was taking deep breaths and getting a hold of herself again.

"You know I hate those damn things. I'll be up for days," she said.

"Uhh… that's kinda the point?" I said.

"I'm rested enough to hear you trying to change the subject," she said through clenched teeth.

"There's nothing to say. We played our best hand and now we're screwed."

"No way Maker. I won't."

"We don't have a choice," I sighed.

"I am not raiding with Vermillion Falls." She growled

"You *have* to go. I *have* to go, and when we go, we're gonna kick them in the nuts."

Chapter: 20

Rollo was not a happy man. I don't think he was happy in general, but particularly today. He seemed the type to engage in misery to save the people he cared about. Maybe we had as much in common as he always tried to get me to believe.

The current situation wasn't going to help matters. It wasn't two children missing this time. It was an entire family, some homeless people, a secretary in some state government office and probably ten more I knew nothing about yet.

He sat in the light of a Tuesday morning looking more stressed than usual, but that could've been my fault. This was the first time I'd ever come to him. He smiled and made pleasantries, but there was no way I would ever represent good news. We both knew that.

"Morning, Maker," he said, settling himself behind a desk. "Coffee?"

"Nah, I already had mine."

"So, to what do I owe the pleasure? Graid giving you problems already?"

"No. Thanks again for that by the way. I'm here because I need a favor." Rollo only sat back and exhaled. Never good news. "I need you to keep an area north of Hillsborough empty of police activity and people as much as possible tomorrow night. Also, if you can be ready to move in with swat and everything you got on… a certain address." At the last moment, I reconsidered telling him where the place was. I didn't need him running off before I was ready. "If you do have to go in, you shoot to kill. There is nothing in there you want getting out alive."

"There's a long story in there. I suspect I'll need to hear it. All of it."

Now it was my turn to exhale and ask myself that most asshole of questions: how much truth do I tell? I hadn't slept much. The power from the ankh found a way to seep through all the wards I'd built around it. Which was a problem… not to mention terrifying. I'd drawn a circle and put my pack in it; when that didn't work I took it to Zora's apartment and passed out on her floor. Damn thing was beyond powerful. I'd need a gold circle of my own at this rate. I'd spent the last twelve hours adding even more wards and traps around the thing. It was quiet again for now, but too late to reclaim my lost night.

I told Rollo that I had my coffee. What I didn't tell him was that I was up to six cups so far. Perhaps that's what led to my misjudgment. I told him everything.

"I caught up to one of Blackstar's people. Actually, she caught up to me. Wanted to defect for more magic. She's basically a junkie at this point. Broken, not even thinking about life beyond her next fix. I told her I'd give her one if she went to talk to Blackstar for me. She went."

"What'd you have her say?" Rollo said, staring at me in confusion.

"That I wanted to meet up with him to surrender." Rollo's eyebrows went up at that. I pretended not to notice. "I got a wildcard in the hole, and I need to play it. Not sure if you noticed, but homeless people are disappearing. Seven so far—and those are just the ones I know about. Blackstar's amassing power. I need to finish this before he does."

"I don't know about magical junkies, but the regular ones aren't trustworthy," he said.

"They have that in common. Zora put a sensor on her shirt so she could hear everything. We elected not to tell her that part though." Rollo laughed at that.

"I love that gal," he said. "When you gonna let me get some of those sensors?"

"When someone burns the 4th Amendment out of the Constitution," I said. To that he shrugged, but didn't stop smiling.

"She set up the meeting. It's tomorrow. I think this is their only hideout; when she walked in, everyone was there. I don't know how many exactly, but she said there were people being held in the basement as well. It's a farmhouse out in the middle of nowhere, so they don't have anyone that's gonna stop by and ask what's going on."

"There's a whole family being held hostage by maniacs, and you want me to just wait a day?!" He was out of his chair and out of his mind.

"Blackstar has been holed up there for weeks. Those people are dead," I said. "I'm certain of it, and if I'm wrong, they should still be alive tomorrow. Blackstar wants to sacrifice them to summon a demon. Either he's summoned it already, or he hasn't. If he has, then we're too late to save those people and the whole city is in danger. If he hasn't, then you still can't save them. Blackstar will just bail, take the people with him or kill them, and we're back to square one again. I'm trying to stop him for good. You're trying to be Captain America."

Rollo calmed down, but he was still standing. I think I was starting to like him. He grasped cold hard logic better than most. As much as neither of us liked it, those were the rules we had to play by.

"What do we do if he's already summoned it?"

"That's what the evacuation is for. I'm not sure if there's anything I *can* do, but I already set up something that might work. If it doesn't, then I'll probably be dead… and it's your problem. Fire works well most of the time."

"So, you need me to evacuate a few square miles, without telling anyone why. Keep the local police in the dark, again, without giving a reason. Have a special weapons team available. I assume I can't tell them anything either, and somehow have them ready to take out a demon in case you blow it—which we don't know how to do. All without the evil wizard sitting in the middle getting wise. That about right?"

I felt my face darken. "I finally bring you in on something and you bitch about it?! You said you wanted to be involved; you didn't say 'only bring the easy jobs.' For the record, wizards act like we're badasses, and compared to one of you, we are. But nothing keeps us up at night more than the thought of seven billion normals armed with torches, pitchforks and prejudice."

"Maybe that scares you. What about the ones that wanna rule us all?"

"I think they're even more scared. Amassing power has never been a means unto itself, no matter what the storybooks say. Why amass power if not to control? Why control if not to feel safe? It's a fantasy. It doesn't matter how strong you get, if you think you're safe, it just means you haven't seen what's trying to kill you."

Rollo sat down, shaking his head. He was trying to reconcile something, but didn't say what. Finally, he spoke with a sigh.

"My priority tomorrow night will be getting those people out alive, and I'm not signing on for this unless it's yours too."

"Then you aren't signing on," I snapped, so much for Rollo's sense of cold, hard, logic. "This is bigger than a few people. It's bigger than your duty, my pride, or any other bullshit we can dream up in this office. People are going to die if we don't act, and people are going to die if we do act. The question is, which choice can you live with?" Now it was my turn to walk out in a cinematic cliché moment.

"Let me put this another way," he said as I reached the door. "If it was your family—"

"If it was my family you can all go to hell and I'll see you there," I growled. "Now ask yourself, is that the world you wanna live in? Where every person in danger is somehow special and we're willing to sacrifice a million unwilling people to save them? Do you wanna live in a world where whoever has the power is willing to sacrifice your family to save theirs, or should someone be constantly looking at the big picture?"

Rollo stared at me like he'd never seen me before. That rant had dredged up emotions I thought I'd dumped a long time ago. I might've had a normal life if the Martinet thought like Rollo. Shit happens. That time it happened to me. I took a deep breath. The emotional detritus of being human just came with the territory.

I took another, picturing myself sweeping up my emotions like so much dust and debris and dumping them in the trash where they belonged. They would get me killed otherwise. I opened my eyes, and Rollo was still looking at me, sitting back in his chair.

"Ya know son, I just realized something."

"What's that?" I said.

"You're older than you look."

* * *

I shut the door on Rollo's office. I guess it was too much to ask. There were folks who could look at the big picture. I do it all the time. Rollo had likely never practiced that particular skill.

What choice could I live with? The trick to that question is that you had to live beyond making it. A dead man could live with anything.

I climbed in my Toyota and went for a drive with the windows down. Rania's prediction was set to take place about now. If it were true, then Blackstar would summon his demon and I was boned. Summoning a demon was crazy.

The summoning itself wasn't the reason no wizards ever did this, though the effort required was considerable. Controlling the summoned thing was the real issue. It would take the entire Constellation working together to control something even remotely powerful, and if anyone's focus slipped for even a moment the demon would tear them to shreds. Even if their focus never wavered, they'd have to sleep eventually. Everything a wizard could summon was either too powerful to control or too weak to pose a threat. Otherwise some idiot would've summoned a demon, and the earth would be Hell's penthouse by now.

Evil wizards didn't have a good track record of working well together, and The Constellation was no different. But maybe Blackstar and company didn't know that, or they were all working towards one goal. That could mean there was no benefit to one of them betraying all the others, but that thought was truly crazy.

Shroud was only keeping Blackstar in line through fear and Blackstar was doing it with everyone else, but it was impossible to instill loyalty that way. Fear wasn't enough to keep a lackey from stabbing you in the throat if they were certain they'd get away with it.

I kept driving while my mind ran in pointless circles on an emotional rollercoaster that only went down. I was on an empty tank and two hours of anxious brooding by the time my meandering path led me back to Miles'.

I'd sent Zora to scout out the place Blackstar was holed up. After asking the locals a few questions, she found out the family that lived there was on vacation. That would've been nice if it were true. She was getting back from another trip when I arrived. She couldn't tell me if the people that lived there were alive though.

"Still couldn't get close," she explained. "The place has wards like Rikers Island. Ya know… if Rikers Island were full of wizards." I sighed. I knew where they were, but there wasn't much I could do. I was much too weak to walk into The Constellation stronghold and take back a dozen innocents no matter what tactics I employed.

I nodded and walked past. Zora followed me in. Miles was making something that smelled good. I saw chicken burgers as I sat down. I decided I wasn't hungry. I just wanted enough beer to knock me out for a dozen hours or more.

"Is everything set?" She asked.

"Yup." I nodded.

"You alright?"

"Nope. But I'll be alright," I sighed.

"Maker," Miles said, without turning around. "Officer Rollo called, said he would get you what you needed. He wouldn't say more than that."

"That's good news," Zora said. I nodded.

"Yeah, 'Hey Rollo, we're all gonna die anyway so come walk into a war with us.'"

"And end another before it starts." She smiled.

"And end another before it starts," I conceded.

Chapter: 21

It was the eve of battle and still no Gomez. I was back in the phone booth on the corner for what seemed like the tenth time today. Felt like I was back where this crapfest started. Gomez didn't pick up. As a testament to how desperate I was, I even left a message.

I didn't want to be famous, well-known, or even respected like some wizards. I wasn't Merlin. I did want the cavalry to come when I called though. Maybe that was asking too much. To say that it was all frustrating was the understatement of the year.

It didn't matter that I was angry. I had to bring everything, or everyone would know I was bluffing instantly. Carol was certain the whole Constellation would be there, coming to treat with me for Neka, and planning to take Zora and me to subjugate and make up for their losses. There wasn't much talk of the demon. According to Zora, Carol was sent away just when the conversation was getting interesting, but it was enough to confirm what they were planning.

Carol didn't report back any talk of the demon summoning. I couldn't blame her for playing both sides. She was on her side, not mine. Since I knew what the big secret was, it didn't make much of a difference. Except that having a demon on your side made all the difference in the world. Duke was probably only responsible for half the disappearances, which meant that Blackstar had snatched the other half.

Human sacrifice was beyond powerful. If you were going to summon some major demon and actually have a chance of controlling it, you needed that kind of muscle. With Blackstar, Shroud, Firehag, and the Executive all there focusing, they could get it done. Explaining that to the Martinet should've gotten me somewhere. Dammit!

* * *

We were all in Zora's apartment. Zora was stretching, and Neka was meditating. I was in a chair shoving everything in my pack. I'd made three batches of potions, Molotov cocktails, homemade thermite, and four bandages, which I gave to Zora. There had been a lot of stove-top chemistry over the last few days. I'd also finished some new summons from my pack. It might've been a waste of time and power, but I didn't have the days it would take to make anything else.

Physically, I was mostly healed by now. The mental scars would take forever, or they wouldn't heal at all. Wouldn't be the first time. "That's what wars *do*," I whispered. It wasn't what I wanted my new mantra to be, but Miles' words had found a way into my vocabulary.

My mind was going over scenario after scenario. Hoping to find some way to get through this alive. I didn't see one, unless everything went perfectly… which was laughable. No plan survives the first strike.

Meeting on the field of battle like some old civil war battalion wasn't what magical forces did. It certainly wasn't my style. If I sided with Duke, we might get Blackstar. At the same time, that would be a wonderful opportunity for Duke to kill me.

There would always be another wizard he could use as a pawn. If Blackstar was summoning a major demon—and I was ninety-nine percent certain that he was—and I sided with him, I could kill Duke. The disadvantage to that plan was that I already knew Blackstar wanted me dead. Duke *might* kill me if the opportunity arose, Blackstar would be trying to kill me from the start.

According to Carol and Zora's surveillance, Blackstar didn't know much about Duke. I had the element of surprise there. Surprise could do a lot. The concept of the ambush was what I always used to level the playing field. That, and perfecting the art of the tactical withdraw. "It's not running. I'm finding a better place to kill you." I said it, but it didn't have the confidence it normally had.

Carol and her two shape shifters didn't know I'd bugged her, and Blackstar didn't know I'd made a deal with Duke. As long as Duke didn't figure out the demon summoning, I was holding all the cards. I just had to hope no one had any nasty surprises for me.

I had rationalized to Rollo. Everything I said was true; I just wish I could believe it had nothing to do with being scared. The truth was, Blackstar petrified me and Duke gave me that feeling only a third grader can get. That sinking, stomach sick, that happens when four larger children suddenly appear in front of you.

Now, I was getting ready to face them together, and it was hard to focus. My mind kept racing back to the fear, and I had to drag it away. I kept in venting worst-case scenarios where they put aside their differences over tea and realized that I was behind it all. The mental image of them having tea was accompanied by me roasting on a spit in the background.

"Hit and away," I whispered. The mantras were helping. They were a code. The rules Zora and I had used for the last four years to keep us alive. There was only one that we hadn't had to learn the hard way.

"Attack from ambush," I whispered, shoving things angrily

into my pack. I didn't want to attack at all. I wanted to run. This city wasn't even that great, and I couldn't save everybody. There is a family being tortured to death right now that I can't even save. How many others across the world?

It didn't matter where I went, I would always have the same issues. That meant this fight didn't matter either. I could set up Duke and Blackstar to meet and just run. Take Zora with me, use magic to get rich, buy an island somewhere, and fuck this place.

I wanted that, Christ, I wanted that. I didn't have a family. I had Zora and Miles. I had brought them into this; I had brought that faceless family into this. Blackstar wouldn't be running wild if I were stronger. If I'd managed to kill him last month in Durham. Was that a month ago? Seemed like last year. So much had happened.

"Dammit," I whispered. All the good barbeque was here I guess, and I liked the peaches even better than Georgia's.

I had all the rifles in my pack, full magazines on demand, seven of the fourteen grenades we had left, all our latest chemistry experiments, and every magic item and potion I'd ever made or stolen. The last items were in and I started reversing the enchantment.

Still wasn't ready.

It was evening by the time I finished. I summoned my light and sat there, dispelling my fear, breathing deep and thinking about quarks. I was trying to calculate exactly how many photons, at what density, it took to make the slow-moving light between my hands.

Zora's phone started blaring Ignition by Toby Mac to signal that the sun had fully set.

Everyone knew their parts to play in this madman's gamble, so there wasn't much to say. I tossed Neka the keys, and he caught them without opening his eyes. He rose without a word and went to go start the truck. He'd learned to start it at least. Zora rose, holding her sword, and checking a blade that didn't need checking. On her hip was my old satchel with the other seven grenades.

"I need you ice cold tonight," I said, not sure who I was saying it for. She looked me in the eyes and let out a deep breath.

"Yeah."

"I may tell you to run. If I do, you take my pack, start running, and don't look back before morning."

"South is nice this time of year," she shrugged.

"If you see a chance to kill Broc without trashing the plan… take it." I had a feeling I would regret those last two words. I was going to tell her not to take it, don't do anything reckless or stupid, but this entire night was reckless and stupid, and there would never be another chance to kill Broc without Duke stepping in.

Zora didn't brighten up at all. She just nodded. Ice cold, as promised. I still think not having such passion is better, but if you have to have it, be able to turn it off. Zora needed that passion in a way I didn't understand, but it was to her credit that she didn't *always* need it.

We walked downstairs past Miles reading a paper. "I… uhh…" I wasn't good with goodbyes. "I might be back. Umm… if I'm not then, thanks… for everything." He didn't respond. The paper didn't move. Thank God Zora ruined the moment.

"*I'll* be back in time for breakfast. Strawberry banana pancakes and steak, old man. And don't skimp on the steak." He grunted a laugh, and with that, we walked out to my truck.

A goddess of the sword climbed in the back, lord of shapes at my side and a laughing goddess in my head. On the field before me were a god of magic and a god of death gearing up to clash, and driving off like an idiot to get in the middle was me…

Just a man.

Chapter: 22

We were getting off the freeway when I felt the thump. Zora had jumped off the truck to go do her part. I thought about the trap I had laid a few days ago and quickly put it out of my mind. I didn't want this night to come to that. Better just to not think about it.

I parked the truck at a McDonald's about a half mile out from our destination. Neka and I started walking through the woods. It was closer to a mile than I thought, and there was no trail to where we were going. I had counted on that. Humans wouldn't move through the underbrush well, but vampires, Neka, and Zora would be fine.

As for little ol' me? Well, if I had a chance to run I was taking it. The problem with that plan was there were at least two powerful beings that were not going to let that happen, and I wasn't so confident in my ability to get away despite them.

Neka was moving behind me, silent as a snake. There was an occasional rustle to remind me he was there. The big man had become quite solid in a short period of time. I didn't trust him per se; it was that I was more certain now our goals aligned. You couldn't easily fake the anger I saw in those eyes when I brought him up to speed. Zora had it right. He was here because he was pissed.

"You have to run if I tell you," I said.

"I already told you. None of them are leaving here alive. I'm not concerned with anything else."

"Listen. There's no reason for anyone else to throw their life away for this, and Carol and the others still need you."

"If I live, I will do what I can to help them. They didn't use your blood. I do not expect you to understand. I agreed to the first part of your plan because it's a fine ruse. Don't count on me for anything after. I'll be busy."

I wanted to argue some more, but I knew that look. Neka was angry. He was also right in that I didn't understand his anger. No one had used a part of me to kill, maim, and spread panic. I didn't know what that was like. My imagination told me that I wouldn't be handling it nearly as well.

I stopped at the edge of the clearing and scanned the treeline. I looked back, and Neka had on a pair of thick, steel shackles I ordered from a BDSM store online. They looked heavy enough to be formidable. I had etched a few large meaningless arcane symbols on them that pulsed with a muted blue light.

Blackstar's hideout was a few miles further on. I didn't know exactly where, but Zora had scouted it yesterday and gave me directions. I let out a breath I didn't realize I was holding. It was a good plan, though my intense need for self-preservation made me biased. I stepped into the field, moving to my assigned spot. I hoped I wasn't deluding myself.

Enter Maker, stage east.

I drank a charmer potion and resisted the urge to move some dirt and make sure the five foot, nearly perfect silver ring was underneath. I had a lot of back up plans. I hoped I wouldn't need that one.

I didn't have to wait long. Less than five minutes. Wasn't easy to stand fast when I saw The Constellation was out in force.

The short one-armed Executive with his balding head. The Hag with her wisps of white hair and boils—not to mention the skin and chunk of jaw hanging from her face. In the middle was Blackstar himself. Behind them were Carol and the two other shapeshifters I didn't know, in their animal forms, seventeen men and women with guns and a partridge in a pear tree. I asked that everyone be here, but I was in no position to make a fuss about Shroud off-guarding the hideout.

Even if I hadn't asked, I figured they would've brought out the big guns anyway because Neka was here. It certainly couldn't be for me.

Nothing they were wearing appeared different. Firehag was in her black robe, and the Executive in slacks with a cream button down shirt, straining to hold the buttons closed at the belly. Blackstar was in jeans, white, button up, shirt and a purple, cardigan vest. Wizards often used magical tools, they were labor intensive, expensive, and for everyone but me, they took forever to make.

Most wizards used them; I relied on them. As a result, I paid close attention to wizards who got a new ring, wore a different colored robe, or carried an ash staff when the last one was oak. I didn't see anything the passing of a couple weeks could not explain.

The thing I saw that made me think were the injuries. Blackstar still had his limp from last month, Firehag looked a wreck as always and the Executive still had one arm, but it was more than that. They moved… stiffly.

Firehag looked like she hadn't slept. She seemed excitable, almost nervous with the way her eyes darted around. The Executive had a limp he was making no effort to hide, and he walked through the clearing with a roll to his step. Perhaps the fight in Durham had taken a greater toll than he let on, but that didn't explain why Blackstar had a small bruise at the side of his mouth. If Duke had gotten close enough for any of that, he would've taken their heads off—which meant that Shroud was in a foul mood or just dishing out punishments for the fun of it.

I wondered why Shroud might be upset this time, but didn't dwell on it. I had a performance to put on. I took a long blink to steady my nerves. Raise the curtain.

The key to getting the drop on your enemy was to know everything they knew or at least one thing they didn't—more if possible. Blackstar knew loads more than me, but I knew one thing he didn't.

I hadn't been broken by Rosenthal.

The message I had Carol deliver sounded desperate. Whatever Hawknose did felt good. It was obviously intended to act as a drug. Who's to say it didn't work.

"I'm letting them think they are succeeding…" Arta had said. If they bought that, then this might work. I hadn't seen any sign that they had excavated the base that I'd collapsed. If they hadn't, then I had a chance. No matter that it was small.

When it was all said and done, my life and the life of everyone I knew rested on a charmer potion that I normally sold for twenty bucks.

They approached, and I knelt down. I'd requested they not send projections; I didn't need Blackstar using an illusion to get the drop on me again. I tossed a small pebble at each of them in turn. The pebble hit and rebounded off the Hag. Blackstar tapped his back with a foot.

Steven caught his and crushed it, letting a fine dust fall from his fingers. The Executive, dammit! I fought down a torture flashback. If I thought of him as Steven Mendon, then he was the man who had a fetish for the sounds of my bones slowly cracking. The Executive was some shit wizard with a target on his back I was determined to hit.

My anger came in a rush so strong I had to stop myself from taking a step forward. I had visions of the Hag flaying the skin off my chest with an oversized scalpel. Stupid emotions.

Suddenly I wasn't feeling so meek. In this situation, too much anger was just as dangerous as too much fear. I breathed out and hoped it came as relief. The plan, at least this part of it, was predicated on the assumption that I would be afraid. I focused on Blackstar. I was terrified of him. Blackstar and his steel spikes that he loved to hammer into my arms and legs.

I lowered my eyes and thought of Tema. There was nothing but fear there.

"I'm here to sell information and return what was stolen." I heard Neka shift, and every eye turned to him with hunger. All three looked to the manacles also. I didn't turn around, just said a silent prayer that they looked convincing from ten feet away. I also hoped Neka looked significantly weak; it wasn't easy with a man bigger and wider than me. Dammit. This wasn't going to work.

"What is your information?" Blackstar said. He didn't sound suspicious, but I couldn't tell with that accent. His eyes didn't narrow, at least. They didn't know what I wanted. Only a stupid or desperate man would give up information before at least a promise of payment. Luckily, in this scenario, I played the part of a stupid and desperate Maker. It was a test. I allowed my fear to win and failed it.

"Vermillion Falls is on the move, and they're hunting you. I know that the local lord, a powerful vampire named Duke, is angry enough and powerful enough to see us all dead. I can lead you to him." See us all dead. Ha! As if there was an "us."

Firehag made some noise in her throat that sounded like a hiss. She was probably still upset about her face. I flinched at the noise and continued. "I didn't kill Gerod. The vampires attacked and…" I sniffed. Not sure what that accomplished since I was looking at my feet. "I barely got away." I blinked hard and summoned a bit more water for my eyes, thinking of one of Tema's surgeries to summon the tears. She hadn't believed in anesthesia.

Blackstar was looking at me and *through* me. Looking me in the eye, then not. I tended to focus on the bridge of the nose or the eyebrows. "I want to come home," I choked out. A finer act had never been made. I was properly motivated since my life depended on it. Eat your heart out DiCaprio.

This was the moment of truth. If they didn't believe me, I would be toast. If they did believe me, I would only probably be toast. They weren't there that night. They didn't know that Hawknose had failed to break me. If they were there, then all they knew was that the whole place came down randomly. Even if they did know, there was still no guarantee that Hawknose had failed.

I could be a perfectly good thrall. They were down several assets over the month, and I just told them they had a major fight coming. There was no way they didn't at least know about Duke by now. The odds of operating in the area without crossing him were exactly zero, and they had to know that by now too. This was a fight they were expecting, but they didn't know I knew… I hoped.

There was a long silence. The Hag was smirking. Blackstar was thinking. The Executive broke the spell.

"The woman," he growled. "I want her dead." He and Blackstar exchanged a look and the Executive growled something so low that only Blackstar could hear.

Blackstar thought for a moment and nodded. "Where is your apprentice?"

"I don't know. On my power, I will find her when the current threat has passed," I said. The Executive didn't like it, but he didn't speak again. He merely looked at Blackstar, who was still thinking. Must've been the oath that did it. Of course, I would find Zora after this current threat has passed. I'd find her at Miles' eating pancakes. This was the reason I always made the wording of any oath specific.

"Return to us what was taken first. Afterwards, The Constellation will decide your fate. It may not be a merciful one."

Good thing I'd planned for this. If the goal was subservience, then I had to return Neka.

I stepped back and pushed Neka towards them. The big man made a show of looking weak; tripping and stumbling into Firehag, who caught him despite her frail looks. She also threw him over one shoulder and rose as if hefting a sack of laundry. A flare of red shot above the tree line in front of me. Right on time.

The flare arced higher, and as I was about to turn and run, it stopped. Just… stopped. I turned my attention to Blackstar; he and his cronies were just as frozen as the new red star in the sky. In the red light I saw a bird, obviously disturbed by the commotion, suspended in flight. "What the hell?" I breathed.

A woman appeared in front of me, as if fading into reality. Short brown hair framed her ageless face; a white dress wrapped loosely around her body

"What do you want?" I snapped. The tension of the moment had me on edge. According to the plan, I was supposed to be running like hell and hopefully getting away. Arta paid no attention to me; she was too busy studying Blackstar.

"Good to see you Maker," she said. "Kill him."

Chapter: 23

"What?!" I said, incredulously. "Why the hell would I try that?"

On the surface, it wasn't a bad idea. If time were frozen I could stab them all and let the damage hit when time resumed. Unfortunately, I couldn't move. I tried to cast and summon a flame potion, and that didn't work either. Arta showing up was the final piece to the puzzle: this was only going on in my mind.

"I didn't say try," she smiled. "I said kill him."

"Even if that were possible, which it isn't, that's not the plan. The plan is—"

"I know the plan," she said with an edge in her voice that shut me right up. "Kill him."

"You claim to have been paying attention, and yet you don't know how stupid that sounds. It'll be Durham all over again, only this time I'll die." I felt stupid standing there. I struggled against whatever was holding me but it was no use, I couldn't move anything below my neck.

"Why did you give Zora all the bandages?" She said, smiling again. Why did everyone smile at me like I was a meal?

"Because her part is more dangerous," I said.

She scoffed, "And yet, you're the one standing here facing the entire Constellation alone. You cannot hide anything from me. You planned to die here, even if you did not realize it before now."

"I made peace with the fact that I might die a long time ago. The possibility tonight is just... higher than normal."

"Then if you believe you're going to die, take him with you." I looked at Blackstar and felt the terror in my chest. He was looking at me with a superior smirk. Even though he was frozen, If I could've run, I would have.

"No," I said, with a tremble in my voice. "That's... that's not the plan."

"Plan," she scoffed. "You're already dead, Maker. You may as well die for something worthwhile." I didn't answer. Another glance at Blackstar and I just shook my head.

"Something worthwhile, like revenge? Like indulging my petty emotional bullshit? Very constructive." I added a sneer just in case she missed the sarcasm.

"All you have is this... infinitesimal slice of time. If you will not think of yourself now, then when? It cannot be the past, for you that doesn't exist anymore. It cannot be the future, for a mortal that's not yet written. So it must be now, or it's never."

"Then it's never," I said. It came out hotter than I intended. It was wise to monitor your tone with beings that could exhale and kill you, but unwise seemed to be the theme of the evening. "Violate the plan and screw everyone else because I'm an emo bitch and I can't handle a little torture! Yeah, they took a dump on me. It was my day to get burned, but they'll get theirs... sooner or later." Arta had a point. I'd love for it to be sooner, and I'd love to be the one who made sure they got it, but that was about as likely as me flapping my arms and flying away like Neka.

"A little torture?" She laughed. "A little? How long did he take draining your blood and putting it back?" I didn't remember that... and then I did.

The memory came in a flash, and with it came the pain. Burning, stinging pain all over my body and a cold more terrible than any spell. "How many of your bones did they crack?" I grunted at another flash. I was pretty sure they tried for all of them. In my mind, the Executive was slowly fracturing each one with a vice.

"Stop!" I yelled at her. I still couldn't move anything more than my head.

"No need," she said. "After all, it's just a little torture." My mind showed me four long thin spikes being driven through my abdomen, carefully done to miss most of my internal organs. They came out of my back and through the chair I was lying on. Then I was left to bleed for an hour. Taking them out hurt even worse. I felt it like it was happening all over again. Blinding agony with colorful illustrations.

I screamed and tried like hell to breathe. It wasn't working. "Stop." I choked out through the pain.

"I have stopped," she said, looking up at me. "Before I was holding back the memories of all they've done to you."

"Start!" I screamed. In my mind the Executive hit me in the sternum with a hammer, and just before I was able to catch my breath, he hit me again. He went on like that for hours—even after I'd passed out.

"You don't care that you were flayed? Tema wasn't nice to you either. How many times were you operated on?" Suddenly I was remembering things with Tema also. Each memory more gruesome than the last. All my old scars were getting brief, abrupt explanations and lighting up with a dull ache, but it was all the new ones that made me scream.

"Make it stop!" I screamed, trying to bear it all. It wasn't nearly so easy without Arta unplugging my brain over tea.

"Are you begging or demanding? I can't tell," she said with a fair bit of scorn. In my mind, Firehag was burning holes in my arms. I could remember the smell of my burning flesh and the sound of me moaning. I couldn't see through the tears in my eyes.

"Please!" I yelled.

"You claim to forsake the emotional path, but all I see is emotion," she said. "You don't want to attack because you're afraid you'll die, but you arranged this whole night with the expectation that you would. I don't see reason. I see fear. You're weak, Maker. Kill him." I didn't answer. I couldn't answer. My focus was shattered into a montage of pain, screeches, and tears. "You're helpless. Worthless. It takes conviction to be anything else. It takes resolve, and if rage is the only way you're going to learn it, then so be it. Kill him."

Arta disappeared, and I dropped to one knee with tears streaming down my face. I hated that helpless feeling. I hated all feelings. The pain was gone, but the anger and hatred stayed. I was livid with Arta for making me remember at the worst possible time. I was angry at Tema, pissed at The Constellation, but most of all…

I was mad at myself.

Anger is the first step in progress. If I wanted to ever forgive myself, I knew what I had to do.

"*Staff*," I said under my breath. I snapped it to its full length. Blackstar and company turned their heads, noticing the flare behind them almost as one. I grabbed my staff in both hands, tossed in some magical oomph and swung as hard as I could. I was so angry I couldn't think.

For days I'd sat at Miles' going over every detail in my mind, and all my grand scheming at the moment was reduced to grabbing the nearest stick and beating them to death.

I heard somewhere that revenge is a sucker's game. Sending my staff at Blackstar's head and screaming in rage might've made me a sucker, but damn if I was going to be the only one to die here.

Blackstar ducked his head back just in time and my staff embedded in his shield. It wasn't what I wanted. I wanted the force

I put behind it to take his head off, but plans were forming in my mind faster than even I could keep up with—and I had a plan for this.

"*Resonance.*" My staff vibrated the air that made up Blackstar's shield and the air inside quickly achieved resonance. The same thing a good opera singer uses to shatter wine glasses can be used to shatter eardrums. I grinned as Blackstar's ears and eyes started bleeding.

Attacking was crazy. It was suicidal. Everyone present knew that, which was probably why they were in shock for the first second or so. That was over now, and so was my advantage, but the rage still had me screaming about killing them.

Blackstar dropped the shield with a scream of rage and pain, blood pouring out of his eyes and ears. Unfortunately, he didn't need to see me to send a blast of semi-solid air that hammered me into the dirt. Something ruptured. I felt it in my chest, but I was full of adrenaline and back up before the pain fully registered. Everyone seemed to be entertained, hanging back and watching the wizards fight it out. Good—I didn't need the interference.

I rolled away and coughed as the air got thick. Saw this trick coming too. I raised my hood and mask. It wasn't easy; took me two days, but I had managed to add an enchantment to it after the scuffle in Durham. Now my mask filtered out anything that wasn't air. That included Blackstar's tear gas but didn't include the Hag's fire—which I dodged by a very warm few inches.

"***OOOOOOOO!***" Arta bellowed in my head. Which meant whatever the Executive just cast was mind magic.

"...*Raken scarinto!*" It was Firehag casting this time. I heard lightning crackle and smelled ozone—which was technically oxygen—so my mask needed adjustment. I looked and Firehag was holding a ball of lightning. The bitch could make ball lightning?! I didn't have a plan for that.

I heard a roar, and suddenly a giant grizzly was there and barely missed biting her head off. I'd forgotten all about Neka.

Firehag released the lightning at Neka instead. It hit and charred one of the massive paws up to the elbow. I thought Neka was done for the night, but he shifted into a moose that didn't have any debilitating injuries and attacked again.

I didn't have any more time to admire Neka's fighting prowess. The ground at my feet exploded in a spray of earth and rock that threw me thirty feet in the air.

There was plenty of grass in the air with me. That was advantageous.

"*Hydrate!*" Water came to my hand from the grass, the air and probably even me. It was the size of a basketball. I was putting a lot into this.

"*On the rocks.*" The penny appeared in my hand and turned the water to ice. I sent it at Blackstar as hard as I could. "*Move!*"

Blackstar threw up a hand to block, and the ball of ice slowed as it approached him. "*Move.*" The ball of ice shattered and sprayed everyone was fast moving shards of ice. Firehag screamed. The executive howled. My clothes protected me. Neka shifted into a coyote and kept coming.

Christ, who knew I could be so angry. Four spells and I hadn't even hit the ground yet.

Blackstar wiped the blood from his hate-filled eyes; the only sign of pain was the twisted grimace he wore. The ice shards that hit him were melting from the heat of blood.

"*Finalem arrestium!*" He was smiling with his hand outstretched towards me. He made a fist, and the air around my chest tightened like a vice. I was still about four feet above the ground and running through everything in my pack for something to summon. Then the crushing pain cut off all thought.

"Less tedious than last time," he smirked. "Have you nothing more?" My jacket and shirt were doing what they could against the air squeezing the life out of me, but I heard my ribs crack and in a few moments I'd be dead.

"B... Bur..." I grunted. It wasn't the whole word, but it still worked. The burn potion couldn't come to my hand, but before it could drop to the ground, I kicked it at Blackstar's face.

The bottle shattered and I screamed as my foot caught part of the fire. Blackstar was laughing as the rest of the flame went sailing past his head. The Executive was on his way to help Firehag, who was still holding her own against Neka.

I felt the magical energy in the air suddenly disappear. The flames died over a few seconds. The grass over the entire clearing was starting to frost over, and the air holding me became softer and more like air. I fell to the ground gasping; at least Zora was sticking to the plan.

Zora and I knew circles. A nearly perfect circle could do amazing things with almost no power, and we had two. A circle didn't have to be gold or copper—it could be anything.

Zora's circle was a furrow in the ground, a few yards into the trees, which enclosed the entire clearing and grounded out any energy inside. Nothing magical could cross to the outside, and any spell inside was grounded out almost instantly.

The downside of a circle that large carved into the ground was that Zora would have to stay there and power it, making sure a leaf didn't fall somewhere and break it.

Physical things could move in and out of the circle just fine. The ferals stormed in from north and south. They were screaming and hissing. Mad things finally given the chance to feed. Even the vampires weren't violating the plan. Somehow that made things worse.

The gunfire from Blackstar's people was nearly instant. The vampires fell one after another, but their numbers showed no sign of thinning. Bullets were a temporary measure. The shot and trampled vamps got right back up to continue the charge.

I was free of Blackstar's air prison and gasping for breath when he cast. "*Arcunus Fothenium Thaalo!*" An inferno came for my head and hit hard. I screamed and ducked away. Another came for me and I rolled, getting caught in it again. My face was numb, and my right eye was blurry as if I was looking through water. The heat had done that, inside a circle, and through the protection of my clothing. I was so outclassed.

I ran the few steps back to where I'd been and summoned every scrap of power I could gather in a half second. It came out with the same ferocity as my fear.

"*Blow!*" I screamed. The dirt and grass were blown off the thin silver ring and I simultaneously shoved everything I had into powering it. My breath condensed in front of me for any wizards that didn't already know I was casting. The silver ring hummed as the next flamethrower from Blackstar's fingers hit.

The ring stopped magical things entering from outside, creating a no-man's land inside Zora's circle. I still got enough of the blast to knock me flat.

"*Rifle,*" I grunted. My AK appeared in my hand. I took aim at Blackstar and fired. It was on full auto. The bullets bounced off his shield, though I could tell keeping it up was an effort for him. "*Mag!*" I yelled above the din. All hell was breaking loose. I was supposed to be a hundred yards away by now.

I was on my back, fighting to hold the rifle steady. The Executive was pummeling Broc with one spell after another. Neka had turned into the biggest cougar I'd ever seen, with claws to match. The Hag was dodging his blows or burning anything that got close, causing Neka to keep shifting forms. A reindeer, which had to be Carol, and a large black wolf were helping him out. I didn't have time to back them up—Blackstar was advancing. I switched out mags in the span of a breath. Not fast enough.

"*Pechio Forma Hasuto Conia Mecheia!*" I rolled and cleared the circle. Dammit, too early. Much hotter flames hit the earth three feet away from where I was lying, and some of them caught me. Suddenly, it was a warmer night. I kept rolling to put out the fire and aimed the rifle again. Semi-auto this time, but I didn't stop shooting.

Blackstar threw up his shield, but he was inside the silver ring and it was much less effort now. I was supposed to be running. Check that, I was supposed to be long gone, but I wasn't leaving. Anger was going to get me killed. "You're already dead Maker…" I remembered Arta saying. Screw that! I was alive, and I was gonna to stay that way.

"*Brick!*" The concrete failure dropped to the ground next to me. It'd been worthless until about four seconds ago.

"*Move!*" I screamed. The pile of viscous concrete hit Blackstar's shield and spread out to cover the whole thing in an instant. I could finally see the full outline. "*Solid!*" The concrete hardened into what concrete should be but it would only stay that way for a few seconds. It was enough.

"*Boom!*" I screamed. I threw the grenade that dropped into my hand and ran like my life depended on it.

Blackstar wouldn't be able to see it, and for all he knew, that concrete would stay solid. If he wanted to get out he would have to drop his shield and cast something. That plan had worked at least. I heard a scream of "Grenade!" behind me, but I didn't stop running until I heard the explosion.

Chapter: 24

Most people don't know the first thing about grenades.
They think that a grenade explodes, James Bond gets up, brushes off his still immaculate tux, grabs the girl and saunters away for another martini. I wish I were James Bond.

In reality, the grenade explosion isn't all that big a deal. It's just used to shatter the metal casing into a million fast-moving, knife-edged shards of death that rip through thin pseudo-concrete shells like wet tissue paper.

The kill radius on the average grenade is about three to five meters. I was further away than that. Not far enough.

Pieces of shrapnel hit my jacket and pants. My spell worked clothing did its job, taking the momentum and spreading it out over a wider area and greater time. Instead of a sharp piece of metal that would go right through me, it hit like one hammer after another.

I only remembered the first two, and I went down. I managed to land on a shoulder and roll onto my back. I fired my rifle at Blackstar, who was down on a knee holding his shoulder. The bullets still bounced off a shield I couldn't see, but his left leg and right arm were stained with blood. I hadn't missed every time.

Firehag, the Executive, and two of the gunman were covering Blackstar's back. Both were throwing spells for all they were worth at the oncoming vampires. Clustered inside the ring, they were able to mount a successful defense. Their spells still grounded out eventually, but they went much further from inside. I rolled to my feet and took off. Neka and Broc were nowhere in sight; neither were the other shapeshifters.

I got into the treeline and took cover to breathe for a moment. I chose a tree and clicked my heels together once to activate my boots. I jumped twenty feet straight up onto a large branch and got comfortable.

"*Owl*," I said and put on the sunglasses that dropped into my hand. Through them I could see as well as if it were daylight, except everything was cast in shades of faint blue. There was very little color to be had in night vision. There was very little vision to be had at all. My face was burned and my right eye was still a blur.

I let out a sigh. That was stupid. I didn't know if I was more angry at myself for not killing Blackstar, or ashamed for violating the plan in the first place. I breathed while the cynical voice in my mind teased me about self-control. That I was no better than Zora.

"Shut up, brain, or I'll stab you with a q-tip," I growled at myself. Some of the best wisdom in the world came from Homer Simpson. I summoned a scope from my pack and screwed it on the rifle. I had to look through it with the wrong eye.

Everything was working out well enough so far. I tested the aim by shooting one of the dead vampires. It wasn't perfect firing with the wrong hand and eye, but after a few shots I managed to hit what I aimed at.

I could see the whites of their eyes now, literally. I was still inside the circle but only just. I wanted to be close for this part. Blackstar was back up and throwing fire at the vamps that were closing in.

I fired at the Executive and hit a shield. Firing at the Hag got the same result. I suspected all of them were under Blackstar's shield. I was sure the shield was something like the silver circle, only much stronger. Physical objects could leave, but it kept me out. The specifics didn't matter so long as there was a shield up and they were feeling safe.

Time for the next step. I reached for the detonator in my pocket. I was hoping it hadn't been fried. There was a lot of energy flying around. If you get enough power in the air, electrons flowed and everything shorted out. Hopefully it was still good, but if not, I had a plan for that.

The vampires had surrounded The Constellation and were starting to close in. Duke was there directing them forward. I couldn't help but smile.

I pressed the button, and there was a deeply satisfying pair of booms. I surmised that only about half the homemade C-4 had gone off, and that blew the other half. As a result, Blackstar, his people, and twenty or so vampires were blown a few dozen yards to the southwest. It wasn't the most potent stuff—it was difficult to make military-grade C-4 on a kitchen stove—but I wasn't relying fully on explosives either.

The wizards were thrown out into the circle. The silver ring of protection was gone, along with most of the feral vamps. The charges were lined with steel balls that flew outward at the blast.

Only about ten or so vampires were still standing; I saw with a smile that Broc wasn't one of them. I took aim, fired at Blackstar, and hit the Executive instead. Right in the gut. My scope showed me his look of surprise and pain. I fired twice more. Both shots took him in the chest. He fell to his knees with blood oozing from his mouth. Two nearby wounded ferals were on him in moments, ripping at arteries to get at the freshest blood.

"Now you can be Steven Mendon," I said.

Firehag screamed, and I panned over to see Duke himself feeding on her. The scream cut off as her throat was torn out. More ferals were drinking from both the recently dead and the few left living.

Zora was right on time dropping the circle. In Duke's mind she would be early, but if he was stupid enough to think I'd stick to our deal, then he deserved whatever he got.

Blackstar felt it just as I did and he lashed out at Duke with a fan of flames that lit up the night. Duke moved with a grace and speed I didn't follow. The Hag's body dropped, and it was still on fire when the smoke cleared.

They faced each other for a moment, the god of death and the god of magic. The night seemed to settle even though there were still gunshots and screams on both sides.

Blackstar cast and I sighed. It was that euphoric feeling that comes when a strategy works. I had a lot of Plan B's. Most had died a quick death by now, but I had gotten to the ultimate goal of the evening; lounging in a tree, patiently watching Duke and Blackstar fight to the death so I could shoot the winner.

An eight-foot tall spire of rock erupted from the ground to Blackstar's right, and Duke moved just in time. It started firing rocks at him that hit the ground, leaving tiny craters everywhere. Duke was staying ahead of rocks that were faster than bullets, but he made it look graceful—almost casual.

The few remaining vampires were moving to surround Blackstar while Duke kept his attention. Worse than that, many of the vamps were getting up. I didn't know any by name, but there were enough for Duke's inner circle to have survived. A few ferals, and of course, Broc.

Blackstar tossed some fire at a vamp that got too close, setting it alight in the night air. A second vampire screamed, holding its head and then jumped in front of Blackstar, blocking an attack from Duke that could've taken his head off. Duke grabbed the vampire by the neck while Blackstar retreated. Duke used the vampire's body to block the incoming rocks and did something I'd never seen before.

The vampire he was holding grew sickly looking and got steadily thinner until just a skeleton with skin remained and fell to dust. What the hell was that?

Bolts of pure darkness shot from the air in front of Duke and hit Blackstar's shield with so much force I could feel it from where I was. The sounds came too—high-pitched thunder like Hephaestus pounding on the earth.

I didn't know how Duke was able to use magic; for a vampire it was supposed to be impossible, but he did it anyway and did it well. Just not as good as Blackstar.

The ground around the warlock froze solid, stealing away some of Duke's ridiculous mobility. It was a good plan, but it didn't work. Duke wasn't affected by the slippery grass underfoot, and the shots from the earth spire weren't any closer to hitting him. He was still held at bay by the thing. Getting closer would mean less time to react, and likely getting hit. I'm sure Duke was already as close as he dared.

A moment after the ice formed a yellowish haze spread over the area where they clashed. The dark bolts from Duke stopped, and he retreated beyond the cloud. Whatever it was had to be acidic. Duke's suit was smoking and already eaten away in places.

Blackstar was smart to keep Duke at a distance, but it backfired in that moment. Neither of them could see through that cloud. Duke took a deep breath and blew out what looked like dust. It covered the area of Blackstar's yellow acid and then some.

I couldn't see Blackstar, but if he had any sense, he'd be running. Duke reached into his pocket and pulled out an old silver lighter, flicked it open and threw it in the cloud. The dust ignited like a coal mine blast and nearly shook me out of my tree. I regained my balance just in time to see Blackstar being blown back and Duke moving like Zora to catch him on the ground.

They had traveled beyond the range of that spire of earth. At least that's what I assume since it stopped firing and crumbled.

Blackstar landed and cast something that forced him immediately back into the air.

Duke landed a split second later. His punch into the hard, North Carolina clay embedded his arm up to the elbow. Blackstar would've been dead several times over if he didn't cast so quickly.

The earth rose up and wrapped around Duke by the arm and both legs. Blackstar grinned in triumph. I got ready to shoot him. Just after he killed Duke, his guard would drop. I didn't see the air solidify around Duke, but the earth fell away from his arms and legs and he stood up doing a quick street mime routine that would be funny if I weren't terrified. The air around him was a sphere. I know that because it started to fill with water as Blackstar stood and laughed. Duke crossed his arms and waited.

I supposed there wasn't much he could do. Drowning is a perfectly valid way to kill a vampire. As long as Blackstar kept the water flowing and the shield up, Duke was in was in checkmate.

I watched the water rise over his head, filling the bubble. I moved my finger to the trigger. I didn't know how long Blackstar would keep it up, but I wanted to be ready. A few feral vamps had gotten around him, but he seemed to pay them no mind.

The shape inside the bubble moved, and it shattered. The water rushed out onto the ground and in the center stood Duke with one arm stretched out to the side where he'd swung so hard the sphere of air cracked. Blackstar wasn't laughing now. This was the psychological warfare portion of the program.

I sat there amazed. What kind of monsters were these?! I was even more relieved now that I wasn't down there.

Duke let the fact that he had taken Blackstar's best shot sink in a moment and attacked. I blinked, and there were five Blackstars all moving away in different directions. Illusions were the height of difficulty. It wasn't just a picture. To fool someone, you had to imitate sounds, smells—everything. The level of detail involved is astounding, and Blackstar had done it five times in a blink. I didn't even know which one was real.

Duke was only fooled for a moment. He whipped his head around studying each one a few times and then launched himself after the one going south. Blackstar ducked and got a gash on his chest that would've hit his neck.

Blackstar cast again, and five daggers made of rock sprung from the earth and hovered around him, slashing at Duke and driving him back. Another vampire took this moment to throw himself at Blackstar and paid for that mistake with its life. One of the daggers veered off and blocked a chain thrown by Broc. For the second time tonight, Blackstar was surrounded.

Most fights were seconds long; you could live a lifetime in those seconds. This fight was going on two minutes.

Blackstar and the vampires were engaged in an elegant dance; each time one would get close a new spell fended them off. Blackstar used everything in his arsenal; tear gas, rocks, fire, air. There were sharpened blades of grass and some kind of black ooze. One of the vampires screamed, grabbing his head and throwing himself in the way of Broc's chains.

Spells flew, and vampires twisted to dodge them. They were jackals. Biting and maneuvering, trying to gain advantage from every side. The vampire forces were being thinned out. Less than thirty were left out of the hundred that started the fight.

Any that got close enough found Blackstar's shield and a nasty spell waiting. It was a deeply impressive spectacle. Of course, I could only say that because I was hiding in a tree.

Duke was watching, as the other vampires wore him down. Blackstar would be dead soon, and I wouldn't even need to do it myself. The plan had worked better than I'd hoped, except for him being the last Constellation wizard left. Still, all the vampires had to do was chase the king around the board until the game was over.

I spotted Zora weaving rapidly through the trees, meaning she must have taken care of the other Constellation members. It took a second to process that she wasn't going the way we planned. With a sinking feeling, I looked up to where she was headed.

She must've felt the demon before I did. I felt it before I saw it—felt it and cringed inside. I screwed up. I put Blackstar's back to the wall. Worse, I gave him the time to realize he'd been backed into a corner. Of course, he'd call out the demon now, even if he couldn't control it. He had nothing left to lose.

Summoning a demon was beyond difficult, but that was child's play when compared to actually controlling one. Getting a demon to do what you want was being so powerful that you didn't give the beast a choice. Most people couldn't even get their teenager to do the dishes. If Firehag and the Executive were alive and they were all on the same page mentally, they might have been able to get it done.

I took three shots at Blackstar. One missed, and two hit his shield.

The shadow of the night coalesced into a beast horrible enough to be spawned from my nightmare's nightmares. It was twenty feet tall and had four arms with three-fingered hands ending in claws that were proportionally larger than talons should be. Its head was a perfectly round black ball with a vertical split full of what looked like stained black fingers.

As it reached out, I saw that the palm of each hand had something similar. There was another mouth that ran the length of its torso, and one on each thigh. When it ran on all six limbs, I could see there were two more on the bottoms of its four-toed feet.

I wanted to run just seeing it.

The retreat signal was in my pack, but I didn't bother. Running was a joke with a demon around. It wasn't like I could vacate the planet.

Only someone who summoned it could know its name, and

only someone who knew its name could send it back to whatever hell spawned it. If what I knew about demons was true, then it would go straight for anyone that knew its name so it couldn't be sent back. Then it would start killing or torturing everything in sight. Maybe it would kill Duke after it ripped Blackstar to shreds.

Some of the vamps were not so quick on the uptake as I was. Two went down instantly, and the creature snapped up, and swallowed another four before I had time to process what I was seeing.

Blackstar was yelling orders to the demon. Worse, the demon was following those orders. Blackstar was controlling that thing by himself?!

I felt like I was about to puke. I was so out of my league.

The demon cleared another few ferals off Blackstar. Even Duke dodged an attack. In his haste to save his own ass, Blackstar was nearly gutted by the thing.

As large as it was, it moved like Zora. It just blurred and was somewhere else. I took aim at Blackstar. If it was gonna go for Duke again, it was gonna happen fast. The beast roared, only there was no sound. The roar was inside my head, and it hurt like one of Arta's bellows.

I heard screams as the sound resonated in the minds of anyone left alive. Duke seemed to be immune, zipping up to Blackstar and going right for his throat. He missed and got the injured arm instead. Even at this distance I clearly heard Blackstar scream. I took a shot at his chest as he jumped back from Duke and hit his shield again. Dammit.

"Maker." I turned at Neka's voice and saw a small man, whose obsidian skin clung to his skeletal form, with the dark feathered wings of a crow. Zora was crouched near him on a different branch. "What do we do about that thing?"

"First pass me a bandage." Zora handed one over. I dropped my hood, slapped it on my eye, and put my hood and mask back up. "If its name is at Blackstar's, then I could command it to leave, but there is no way to know if he wrote it down. Probably didn't. I wouldn't."

"So how do we kill it?" He asked.

"Fire should do it. Lots of it. I can provide the fire, but it won't work if Blackstar is still alive giving it orders. Have to kill him first. For now, help Duke, but stay away from that thing and don't take any chances trying to close. Let Duke take the risks."

"Why? I'm no coward!" Neka snapped. What the hell did that have to do with anything? If there was a risk to be taken, let your enemies take it. Zora spoke before I did.

"No worries Neka. When they're all dead, and I'm writing history, we'll leave this part out."

She jumped down and landed soft as a feather. A moment later they were gone.

In the time that took, the vamps had moved the creature off and harried it to the far end of the clearing.

The fight between Duke and Blackstar was near the center. Blackstar had produced a staff from somewhere and was swinging as he cast certain spells. Duke twisted and dodged as acid and sharp rocks sprayed the air. Duke could avoid a ball of flame, but a rain of acid was trickier. His suit was damaged to the point he'd ripped off the top half of it, and the burns on his skin were evident even at this distance.

The vamps with the demon were down to five. The demon had surprised them before; now they were keeping their distance. The beast was much faster, but if they had a second head start, they could stay ahead of it. They were also slowly burning it with torches, darting in to attack the flanks like a pack of wolves attacking a bear. Broc was there, whipping the thing with spiked chains each time it turned its back.

Neka swiped at Blackstar from above in the form of a giant hawk. One set of talons raked his right shoulder, and the other savaged his face. Blackstar struck with a flame that burned Neka out of the sky. Zora caught him and blurred away. Dammit, I said no risks. I took a shot at Blackstar and hit him in the leg. The second shot hit his shield and so did Duke as he attacked from above.

Blackstar was back up and bleeding heavily now. I must've hit an artery; bright blood was pumping out and splattering the ground, and Neka's strikes weren't trivial either. Blackstar still threw spells at Duke—he hadn't slowed his pace at all.

A fog came up where Blackstar was standing. Like the earth was breathing heavy. With each inhale the fog contracted a bit, and with each exhale it greatly expanded. Soon it would cover the whole clearing. I knew what this was. I had run away more than enough times to know. From inside the fog I heard Duke yell something indistinguishable. Broc reacted instantly, dropping his attack on the demon and running towards the noise.

Zora was there from nowhere and sliced open the backs of his legs. The big vamp went down and Zora took a second to impale him through the back. I couldn't see what else she did from the angle I was at, but she was gone just before the demon got there. It used one hand to throw Broc into its chest mouth. The fingers clutched at Broc and drug him in, despite the chains lashing at the inside of its mouth. God that thing was weird.

There was the sound of an explosion. Zora had apparently planted her grenades on Broc before he was eaten. Not enough fire to kill it, but it was damaged. It roared again; the sound was in my head again. Dare I say I was getting used to it? This time it didn't hurt at all. Felt kinda good actually.

The fog dissipated in moments and Blackstar was gone. I took my eye off the scope and looked around. I didn't see him anywhere. There was nowhere he could've run to for cover that quickly. Moreover, Duke was also looking around, and he'd only been a few feet away. No way he had gotten away from a determined vampire.

Could Blackstar have teleported? That was the only way I

knew to get away that fast. It was against Merlin's laws to physically traverse another plane, but Merlin's laws had never stopped Blackstar before.

If I were Blackstar, I would be thinking this night had gone to hell. Crew gone, demon maybe gone… at the very least he knew he was being hunted and he'd lost almost everything. I'd be trying to cut my losses, bail, heal and find somewhere else to set up shop.

I jumped to the ground and rolled. At least I knew where his first stop would be, but I didn't have much time.

"*Kitty Pride.*" The potion appeared in my hand, and I drank on the run. It took forever for it to activate, but once it did I was moving. I covered the two miles to Blackstar's hideout in two minutes. Running through the woods at that speed is downright reckless. I almost fell and broke my neck a few times.

I got to the tree line and spotted the farmhouse. This had to be it; there was no other house in sight. There was a barn and fence where some running horse might be if it weren't the middle of the night.

I walked right in. The furnishings were nice. Something you might find in a *Better Homes and Gardens* magazine. I waited for the wards to turn me into Jell-O or maybe explode, but that didn't come. The people that had lived here were dead. I could tell from the smell.

There was a trail of blood on the wood floor, and it ran to a door that I assume went down to a cellar of some kind. I could hear someone yelling down there.

I had my rifle at the ready, with a nearly full clip I was just waiting to burn. The door wasn't shut fully, and I edged it open with the barrel, hoping the door wouldn't creak. I went down the stairs, confident that the potion would silence any noise I made. That would include creaking stairs, but for some reason, it never extended to creaking doors.

The basement was huge. The ceiling was eight feet, and

everything was cement or drywall. Bullets went through drywall. Cement not so much.

I proceeded down the hall towards the noise. There was still screaming from someone in a language I didn't know. I passed one room and ignored the bodies in it—well, tried to anyway. I would never be able to fully ignore the faces of dead people I couldn't save, and these were children.

Well, there were children among them. There were more than ten bodies stacked in the room against one wall. It was human sacrifice made efficient. The Constellation had taken these people and turned them into a commodity. Like bags of corn stacked in the corner until the bodies could be used for something or disposed of.

There were more accusing eyes in the room on the other side. Both were murals of blood and human entrails. I was walking faster now; I didn't want to look in the next room, but despite myself, I did. This room only had one body. Cut down the middle and every organ set in a circle drawn in blood around it. The kid couldn't have been more than two.

Something snapped. I lost it. Whatever "it" was. You hear about it sometimes. When you've seen too much, and can't see anymore. Your brain just shuts off. Everything was suddenly quiet. I knew someone was yelling, but I couldn't make out the words. I was moving, but I couldn't feel the floor beneath my feet.

The final room came into view. Blackstar and a shorter person in a black robe that covered all but their eyes. Their eyes were white completely. No pupil or iris, just white sclera all the way across. Shroud. They went to cast spells, both of them, but I didn't care. I didn't care about anything as long as they died.

As long as I killed them for everything they'd done.

They started to speak. Their hands moved, but they were moving so slowly, I had all day to decide what to do with them. A far-off part of my mind wondered If this was justice or revenge. The answer didn't seem to matter. As long as a trigger was squeezed. As long as this never happened again.

I fired into the room. I didn't care that I was on full auto. I emptied the clip.

I heard someone say "*Mag*." There was another clip in the rifle, but I didn't remember the motion I took to put it there. I was ready to fire, but there was no one left standing.

My world lurched back into normal speed when I bent over and puked.

I stood again, spitting bile and breathing heavy like I had just run all the way here holding my breath. I noticed a hole in the air zip closed before me. Shroud must've escaped the bullets by ducking through it. Not likely, but possible. Blackstar was on the ground with a hand holding his torn up stomach. He was holding in his guts, but it was pretty clear he was finished.

"What's the demon's name?" I demanded.

Blackstar coughed up a laugh. Some blood escaped his lips. "What will you do if I not tell you eh? Kill me?"

"What am I, one of the bad guys?" I said flatly. "I'm going to give you an opportunity to do the right thing. *Heal me*." A potion dropped into my hand. It was green and glowed slightly. "This will heal you. I've never taken one because I'm pretty sure it will also shorten your life by a few decades. On my power, it's yours if you give me the name of the demon." Blackstar stared at me for a long moment.

Apparently, he decided something. His lips parted, and I brought up the rifle. His smile dropped and he parted his lips again, speaking each syllable slowly.

"Lansavaknen." Somehow just hearing it I knew it meant 'that which slaughters the innocent lambs.' Weird.

I tossed the potion into Blackstar's lap, and he drank it. At once his bleeding stopped. He screamed as bones reknit and skin brought itself together. Recovery could be just as painful as injury, apparently. I was fascinated. I'd never seen anyone drink one before. I'd came up with the recipe years ago, and after using it on a few dogs, cats, and mice, I decided against ever drinking one.

Taking a pill medicated the entire body—whether it needed it or not. Same principle here. That potion put so much stress on the body fixing everything wrong with every cell that the mice died within a few days and the cats and dogs lasted less than a year.

Another failure in a line of dismal failures, but it had given me the base knowledge needed to make the magical bandages I was so fond of. No way I was giving Blackstar one of those.

The warlock slowly got to his feet.

"My thanks, friend." He was trashed. He fell back to the floor with a grunt, barely able to stand. Barely form words either. The accent had gotten much heavier. I could tell now that he was from Russia or Ukraine somewhere. I was still between him and the doorway.

The smell of blood, puke, and death hung around me. Hung around the whole house. I stood in the doorway of a room in hell. I didn't move. I still saw the faces of the dead in those rooms. The only living thing was the man who made them, sitting down there helpless and looking like he'd fall asleep any moment.

"Do not worry my friend. I will be well. Leave me," he said. His eyes grew wide as I raised my rifle. "NO! NO! You gave your word!" He was trying to scramble away, but the room wasn't that big.

"What am I? One of the good guys?"

Chapter: 25

Blackstar was dead.

Thirty rounds of 762 mm slugs to the chest tend to do that. I snatched a gas line out of a wall and left the basement. Anyone paying attention would notice a small wooden doll strapped to the outside of my pack. If I lived, it would make a wonderful surprise for Shroud. Only if I lived, though. I put it out of my mind. "One thing at a time Maker." This night was far from over.

"*Burn.*" The potion dropped into my hand, and I threw it at a wall near some curtains on the first floor before I ran out.

No one wanted to see what was in that basement. I wasn't going to make some poor coroner go through what I just did. Certainly not. Rollo could make everyone believe they died in a fire. That was better for everyone living. I could only hope that what I'd done already somehow helped the dead.

Speaking of Rollo, he was probably around somewhere. The area had remained clear, but this would change that. The fire department couldn't ignore an obviously burning residence, no matter what he said.

It didn't matter. He'd done his part; now I had to finish mine.

"Lansavaknen." I whispered. My mind flooded with images.

Images of death, torture, the screaming of innocents. I knew things about the beast just by uttering its name—things no sane person would want to know.

I knew its rage, its passion, and its thirst for death. I also knew somehow that I couldn't send it back just by knowing its name. The beast was already moving this way, but slowly. It was injured, and it was chasing the annoying lamb that was too fast to catch.

"Zora!" I took off into the woods. I was moving as fast as my boots and the potion could carry me. It had to be nearly spent by now, another few minutes maybe. This was a great batch; you could never tell with potions before you drank one.

I found the demon crashing through the woods after Zora. I ran right past, and she turned and followed. The creature wasn't slowed by the underbrush. The grenade I dropped didn't hurt it. My pistol didn't work either. Zora fell back, slicing at its legs and flanks with the flaming dagger. That worked, just not very well.

I moved behind trees at every chance. It knocked them over, but it had to stop, and by then, I was gone.

I stopped trying to fight and ran for the field I picked out. Between my boots and the potion in me, I was just a little slower than it was. If not for the trees it would've caught me in the first few seconds.

The field was roughly circular, and I was at the far end when I heard it crash through the treeline. The fiend roared that insane, silent, roar in my head.

"Lansavaknen!" I yelled. "Leave this world now, and never return!" The beast roared but stayed where it was. "It was worth a shot anyway," I growled, looking up at the sky. I didn't see anything except a couple light puffy clouds and a sea of stars.

Zora appeared at my shoulder and dropped my staff. She had the pommel of the hydra tooth wrapped in white tape and held it in one hand with the heat dagger in the other.

"I told you to leave that at home!" I yelled. The last thing we needed was Duke—or anyone for that matter—recognizing it and turning on us.

She looked at me incredulously. "You wanna talk about this now?" She was away and sliced into the demon with both blades, getting away with a graze that almost took her off her feet. She was back next to me after a second, bleeding at the shoulder. "Plan?!"

The tooth was spiderwebbed with tiny streaks of black that seemed to be pulsing and getting bigger.

I stared at it for a moment. "Why's it doing that?" I asked.

"Don't know," she said and charged again. Lansavaknen missed her head, but roared at the injuries being inflicted. The tooth opened wide furrows in its flesh that didn't close and heal right away.

"Zora, you have to—"

She rounded on me screaming. "Will you please fucking focus on the task at hand?!"

She was away again, slicing across the demon where its hamstrings would be. She was right of course. No sense worrying about something dangerous tomorrow when there was something right here that will kill us today.

"Stay on opposite sides and keep it off balance," I said when she returned. "When we leave it's gonna happen quick." I said.

"*Boom. Burn. Air is not soft.*"

I said the commands one after the other. The beast blurred and so did Zora. They met in the middle and I heard her scream. I was already firing. The air pistol hit the demon in the head. That vertical slit of a mouth turned to me. At least that got its attention. I threw the grenade and missed getting it into one of its mouths. The explosion seemed to hurt it, but not as much as I'd like.

Zora took the chance to slash across its lower back. She screamed its name right before she ran in. The thing couldn't help but stop and listen at the call of its name.

It made no noise but turned to her. I fired again. Three shots, three hits, and nothing.

"*Digger!*" My wand was in my hand looking cracked and frail. With my wand in one hand and air pistol in the other, I hammered at the thing. It healed from Zora's strikes almost instantly. Mine too, but there was nothing it could do without balance.

Keeping it up on two legs, with stones to the head, attacks to the triceps and hamstrings, while yelling its name was difficult enough. I didn't know how long we could keep it up.

Zora got in a great hit, nearly taking the creature's leg off. It reattached even as she cut through, but that was the half second I needed. I rushed the demon and got to the center of the field when the potion died.

Suddenly I was running in the other direction as fast as my enchanted boots would allow. It was lightning fast by human standards, but in the realm of supernatural monstrosities, it didn't even register.

Lansavaknen turned in time to hit me. If it had struck on balance, it would've torn me in half. As it was, I was nearly gutted and sent flying. I got on my feet before the pain could hit and realized it wasn't that bad. I looked down to see a bloody mess of stomach tissue. I had enough time to wonder if I was in shock.

"Maker down!" Zora screamed. The demon was looking my direction. That was all the warning I was gonna get.

"*Expel!*" My wand shattered and fell to dust. Luckily it released a few tons of rocks, dirt and debris onto the creature. That hurt it. It screamed in pain, which oddly felt pleasurable to listen to in my head. It still made no actual sounds as it thrashed around.

"*Multiburn.*" I'd made a batch of fire potions specifically for this occasion, and fourteen total appeared at my feet, along with some homemade Molotov cocktails, homemade thermite, and a few milk jugs full of gasoline. I wasn't holding back anything tonight.

Zora ripped open my shirt and slapped on a bandage at her full speed. I stumbled back and screamed at the pain. She scooped up five bottles and ran. I threw, and she threw. Each of us grabbing more from the pile whenever we ran out, making a death pyre in the rocks and stone.

Inside my head was a euphoric feeling each time a fire potion hit. I could see skin charring and healing slower than it had only moments before. As I planned, the rocks heated up quickly and with that many potions, even granite started to melt.

Zora cut deep with the tooth and shoved a potion inside before it could heal. She paid for it in the form of a backhand from the thing that took her off her feet. She managed to cut a finger with the dagger on her way down. I threw the last three as a distraction and she was able to get away.

Zora was back by my side in a flash. The tooth was nearly all black by now, and the black veins ran up her arm to the shoulder. She was bleeding from her other shoulder, her leg and she had a nasty gash on her chest. Her eyes were determination, but her face was all fatigue. We had never pushed this hard before.

"*Salute!*" I screamed. Normally there was only a slight chill when I summoned from my pack. Not so this time. The rifle on my back flew into the air and joined nine others about twenty feet up. They made a circle around the demon and all fired at once. On full auto, they went through bullets quickly, but each time one was fired another was summoned from my pack. Took hours to convince the universe to behave on that one.

I only had a few thousand rounds so this wouldn't take long. I could already see a few of the barrels starting to glow red. Next, they would melt, and after that, we would die.

"We're done here. Get Neka and go—this place is about to get unpleasant." Zora didn't ask questions, didn't think, she just moved. The beast showed its face and Zora shoved the tooth in its chest and cut through on her way out. It healed almost instantly, and there was no blood. I ran over and picked up my staff. The salute spell had drained it some.

"*Move!*" I shouted. All ten rifles had red hot barrels, and every one stabbed through Lansavaknen and pinned it to the piles of once-melted, slowly cooling rocks. It could barely move, but that didn't keep it from struggling.

"*Boom.*" With both hands full, the grenade dropped to the ground, and I hit it with my staff to send it flying at the demon. I'd hate golf even more after this.

It was able to free one of its arms with a great ripping of flesh. The arm was healing already, but slowly. "Lansavaknen!" I screamed, and a rage of flame from my staff burned its one free arm. This was my flame that consumed magical energy. Lansavaknen was giving off so much it engulfed the demon in seconds. I cast again, trying to make it even hotter. It's euphoric screams in my mind felt better and better. Go home!" That same arm was again consumed in flame, and I was straining to keep it that way with grenades and fire from my staff. I was circling around, moving away and still trying to keep the arm that it would use to free itself in sight. "Go home Lansavaknen! Never return!" The next flame from my staff hit it in the head.

Soon I was out of grenades, and my staff was empty. Evocation drained it faster than anything else. No matter, I'd bought the time I needed.

There was no fire I could make that was enough to burn this thing out of existence.

Luckily, I wasn't bound by fire only I could make.

I knelt down and picked up what I had been circling around for. I had to "unhook" my spring failure from the Earth. Small force at a far-off distance. Even I didn't realize just how far off until I tested it. You didn't need much force to move things in space. Gravity was always happy to do work. Ha! At least I'm going out on a physics joke.

"*Move.*" The spring fired off and embedded in the thing's back.

"*Poke'ball,*" I said, and the ankh appeared in my hand. Before I could register the horror of holding that much power, I threw it in the pile beneath the demon. Fire or the ankh, one of them had better work.

The sky got ever so slightly brighter behind me, and I ran like hell.

The edge of the field was a few steps away when I finally gave in and looked up. A huge ball of flame and rock was coming down through the atmosphere, straight at the demon. If my calculations were right, it would be about the size of a baseball when it hit. It only looked so big now because it was about to kill me.

I jumped into the hole I had dug two days ago. It wasn't deep enough, or far away enough—not nearly. What the hell had I been thinking?!

"*There is no spoon.*" The silver tablespoon appeared in my hand and I set to work, desperately heaving large rocks into a wall in front of the hole. I was on my third scoop when I heard the screaming start. Like incoming artillery only louder and more menacing.

Then the world went white.

* * *

Screaming didn't help. My whole body ached and one of my legs wouldn't work. I was coughing up blood, and I couldn't hear anything that wasn't a loud, persistent ringing. Everything smelled burnt.

I was a dozen yards or more away from my shelter. The ground itself had been torn up so that only a small indentation remained. I must've hit a tree. I couldn't find my spoon anywhere.

I limped back to the field. I didn't think it was this way; I was dizzy and disoriented. The whole world was blurry. All the trees were lying pointing towards me, so the field must be this way, right? I drug my worthless leg along and realized that my side was bleeding. My right arm wouldn't move, so I used my left to apply pressure. I was too numb for anything to hurt.

I didn't see my staff anywhere; I didn't have a hand to pick it up, but I still looked. The field was now a larger field. Everything was charred or smoking or on fire. The center of it had a black form in the middle that the flames still licked at. I leaned on a tree and felt the charred wood searing my shoulder. That wasn't right—my clothes were supposed to be fireproof, even if they were mostly burned off.

When I got to the field, Lansavaknen was violently lurching to and fro. I was mouthing words, but no sounds came out. "No, no." That was everything I had.

Somehow I got to my feet and just stood there. I couldn't run; not sure I had anything left to fight with. Was I wearing my pack? The demon beast wailed in pain and gave me that feeling of immense pleasure. It clawed at the ground while it burned, but it was too weak from the fire to resist being pulled into the little black rock. Lansavaknen grew smaller and smaller. The final wail cut off and the night was silent.

"*M... mov...*" I could barely speak. My throat felt burned, but the ankh flew from the rubble and I shoved it in my only remaining cargo pocket before I could think too hard about it.

I collapsed. It was done. *I* was done. I didn't know what to do. It was funny. I usually had a plan. Zora was still good. If Neka hadn't been burned too bad we could… I laughed. I couldn't think of one idea. Not a single one.

It was a stupid thought. I just kept laughing.

Fallout

I couldn't say the last week had been fun. Sitting in my attic apartment with an ace bandage wrapped around my head, trying to preserve my dashing good looks. Most of my body was burned. My whole left side had one burn or another. The inside of me probably didn't look much better.

I woke up in the hospital with no idea how I'd gotten there. I had a list of all the people I would expect to be standing vigil by my hospital bed. Duke was not on it. I was startled at first; I was certain he'd come to kill me, and he had the perfect opportunity—Zora couldn't stop him, and I was useless.

Daylight streamed through the windows. There were beeps coming from some machine that was turned away from me. It was daytime, but there didn't seem to be much activity around my room. Of course, I didn't notice any of this as I immediately got to work pulling the tubes out of my nose and throat, thinking of how I was going to sneak out of there—dodging the undoubtedly enormous bill.

"There you are," said a hypnotizing baritone. Duke was sitting in the corner in one of the two chairs. His teeth shined in the daylight. I looked past him; through him. I didn't dare meet his eyes in the condition I was in... whatever that was.

The gasp hurt. I grunted and clenched my teeth, which also hurt. In the daze that followed, I noticed that several of my teeth were missing. My whole head was in a fog, and I was dizzy even while laying down. Focus quickly became an endurance trial, which was great since I assumed Duke's gaze could only work if I were mentally capable enough to have thoughts.

From my head down was a mass of tingling muted pain. Must've been good painkillers. From what I could see, everything was covered in bandages. Everything I couldn't see also. I felt them wrapped tightly around my head, with only one eye uncovered. My ears hurt and Duke sounded like he was much further away. I'd had internal bleeding enough times to know what the fatigue, body chills, and pressure in my stomach meant. I was in bad shape to be sure.

Duke only smiled larger at my additional discomfort. "You betrayed me," he said. A prelude to death if ever I heard one.

My mouth didn't want to work. I summoned every scrap of willpower—since that was apparently all I had—and managed to make words.

"True," I croaked out. "But in my defense, you're an asshole." I gathered some spit, which felt like dust, and swallowed a few times. It didn't help. "Come to finish me off once I woke up? Why does that strike me as weakness?"

I still sounded like a frog. My throat was a clone of the Sahara. Still, I tried to make it sound confident. If this was the end, there was no way I was gonna give him the satisfaction of knowing I was two seconds from filling my bedpan.

I thought about those emergency buttons they put on hospital beds. All that would accomplish is getting some poor innocent nurses killed along with me.

Duke merely laughed. "If ever you prove incapable of treachery, I will be forced to reconsider your utility."

"Well, we can't have that, can we?" I said dryly, even though I had no idea what he meant. "I'm sure the burns and internal bleeding will finish me off then. Now, if you would ever so kindly get the hell out and let me die in peace." I realized that I didn't feel any pain. The drip must've had morphine in it. If the injuries were that bad, it bode ill for a speedy recovery.

"A cynic at such a young age." He hadn't stopped smiling. It was unnerving. "I'm afraid I can't allow that either. All the best trauma surgeons saw to you yesterday. I'm happy to report all the surgeries were a success. They weren't able to repair all of the damage of course, but I'm sure you can take it from here. No, Maker, you will be alive another day to enjoy your spoils. What is the expression… you owe me one?" The way he said it made the hairs on my neck twitch. Well, it would have if they hadn't all been burned away.

"I don't owe you anything. " I said." If you wanna go around saving your enemies, then go ahead, but I'm not accepting responsibility for your poor life choices."

"Do you still not understand?" He grinned. "Take more care choosing your enemies than your friends, boy. Enemies are more important." Before I could come up with a retort, he was laughing and falling through the window.

"Well that's disturbing," a voice said from a corner behind me. I tried to turn and sit up. A spell died on my lips and I reached for my pistol as if I weren't wearing a butt-out hospital gown. When I saw it was Zora, I fell back with a groan and decided to stop testing the limits of my painkillers.

"You just don't wanna hear powerful vampires saying things you agree with," she said, setting my pack on the bed next to me. "Little fucker makes my skin crawl."

She went over to the two chairs, and after a moment picked

the one Duke had not been in and pulled it up to my bed. I'm not sure what the look on my face was, but Zora seemed to think it meant something.

"What? He agreed to safe conduct, and he paid all your hospital bills. It was either let him in or have it out in a hospital room." I nodded. I must look grim indeed. "Spoils?" She asked. "Did we get something out of this other than another sunrise?"

"I wish." I said. "I'd kill him with it. Maybe Blackstar had something to salvage, and he thinks I picked it up or something." I shrugged, or at least I tried to. That was for Duke's benefit, in case he was still around. We wouldn't be talking about the tooth or the ankh unless we were behind a threshold where a vamp couldn't hear us. "Check the window."

Zora went over and looked, but apparently she didn't see him anywhere, because she shrugged.

I knew he'd already gone through the house. That fire would've destroyed anything magical. I'd never tried it on anything as powerful as the ankh or the tooth, but Duke didn't know that.

What he knew is that some heavy magic had gone down to summon that demon and there was not a trace left in the rubble. After his fight with Blackstar, he'd searched it. I could smell the stink of charred remnants in the room, even over the stink of vampire.

"How long was I out?"

"This is the third day now. How you feeling?"

"Like I just prevented a war?"

She shrugged. "The demon is gone. It won't be happy with us if it ever gets summoned again. No one has heard anything from Blackstar. I've been out looking for him a couple times. Nothing. The farmhouse is a pile of ashes. Rollo still has it taped off. And that man is pissed by the way. It's hilarious, never seen him so upset."

"Then I'm doing just fine. How are you?"

"As well as can be expected." She held up a wrist that was covered in a tan cloth cast; the ones they give out for light sprains. "I heal quick these days, though nothing like having a bandage. Neka caught the worst of it."

"I saw the pyro Blackstar threw. How bad is he?"

"Bad," she said. "I thought it was just fire, but it couldn't have been. Neka has been in giant demon bird form ever since. I figured he could shift into something that wasn't burned and that would be the end of it, but he hasn't woken up. He's sprawled on a bed back at Miles'. Hasn't eaten; barely moved since the showdown. I only had a few bandages left and I used them all. No help."

"Dammit," I said. "As least he's still alive. We'll have to find a way to fix him up. Maybe there is some special medicine for shapeshifters or something. How bad am I? What time is it?" Zora checked her phone.

"About 1300. Massive internal bleeding. Pretty much every organ in you has a busted artery or two, and the worst concussion the doctors say they've ever seen. I saw an x-ray of your leg and it looks like gravel, so you were bleeding a lot there too. For some reason, they wanted to see if you woke up before they bothered with drilling holes in your head to relieve the pressure. The bandages spared you that I think. The x-ray says only one side of your skull is full of cracks. If you don't feel any of that, it's because you have a morphine drip so strong it made me jealous. I probably can't raise enough hell to get you discharged today."

"No, need," I said, "If Duke paid the bill—and man that's weird—we can just leave."

Zora nodded and yawned. Three days? She had probably not slept the whole time. Worse if she was standing in a room with Duke for three days. I couldn't imagine how terrible that would be.

Zora drank a charmer and sweet talked a couple nurses, but no one raised more than a token argument to stop us. It was amazing that my pack survived. Zora found it not far from the burnt-out field. All my other magical clothing was gone. I'd have to enchant a new shirt, pants, jacket, and boots—even my socks were gone. My clothes could stand most things, but being half burned to a crisp and then having the rest cut off me was a bit much. There was no way they survived that.

Zora carried me and my pack back to my place and left me there. I told her everything that happened and she gave me the ankh back. With a story about having to root around in a dumpster full of medical waste to get it out of the pants they'd cut off me

I wrapped my ace bandage around my head, all the way down to my neck. Turns out my left eye was gone. It had popped in the heat, or melted… or whatever eyes do. I was less concerned with my face and more with the massive brain damage. My thoughts were slow and disjointed. Foggy didn't begin to cover it. As I wrapped up my head, I was concerned; I'd never healed this much damage before. "Don't fail. Please don't fail," I whispered as I wrapped.

My staff was nowhere to be found, and I wouldn't be able to make any more with just the meager magic I brought to the table, so I sent Zora to look for it. She'd found my pack after all. My staff must be around there somewhere.

Once I was in my bed, I passed out. I shouldn't have been tired since I'd just slept three days, but in my apartment, I felt safe like I didn't feel anywhere else. Maybe subconsciously I couldn't fully rest in a hospital.

That was day one after Blackstar's demon had taken a hammer to my life. I guess I had also done it to myself, but I didn't like that thought, and the incessant itch and brain damage was making me irrational.

Days two and three were clones of each other. Zora brought me food, avoided the Masons, and reported on Neka's condition which was getting slowly worse. Meanwhile, I moved the sports wrap around, took five cold showers a day and tried not to scratch.

My whole left side was one giant itch. On the second day, I took the bandage off my face with Zora's help. A mirror showed that I didn't look like Jack Napier, but I so seldom looked in a mirror, the face that stared back still looked weird. The fortunate thing is that it wasn't covered in scars, had two eyes and all my teeth. Going even deeper, there was no brain damage.

On the third day, I sprouted some stripes of normal looking skin on my stomach amongst all the charred and exposed flesh.

"I'm done. Take it to Neka and get me as many sterile bandages as you can. I'll be exhausted, and they'll be weak, but we're going to need more."

"No," she said. The concern in her voice was obvious. Below the neck, with the exception of my abdomen, I still looked like a half-melted wax statue. "I like Neka fine, but you aren't even healed yet."

"True," I said, "but I'm not dying anymore. The rest of this is cosmetic. If you wanna help, find my staff. Then I can take a couple days and we'll both be fine."

Zora didn't argue and left. I ate the food she brought without tasting it. It had something to do with chicken. I was distracted because I was staring at my pack and plotting. Against all odds, a small wooden doll the size of my palm was still strapped to the outside.

Voodoo is actually a thing. Magic that was more ancestral, passed down from grandparent to grandchild through generations with no formal structure at all. That made it more fluid in how it worked—and a lot less predictable. The power of killing someone with voodoo, Santeria, or any other African originated folk magic was that, if you knew what you were doing, your opponent would never know the strike was coming. You could strike them as often and as many times as you wanted without fear of reprisal. The dangerous part was getting what you needed to make the connection in the first place.

Sweat was terrible. It took a master to cast through it, and the connection wouldn't last a day. Hair was better; blood was better still. Bone and heart flesh were best.

We'd taken on a witch doctor a couple years ago in South Carolina. It was as simple as a bullet to the head from a hundred yards away. When we looted the place, there was almost nothing we wanted. Just a shack in a swamp. The doll was the only thing we hadn't sold.

We did some experimenting. I made Zora sick for a week with it. She returned the favor, and we both knew it could work. We brainstormed ideas on how to block it, but neither of us was keen to volunteer.

It was purely an intellectual exercise. Mostly because neither of us could fathom a situation in which we would get close enough to someone to steal their blood or heart flesh and not just kill them while we were at it.

Tema told me it was often used for blackmail. Keep the person alive, and if they didn't do what you say, then you could kill them. That didn't make sense to me either. Why blackmail anyone for anything? Better to kill them than live in fear that they will one day track you down, reclaim the doll, and exact revenge.

None of it ever seemed like good strategy… until now.

The little wooden, slightly scorched doll sat on my pack staring at me with its potential. I'd had three days to think about what to do with it. The head of the doll was stained dark reddish brown with smudges of caked blood. When I'd shot Shroud and Blackstar, there was plenty of it on the walls. A few drops from Shroud were easy to get for this. Normally, blood would lose its connection to a person the moment it fully dried—but this doll was special. It kept the connection the blood had to anyone, and I hadn't touched it since I made the link, so hopefully Shroud didn't notice. The connection would still weaken and disappear eventually, but that wouldn't be anytime soon.

I didn't know where Shroud was or what he was doing, but I swore I'd kill them all, and I was happy to do it from a distance. If I caught Shroud in a weak moment, or maybe asleep or something, I could kill him from here. If it didn't work, I could strike again. I could send as many magical attacks as I wanted. All that mattered was how much power I put into each strike vs. how much power Shroud had to block it.

I was thinking about what spells I could throw. It couldn't be anything major. I didn't want Shroud to notice and come looking for me. I would have to watch and wait for just the right nudge at just the right moment. If I did it right, it could be fatal.

I laid down. Lying down had become a careful and delicate process lately, filled with lots of groaning and sighing.

There was another reason I was procrastinating. The trouble was this was killing with magic. No ifs, ands, or buts. No way I was going to be able to sell this to the Martinet as a magical trap or self-defense. If they found out, I was dead.

Of course, I do believe there's no way Shroud isn't coming to find me. I'm the reason his lackeys are dead, and worse; I tried to kill him. I'd bet pennies to pounds Shroud was hunting me. Come to think of it, it's probably a stroke of obscene luck that I even made it out of the hospital. Still, I couldn't sell that to Gomez.

I was lying down, and I still got a horrible sinking feeling. Was Duke there protecting me from Shroud? Did Duke even know about Shroud? No. That was silly. Lying in wait for any surviving Constellation members and using me to bait the trap was far more likely. That made sense; it made paying the hospital bill work too. Any member of The Constellation that showed up to finish me off would find Duke there in a bad mood with a few dozen uncomfortable questions.

Good. That meant I didn't owe him anything. Then again, even if Shroud had a knife to my throat and Duke bit his hand off,

I wouldn't admit to owing him anything. In that case, I would owe him, but I would never pay up.

I made a decision. It may not have been the right one, but it was a choice I'd own when the consequences inevitably came.

I picked up the doll and gathered everything I had. It wasn't much, but I didn't need much. I didn't know where Shroud was or what was happening. I couldn't see through his eyes. All I knew is that he was far away, and feeling what could best be described as amused.

The information I got from the doll was pretty useless. When Zora and I were experimenting with it, there was a lot more detail. I didn't know if it had something to do with Shroud's power, or with how far away he was. I was far from a master at attacking warlocks through little wooden dolls. All I could do was hope this was a good time.

The chill from the power in the air I was gathering rushed in every pore. I felt cold to the bone; so much so I saw my breath on the next exhale. "I'm coming Shroud."

I attacked. I sent every scrap of power I had through the doll and into Shroud's mind. I felt the amusement die and gathered power for another strike.

I assume he cast some kind of spell. There was a great effort he expended. I didn't know what he did, but I knew it didn't work.

I attacked again, and before the strike even hit home, I was gathering for the next. The doll was sending me what I wanted; what I'd hoped to feel from Shroud: fear.

I gathered my power again. My breath was a white cloud before me, and ice crystals started to form on the floor. I was chanting some meaningless syllables to help me focus. The presence in the doll kept trying to slip away. Shroud was trying to escape. I had to spend half of everything I gathered maintaining the connection.

Something else hit him. I didn't know what it was, but it was strong. Now there was lots of pain and even more fear. Had

I caught him in a battle with something else? I couldn't believe my luck.

My attacks were getting weaker. Maybe I should've waited until I was fully healed for this.

No, Shroud had to be hunting me, and I had to kill him before he found me. I struck again. My attacks were weak enough now that he was blocking them or shrugging them off—I couldn't tell which, but it was still enough to be a distraction. It was still taking something out of him. I had to keep going until I'd whittled him down. I struck again.

There was no way to tell what my attacks were actually doing with the doll giving me so little feedback. I didn't know if his bones were breaking or blood was congealing; he could be on fire for all I knew. I wasn't being specific because I wasn't that good at voodoo. I just set the spells with the intent to harm, and fired them off as hard as I could. The next strike was ready. The sweat was pouring off of me and turning to ice against my skin. What was this? Strike number twenty? Twenty-two? So cold! I was losing focus as I sent the next one.

It was like throwing a punch with everything you had and having the person disappear right before your fist made impact. The doll had no connection; nowhere to send the power to, and it came back at me with a vengeance. I screamed as my own strike hit me and tore open my already burned flesh. My mind was assaulted with images I couldn't understand, and I screamed.

"*MMMMMMMMAAAAA,*" Arta bellowed in obvious pleasure. As for me, I blacked out.

* * *

I woke up on day four bleeding again. My veins felt like they were filled with ice, and I had a headache that demanded I stay right where I was on the floor, but instead, I crawled over to where I'd dropped the doll.

I had to kill Shroud. He was probably on his way. Even if I couldn't use the doll to kill him, it could at least tell me if he was still far away. Maybe I could keep him there until I thought of something.

The moment I put my shivering finger on it, I knew. The doll wasn't failing; it was perfectly fine. The few smears of blood were still on its head, but the connection was gone. There was nothing at the other end. I collapsed on the floor again. Shroud may not know it was me casting at him, but he'd still be hunting me.

I was still a target, but that wasn't anything new.

but that wasn't anything new.

Tomorrow, I'd likely be dead. I grabbed my heating blanket off my cot and wrapped it around me. What was the point of getting warm if Shroud would be here soon to trash the whole block? I laughed suddenly, "because I don't wanna die cold." I said to the empty room. Dead tomorrow, but at least I could be warm today. Then it hit me. Like a freight train made of joy, sunlight and chocolate ice cream.

I'd survived.

Tomorrow I may be dead, but today I was alive and… cold, and itchy. Arta said that all a mortal had was the moment they were in. I'd heard that idea a million times from a million places, but in that moment, it struck home.

The Martinet would be coming to kill me, or maybe Duke would find out about the ankh and come kill me. One day soon the Shroud would fall and that would kill me, but today—

"Today I'm alive… and itchy."

* * *

Zora came in when I was standing under the water streaming from my shower. I'd have to find some kind of mittens to keep from scratching in my sleep. I desperately wished the water were colder.

I'd been casting spells all week to make it ice cold, but I had nothing left.

Zora made mock appraising noises until I shut the water off and grabbed my only towel. One thing I learned from my multi-shower days was that rubbing with a dry towel was greatly overrated. I patted myself with the weight of a feather and still winced each time.

"Got a surprise for ya!" Zora said, tossing my staff on the bed with a plastic drug store bag. I didn't remember putting it back in baton form, but I didn't dwell on it. I picked it up, and it was nearly a quarter full. "I charged it a bit. Should be enough for a stack of bandages, right?"

"Yeah," I nodded, holding my staff like I would a baby. I'd felt naked without it… and I was actually naked. "I don't suppose you found my pistol?"

She just shook her head in a, "why would I be looking for that?" sort of way. Ahh, well, I could buy and modify another pistol tomorrow if I wanted to. My staff had taken me months to make.

Zora left and I got started. In the bag were sterile bandages. The itching, the pain and the seeping wounds may have been a distraction any other time. Now, it was motivation.

I worked on bandages all day, only taking a break when Zora brought me food. I handled each pack carefully, but I was zipping through them like I never had before.

Normally a pack of twenty bandages would take me a few days. When I finally passed out at my desk, I was almost half done.

I woke up on day five feeling like I got hit by a truck. My staff was gone, and I was in bed. My sports wrap and all nine bandages I'd completed were spread over me. Zora must've come in last night and done it all. I didn't want to get out of bed, but I needed to…

When I woke up again it was afternoon. I drug myself out

of bed in considerably less pain than before. I was gonna shower, but I couldn't get the bandages wet. I threw on a pair of mundane jeans that I hadn't worn in years and a t-shirt I enchanted long ago. It changed color each day. It was a prototype of the one that got burned up.

I'd need to make more clothes soon. I only had one other pair of jeans and a few t-shirts. Everything still itched. If anything, it itched more since the skin was knitting itself together faster.

I grabbed my pack and headed out. I went straight to Miles'—I was starving.

When I walked in, the man himself was behind the bar, as always. Cooking something delicious, as always. I went to my usual stool, third from the end, as always. There was a beer when I got there, as always. A few minutes later came a steak, loaded mashed potatoes, and steamed broccoli with melted cheese.

I let out a sigh I'd been holding in for weeks.

"Back to normal."

Made in the USA
Middletown, DE
16 January 2018